RED DEVIL TALES
A Son's Journey to Discover His Father's Legacy

RONALD SEXTON

Copyright © 2017 Ronald Sexton
All rights reserved
First Edition

Fulton Books, Inc.
Meadville, PA

Published by Fulton Books 2017

ISBN 978-1-63338-388-3 (Paperback)
ISBN 978-1-63338-389-0 (Digital)

Printed in the United States of America

Coach Amos Sexton

March 1957—Amos Sexton's last season to coach. Under the title, Count 'Em, There Are 24 with One to Come, the caption reads, "Grainger High School basketball mentor Amos Sexton, poses here with the trophies that his basketball teams have won since he came to Kinston nine years ago. There are 24 trophies pictured here, including the 1957 northeastern conference regular season championship award and the loop tournament award. The district trophy for 1957 is not included in the picture."[1] (Photo by George Denmark, Jr. staff photographer for the *Free Press* and used by their permission.)

To My Son David

Who is courageously fighting to beat cancer
With the same determination and fierceness
That his grandfather had in winning ballgames

ACKNOWLEDGMENTS

Writing a book is a community effort. The author may be the one who puts words on a page, but there are many others who contribute and help shape its outcome. This is a book that involved dozens of people who knew and admired Coach Amos Sexton. Without their stories and willingness to share their memories, this work would never have been possible.

In Amos Sexton's nine-year run as the head basketball coach of the Red Devils of Grainger High School and as an assistant football coach, there were many boys who came under his tutelage. The former players and friends I was able to visit with were invaluable in their accounts of this most amazing era.

As I made my way around the country to interview these former players and friends of Amos Sexton (most now in their eighties), it was not unusual for them to see an uncanny resemblance between father and son. Their faces would light up, and some embraced me with a big bear hug. I knew their affection for this man was great. Everyone was gracious, and many invited me out to eat as if to say, "Thank you, Coach, for the great memories." To everyone I met, I thank you for the warm reception, the stories, and the gracious hospitality.

Everyone took time to tell me their story. Although some of their accounts were not included in this work, I thoroughly enjoyed listening and remembering. The former basketball players I was fortunate to visit were Bobby Hodges, Doug Bruton, Fred Williams, Eugene "Red" McDaniel, Amos Stroud, Graham Phillips, Joe Whaley, Frasier Bruton, Tommy Cole, Bryant Aldridge, George Whitfield, Alley

Hart, Charlie Lewis, Poo Rochelle, Lee Becton, Roger Hobgood, Robert Whaley, Marshall Happer, Claude Kennedy, Ray Barbre, Eion Faelten, Fletcher Baker, "Bud" Bradshaw, Bobby Stanley, and Pat Wright. All had great stories to tell and helpful insights into that special era of Red Devil history.

Red McDaniel and Doug Bruton live in the Washington, DC. area. I spent several days visiting Doug and Ginny Bruton and then Red and Dorothy McDaniel. They were gracious hosts and gave me an experience I will never forget.

Dorothy McDaniel was especially helpful in taking the time to proofread the manuscript. I would send her a chapter via e-mail, and she would return it with corrections and suggestions. Her help was invaluable. Both she and Red have written powerful books about their experience during the years when Red was a POW (prisoner of war) in Vietnam. Red's book, *Scars and Stripes,* and Dorothy's book *After the Hero's Welcome* have recently been reissued.

Reid Parrott and Talmage Jones are two Red Devil alumni and avid sports enthusiasts who were especially helpful in their accounts. Each of them brought a unique prospective on Amos Sexton and the Kinston Red Devils. There were others who played football, or they were graduates of Grainger High School who simply knew Coach Amos Sexton. I enjoyed visiting with Vincent Jones, Jimmy Bryd, Bob Church, Bryd and Pat Humphries, Jerry Kanter, Becky Mull Templeton, Gary Hocutt, Alban Barrus, Gary Baldree, Buck Fichter, James Sanderson, Harvey Whitfield, Buddy Holt, and Sam Stapleford—(class of '34). Some like Paul Popov and Robert Whaley I visited with over the phone, and others like Michael Gaylor, Alfred Earl Howell, and Bill Wells corresponded via e-mail.

Several former players became a little more engaged in the process for which I am especially grateful. Eion Faelten sent newspaper clippings and corresponded faithfully via e-mail. He also proofread the manuscript and provided helpful suggestions and corrections as well, and, of course, like Alley Hart, he made sure I got his chapter right. Fred Williams also reviewed his chapter and made helpful suggestions. Fred was the oldest boy of four brothers who played for Amos Sexton. All of them were good athletes. Charlie Lewis read through his chapter and also sent some photos. He was very helpful as well.

Alley Hart put his reflections on five pages of notes that he gave me. He proofread several chapters and made helpful suggestions, especially with his chapter. Alley occasionally called me on the phone to see how I was progressing and reminding me to hurry up and publish this before they all died.

When our family moved to Louisiana, Dad established a friendship with Scotty Robinson, head basketball coach at Louisiana Tech University. In Scotty Robinson, Dad found someone with whom he could talk basketball. Coach Robinson would go on to become the first head coach of the New Orleans Jazz and later coached the Chicago Bulls and Detroit Pistons. He returned to Ruston when he retired, and I always seemed to run into him at Backus True Value Hardware or Super One food store. He had a few stories to tell himself about Dad. In his last few years, he would always ask me, "When is that book coming out? I sure want to read it." Then he would tell me an Amos Sexton story. Also, Dad befriended Leon Barmore who played for Scotty Robinson at Louisiana Tech University and who latter became the legendary coach of the Lady Techsters.

Clyde King, a native of Goldsboro, North Carolina, had been a professional baseball pitcher for the Brooklyn Dodgers and Cincinnati Reds in the 1940s and continued to work in baseball as a general manager or pitching coach for numerous baseball organizations. From 1976 until his retirement from the game, Clyde was with the New York Yankees as a scout pitching coach, manager, general manager, and, finally, as a special advisor to George M. Steinbrenner III. Clyde King had become close friends with George Whitfield, and as a result, I got to know Clyde as well. Every trip I made to North Carolina, George and I would go by and visit with Clyde. He was always interested in my book, and he always asked me how my research was going.

The first time I met Clyde was when he was a pitching coach for the Pittsburg Pirates. In 1966, when I was a young teenager, George took me and my brothers to Houston to see the Pirates play the Astros. We were able to ride with the team on a bus from the hotel to the stadium.

9

I sat by a player who was rather shy and very quiet. When we got off the bus, Clyde asked me if I knew who I was sitting with. Of course, I had no idea. Clyde told me that it was Roberto Clemente. That night, I saw Roberto Clemente hit a straight-driving home run over the centerfield wall in the Astrodome. It was the longest home run ball I believe I have ever seen hit. Clyde King was an incredible man, and I always appreciated his words of advice and encouragement.

Dad loved to fish, and Tom Briley who worked for the City of Kinston was his faithful fishing partner. I visited with Mr. Briley several times before he passed away in April of 2011. His stories of him and Dad fishing and some of their exploits were very entertaining. They fished mostly in the outer banks off the North Carolina coast. Mr. Briley said Dad was always running on a sandbar, getting lost, and getting home late at night, which worried Mother to death. He said Dad was always tinkering with the motor. Nevertheless, they always managed to catch fish.

Tony Kelly, former Red Devil football player, was gracious enough to give me a tour of the historical sites of Kinston and Lenoir County. His perspective was very helpful, and the tour was a wonderful experience for someone who loves history as I do. On my first research trip to Kinston in 2008, I stopped by the Kinston Visitor's Center to check out some of their local history. I was admiring a display of Civil War artifacts when I heard this voice across the room bellow out, "If you have any questions about that stuff, just ask me and I will help you." I turned around and saw a man with a cane in an old rocking chair and looking like Grizzly Adams. It was Tony Kelly. I asked him if he remembered a man named Amos Sexton. He said, "Oh my god, do I? That man liked to kill me. I played football under him and Frank Mock, and I tell you they would run us to death." I laughed and introduced myself and told him what I was doing. A few days later, he gave me a tour of Kinston and Lenoir County showing me all the historical sites in the area. It was very informative.

Bill Rowland, a local historian in Kinston, put me in touch with hard copies of the *Free Press*, Kinston's local paper and formerly known as the *Kinston Daily Free Press*. The hard copies were located at South Lenior High School in Deep Run. It was much easier to peruse through years of newspapers gently turning fragile pages than sifting through years of microfilm using a machine. At South Lenior High School, Tanya Cahoon, media coordinator; Mrs. Daphne Pollock, assistant principal; and Pat Moore, bookkeeper, were very helpful in giving me access to the hard copies of the *Free Press*. Tracy Banks, librarian at Kinston High School, was very helpful as well.

My mother's family still lives in North Carolina and continues to maintain the family farm outside of Newton Grove. They provided a lot of help with family background and stories, as well as being gracious hosts, taking me in and feeding me from time to time. Mother's brothers Theron and Sherroll and his wife Janice; mother's sisters, Janice Todd and Sandra and her husband Billy Boyette were all very supportive and encouraging.

I received an invaluable amount of help from Mrs. Frank Mock who, on June 1, 2016, celebrated her ninety-ninth birthday. She had been a graduate of Grainger High School in 1934, and she knew and kept up with all of Coach Mock's boys as well as many others.

Mother and Dad had many friends in Kinston, and I was able to visit with several of their friends who were dedicated Red Devil fans. Jim and Barbara Anne Hartis and Myron and Betty Hill were two couples who were good friends with Mom and Dad when they lived in Kinston.

Dan Perry, a lawyer in Kinston and former Red Devil, provided encouragement and advice having published several books himself. His books provided a worthy model for publishing.

George Whitfield provided the names and addresses of over three hundred people. I was pleased with the response. Two Red Devils sent me their entire scrapbook, which contained pictures and newspaper clippings. Zollie Collins sent his scrapbook and a nice letter. Unfortunately, Zollie passed away before this book was completed. Marjorie Moore sent me the scrapbook of her husband, Bob, who played football under Frank Mock. Joyce DuBose Patrick sent me the scrapbook of Carroll DuBose.

Most of the photographs in the book first appeared in "Kinston's local newspaper," *The Free Press* . . . Bryan C. Hanks, managing editor, was gracious in giving me permission to use these photographs. Bryan was the sports editor for years and did a lot to promote athletics in Kinston and Lenior County. He also was very supportive and promoted the Kinston-Lenoir County Sports of Fame. I read every sports article in the *Free Press* from 1948 through 1957 and many other years as well. This newspaper has always been a positive influence and supporter of Kinston, Lenoir County, and North Carolina athletics.

Many former Red Devils responded via e-mail, and others wrote letters and sent articles, who I would like to thank: Blanch Miller, Sylvia Wheless, Jerry Kanter, Maude Stanley Speight, Betty Keaton, Patrick Leonard, Eddie Martin, John Laws, Buddy Holt, Eddie Martin, Dorothy Mills, Paul Papov, Wilbur Mozingo, Gene and Darlene Handy, Bob Church, and Alfred Earl Howell.

Finally, if there was one person who was most responsible for this book, it was George Whitfield. George came to live with our family during his teenage years, having lost both of his parents. George provided the impetus for the book, and I absolutely could not have pulled this off without him. He is the consummate Red Devil. And he is a Red Devil encyclopedia. I believe he knows every Red Devil and where they now live and what they are doing. He spit out names, phone numbers, vital statistics, and pertinent information like a computer program. All of this from a man who does not even own or know how to use a computer. If I ever had a question about anyone or anything related to Grainger High School or needed to contact someone, George was the person who knew the answer and could arrange the meeting.

The story of how George, a young teenager, came to live with us is a part of the Red Devil story. When George married Mary Lou Ward in 1961 (I was nine years old), she too became a part of our family. Mary Lou read through the manuscript and made some helpful suggestions, especially on George's chapter.

I made more than a dozen trips to North Carolina over a five-year period, and every time I stayed with George, he not only provided room and board but also took valuable time to help me. On many occasions, he would go with me to interview other players. I dined at some of the finest restaurants in North Carolina, and in between interviews, I saw more baseball games than Babe Ruth ever played, all graciously provided by George Whitfield.

FOREWORD

The ancient Greeks enjoyed the golden era of Pericles, and in the early nineteenth century of the United States, our nation's citizens lived in the era of good feeling.

The time we spent as students at Grainger High School was our memorable time, and as we grow old, we relish our memories. We have come to the realization that the years from 1948 to 1958 was a time that bears reflection and instills a sense of pride. We were fortunate to have been Red Devils during those years. *Near the end of his life, former superintendent Jean Booth urged George Whitfield that he should find someone to write about these golden years of Grainger High School and the Kinston Red Devils. Ronald Sexton has done just that.*

We have chosen the decade of 1948–1958 to parallel the remarkable achievement of our athletic teams under the leadership of two men, Frank Mock and Amos Sexton, who left us with much success in high school sports.

This book was written by Dr. Ronald Sexton in an effort to understand his father's legacy as a coach and teacher at Grainger High School.

Ronnie was born in Kinston and moved to Ruston, Louisiana, when he was five years old. He took a leave of absence from a college teaching position to visit with former players and get primary answers to many experiences he had heard about his dad's time in Kinston. Several of the folks he interviewed have since passed away, which makes this book all the more timely. It is important that it was written while there were principal characters still alive and were so important to his text.

As two former students at Grainger High School, we were privileged to encourage Ronnie to write this book and to assist him with interviews, documents, newspaper articles, yearbooks, and statistics.

We encouraged Ronnie to push forward and we served as cheerleaders, but he was determined to learn of the time that his dad lived in Kinston and to offer a lasting tribute to the legacy of Coach Amos Sexton.

The Scottish writer James M. Barrie wrote that God gives us memory so we can have "roses in December"! We trust that when you read this book, you will remember this amazing era of history and have roses in December.

Reid Parrott, '56
George Whitfield, '54

PREFACE

I was in Oxford finishing up a postdoctoral study in local history when I received an e-mail from my older brother Edison: "Dad is being inducted into the Kinston-Lenoir County Hall of Fame." Neither he nor my younger brother, Don, would be able to attend. He added, "We hope you can go to represent the family." Well, they didn't have to ask me twice; I was excited to go. Dad had passed away in 1989, so now, almost twenty years later, I had the opportunity to revisit a part of family history I was too young to remember.

The induction ceremony was held on April 28, 2007, in Frank Mock Gymnasium, ironically the very place where Dad had directed many Red Devil basketball games. The basketball court was filled with dozens of round dinner tables elegantly decorated for the evening. Each inductee's family was given a table, which accommodated about eight people. The gym was full with over five hundred guests. George Whitfield had invited Mother's family to attend the ceremony, and they all came.

I marveled as I looked around the gym, which I hadn't seen since I was about nine years old. Dad had returned to coach a game of his former players in an exhibition game in the early sixties. The gym still had a familiar aroma that triggered memories from my childhood. *So this was the place where many Grainger High School Red Devils had raced up and down the court,* I thought, running that indelible fast break Dad was famous for using. Now fifty years later, it was ironic to be occupying the same space where the Red Devils had played.

In receiving the reward on behalf of Dad, I was given about five minutes to say a few words. I had prepared a few remarks in response. What I was not prepared for was how this experience would affect me emotionally, in part because, I think, both Mother and Dad were gone.

When the moment arrived to introduce Dad, the master of ceremonies read through the list of accomplishments achieved by Amos Sexton as the head basketball coach of the Kinston Red Devils. When all strung together, his record was impressive, especially for someone who was a novice to the game and only twenty-seven-years old when he began his coaching career.

Along with Dad, there were eight other people being inducted into the hall of fame. Hanging high from the rafters was a larger-than-life poster of each new inductee. The picture of Dad hung in the middle. He was sitting in the bleachers among all the trophies his teams had won over his nine years of coaching (see front cover). The picture was taken in 1957, his final year and just before the state championship playoff. Winning the state championship that year would have given the Red Devils an unprecedented three state championships in a row.

My two brothers and I were all born in Kinston, so when Dad retired from coaching in 1957, I was only five years old. Edison was seven, and Don was only seven months. Edison, of course, has a better memory of those years than I do. Being the oldest, he was Dad's sidekick, often accompanying him to basketball practices and on fishing trips. Dad's success as a coach and the legacy he left were never fully understood or appreciated by me until I attended his induction into the Kinston-Lenoir County Hall of Fame. I had, of course, heard Dad tell many stories growing up, but those had been some of the humorous things that happened on road trips, which he always laughed about. He never talked about his record and skills as a coach.

In 1981, several of his former players honored him at a reunion and appreciation banquet. It was an event that meant a lot to him, and he never forgot it. Many of his former players, cheerleaders, school officials, and teachers were there. Dad flew all of us and our families up to North Carolina for this event held in his honor. I was twenty-seven at that time and mostly just an observer. I didn't interact with the players, and the banquet was more or less a "roast" with everyone having fun and remembering old times. It was a great weekend, but I still didn't grasp the significance of his years as a coach.

In the days following the induction ceremony, I began thinking about visiting these former players to try to discover what those years were like for them and what kind of coach Amos Sexton was to them. For someone to be remembered and honored for their accomplishments fifty years later (1957–2007) is worthy of a second look. So I set out to see as many former players as I could and listen to their stories. I wanted to know what Amos Sexton was like and what made him such a successful basketball coach. I intended to eventually write something down but only for family history, not to be published.

Fourteen months after the induction ceremony, I made my first trip back to North Carolina from Louisiana. It was August 2008. I made seven more trips to North Carolina in the next four years, and each time, I learned a lot about the legacy of Coach Amos Sexton and the Kinston Red Devils and met many wonderful people. I continued to record and put down my thoughts until 2012. Then I just set it aside for three years. I got a call from Alley Hart who told me that I need to get off the bench and get back in the game and publish this work "before we all die."

The following is a product of those visits. It is my notes and impressions from those encounters with former players and friends. As we get older, the stories of our youth tend to become more or less mythological. We seek to give meaning and value to events, and in doing so, facts tend to bend a little to fit our narrative, sort of our spin on history. "That's my story, and I'm sticking to it." I trust the reader's ability to discern where history stops and "to the best of my knowledge" begins.

1

NEVER PLAYED THE GAME

In the fall of 1948, Grainger High School needed a new basketball coach. Bill Faye who had directed the Grainger High School Red Devils for three seasons was taking a new position as director of the city recreation department in the small town of Kinston, North Carolina. Bill Faye knew basketball and had been an excellent basketball coach, but being director of recreation gave him the opportunity to work with more kids of all ages in a variety of sports. When the position became available in October 1948, he took the job.

Now with basketball season just around the corner, someone had to be appointed in short order. The 1947 Red Devils had come within one shot of being state champions, and the same group of players, with one exception, was returning. Everyone had great expectations for the 1948–1949 season.

The task of finding a new coach fell upon Jean Booth, superintendent of education. Mr. Booth was a tall and stately gentleman who had served as principal of Grainger High School from 1928 to 1945. But now as superintendent of education, he had the challenge of finding a new man to fill the shoes of a coach who had brought the Grainger High School Red Devil basketball team within one game of winning the state title in the spring of 1948.

The football season was well underway by the time news came to Booth that a new basketball coach was needed. The boys of the 1948 football squad were having their best season ever under the direction of Frank Mock, a coach who had been at Grainger High School since 1934 and was already rising to legendary status.

The football team finished the season undefeated, the only undefeated football team in Grainger High School history. It was an exceptional and gifted group of young men. Every player on the basketball team was also on the football team, and most of them played baseball as well. It was the era when an athlete played all three major sports, and most of them made the transition to the next sport without a hitch.

The football season would soon be drawing to a close, so time was a factor. A new basketball coach had to be in place before the end of November. Jean Booth called the director of personnel at East Carolina Teachers College in Greenville (about thirty miles north of Kinston) and asked him to send four young men down for an interview. East Carolina sent four boys down to Kinston for Booth to look over.

The first gentleman to walk into Jean Booth's office for that interview on a bright and crisp November day was a rather small but strapping young twenty-seven-year-old and ex-marine, who immediately impressed the superintendent with his positive attitude and commanding presence. He was an aggressive but charming young man who seemed to have the maturity that could only come from a seasoned Marine veteran.

Jean Booth would later say that Amos Sexton stood out like a mighty oak, and after this first brief encounter, he knew then that he had his man. As a matter of professional courtesy, the other young men were interviewed, but Booth already had made up his mind on Amos Sexton, who he said had the two qualities that he was looking for—personality and determination. "Amos Sexton," he would later recall, "had charisma." Mr. Booth believed that Amos Sexton would be just the person needed to continue rebuilding a promising athletic program.

RED DEVIL TALES

However, what made the appointment of this young man as the head basketball coach most unusual was the fact that Amos Sexton had never coached basketball. In fact, he had never even played the game. He played football as a guard at East Carolina Teachers College in Greenville, North Carolina, but knew virtually nothing about basketball.

Anxious to know who had been selected as the new head basketball coach, the principal John Horne Jr., called the superintendent to get a report. I am not sure exactly how the conversation went, but by all accounts, it went something like this:

Jack Horne blurted with anticipation, "Jean, John Horne here. So tell me how the interview went. Did you find what we are looking for?"

"Yes, John, I believe I have. I have selected a young man named Amos Sexton," Booth reported enthusiastically.

"That's great, Jean," Horne responded. "Now give me his resume. Where did he play basketball, and how much experience does he have coaching?"

"Well," Booth continued, "actually, he never has coached basketball, but I believe he is the right young man for the job."

"Really?" Horne replied. "Well, did he play basketball at East Carolina?"

"No, John"—Booth now somewhat apologetic—"in fact, he has not even played basketball, but—"

"What!" Horne interrupted with great incredulity, and after virtually picking himself off the floor, he continued, "You mean to tell me that you have hired someone that not only has never coached basketball but has never even played the game?"

"That's right, John," the superintendent confidently responded. "But Amos Sexton has charisma and personality. He has enthusiasm and sincerity about what he wants to do, and I think he will be a great motivator of young men. I think he is exactly what this program needs."

Jean Booth was right. In the nine years that Amos Sexton coached basketball at Grainger High School, he would leave quite a legacy. His teams won three-state championships and were state runner-ups for three other years. He left an impressive 202 wins with only thirty-nine loses.

His 1950 championship team would also set the Grainger High School record for the most wins in a season (thirty). His teams won the northeastern conference regular season championship eight times, the northeastern conference tournament title five times, and the district championship six times. For a man who had never played the game, his personality and determination paid off. He would eventually learn the game, and by the time he ended his brief career, he was one of the top high school basketball coaches in the state of North Carolina.

Amos Sexton graduated from East Carolina Teachers College (now East Carolina University) in Greenville on November 24, 1948, and moved to Kinston the following week to assume his duties as head basketball coach of the Kinston Red Devils. Fresh from a successful undefeated football season and winning the northeastern conference championship, the Red Devils of Grainger High hardly had time to catch their breath before having to retool their talents toward winning basketball games. Last year's team had come within a hair of winning it all but fell short of being state champions. The new coach had inherited a very talented and seasoned team. The question was could he fine-tune the talent and take them to the next step of being a championship team, or would his inexperience as a coach and ignorance of the game sink the program into a lost cause?

Amos Sexton was first introduced to the city of Kinston in a small insert in the *Kinston Daily Free Press* on Tuesday, November 30, 1948, which notes that he had just arrived in Kinston that week "to assume his duties" as a member of Grainger High School faculty and was replacing W. L. (Bill) Fay as the head basketball coach. There is no hint of his inexperience, and after the team's first scrimmage against Contentnea High School several days later, the next article to appear reflects his confidence and emerging philosophy: Red Devils Need Many More Drills.[2]

His major in college had been physical education, and as football player who played right guard, physical conditioning was one of his cardinal principles. After the team's first scrimmage, the coach

22

would also began to stress another rule, which would define his coaching philosophy—playing as a team.

From the very beginning of his career as a basketball coach, Amos Sexton modeled his teams after the then popular St. Louis Billikens who were famous for running the fast-break offense. The Billikens, under coach Edgar S. "Eddie" Hickey, won the National Invitational Tournament (NIT) in 1948, so this was one of the hottest and most popular teams in the country at that time. Eddie Hickey was the first coach to take three different schools to the NCAA tournament. He is also credited with developing the modern three-lane fast break in which the player with the ball heads down the middle of the court toward the basket, flanked by two wingmen.

Sexton incorporated the fast break into his basketball program. The fast break would become the Red Devils' signature offense and one that many opponents feared. However, in order for this offense to work, the players had to be in top physical condition because they were running up and down the court for the entire game. Timing and teamwork were paramount, and the Red Devils executed this to perfection.

By the end of 1948, three years after World War II had ended, the world was rapidly changing. The new technologies that would forever alter our world were in their infancy. The United States now possessed a weapon that could destroy civilization itself, and the power struggle between nations to control their own destiny and dominate world affairs was well underway. With the creation and use of the atomic bomb, a new but dangerous era emerged. The cold war was just beginning, but America was entering a golden age of peace and prosperity unlike any time in its history. It was a time of great optimism as our fighting soldiers returned home and settled down to raise families and live the American dream.

In 1948, you could buy a new home for fewer than $8,000. You could purchase a new car for $1,230 and put gas in it at 16 cents per gallon. The average movie ticket cost around 60 cents, and US postage stamps were 3 cents each. Tuition to Harvard University was $525 per year, and the average rent on an apartment was $70 per month. Milk was 87 cents a gallon, eggs 23 cents a dozen, and a loaf of bread was 14 cents.[3]

In 1948, there were only about one million households that owned television sets. So rare was this new technology that in January of 1949, it was news when the first television set was purchased in the state of North Carolina. The *Free Press* of Kinston noted the event, First Television Set Purchased by E. E. Rowe of Jacksonville. The article noted,

"What is believed to be Onslow County's first television set was purchased by E. E. Rowe, proprietor of Rowe's Radio Shop in Jacksonville, this week. The set arrived here Thursday and Rowe tried out his new television outfit. He reported and, as was expected, that he could not pick up any television stations. Rowe said, "The only town in North Carolina that has been able to pick up television is Henderson, which can receive the Richmond, Va., station 102 miles away."[4]

Harry Truman unexpectedly had just won the Presidential election over Thomas Dewey on November 2, 1948. On the world scene, the Marshall Plan was initiated with $5.3 billion for aid to war-torn Europe. In newly independent India, Mahatma Gandhi is assassinated, and the United Nations recognized the state of Israel. There was no vice president in 1948, and the Nobel Peace Prize was not awarded. But James A. Michener won the Pulitzer Prize for his book, *Tales of the South Pacific*. The life expectancy was 62.9 years.[5]

In football, the Michigan Wolverines were the college champions in 1948. The pro-football champions were the Philadelphia Eagles. The Heisman Trophy winner in 1948 was Doak Walker from SMU. In baseball, the World Series champions were the Cleveland Indians. They won with the help of pitchers like Bob Feller. Pat Seerey, outfielder for the Chicago White Soxs, hit four home runs in an eleven-inning game over the Philadelphia Athletics. The final score was 12-ll and interestingly enough, Pat Seerey had only a total of eighty-six home runs in seven Major League seasons.[6]

In basketball, the Kentucky Wildcats under legendary coach Adolf Rupp won the NCAA basketball championship. They would go on to win again the following year. Baseball in 1948 and 1949 were golden years for that sport in America. Although baseball lost one of its greatest, Babe Ruth, there were other legendary names still playing—Joe DiMaggio, Ted Williams, Bob Feller, Yogi Berra, Stan Musial, just to name a few.

In the spring of 1949, the Red Devil basketball team would come within one game of winning the state basketball championship under the new and inexperienced coach Amos Sexton. But the baseball team that spring did win its first state championship under Coach Frank Mock.

"Sexton came to Kinston fresh out of East Carolina College in Greenville," wrote one sportswriter, "and although he had some offers for jobs paying more money, he felt that there was more potential in (Kinston)."[7] In his ninth and final year of coaching basketball, Lloyd Whitfield of the *Kinston Daily Free Press* noted that "because his basketball teams have competed in eight state tournaments, won three of them, been runners-up in three, captured northeastern conference laurels for seven years and won eight district championships, Sexton has been termed by many 'the baron of prep basketball in North Carolina."[8]

He explained his basic coaching philosophy to the *Free Press* sportswriter, Lloyd Whitfield:

"I try to have my clubs well-drilled in the fundamentals. Think, run and shoot is what I tell the boys to do. Conditioning is the top thing on my list. When the boys are conditioned, I'm satisfied we will have a good season. Conditioning has paid off for us. I could name game after game where we have whipped the opposition in the last quarter because of our physical shape."[9]

Discipline was a critical component for any successful program. "Discipline is a must for boys interested in playing with the Red Devil cagers," Whitfield went on to note, and, "Sexton lets it be known that he does not care how good a person can play basketball, without discipline there is no place for an athlete on a Kinston club."[10] Having disciplined teams, along with his determination to learn the game and his fight to win, would pay off.

At the end of nine years when he decided to move on to other opportunities, he had carved out a unique legacy. The *Free Press* gave him a stamp of approval:

"Coach Sexton deserves a large share of the credit for putting basketball on the map in Kinston. Year in and year out he has taken the talent as it came and made the most of it. He has had great success with team units, and his cagers have been better known for their teamwork than their individual powers."[11]

After winning the state championship in 1955, the *Free Press* said,

"Kinston is proud of its champions, its coach and the school. The title rightfully belongs to those who went into the Sanford tournament as heavy favorites and played together like real champions to bring home the crown. The State Class AA schools have never been represented by a finer group of cagers nor a more able coach."[12]

In 1956, the Red Devils won another state title, and the local paper praised the team and the coach.

"Kinston has had many outstanding cagers in the past decade, but its title winners have been, as a rule, well-balanced squads in which there was no dependence on any one star. Coach Amos Sexton has the ability to inspire his teams to go after the big ones and to stay in there and fight when the chips are really down."[13]

And finally they noted,

"(The city of Kinston) is proud that the cagers have matched the gridiron greats to bring another title to this community this school year. It is really the home of champions and what community would not be proud of such fine boys as make up the 1956 cage squad? Congratulations to the entire squad and to Coach Sexton."[14]

By all accounts, Amos Sexton was a quick study when he began his coaching career in 1948. He absorbed basketball fundamentals, strategies, and tactics from any and every source he could. He studied books, attended clinics, and befriended other coaches who knew basketball. He was always willing to learn more, even from his players. Amos Sexton came to Kinston "fired up" and ready to go. He hit the ground running, taking the reigns as the new basketball coach of the Grainger High School Red Devils.

2

LEARNING THE GAME

When Amos Sexton walked out onto the basketball court for the first time in November of 1948 and introduced himself to the players as the new head basketball coach of the Kinston Red Devils, he stood among giants. To be sure, they were physically tall, but they were also giants in athletic talent. Virtually, all the players were three sport athletes, and they moved from one sport to another with ease and grace as each new season emerged.

For these boys, football season ended on a Friday, and basketball practice began on Monday with the first game only days away. In one year, for example, after playing in a championship basketball game on a Saturday night, Tommy Cole, with one day of practice on Monday, hit three line drives off the left-field fence in the first baseball game of the season the following day. Through the years, Kinston seemed to have more than its share of athletes who were great players in all three major sports. They were talented athletes on the gridiron, the basketball court, and the baseball diamond. These boys were just good athletes, and it didn't matter what the sport was; they had certain natural abilities common to all sports. They had been playing together in backyards, playgrounds, and city parks since grammar school. Their heroes were high school, college, and professional athletes, not rock stars. And most came from families who

27

scratched out a living on a farm or a barbershop or a hardware store. Some grew up without a father, and they found worthy models of manhood in their coaches who understood their plight.

In those days, the line between playing one sport and another sport was not as distinct as it is today. This may be one reason the new coach felt reasonably comfortable coaching a game he was not familiar with. He could learn the game, but he knew an athlete had to be in shape to play, and in a team sport, they had to learn to play together as a team. Amos Sexton knew he had a group of talented and seasoned athletes, but he also knew that they needed direction and structure, someone who could bring out the best in them and instill confidence. He believed that he could do that.

Most days, these boys were working somewhere to help defray expenses or just fulfilling their family responsibilities like Red McDaniel plowing fields for his dad, a tenant farmer, or Fred Williams who threw newspapers daily to help support three younger brothers and a single mother struggling as a low-paid seamstress. Coach Frank Mock offered Bobby Hodges odd jobs around his house so he could buy his own athletic shoes. They all grew up working hard and competing hard, two traits that would serve them well in athletics and later in life.

Virtually, all of the players were six feet or over. Bobby Hodges was the tallest standing majestically at six feet five inches, while most of the other boys were at least six feet to six three. The one exception was Joe Whaley who was five feet seven, but he was quick and could hold his own on the court, not to mention that he was an outstanding fullback on the football squad. The new coach stood only five feet eight inches, but everyone knew he was an ex-Marine and had been an outstanding guard in football at East Carolina Teachers College.

The new coach walked onto the court with some spunk and authority even though everyone knew of his inexperience as a coach and that he knew virtually nothing about basketball. He dribbled a basketball with two hands as he approached the boys who could see right away he was not a basketball player. Nevertheless, this twenty-seven-year-old former Marine left no doubt that he was in charge

RED DEVIL TALES

and inexperience notwithstanding; he was determined to bring home a state championship.

Both the varsity and junior varsity players sat anxiously in the bleachers wondering how the new coach was going to direct the team. The air was filled with some apprehension and uncertainty among the players. Was the new coach going to make drastic changes to an already successful program? Was he going to set new rules in place that would work against a team that had come within seconds of winning the state championship in the last two years? Having a new coach certainly meant changes, and any change could upset the delicate balance of a team that had taken years to build. Fred Williams, who played in the previous year's championship game, said that in the final moments of the contest, he had stolen the ball and thrown it to Bobby Hodges who broke away down the court for a game-winning layup. However, the cheering crowd of Kinston fans was silenced when the referee blew his whistle and called a traveling violation. Fred said he knew he wasn't traveling, and he believed that Bobby Hodges wasn't either, but the call was made nevertheless. The points were voided, and the game was lost. It would have been Grainger High School's first state championship.

The new coach did not try to hide the fact that he was new to the sport. He told them that they were going to do what they had always done, which came as a relief to the team. He gave them a lot of latitude, but he left little doubt that he was the coach. He was not intimidated by playing the role as a learning student of the game and sought players' advice and suggestions. Nevertheless, the practices were still intense and relentless drills became a part of the team's daily routine.

Everett Case—known as the Grey Fox—who coached North Carolina State University (1946–1964), commented on one occasions that the Red Devils ran the best fast-break offense he had ever seen, even better than any college and professional team. The fast break would become the signature offense for every Amos Sexton basketball team. Eddie Hickey, known as the Little General, wrote numerous articles on basketball and conducted clinics all over the United State and around the world. He coauthored a book, *How to*

29

Improve Your Basketball, a book that was seriously studied by the new coach. He never stopped learning the game.[1]

George Whitfield, who lived with our family through his high school years, remembered that he often saw Coach Sexton late at night or early in the morning studying his basketball books at the kitchen table. He said, "Sometimes when I had to get up late at night or early in the morning to go to the bathroom, Coach Sexton would be at the kitchen table studying his basketball books and drawing up plays." George said that Dad had about three books on basketball that he constantly studied. Eddie Hickey's book was one of them. Of course, Amos Sexton also had Bill Faye close by to consult with and learn from as well.

The coach's first year was very commendable, taking the Red Devils again to the state championship game only to lose a close one to Hendersonville. The Red Devils had plowed through the regular season with 17–3 record. They won thirteen of fourteen conference games, losing only to the Washington Pam-Pac but winning the conference title nevertheless.

In the conference tournament, the Red Devils blew past Roanoke Rapids 59–40, but met a stiffer challenge in the semifinals against all-conference Sonny Russell and the New Bern Bears. Bobby Hodges and Sonny Russell would eventually end up as teammates at East Carolina, but as high school players, they were fierce competitors. On this night, the contest was close the entire game, and with three minutes left in the game, the Bears were up 30–28. Z. A. Collins made a set shot to tie the score followed by a long shot drilled in by Joe Whaley. The Red Devils now had a two-point lead. Bobby Hodges then intercepted a pass intended for Sonny Russell and then breaking down the court only to miss a layup. Doug Bruton rebounded and passed off to Joe Whaley. Whaley shot and missed, but Bruton rebounded again and pushed in the final two points. The game ended with the Red Devils on top 34–30.[2]

In the final game against Washington, the Red Devils were on target and steamrolled the Pam-Pac 46–34, winning the conference title. It was the first time in the history of the conference that a team had taken the conference title and the tournament finals in the same

RED DEVIL TALES

year. Even with a new coach at the helm, the Red Devils didn't seem to miss a lick.[3]

The Red Devils next headed for the regional tournament at Wake Forest to meet Roxboro. Bobby Hodges led the team with twenty-six points, winning the game 33–24. In the regional finals, the Red men beat Chapel Hill 31–23 even though the first quarter ended in a 5–5 tie. Their next opponent was Hanes from Winston-Salem in the state semi-final game.[4]

Hanes gave the Red Devils a run for their money. The first half was nip and tuck with the second quarter ending with an uneasy 28–27 Red Devil lead. By the end of the third quarter Hanes had the advantage with a four-point lead 36–32. Near the end of the fourth quarter, the Red Devils edged their opponents by three points 44–41, but Hanes tied it up with just over a minute to play. But then Bobby Hodges dropped in a layup to give Kinston a two point lead 46–44. "Hanes threatened when (they) made good on a free throw, but Kinston froze the ball for the final 55 seconds to take the victory."[5]

The championship game was a repeat from the previous year when the Red Devils had loss to Hendersonville by two points. Now it was their chance to take home the bacon. Both teams virtually had the same players from the previous year. With over 2,000 fans crammed into Duke Arena, "the game started off as a duel between two lanky centers—Bobby Hodges of Kinston and John McGraw of Hendersonville. The lead changed hands four times and was tied three times in a thrilling first half. Kinston spurted near the end to take its 23–20 advantage."[6] Kinston was on top 29–22 early in the third quarter when the Hendersonville staged a brilliant comeback to beat the Red Devils 52–38. It didn't help that Bobby Hodges had to leave early in the fourth quarter with five personal fouls; nevertheless, his outstanding performance throughout the year earned him a berth on the all-state team. An editorial in the *Free Press* underscored the new coach's successful first season:

"Coach Sexton is making his debut as a local coach. His lads, although not considered as strong as they were last year, did equally as well and deserve the plaudits of all local fans. Kinston's record in all local sports has been an enviable one for the past three years, and we believe the auspicious beginnings Coach Sexton made this season means that local fans have many victories in store for the future."[7]

In December of 1949, the recreation department of Kinston started a city basketball league for boys. The league was organized on two age levels. One league was for the fourth, fifth, and sixth grade boys, and the other league was for the seventh, eighth, and ninth grade boys. Games were scheduled for two nights a week. Before the season started, there was a three-day basketball clinic in which the boys received instructions in fundamentals such as dribbling, shooting, passing, and foot work. Over 180 boys signed up just for the elementary-school basketball league. All sessions in the basketball school and play in the league was under the supervision of Tracy Hart, director of men's and boys' activities; Bill Fay, now director of recreation and former Red Devil head basketball coach; and Amos Sexton, the new Red Devil coach.[8] Alley Hart and Eion Faelten were seventh graders at that time, and their team won the championship. Both would go on to play on the Red Devils' 1956 state championship team.

The strength of the Grainger High School Athletic program was its cooperation and coordination with the City Recreational Department. By the time the boys of Kinston had reached the varsity level, they had been playing basketball and been trained and coached since the fourth grade. Basketball goals were set up at Emma Webb Park where kids could play basketball year-round and many did.

The city recreation department became a farm league for future Red Devil teams. Grainger High School went from grades seven through twelve. As the physical education instructor at Grainger High School, Amos Sexton used his class time to scout out potential basketball players. During his PE classes, he regularly selected boys who he thought looked promising. He directed these boys to go to the gym to practice basketball. The rest of the students played volleyball or did something else. Coach Sexton was always thinking about building a stronger team and looking for opportunities to improve his chances at winning ballgames. In the process, he developed a real eye for talent, and he would have plenty of material to work with. For the first two years, he pulled double duty and also coached the junior varsity team. During his tenure as a coach at Grainger High School, he also coached the junior baseball team; he was an assistant football coach; and, in 1956, he took the reins as a tennis coach after Charles Lee, the Red Devils' junior varsity basketball coach who left Kinston to become the head basketball coach at Goldsboro High School.

The 1948–1949 starting five. From left to right—Zollie Collins, Fred Williams, Bobby Hodges, Doug Bruton, and Joe Whaley. Courtesy the *Free Press*.

The 1948–1949 Red Devils. Left to Right: Front Row—Joe Whaley, Z.A. Collins, Lloyd Whitfield, Charles Larkins; second Row—Frank Seville, Fred Williams, Joe Aldridge, Sherrill Williams; back row—Eugene McDaniel, Bobby Hodges, Coach Sexton, Doug Bruton, Ed Bradshaw. Courtesy the *Free Press*.

3

WINNING CONFERENCE
BUT NO CIGAR

As defending champions of the northeastern conference in the previous two years, a third repeat could not be taken for granted. Every school in the conference was anxious to dethrone the Red Devils. Fred Williams and Z. A. Collins had graduated the previous year, so two new players had to move up to fill the void. New personnel required time and practice to make a team run smoothly, not to mention just having the right combination of players to make a team.

The first conference game was not scheduled until January 5 against the Greenville Phantoms. Until then, the Red Devils were playing eight games in December to get ready for conference competition. Sexton knew enough at this time to schedule games against teams that would challenge and sharpen the team's basketball skills. Three games were against class AA schools: Fayetteville, Wilson, and Goldsboro. At the time, Kinston was class A. Two other games would be against the East Carolina Freshman squad.

The coach knew that to become a better team, you play against the best. Unlike today's high-scoring shoot-outs, the basketball games during this era were noticeably lower in score. It was not unusual to

35

see a final score of 44–36 or 38–31. It was not because the players of this era were poor shooters. It was because the game was a little different. Over the years, basketball has evolved. Rules have changed, and athletes today benefit from the advancement of sports conditioning and technology. But there are at least four noticeable changes in the game that help explain the difference in scoring.

First, the "one and one" rule at the foul line had not been invented yet. A player got only a single shot even if he made it. Second, there was no limit to how long a team could offensively hold the ball. If they wanted to and often did as an offensive strategy, a team could freeze the ball and force the defense to come out to get it. This often ended up in a foul. Finally, unlike today, there were no three-point shots. There were many excellent long-ball shooters in those days whose statistics would have soared if allowed three points for their shots. It was not unusual for a game to be very low scoring, especially when it was a tough defensive battle.

The opening game of the 1949–1950 season was against Snow Hill on December 7. Snow Hill was a small school not far from Kinston and not expected to be much competition, but the new coach was not going to be overconfident. Bobby Hodges and Doug Bruton dominated the scoring, shoving in nineteen points each. The team looked better than expected this early in the season and mauled Snow Hill 46–27. Before the game in Kinston's local paper, Coach Sexton had rated the game to be a toss-up.[1]

Not wanting his team to be overconfident and making a sales pitch to the fans that this game could go either way, he had learned the psychology of getting into the players' heads while at the same time selling the game as one worthy to be attended. Even with such a lopsided victory, the coach could still see work to be done. The first conference game would be against Greenville on January 5. The Red Devils would play five more games to sharpen their skills before the regular season began.

The next warm-up game was against the undefeated class AA Wilson Cyclones. This was a legitimate challenge. The same Wilson team had entered the class AA state tournament the year before. The Cyclones were not going to be a pushover. In this game, Bobby

RED DEVIL TALES

Hodges was starting at center. Red McDaniel and Doug Bruton were the forwards. Joe Whaley and Bryant Aldridge finished out the lineup as the two guards. As the game opened, the Red Devils started slow and were somewhat sluggish.

By the opening of the second quarter, they had fallen behind by ten points (20–10). It looked like the game might be a rout for the Cyclones, but Joe Whaley hit two long set shots and drove down the middle from the free throw line to sink a third. At the half, Wilson held a slim 27–24 lead. In the third quarter, the Devils seemed to find their mark and fought back to take the lead 39–31 by the end of the third quarter. Joe Whaley broke up passes as Wilson tried to move down the court, and by the game's end, the Red Devils gave Wilson their first defeat 47–38.[2]

The Red Devils faced another class AA team in Fayetteville on Monday, December 12. In this game, both Bobby Hodges and Doug Bruton, the Red Devils' top scorers, were absent. These two Red Devil football standouts were in Greenville attending the all-state banquet honoring all state high school and college football players. However, Red McDaniel and Graham Phillips stepped up to the challenge and gave the Red Devils a 51–39 victory. McDaniel was the high scorer with nineteen, and Phillips had thirteen, and both controlled the backboards.[3]

By the end of December, the Red Devils had defeated Wilson for a second time (49–41), as well as Rocky Mount (53–34). Their only preseason defeats came at the hands of the East Carolina freshmen (49–41), who avenged an earlier defeat by the Red Devils a week earlier (35–24), and Goldsboro, a class AA team, who beat the Red Devils 49–46.[4] However, it was in the games lost that the team discovered its weaknesses. Getting beat by the East Carolina Freshmen and Goldsboro helped the Red Devils to do just that. The season was young, and the team had a lot of work to do to get ready for conference play.

East Carolina had a former Red Devil, Vincent Jones, on the team. Vincent scored eleven points for the Pirates against his old alma mater. However, it was East Carolina's center, Ray Everett, a native of Wilson, who dominated the Red Devils, putting in twenty

37

points. Defensively, he stole the ball, deflected passing, and generally dismantled the Red Devils' ability to score. Without Everett, in the opinion of one sports writer, Kinston would have won. He wondered why this player wasn't on the varsity. Hodges again had the top score for the Red Devils with seventeen points, but it wasn't enough to overcome the play of Everett.[5]

However, the losing experience would have its benefits. The Red Devils needed to work on the fundamentals of basketball and learn more about how to play as a team. The only other loss Kinston had during its preseason warm-up games was against the class AA Goldsboro Earthquakes. It was Kinston's first high school loss, and it was only by three points (49–46). It was the last game before the Christmas holidays, and it was being played on the Red Devils' home court.

The game started out promising, with both Bobby Hodges and Red McDaniel each scoring quick field goals before Goldsboro could get on the board. However, with the sharp shooting of the Earthquakes' guard, Ronald Percise, Goldsboro held a 30–21 lead at the half.

"For the first moments of the second half, it looked as though the Earthquakes would make a runaway affair of the game, but Aldridge tossed in three long set shots and McDaniel put in six points from down under the basket to bring the Red Devils back into the game. But Ronald Percise worked his magic scoring a total of 20 points, and put the Earthquakes out front, ending the game with a 49–46 victory."[6]

With a second loss in preseason, the road to the championship seemed more treacherous than anyone had anticipated, as the local sportswriter indicated, "It becomes more and more evident that Kinston will have a struggle on its hands to take its seventh straight northeastern conference title."[7] In frustration, after one of his shots rolled in and out of the basket, Doug Bruton complained, "Nobody else is as unlucky as me!"[8] The Red Devils were improving but still had a lot of work to do.

The first game in the New Year was on January 4, 1950, against the Fayetteville Bulldogs, a Class AA team that the Red Devils had

RED DEVIL TALES

beaten 51–39 in December. It was also one day after Dad's twenty-ninth birthday. For this game, the Red Devils had to play without Red McDaniel, who, along with Bobby Hodges, had been injured in an automobile accident over the holidays. Red had received a severe cut over his left eye and had hurt his ankle. Bobby Hodges injured his left ankle in the accident. Both boys were thought to be out of play for a while, but Bobby managed to recover enough to start in the game against Fayetteville.

Graham Phillips was inserted as a forward to replace Red McDaniel. Despite his ankle injury, Bobby Hodges led the Red Devils with seventeen, points and new comer Graham Phillips was close behind with sixteen. Graham Phillips, a recent transfer from Warsaw, showed a great deal of promise for the Red Devils as he gave Kinston control of the boards throughout the game. Bryant Aldridge, Joe Whaley, and Sherrill Williams played well defensively and helped hold Fayetteville to two points in the third quarter as the Red Devils continued to walk away with the game. The class AA Fayetteville team fell to the Red Devils for a second time, 61–38. Kinston was beginning to look like a team.

January 5 finally arrived, and the Red Devils faced their first conference contest against the Greenville Green Phantoms. From the start of the game, it was obvious that the Red Devils' shooting was off. Doug Bruton, playing at center and forward, was high scorer for the team with thirteen points, and newcomer Graham Phillips was second with eight. Bobby Hodges had seven points for the night. The halftime score was only 29–21. Greenville was aggressive, but the Red Devils had the advantage in height, forcing he Phantoms to shoot from far out. The game was progressing rather rapidly until midway into the second quarter when both teams seemed to lose sight of the basket. Scoring was held in check until the final minutes of the game when Greenville began to cut into the Red Devil margin. The final score was 42–31.[9]

In the opinion of their coach, the Red Devils had played their poorest game of the season. This performance had come on the heels of one of their best games at Fayetteville the night before. Coach Sexton was not pleased and showed some consternation. Some of the problem, the coach believed, was fatigue from having to play games on successive nights. But the Red Devils had no time to rest. They faced Rocky Mount the next night.[10]

Fatigue must have finally caught up with them. On January 6, the Red Devils experienced their third loss of the season to the Rocky Mount Blackbirds in a close 45–44 final. It was sweet revenge for the Blackbirds, who had been trounced by Kinston in December 53–34. The Red Devils' shooting was off but then had moments of good basketball with Doug Bruton's hook shots keeping Kinston in the game and Williams, Phillips, and Hodges showing outstanding floor play. A free throw in the last minute of the game made the difference.[11] Had the Red Devils been given a few days' rest, the outcome would have probably been different. The next game was against the New Bern Bears the following Tuesday. The team had the weekend to rest, and it made a difference.[12] Their best games so far had been away from home. This was going to be a home game, and they needed to have a good performance. For this game, Hodges was at center, Aldridge and Whaley at guards, Bruton and Phillips at forwards. Red McDaniel was still recovering from his injuries, although he was ready to play. He had a protector put on his head to cover the cut over his right eye. He did enter the game and contributed four points to the final score.[13]

New Bern was not as strong this year as they had been the year before when they had Sonny Russell, the Bears' outstanding center, who went on to have an excellent career with the East Carolina Pirates. Bobby Hodges would join him at East Carolina the next year, and the Pirates became a formidable force to contend with in their conference. Doug Bruton was the high scorer in the game against New Bern with thirteen points. Graham Phillips continued to show he could play, putting in ten points for the night. Kinston beat the Bears 43–36.[14]

Kinston's strongest opponent in the conference in 1950 was up next—the Washington Pam-Pack or Little Washington, as they were known to the Red Devils. The game was set for Friday, January 13, in Washington. The Washington team was traditionally hard to beat on their home court, although early in the season, both teams were

RED DEVIL TALES

undefeated in conference play. The entire Pam-Pack starting five were holdovers who saw much action for the conference runner-up last year.[15]

As the game got underway, it became clear that the Pam-Pack was never a real threat even on its own home court. Graham Phillips led the scoring for the Red Devils with thirteen points. Doug Bruton had the next highest score with ten, and Hodges had eight. Phillips, Bruton, and Aldridge paced the Red Devil defense, and although Kinston's play was considered slightly off, it was still good enough to beat the Pam-Pack, 47–34.[16]

As the junior varsity coach and PE teacher, Coach Sexton was always on the lookout for new and talented players. In one of his PE classes, a new student appeared who had recently immigrated to America from war-torn Europe. He was a sixteen-year-old displaced refugee from Latvia who somehow had ended up in Kinston in December of 1949. He was enrolled at Grainger High School even though he could not speak or understand English. His name was Bonifacys Madelans, but his fellow students simply called him Barney. One of his scheduled classes was PE. Of course, one of the physical activities in Coach Sexton's PE classes was playing basketball. The sport was strange to Barney, but he seemed to catch on quickly, showing good coordination and ability. Barney did so well, in fact, that Coach Sexton decided to try him out with the junior varsity squad in the preliminary game scheduled for Tuesday night against Edenton. Unfortunately, both the varsity and junior varsity games were postponed due to sleet and ice. Barney's debut would have to wait.[17]

The Red Devils had a perfect conference record going into the next game with Roanoke Rapids. Roanoke Rapids had a team that was showing much improvement as the season progressed, and they were expected to give Kinston a good battle. After Tuesday's cancellation with Edenton, the Red Devils were getting a well-deserved rest. Red McDaniel reinjured the cut on his head during practice on Monday night, so his participation in Friday's game against Roanoke Rapids was doubtful. He was one of the Red Devils' leading point makers, but since his automobile accident over the holidays, he had

41

seen little action.[18] Bobby Hodges was back in form against Roanoke Rapids, leading the scoring for the night with nineteen points. Joe Whaley, Kinston's scrappy little guard, put in ten points, while Doug Bruton and Graham Phillips each had seven points.

The Red Devils had little trouble with Roanoke Rapids, beating them soundly 55–28. Four players for Roanoke fouled out of the game as they struggled to hold off Kinston's offensive attack. At the end of the first half, Kinston held a 21–9 lead. The reserves were put in during the second half and played on fairly even terms with the Roanoke Rapids starters. Roanoke Rapids was forced to shoot most of its shots from the outside while the Red Devils consistently scored within two feet of the basket.[19]

The Elizabeth City Yellow Jackets were the next team on the schedule. The game was set for Tuesday, January 24, in the Grainger gym. The Red Devils at this point were undefeated in conference play with a perfect four-game record. They had scored a total of 201 points, averaging just over fifty points per game in conference play. Elizabeth City and Washington were tied for second place with three and one records. Coached by Bob Brooks, the Yellow Jackets' performance could be unpredictable.[20] Coach Sexton indicated that the team was notoriously hard to beat on their home court, so the Red Devils really needed a win against them at home.[21]

When the Red Devils played Elizabeth City, it was a rout. Sportswriter Bob Lewis said,

"It was strictly 'no contest' at Grainger High School Gymnasium here Tuesday night as the Kinston Red Devils played brilliant basketball to snow under a highly regarded Elizabeth City team, 73–24. Displaying their best shooting of the year, the Red Devils made good on 31 of 52 goal attempts for an amazing average of nearly 60 per cent."[22]

Bobby Hodges, as was his habit, turned in the highest score with sixteen points. Bruton had ten points, while Phillips, McDaniel, and Amos Stroud all had nine points each. The entire bench was emptied, and everyone managed to score.

On Friday, January 27, the Red Devils were taking a break from conference play to face Goldsboro once again, seeking to avenge an

RED DEVIL TALES

earlier loss against the Earthquakes in December. Goldsboro had a defense much like the Red Devils. It consisted of a three-man zone with two men drifting out on the floor.[23]

Kinston had prepared to face this kind of challenge, and it paid off. Graham Phillips was beginning to make his mark, and he played an excellent game against Goldsboro. He, along with Bobby Hodges, effectively controlled the backboards, limiting the opposition to one shot. Graham Phillips was high scorer with nineteen points. Bobby Hodges had eighteen, and Doug Bruton was the third man in double figures with fourteen. These three players played the entire game, and together, they dismantled the Goldsboro defense. The score had seesawed back and forth, until Hodges tapped in a follow-up shot to give the Devils a 21–19 lead. It was a hard-fought game, but the Red Devils held their lead and finished with a win, beating Goldsboro 56–46.[24]

Beating Goldsboro was a confidence builder. The Red Devils had gone up against a good class AA club, controlled the boards, unraveled their opponents' defense, and had a good shooting percentage from the field. Still undefeated in conference play, the Red Devils seemed poised to finish the remainder of the conference schedule in top form. They had seven conference games left. The next week, they had two conference games, Greenville and New Bern.

On Tuesday, January 31, Kinston traveled to Greenville to face the Phantoms. They had beaten Greenville in the first conference game of the year 42–31. Bobby Hodges set the nets on fire with a game total of twenty-seven points. Within three minutes of the first quarter of this game, the Red Devils had an 11–0 lead. They hit on 68 percent of their shots in the first half, which ended with Kinston on top 35–15. In the second half, the Phantoms went into a pressing defense in an effort to stop the Red Devil attack. It didn't work. Kinston held on to their lead and beat Greenville 61–42.[25]

The game was hard fought and rather intense with the referees calling four technical fouls. Kinston suffered one such foul when a player from the bench went into the game without reporting to the scorer. Another technical foul was called on the Greenville team for booing a Kinston player when he took a foul shot. The other two technical fouls were called on individual Greenville players for unsportsmanlike language. The competition was intense, to say the least, and the Red Devils would eventually meet them again in tournament play.[26]

The Red Devils traveled to New Bern Friday night, February 3, in their second game against the New Bern Bears, who they had mauled 57–28 early in January. New Bern was seriously lacking in height, and height had been a major factor in the Kinston string of victories. Bobby Hodges, Graham Phillips, Doug Bruton, and Red McDaniel gave the Red Devils control underneath while Joe Whaley and Bryant Aldridge provided excellent floor defense, and both guards could pull out the opposition's defense with long set shots when things got too crowded under the basket.[27] However, Joe Whaley would not make this trip, having to take part in the minstrel show currently being presented in Kinston. Sherrill Williams would replace Whaley for that game.[28]

Because Bobby Hodges was such a dominant player, his substitute, Bud Bradshaw, was somewhat overshadowed. But Coach Sexton noted that he was particularly pleased by the way Bud had been playing when he relieved the all-state center. The Red Devils' shooting accuracy was also improving. During the Greenville game, the Red Devils' accuracy averaged 55 percent for the game, and they made good on 65 percent of their foul shots. The next two games were critical. The Red Devils faced the New Bern Bears and then the Washington Pam Pac. Coach Sexton was afraid that the Red Devils were due for a bad night which would be coming at the wrong time. The coach felt that he might be able to afford a loss if he could get through the next two games against New Bern and then Washington.[29] The game against Washington the following Tuesday was looking more and more like the game of the season, with both clubs now fighting for top position in the league.[30]

The Red Devils beat the New Bern Bears again 44–32, but the final margin wasn't gained until the last quarter. The Bears were only one point behind after three quarters of play. The score was 28–27. In fact, New Bern held a 10–7 lead at the end of the first quarter. Hodges had twenty points, while Phillips and Bruton had nine each.

RED DEVIL TALES

New Bern tried a new strategy against the Red Devils, passing the ball around in a circle with no attempt to work into the basket, i.e., holding the ball since there was no shooting clock. Knowing they were they were no match for the Devils under the basket, the Bears were content to shoot outside set shots and long hooks. New Bern managed to keep the ball most of the time until the final quarter when the Red Devils abandoned their zone defense and played man to man, forcing New Bern out of their comfort zone. It was then that Kinston pulled far ahead. The Red Devils' shooting average dropped to 36 percent in this game, which, of course, contributed to the closeness of the score.[31]

Kinston now had a record of 7–0 in conference play. Tuesday's game against Washington, who were 6–1, was being played at home in Grainger Gymnasium. Washington's only loss had been at the hands of the Red Devils, so they were out to even the score. The Pam-Pack was paced in scoring by their talented forward, Garland Holmes, and guard Billy Asby. Defensively, Washington's Dick Cherry, Lee Knott, and Pappy Fowle were the standouts. In seven conference games, the Red Devils had outscored their opponents in points 379 to 219.[32]

Because a capacity crowd, including a large group from Washington, was expected, tickets were on sale in the lobby of the gym starting at 6:00 p.m., and a public address system was installed for the first time to keep fans abreast of what was going on.[33] After a hard-fought game, the Red Devils edged the Pam-Pack by only one point, 63–62.

The Edenton game, which had been cancelled due to weather in January, had been rescheduled for February 8. It was the final home game for the regular season, and the varsity Red Devils trounced the Edenton Aces 51–11. Red McDaniel was finally back after being out since December and led the Kinston scoring with 9 points, with Bobby Hodges close behind with 8. The starters were pulled after the first quarter and the reserves finished up the helpless Aces. At this point, the Red Devils had won nine straight northeastern conference games and had compiled a record of seventeen wins with three losses. The junior varsity game was an even greater slaughter with the Kinston Imps mauling the Edenton Junior Aces, 50–9.[34]

Unfortunately, little Barney Madelans, who had been scheduled to make his appearance in the first JV game against Edenton back in January, missed this game, as well. The game had been scheduled at the last moment. Since Barney couldn't read the daily paper, and no one had thought to inform him of the upcoming game, he stayed home. He would certainly have gotten to play.[35] The Red Devils traveled to Edenton on Friday, February 11, to play their regularly scheduled game with the Aces. Again, the Kinston cagers mauled the helpless Aces. This time, Edenton fared just slightly better, losing to the Red Devils 52–16.[36]

The Red Devils had two out-of-town games left on their schedule to complete the regular season—Roanoke Rapids on Tuesday, February 14, and the final game with Elizabeth City on Friday, February 17. They were 10–0 in conference play with Kinston's closest game coming against Greenville who they had beaten by eleven points. With a win against Roanoke Rapids on Tuesday, the Red Devils would take their third straight northeastern conference title.

At Roanoke Rapids, the Red Devils seemed to be synchronizing as a team with everyone contributing, passing, and shooting with ease and fluidity. The paper noted the difference: Team Play Beats Roanoke Rapids as Kinston Wins. It marked the Red Devils' seventh straight northeastern conference title. Center Bobby Hodges and guard Joe Whaley combined to make up half the score with Hodges pouring in seventeen points while Whaley had fourteen. Joe Whaley hit eleven of his fourteen points in the first half, while Hodges accounted for 15 of 17 in the last half. It was an overwhelming win for the Kinston cagers 69–34.[37]

With the conference title won, a win against Elizabeth City would give the Red Devils a perfect conference record. Elizabeth City could be difficult to beat on their home court, and since the Red Devils had handed them an embarrassing defeat back in January (73–24), the Yellow Jackets were anxious for revenge. Being about a hundred miles from Kinston, Elizabeth City was the longest conference road trip for the Red Devils.

Through the years, the long road trip to Elizabeth City would give rise to many urban legends since the boys on the bus had too

RED DEVIL TALES

much time on their hands, and the usual Pepsi stops along the way were opportunities for devilish mischief. The stories I remember Dad telling about his days in Kinston concerned the shenanigans and rascal incidents that happened on the way to or from a game. I do not remember him discussing championship games, basketball strategy, or techniques. Of course, as children, we would not have the understanding or interest for such matters. I am sure he talked about those things with coaches and players who had an appreciation for the game.

According to Doug Bruton, the Elizabeth City basketball court was one of the worst to play in at the time. The court was some sort of red-and-brown tile, hard as a rock, and difficult to navigate. The lighting was substandard, and the backboards were small, wooden, and half moon in shape, making bank shots almost impossible. As the game got underway, the Yellow Jackets opened up with a delaying tactic against Kinston's zone defense and managed to keep the score low and close. By the end of the first half, the Red Devils were holding a slim lead, 15–12. The coach could see that the game was not going to be a push over. The Yellow Jackets' desperate tactics had their effect. Adjustments were made in the locker room at halftime, and the coach's pep talk fired up the Red Devils.

In the second half, Bruton and Hodges controlled the backboard while McDaniel, Stroud and Williams played their part in keeping the Red Devils in the game. Nevertheless, with only 5:14 left in the game, Elizabeth City was within one point, 28–27. Then Kinston put it in high gear and got hot, making the final score 40–29. Not a rout like the first game, but it was a solid win nevertheless. The Red Devils knew that their performance was substandard, and for a team that just won the conference, they were not pleased.

4

THEY GOT CONFERENCE, BUT WE GOT STATE

If the Red Devils seemed a little distracted during the Elizabeth City game, it was not because they had already won the northeastern conference title and therefore not highly motivated. It was probably because of some disheartening news they had received earlier. Before the game, the team had a pre-game meal at a local restaurant. It was there that Coach Sexton informed the team that there had been a conference ruling made the day before that made Graham Phillips, Kinston's talented new forward, ineligible and declared all games in which he participated null and void. The Red Devils, with a perfect conference record and northeast conference champions, were now 1–11 instead of 12–0 and were stripped of their conference title.

Graham Phillips was a transfer student from Warsaw, North Carolina, and he had entered Grainger High School in the fall of 1949. He went out for football, but in the first game, he seriously injured his back, which put him out for the season. By the time basketball season started, Graham, also a talented basketball player, was well enough to start playing. Graham Phillips would do very well in

RED DEVIL TALES

basketball and eventually went on to Wake Forest on a basketball scholarship.

When Graham was in the sixth grade, his dad was in the Marine Corp and stationed in New Jersey. His father was near the end of his Marine Corp service and was scheduled to be discharged. At that time, Graham came to Kinston to stay with his grandmother for five or six months. He entered the sixth grade in Kinston and made friends with all of the boys he would someday play basketball with. When Graham was in the tenth grade, he was living in Warsaw. Warsaw is a small community less than fifty miles southwest of Kinston. The summer before he entered the eleventh grade, Graham was at Carolina Beach on a house party walking down the boardwalk with some of his friends. He ran into some of his old Kinston friends, Bobby Hodges, Bryant Aldridge, Fred Williams, and several others as they were walking the boardwalk. Bobby told Graham that Fred was about to graduate, and he encouraged him to come to Kinston and live with his grandmother and play football, taking Fred's place as an end on the football team.

When Graham returned home, he started thinking about it. Kinston was a bigger and better school. He had friends there, and they had a great athletic program. Graham asked his mother about it, and she reluctantly let him move to Kinston and live with his grandmother. Within three weeks, Graham was in Kinston practicing football. He lived with his grandmother part of the time and also lived in Kinston part of the time with his aunt, who was Alley Hart's mother. Alley Hart's mother and Graham's mother were sisters.[1]

For some reason, either Coach Mock or Coach Sexton overlooked the necessary paperwork that would have made Graham eligible to play ball in Kinston. After Graham injured his back in the first football game, he fell off the radar screen. By the time he was well enough to go out for basketball, the formal paperwork probably had been overlooked. The *i* had not been dotted. No one had really noticed, and if they had, it wouldn't have mattered. It was just a small technicality. But someone took a complaint to the conference ruling committee, a group generally noted for being rather legalistic.

49

The conference ruling committee took the complaint under advisement and made a ruling. Following the letter of the law, the committee required Kinston to forfeit any games in which Graham Phillips had participated. Kinston was allowed to play in the northeastern conference tournament, but they would have to enter the tournament in last place. It was never officially stated who had reported the violation to the conference ruling committee, but it was generally believed that some administrative person from the Washington Pam-Pack had blown the whistle. They had the most to gain from Kinston having to forfeit their games. One thing is for certain, Frank Mock or Amos Sexton would never have done such a thing to another team. But you don't pull on Superman's cape, and you surely don't jerk on a Red Devils' tail without consequences. The Red Devils had already beaten Little Washington twice in the regular season. The Red Devils were irate, to say the least. They had worked and played hard as a team, and they felt they had won the conference fair and square. The student body of Grainger High School was angry, and the fans of Kinston were fired up. To claim the conference title over such a petty technicality was just an all-time low. The Pam-Pack would pay!

The *Free Press* of Kinston first reported the ruling the day after the last game of the regular season against Elizabeth City. Sportswriter Dick Tyndall stated,

"Playing without the services of regular starters Graham Phillips and Bryant Aldridge, who was out with the flu the Kinston Red Devils still had little trouble with Elizabeth City here last night as they closed out their regular season with a 40–29 victory. The victory gave Kinston a 20–3 record for the season and a 12–0 record in the Northeastern Conference, although through a technicality, 11 of those games may be tossed out by the Conference."[2]

"The Conference yesterday ruled Phillips ineligible and declared all games in which he participated null and void."[3]

On Monday, February 20, Tyndall added his own commentary:

RED DEVIL TALES

"As near as we can figure it out, here is what happened: There is and has been considerable resentment throughout the Northeastern Conference because of the constant winning by Kinston teams in recent years. That's a natural reaction, just as natural as that of some of the coaches, principals, etc., who got hot under the collar about it."[4]

"It is ridiculous to think of a high school principal getting so sore-headed over his school's defeats as to toss out a great team's victories and bar an innocent athlete on a technicality. But apparently that's exactly what happened. Somewhere along the line, a Kinston school official slipped up and failed to send in a statement to conference headquarters to the effect that Graham Phillips, a star basketball player, had come to Kinston of his own free will and not through the influence of Kinston High School. Just the idea of Kinston, 'going out' and getting basketball talent is ludicrous on the face of it. With a host of talent already on hand and a tiny gymnasium that can't take care of the crowds already being drawn, what would be the reason for a talent search? The conference executive committee admitted that this was too unheard of to be considered when it said: 'No fine is deemed necessary, as the Executive Committee feels that there was no intent on the part of the school officials to violate the regulations as set forth in the constitution.' In other words, the executive committee is saying: 'We know you aren't guilty but we are going to declare an innocent (athlete) ineligible and take away 11 victories which we know you would have had anyway. We can win games this way and no other. It's the only way we can beat you.' So Washington High School became the Conference champions with—believe it or not—a perfect record. Kinston ended up on the bottom with a record of one win and 11 losses. Washington, incidentally, was one of the instigators of the affair."[5]

The paper also noted that

"One Kinston coach said that a poll of other coaches in the Conference showed them to be almost unanimous in their condemnation of the executive committee's action. Only one coach,

51

RONALD SEXTON

it was said, had failed to uphold Kinston's right to the conference title."[6]

The whole affair raised numerous questions about how the playoffs would proceed. The ruling complicated the conference tournament seeding, as well as the regional and state tournaments. Before the storm of eligibility broke, Kinston, as the league's number one team, and Washington, as the runner-up, would participate in the regional tournament at Wilson. Conference officials were to meet on Monday afternoon, February 20, to sort out these issues.

"Coach Frank Mock, Coach Amos Sexton and Principal John E. Horne attended the meeting and pleaded their case. It was explained that Graham Phillips had transferred to Kinston from Warsaw the previous fall. He went out for the football team, but was injured in the first two minutes of the opening game of the season. Since it was obvious that he would be out for the rest of the season, Kinston officials neglected sending in the required papers from the schools involved and the question did not arise when he went out for basketball. It was pointed out that while Kinston was not accused of 'bringing in' players, the Kinston school was being forced to take the punishment for that offense."[7]

The following day, the committee's ruling came down, and the paper noted the northeastern conference officials' conclusion:

"Although admitting that Kinston had violated a Conference rule through an oversight and that the punishment involved was unjust, the Northeastern Conference yesterday afternoon refused to change an action by the Executive Committee which forfeited 11 out of 12 Kinston victories. The Conference voted, however, to send Kinston to the State playoffs."

"The Conference meeting by a unanimous vote, with Kinston abstaining, refused to allow Kinston forward Graham Phillips to play in the conference tournament beginning in Greenville Thursday night. The motion, however, was made to hinge on the question of whether or not eligibility rules should apply to the tournament rather than on its own merits."[8]

RED DEVIL TALES

An editorial in the *Free Press* responded,

"We asked for cake and they gave us a crumb.' That might well be the reaction of the Kinston delegation to the Northeastern Conference meeting in Greenville Monday afternoon. Kinston asked for a clean bill, for the return of those 11 games which were taken by forfeit and for the ruling that Graham Phillips was eligible for further basketball play. Instead, the Northeastern Conference voted to give Kinston the right to play in the State play-offs, while in the same breath pushing Kinston down in the bottom spot of the league."

"Coach Frank Mock made an earnest appeal for the spirit of the law to be observed. The law, he pointed out, is designed to punish the guilty and to protect the innocent. That Kinston was innocent of any intent to violate the requirements was admitted by all present. The real question seemed to hinge on the "spirit" of the (league's) constitution. There was no doubt but that the letter of the law had been violated. There was no doubt the spirit of the law had NOT been violated. "But for some strange reason, several conference members, led by Greenville's O.E. Dowd, insisted that rules made by them should not be changed by themselves, feeling, they indicated, that there was something sacred about the present set of rules. Early in the history of the United States, one of the great issues of day concerned the interpretation of the nation's constitution. There was a whole political party—a powerful one which elected several Presidents— which stood for following the (United States) Constitution to the letter. They, too, declared that the spirit was not the thing."[9]

The Red Devils accepted their fate, as seemingly unfair as it was. It only made them more determined. The northeastern conference tournament began on Thursday, February 3, and was being played in Greenville at Wright Auditorium, home of East Carolina Teachers College. The Red Devils were scheduled to play New Bern in the opening round. They were scheduled to play at 9:30 p.m., the last game of the night.

With tensions high and frustrations at a fever pitch, Coach Mock, speaking for the Kinston School, appealed to fans to be "well-mannered," and to show "level-headedness and good sportsmanship." Even in the face of a "raw deal," he called upon fans to show respect for the officials and other ball clubs who had nothing to do with actions taken by league officials. Sentiments in other cities in the conference were generally favorable to the Kinston cause.[10]

At 9:30 on Thursday night, the Kinston Red Devils and the New Bern Bears squared off. The first quarter, the two teams played evenly with both squads using the zone defense. Kinston fans wondered if the pretournament hullabaloo had caused some consternation among the team. Right after the second period opened, New Bern had its last lead, but Joe Whaley scored with a set shot to tie the game. Doug Bruton and Bobby Hodges began to dominate the boards and push in the points. By the end of the second quarter, the Red Devils held a 21–13 lead. The second half saw more of the same with Hodges and Bruton controlling the game. The final score was 47–26 with Bobby Hodges scoring fourteen points and Doug Bruton had ten. The Red Devils' next opponent was the Greenville Phantoms on Friday, who had beaten Edenton earlier in the evening 46–27.

As in the game against New Bern, the Red Devils and the Phantoms battled head-to-head for the first half. Kinston got on the board first with a shot by Bobby Hodges, but Greenville fought to a 12–10 lead by the end of the first quarter. The second quarter was a back-and-forth struggle with the lead changing hands six times in the first six minutes, and with four minutes left in the first half, Greenville edged ahead 21–17. Red McDaniel came back with a jump shot, followed by single free throws by Hodges and Bruton to tie the score 21–21. The half ended with the Red Devils holding on to a slim lead 30–26. In the second half, Kinston seemed to put it in high gear, or as the paper noted, "After what must have been an inspiring pep talk from Coach Sexton, the Kinston Red Devils went rapidly to the front in the second half and what had been a close game became a runaway."[11] The Red Devils routed the Phantoms 72–46. Doug Bruton had the high score with twenty-two points with Bobby Hodges putting in seventeen. Both Joe Whaley and Red McDaniel contributed thirteen points each, and Bryant Aldridge had seven.

RED DEVIL TALES

Amos Stroud and Sherrill Williams got into the game and played excellent defense. The final game of the tournament put the Red Devils face-to-face with their conference arch nemesis, the Pam-Pac. The Red Devils couldn't wait!

If the Red Devils ever had a score to settle, it was against Little Washington in the finals. All of their pent-up frustrations and resentment over the raw deal was going to be mercilessly unleashed against a foe they held responsible. With fire in their eyes and smoke seething from their nostrils, the Red Devils came out and absolutely demolished the boys of Washington 56 to 28. Bobby Hodges and Doug Bruton controlled the backboards, while Joe Whaley and Bryant Aldridge dominated play out on the floor with Red McDaniel doing an excellent job in all departments. Hodges was the top scorer with sixteen, and Bruton and Whaley had thirteen points each.

"In the closing minutes Washington guard Dick Cherry was pressing Kinston guard Joe Whaley rather hard as Whaley brought the ball down the court. Suddenly, Whaley looked at him as though to say: 'Well, if you want it that bad . . .' and handed the ball over to Cherry. The surprised Washington player didn't seem to know what to do with it after he had the ball in his hands. He finally took a long shot at the goal, and missed."[12]

It was sweet revenge. The Red Devils were now the 1950 northeastern conference tournament champions. Both Bobby Hodges and Doug Bruton were placed on the all-tournament team, a well-deserved honor. Having secured the conference championship, Kinston now had to win the Regional Tournament before going to the State play-offs. The regional tournament this year was played in the Atlantic Christian College gym at Wilson. The Red Devils would meet either Oxford or Roxboro in the semifinals, but the Red Devils were not finished with the Pam-Pack.

The Pams-Pack would be the other team representing the northeastern conference in the regional play-offs. There was some confusion due to the ineligibility fiasco as to who would be paired with whom. It was finally decided that Kinston would meet Oxford

55

in the semifinal game while Washington was paired with Roxboro. Oxford was considered the more balanced of the two, but Kinston was ready for the challenge.

The starting line-up against Oxford included Bobby Hodges, center; Doug Bruton and Red McDaniel at forward; and Joe Whaley and Bryant Aldridge at guard. In height, Oxford and the Red Devils were evenly matched, but when the game got underway, Bobby Hodges secured the ball right off and put the Red Devils on the board. Whaley added a field goal, and the Red Devils had a 5–0 lead. Kinston led by the end of the first quarter 13–9 and 23–15 at the half. "Oxford cut the lead back to four points at one time in the third quarter but going into the final quarter, Kinston led 32–25."[13] Oxford had a center, Chappell, who was as tall as Hodges, but in the first half, Hodges controlled the backboard and kept the Red Devils out in front. Doug Bruton picked up the mantle in the second half, providing the spark that kept the Red Devils ahead. Bruton and Hodges were the outstanding performers of the game. Hodges led the scoring with twenty-one points and Bruton with ten. The Kinston *Free Press* noted that Sherrill Williams played very well for the time he was in the game. Red McDaniel and Joe Whaley also had an important role in the Red Devils' win 44–34.

Unfortunately, or maybe fortunately for Washington's sake, Roxboro beat the Pam-Pack 48–41 and so ended Washington's Machiavellian attempt to get to the state play-offs. In the end, the Red Devil cheerleaders would create a new cheer, "Wheaties! The breakfast of champions. Washington got the conference, but we got state!"

The Roxboro Rockets were not as big as the Red Devils. The tallest player was Skippy Winstead, a 6–2 guard who was noted for his ballhandling. Against Washington, Winstead led the attack with nineteen points. As the game got underway against Kinston, it was clear that Winstead was Roxboro's key player. The first half belonged to Roxboro mainly on the efforts of the snappy ballhandling and shooting of Winstead (who put up thirteen points for the game). The Red Devils opened the scoring, but by the end of the first quarter, the

RED DEVIL TALES

score was tied 10–10. The Red Devils were cold from the field in the first half, hitting only 23 percent of their shots.[14]

Up to this point in the playoffs, the Red Devils had trouble getting started in the opening quarters of the game but always managed to pull it together in the second half to win. This game was no exception. With 4:45 left in the third quarter and behind by six points, the Red Devils finally found their mark and started making some baskets. In the fourth quarter with 4:55 remaining, Joe Whaley swished a long set shot and put the Red Devils out in front to stay. The final score was 32–28. Joe Whaley and Doug Bruton grabbed the headlines as the Red Devils' outstanding performers, each putting in ten points. Hodges was close behind with eight.[15]

One reason the Red Devils struggled was a bout of influenza that plagued the squad. After the game, Bryant Aldridge, suffering from exhaustion, was ordered to bed for two or three days, while Bobby Hodges was still weak from the flu virus. Others on the team had similar problems.[16]

Having made it through the regional play-offs, the Red Devils were on their way to the state play-offs for the third straight year. Playing in Durham at the Duke indoor stadium, the Red Devils' first match-up was against Rutherfordton-Springdale on Friday, March 10. The other two teams in the semifinals were Hanes High School of Winton-Salem and Rockingham. The Red Devils had beaten Hanes the previous year by one point, only to fall to Hendersonville in the championship game. This year would be different.

The outcome of the game was never in doubt after the first few minutes. Rutherfordton-Springdale was simply overpowered by the Red Devils. The Red Devils led at the end of the first quarter 13–7 and at halftime 30–13. The bench was cleared, and everyone got into the game. Even the reserves outscored and outplayed the opposition. The final score was 65–29. Bobby Hodges scored twenty-six points, and Doug Bruton accounted for seventeen. Hodges's twenty-six points tied the tournament individual record.[17]

When Bobby Hodges reached the twenty-six-point mark, Coach Sexton, unaware that the Kinston center had tied the record and could break it, started to take him out the game and put in one of the reserves. Maurice Courie, the Kinston scorekeeper, called the coach's attention to the situation. Coach Sexton left Hodges in the ball game. Hodges got an opportunity to break the record when he went to the foul line for two shots. Unfortunately, he missed both of them.[18]

The stage was now set for the Red Devils to win the state championship in basketball for the first time in the school's history. For the last two years, the Red Devils had been the runner-up. They were tired of playing second fiddle. If the third time is a charm, this was their year. Hanes of Winston-Salem had defeated Rockingham in the other semifinal contest, 59–22. The battle for the state championship would begin at 8:15 p.m. the next day, Saturday, March 11. It would be a rematch from the previous year's semifinal game between Kinston and Hanes. The Dragons of Hanes had been beaten by the Red Devils for two straight years in the state semifinal game. In both games, the Red Devils had edged the Dragon(s) by only one point. The Hanes cagers had a score to settle, and they were determined not to make it three years in a row. However, someone forgot to remind them of the old saying that bad luck happens in threes.

The Red Devils, still recovering from injuries and influenza, managed to put those things aside and focus on the game. In the first minute of play, Joe Whaley took the ball down the court for a long set shot. He missed, but Doug Bruton rebounded and scored the game's first points on a follow-up shot. Hanes's forward, Maurice George, came back with a set shot and tied the score, an indication of the "nip and tuck" play between the two squads for the rest of the game. Both Whaley and Hodges would make good on their next shots bringing the score to 6–3. The second quarter was slow as both teams tightened up their defense and scrapped wildly in attempting to rally. After several exchanges of goals, McDaniel hit for five points to give Kinston a 20–16 halftime lead.[19]

In the third quarter, the Red Devils seemed more focused on their game. Being the second-half team they had been all postseason long, it looked as if they might pull away with another wide-margin victory. Bobby Hodges, the Red Devils' leading point maker and

RED DEVIL TALES

rebound artist, came out smoking in the third quarter with a follow-up shot, a layup, and three foul tosses to give the Red Devils a 37–25 at the end of the quarter. The fourth quarter was much the same as the Red Devils continued in relentless pursuit. At one point in the fourth quarter, Kinston built up a seventeen-point lead (44–27) with 5:30 left in the game.[20]

Then Hanes rallied. The Dragons were not giving up so easily. In the final minutes of the game, Hanes would whittle away at the Red Devils' lead and score fifteen points while holding the Kinston cagers to one free throw. With one minute and fifteen seconds left in the game, the score was 45–42, the Red Devils hanging on by a thread. Hanes had the momentum, and it looked like they were going to catch up in short order.[21]

Then Sherrill Williams, who played an exceptional game as a starter at forward, added a free throw, and Joe Whaley laid in a shot from underneath to increase the score to 48–42 with forty-five seconds remaining in the game. Hanes's guards moved the ball down the court and passed off to their center, Jim Stevenson, who then ripped the chords with a left-handed jump-push shot and was fouled by Hodges. He got one foul shot. The score was now 48–44. Stevenson stepped up to the foul line and shot. He missed. In a scramble for the ball off the boards, Sherrill Williams fouled the Hanes forward, George. Now there were only two seconds left on the clock. George came to the foul line for two shots. He made both. The score was now 48–46. The Red Devils took the ball for an inbound play, but the pass was intercepted by Tom Preston, Hanes' agile forward, who attempted a last second shot as the buzzer sounded. The shot would tie the score. For a moment, everyone held their breath as the ball traveled toward the goal. The ball hit the backboard, rolled around the rim for what seemed like an eternity, and rolled off. He missed. The Red Devils had just won their first basketball state championship! And it was a "nail-biter."[22]

The Red Devils played only six players in this game—Williams, Bruton, McDaniel, Hodges, Aldridge, and Whaley. Bobby Hodges was the high scorer for the night with twenty-one points and the tournament's high scorer with forty-seven. His counterpart on the loosing team, Jim Stevenson, had twenty points for the night. Doug Bruton had the next highest with thirteen with Whaley adding seven and McDaniel five.[23]

Three Red Devils were selected on the all-class-A tourney team—Bobby Hodges, Doug Bruton, and Joe Whaley. All three were unanimous choices. Bobby Hodges also was chosen as the outstanding player of the tournament. In addition to this, he was named to the *Greensboro Daily News* all-state squad and selected to the *Durham Morning Herald* all-state team. Amos Sexton was selected as the outstanding coach of the tournament.[24]

The city of Kinston was proud of their athletes. It marked the second time in twelve months that Kinston had won a state championship. Coach Mock and the Red Devil baseball team had won the state championship the previous spring. Many believed that the football team would have won the coveted honor had they entered into state play. The football team did not enter the playoffs because it still had conference games to be played.[25]

The Red Devils returned home Sunday afternoon the following day to enthusiastic fans who escorted the team in an impromptu parade down Queen Street in Kinston. The old Red Devil bus was stopped at the White Owl Café on Highway 70 just west of the city. A convertible pulled in front of the bus to lead the procession, with a number of cars following the bus as they paraded down Queen Street. The boys all got out and piled into a convertible holding high the state championship trophy with Dad getting in the right front seat grinning like a possum. They paraded down Queen Street as proud Kinston fans waved and welcomed home the new state champs.[26]

March was a good month for the city of Kinston, the Red Devils, and for Mother and Dad. Mother was very pregnant during the tournament. She and Dad were expecting their first child. On March 27, older brother, Edison, was born.

Graham Philips would later say that he was very fortunate to grow up in Kinston as a young man. In 1981, at an appreciation banquet held in the coach's honor, Graham said that when Amos Sexton came to Kinston, he found a group of boys who knew nothing else but winning. But winning games was more than just posting a higher score at the end of a contest. Graham said that winning was a way of life and a spirit that embodied the whole community. "Winning is the attitude of always doing your best, at whatever you do," he said. "It is the courage to push ahead when the odds are against you. The people of Kinston had a spirit that was something special. I don't know who put it in them. I don't know if it was people like a Captain Pat Crawford, a Bill Faye, a Colon Byrd, or a Frank Mock or just the air we breathed, but there was a spirit here that is epitomized by a McDaniel man because he could play away from home too as we found out later by the way he survived six years in a POW camp in Vietnam. It was personified in an Alley Hart that played big-time basketball in the ACC in spite of his small size. This is what Amos Sexton found when he came to Kinston. On the other hand, we found a man who had a spirit of his own. One of my earliest impressions of Amos Sexton was at football practice when I heard him instructing a guard by saying, 'If you miss that block, I want you to throw your feet up and your heels up and knock the guy right up the side of his head with those shoes you are wearing.' Now I thought to myself, this is a man I can learn something from. With those two spirits, an indelible mix occurred for nine years."[27]

1950 NC state class-A champions. First row (left to right): Bryant Aldridge, Graham Phillips, Joe Whaley, Bobby Hodges, Douglas Bruton, Eugene "Red" McDaniel. Second row (left to right): Charlie Bland, mgr; George Carter, mgr; Tommy Cole, Sherrill Williams, Edward Bradshaw, Amos Stroud, Coach Amos Sexton.

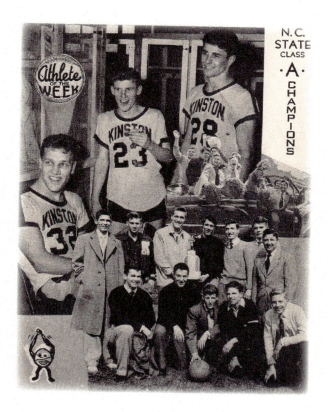

This collage of pictures found in the 1950 Grainger High School annual *Kay-Aitch-Ess* shows the 1950 Red Devil state champions. The three players on top are from left to right: Bobby Hodges (32), Joe Whaley (23), and Doug Bruton (28). The team (bottom right) are from left to right first row, kneeling: Bryant Aldridge, Amos Stroud, Joe Whaley, Charlie Bland, Mgr., George Carter, Mgr., two rows from left to right: Tommy Cole, "Red" McDaniel, Bobby Hodges, Doug Bruton, Sherrill Williams, Edward Bradshaw, and Coach Amos Sexton. The picture in the middle was taken during the celebration parade upon the team's return home to Kinston as the players and cheerleaders along with Coach Sexton beam with pride.

RONALD SEXTON

This picture was taken at the 1988 reunion of the 1950 Red Devil championship team. First row from left to right: Joe Whaley, Red McDaniel, Coach Amos Sexton, and Fred Williams. The back row from left to right: Bobby Hodges, Doug Bruton, Edward Bradshaw, and Amos Stroud.

5

SWEET HOME ALABAMA

It is true, as one of his former players put it, "When Amos Sexton arrived in Kinston as the new basketball coach, he was 'country come to town.'" Of course, Kinston was not exactly high society, but with Amos Sexton's unique Alabama brogue and less than perfect grammar, some may have thought he was not ready for prime time, but he would prove that he was up to the task.

In some ways, his family was like the Beverly Hillbillies, simple country folk with little education. But they worked hard, enjoyed life, and always considered family most important. My grandmother was a lot like Granny Clampett—short, feisty, and full of life. Dad had two sisters who could have passed as Elly May, and I am sure there was a Jethro somewhere in the woodpile.

Granddaddy Sexton, on the other hand, was no Jed Clampett. Unlike Jed, he was short, thin, and small-framed. His personality was more like a Harry Truman and not like the tall, slender, and rather passive, Jed Clampett. Granddaddy even looked like Harry Truman. One look from him, and you knew he meant business. Granddaddy Sexton would tell you flat out "how a cow ate grass." Like Harry Truman, he was a "no-nonsense, tell it like it is" character who had a certain way of looking at life his way. Tactfulness was not one of his virtues. Like Dad, Granddaddy had fire in his belly. He always

65

knew what he wanted to do and had an opinion about everything. He loved to fish too.

Dad was no Jethro either. He was confident and industrious and ambitious and charming with a good deal of street smarts. And he was the hardest working man I ever knew. Dad seemed to be a perfect blend of both his mother and his dad. Both Grandmother and Granddad were down-to-earth, extremely hardworking, and fun-loving people. Grandmother, was part Creek Indian, which may explain Dad's dark hair and olive skin color.

Amos Reddock Sexton was born on January 3, 1921, in Honoraville, Alabama. Honoraville was a small backwater community in Crenshaw County, Alabama, about forty miles south of Montgomery. Dad was the second son of five children born at home to James Thomas Sexton and Gertrude Duffell. The first-born son, L. B. Sexton, died of colitis in April of 1920, less than a month before his first birthday. Dad had two younger sisters, Hazel and Bernice, and one younger brother, Grayom.

My granddaddy Tom (as he was known and from whom I get my middle name) died on my fourteenth birthday, March 17, 1966. At that time, my grandparents lived and worked in Montgomery, moving to the city from the country right after World War II. In Montgomery, Granddaddy worked for Standard Forge and Axel Company until he retired. Grandmother worked as a seamstress for several clothing stores.

Granddaddy Tom was not formally educated and could not read or write. I remember seeing him sign some papers with an *x*. Grandmother would read the newspaper to him every morning. Granddaddy came from a rather large family. He was born September 8, 1890, the eldest of twelve children. I remember him as a serious individual with a dry sense of humor. The family home in Honoraville was not much more than a log cabin, which at one time, I was told, had dirt floors. The family home had been passed down from granddaddy's father, James Marion Sexton. Before moving to Montgomery, Granddaddy was a farmer raising cotton and other crops. He also, at one time, worked with the county, building roads making fifty cents a day. Dad took a lot of pride in telling us how he hitched up a mule and plowed the fields many a day and, of course, walking over a mile to school.

Granddaddy was a tad older than my grandmother, whom he married when she was a very young teenager of thirteen. He was twenty-eight. The age difference didn't seem to intimidate my grandmother. She was a strong woman. I remember several stories about my grandfather, which seem to define his character. Near the end of his life Granddaddy Tom's health was beginning to fail, and he moved rather slowly. The family continued to go to church back home in Honoraville every Sunday.

Granddaddy became a Christian late in life, and his faith was simple but genuine. I remember one Sunday while we were visiting them in Montgomery, Granddaddy was slowly putting on his tie, getting ready to go to church. Grandmother came into the room and, looking at him with some disgust, cried out, "Tom, that tie does not go with that suit." Granddaddy Tom, never looking up at her and continuing to tie the tie, retorted, "If I put it on, it matches!" And that was the end of that.

My grandparents still managed to visit our family in Louisiana even during their elderly years. In those days the trip was a seven-or eight-hour drive. This, of course, was before interstate highways. At our house, we had a rather long driveway, and a ditch ran down the side of the street. On one occasion, I was in the backseat of their car as Granddaddy was backing out. Grandmother was in the front on the passenger side. This was an old car with no power steering, and Granddaddy, unable to turn around to look where he was backing, simply used the rearview and side mirrors. He sat up straight as a soldier with both hands on the wheel and his eyes intently staring into the rearview mirror. As we were backing up, Granddaddy seem to veer to one side, somewhat heading for the ditch. At this point, Grandmother yelled, "Tom, watch it. You're about to run off into the ditch."

Granddaddy, sitting up straight, stiff as a board, with his left hand on the wheel, bringing his right arm in front of his face as if he was positioning himself to slap my grandmother, snapped, "Woman, I know what I am doing. Hush up." Of course, I was horrified.

Grandmother did not flinch and seemed to know that Granddaddy was more bark than bite. Granddaddy was certainly not henpecked, but then again, my grandmother could take care of herself.

Mother's brother Sherrol told me that Grandmother Sexton pretty much ruled the house, and when she would finally put her foot down, that was it. When Mother and Dad lived in Kinston, Dad would occasionally umpire baseball games on the side. Uncle Sherrill remembered the time when he and Granddaddy Tom were sitting in the stands behind home plate when Dad was umpiring a baseball game. He said Granddaddy Tom was proudly telling everyone around them that the umpire was his son. This went on for a while until Dad's calls didn't seem to sit well with the crowd. After a few bad calls, the fans started jeering at the umpire, and Uncle Sherrol said they had to get up and move to the far side of the stands.

I have fond memories of my Grandmother Gertrude who lived until January 1978. She was able to see me get married and to see our first child born. With a very colorful personality, she was always cheerful and could be rather playful and fun-loving. I can see where Dad got his gregarious personality. Grandmother Gertrude's life was her children and grandchildren, and she loved her Bible and her church.

Grandmother read her Bible and interpreted every passage as "matter of fact." Of course, her version was the old King James. On one occasion, she was reading in the book of Leviticus (Lev. 11:9–10), and she turned to Dad and said, "You know that we are not supposed to eat fish that does not have scales,"[1] (implying that we should not be eating catfish)? Dad, looking a little puzzled, simply laughed. He wasn't about the give up eating catfish. Certainly, it didn't mean catfish. Then with her finger pointed to a passage in Deuteronomy, she also informed us that the money you make by selling your dog cannot be given to the church (Deut.23:18). She read the passage out loud, "Thou shalt not bring the hire of a whore, or the price of a dog, into the house of the Lord thy God for any vow; for even both these are abomination unto the Lord thy God."[2] Now we were really puzzled. We didn't have any dogs to sell, so that just didn't seem like a problem. Nevertheless, my grandmother, like many old Bible readers, did not see the distinction between the nation of Israel under the Law of the Old Testament and the church under grace in the New Testament. And they equate the temple of the Old Testament with the church of the New Testament. But Grandmother's simplistic but sincere understanding of the Bible made for some interesting interpretations.

Several of Dad's former players noted to me that he was superstitious, a trait he may have inherited from his mother, or maybe it was just a part of that Crenshaw County culture. On game days, Dad had certain rituals he was careful to observe for fear he might jinx the outcome. For instance, he always wore red socks and his red vest. With regard to my grandmother, I will never forget the night I wanted to build a fire, so I started taking the ashes out of the fireplace. She jumped up out of the La-Z-Boy recliner and, in a voice of panic, told me not to take out the ashes. Somewhat dumbfounded, I inquired as to why, to which she informed me that if I removed ashes from the fireplace at night, someone in the family would die the next day. Obviously, I built a fire without removing the ashes.

For breakfast in the mornings, Grandma occasionally made up a bowl of Cream of Wheat. She put sugar and butter in it, which made it a delight to eat. However, she had one morning ritual that was rather difficult to watch. For herself, she made a hot cup of coffee and toast. First, she toasted her bread until it was burnt. She then took the burnt bread out of the oven and, with the bread knife, scraped the outside of the blackened toast. I am sure this was her way of making melba toast. She next took her hot cup of coffee and burnt toast to the kitchen table, sat down, and poured the hot coffee into her saucer. I suppose this was to cool the hot coffee. She then brought the saucer to her mouth and began to slurp it out. The noise this made was not exactly music to your ears. Anyway, she would put the saucer down and take a bite of her dry, burnt toast. Not exactly an Emily Post moment, but she sure seemed to enjoy it. I didn't leave the table, but I did intently stared into my bowl of Cream of Wheat as I ate.

Grandma also loved to dip snuff and watch soap operas. She often talked about the problems and troubles of soap opera characters as if they were real life situations. At times, it was hard to tell whether or not she was lamenting over wayward life family members or soap opera actors.

Her favorite soap opera was *As the World Turns,* or as we called it, "As the World Churns." But I think she watched them all. There was a time when Dad himself got hooked on watching *As the World Turns* and would watch it when he came home for lunch.

Grandmother did not even drive a car until after Granddaddy had passed away. She took a driving course and got her license. Now in the same old Chevy, she and her older sister, Omalee, would make the long trip to Louisiana to visit us. The old Chevy she drove didn't have power steering or air-conditioning. There was no interstate highway either, but she and Aunt Omalee would make the arduous trip to Louisiana in that old car and stay two or three weeks, cooking, fishing, canning, and watching soap operas. She always had to get back to Alabama to pay her bills on the first of the month.

One of my most vivid memories of Grandma Sexton was watching her and Aunt Omalee fishing off the dock at the family camp on Lake Claiborne (thirty-five miles northwest of Ruston) both wearing bonnets and pulling in brim, bluegills, crappie, chinkapins, and, occasionally, a catfish or a nice bass with their cane polls.

Grandma had no problem baiting the hook with a worm or a cricket, and when she caught a fish, she would holler with joy. "Whew, looky here, Omalee, I got me a nice one." She would gut and clean the fish herself and then fry them up with corn bread and butter beans.

I learned several things from my grandmother Gertrude. She taught me how to put worms on a hook and how to clean a catfish. She also taught how to make her country fresh tartar sauce. It is just a combination of mayonnaise, dill pickles, and purple onions, but it is good. She also gave me two good fishing tips: the fish bite best when the wind is out of the west, and on your way to the fishing hole, pay attention to the cows in the pasture. If they are standing, then the fishing is good. If the cows are lying down, the fish aren't biting. You can take that to the bank.

RED DEVIL TALES

She and Aunt Omalee would sit in the small living room of the camp trailer, shelling peas and watching soap operas with an occasional spit into a Maxwell House coffee can filled with tissue paper. The smell of canning pear or fig preserves or cooking butter beans and corn bread always permeated the whole camp. They loved cooking and canning. This they would do every day until it was time to go back home on the first of the month.

At nighttime, ready for bed and wearing full-length flannel night gowns, she and Aunt Omalee would watch shows like *Barnaby Jones* and *Maverick* and discuss religion or politics while rubbing their dry skin with medicated lotion and their aching joints with BenGay.

Dad went to Highland Homes High School and made the all-state high school football team in 1941. At a recent Sexton reunion, one of Dad's cousins, now in her eighties, remembered how much Dad loved football. In a newspaper clipping of the Highland Home High School football team of 1940, Dad is pictured playing center. The caption lists the players, and beside each player's name is his nickname. For instance, there is Clarence "Red" Mosely, Charles "Hoss" Lansdon, Frank "Sampson" Daniel, Ben T. "Slim" Cauthen, Leroy "Detroit" Cauthen, and even a Woodrow "Hitler" Wilson. Dad is listed as Amos "Sex" Sexton.

One of my cousins remembers Dad telling her the story of when he was in high school and walking to school. In order to impress the girls, he wet his hair and slicked it back only to have it freeze to ice by the time he got to school. After graduating from high school in a class of fifteen students, Dad attended Troy State Teachers College in the school year of 1942–1943.

Dad was the only member of his family ever to go to college. In fact, I couldn't find a Sexton in his family background who ever went to college. Granddaddy Tom, as you recall, was the eldest of twelve children, so Dad had plenty of uncles. When Dad went off to college, one of his uncles told him that he believed the only reason he was going to college was so he wouldn't have to work.

At the end of his first year at Troy, he entered the Marine Corps on July 13, 1943. He completed boot camp at Paris Island, South Carolina, then he went into an aircraft engineering squadron at the

Marine Air Station in Cherry Point, North Carolina. From there, he was transferred to an aviation machinist's mate school in Jacksonville, Florida, and selected as wing leader for his class. He was then assigned to Memphis, Tennessee. There he completed a course of training at the Navel Air Technical Training Station.

During the war, Dad was stationed in China and served as a crew chief on a B-17. I have a photo album containing several dozen pictures of Dad during his time in China. I am sure my mother had put it together. The only story I remember Dad telling me about his war experience concerned his brush with death on a bombing mission. On one particular mission, he got out of his seat for a moment, only to return and find a bullet hole where he had just been sitting. The experience gave him the feeling that his life had been spared for a reason. When the war was over, Dad was stationed at Camp LeJeune, and from there, he entered East Carolina Teachers College in Greenville, North Carolina.

Dad also enjoyed the food he grew up with. Any time I accompanied him on a sales trip, we would stop at some "greasy spoon" restaurant that served corn bread and butter beans or country ham and biscuits. He had a nose for those kinds of places and found many a hole in the wall eatery throughout the states he traveled. There were times he would see a peanut stand along the side of the road and stop to get boiled peanuts. They have a similar taste to butter beans, so I can understand his love for them. As I traveled throughout eastern North Carolina interviewing his players, I would often come across these peanut stands. At home, it was not unusual to see him fix himself a simple tomato sandwich made up of bread, mayonnaise, and fresh ripe tomatoes. Or he would pour a glass of buttermilk and throw in some corn bread. It wasn't exactly fun to watch him gulp it down, but you knew he enjoyed it.

Of course, Dad loved to fish and hunt. We did a lot of squirrel hunting growing up. Mother knew how to make a good squirrel mulligan. Served with hot biscuits and gravy, there is nothing better. It would make a rabbit hug a hound. The first squirrel dog we had was a small and ugly-looking mutt, but he could hunt. He bought the dog from someone who lived around his old home place. We learned early in life how to clean squirrels and scale fish. It was not unusual for us to catch up to a hundred bluegill and sunfish on a single trip. At one time growing up, we had five or six beagles, which dad would turn lose and let them run rabbits in the forty-acre wood lot behind the house.

One night, Dad got a phone call from one of the neighbors who live up the road. He complained to Dad that the dogs were upsetting his pet rabbits. Dad was understanding, and he apologized. The next day, he went to see the man and make sure his rabbits were okay. Expecting to see the man's rabbits in the backyard and caged up, Dad was a little bewildered when he didn't see any rabbit cages. He then asked the elderly man where he kept his rabbits. The man said, "Oh, I mean the rabbits that run in the woods. They are my pets." Dad just laughed.

We always had to clean the fish as soon as we got home. We were usually hot and tired, and when cleaning bluegills, Dad made sure we cleaned every edible part. We ate a lot of fried fish, but occasionally, Dad would make a fish soup, a recipe I believe he acquired while living in North Carolina. Even as a toddler, I remember eating fish stew. It was a dish that was unique to my North Carolina days. In Louisiana, I never came across it. It has a distinct aroma and taste.

In one of my trips back to North Carolina, I visited with Bob Moore and his wife, Marjorie. I discovered that Bob loved to hunt and fish, so I felt a special connection with this Old Red Devil who had played football and graduated in 1958. Somewhere in our conversation, I told him I remembered eating fish stew and that I wish I had the recipe. He smiled and said, "I got one that I'll give you."

When Dad wasn't coaching or selling something, he was fishing. He had a regular fishing buddy in Kinston, Tom Briley, who worked for the city of Kinston. Mr. Briley told me several stories of their fishing exploits. He and Dad fished in places like the Pamlico river and Vandemere Bay along the eastern North Carolina coast. Mr. Briley said they fished mostly for bass and trout\ but caught just about everything. He looked at me and said, "I remember when you went fishing with us and hung a big ole garfish. I told your daddy that he better grab a hold of you, or that fish was going to pull you in. He didn't seem to think you were in that much trouble, so I held grabbed you and held on." Mr. Briley said that they were always getting lost or getting stuck on some sandbar, but they caught a lot of fish. He said Dad was always fooling with the motor and not always paying attention to where he was going, a trait I think he never overcame.

Uncle Sherrol told me another story of one of their fishing adventures. Dad had just bought a new motor and wanted to try it out, so they went to some mill house pond near Mother's home in Newton Grove. Sherrol remembers Dad bringing a friend from Kinston. He was a large man, who couldn't swim, and he owned a Greek restaurant on Queen Street, Sherrol thought. Dad was not doing much fishing but trying out his new motor. He started running the boat in a circle, and at some point, the boat ran over its own wake, and the boat flipped over, throwing all three men into the lake. Thanks to Uncle Sherrol, the man with them, who couldn't swim, was saved. I am not sure who the man was, but I bet he didn't go fishing with Dad anymore.

As a hard-driving football lineman at East Carolina, Dad broke his nose several times. This caused him to have a lifetime problem of snoring. There are many notorious stories, too many to tell, of nobody getting any sleep if Dad was in the room. If he ever had to sleep in the same room with anyone, whether it was a fellow salesman or at a church retreat, Dad ran everyone out of the room. I suppose only someone who was hearing-impaired could have managed to tolerate it. Many times, when we as a family watched television in the den, Dad would fall asleep and start snoring. Of course, we would either have to turn up the television or poke him to wake him up. The only way my mother could sleep with him was if she fell asleep first. Otherwise, I think, she had to go to another room.

The story of how Mom and Dad met has several versions. I am sure that some time in my past, either Mom or Dad told me how they met, but I just can't remember. At that time, it just was not that important. Now I wish I knew the real story. The most believable version came from mother's younger sister, Janis. As the story goes, Dad saw this girl on the campus of East Carolina and was determined to have a date with her. He did not know her name but saw the dorm she enters. Sometime later, Dad went up to the front desk of that dorm and tried to describe the girl he saw. As he was trying to describe the girl to the dorm mother, he looked up and saw her coming down the stairs. He said, "Oh! Never mind. That's the girl." Mother and Dad were married on the twenty-second of June 1946.

At five feet, eight inches, and 170 pounds Amos Sexton was the starting right guard for the East Carolina Pirates in 1946 and 1947. This photo was featured November 5, 1947, in the *Montgomery Advocate*. The article stated that he was the smallest lineman on the team but was considered one of the most valuable men on the squad. "His spirit and aggressiveness leaves nothing to be desired," the caption reads and noted that he had been recently selected as the outstanding athlete among seniors at the college. Courtesy of the *Montgomery Advocate*.

6

TALES OF TWO COACHES

In 1955, the Red Devils of Grainger High School won the state championship in football, basketball, tennis, and golf and came within one strike of winning it all in baseball. It was a year when the perfect combination of great athletes, great coaching staff, and great support from fans all came together to produce one of the most memorable years for the city of Kinston. The successful year did not happen overnight. It was the product of a community strongly invested in its youth, from a well-organized city recreational department complimenting a committed school system that fostered a supporting cast of good teachers, capable administrators, and dedicated coaches all working together to produce some of the best athletes in the country.

The December 24, 1955, Sunday edition of Raleigh's newspaper, *The News and Observer,* celebrated the Red Devils' exceptional year with a special article and summed up the year's accomplishments:

"Here in Lenoir County where the soil is rich and fertile fields produce an abundance of tobacco, they grow some fine athletes too. There's ample proof of this."[1]

"During the past year, Kinston teams won State AA championships in football and basketball. Add the State's high school tennis

RED DEVIL TALES

champion in Marshall Happer, and the No. 1 junior golfer in Larry Beck and you come to the one conclusion: "Kinston is the home of champions, for 1955 at least. Championship teams are a habit in this Coastal Plains community. A winning spirit prevails. A thriving, bustling business district gives evidence of a forward-minded people . . . Folks around here believe in their youth. They like good leadership in that respect. Try to place your finger on the center of this youth movement and it always lands in the same spot. There you will find Frank Mock, athletic director at Grainger High, who coaches football and baseball. Sitting beside Mock is one who adds emphasis to the movement. Amos Sexton coaches the basketball team and helps Mock with the football squad. No two people in Kinston are more highly regarded."[2]

By all accounts, Frank Mock and Amos Sexton as coaches were a perfect match, even though different in personality and coaching style. But one thing seems certain: they both shared the same values and goals as coaches. Winning was the goal but winning according to the rules. Building character and giving direction to young athletes was a part of their shared values. Giving one hundred percent on and off the field was their work ethic. Fair play and teamwork where the hallmarks of their coaching philosophy.

Frank Mock was soft spoken, easygoing, and laid back. Amos Sexton was outspoken, energetic, and aggressive. In his spare time, Frank Mock liked to garden and refinish old pieces of furniture. On the other hand, Amos Sexton loved to fish, hunt, and try new ventures. Frank Mock was a steady but certain driver. Amos Sexton was just driven. After defeating the Washington Pam-Pac one year (1957), the *Free Press* duly noted, "Never have I seen Sexton such a nervous bundle of energy. He was constantly charging from his seat instructing the Devils. He was reminiscent of Wake Forest's Bones McKinney."[3] As a result, combined, the two coaches made a formidable team. "They were always together," George Whitfield said. "If you saw one, you would see the other." Both men loved to win games, and they knew what buttons to push on players to get the best out of them. Everyone understood that if you played for Frank Mock or Amos Sexton, you better give one hundred percent all the time. The last charge Coach Mock said to his players before they went out onto the field was, "All right, boys, let's go get wet."

Coach Mock and Coach Sexton, as his boys remembered, could be tough and relentless disciplinarians if an athlete broke a rule or crossed a line that was not permissible. There were no ten commandments of "thou shalt not" book of rules published and handed out before each season. But every athlete instinctively knew what they were not to do and how they ought to conduct themselves as Grainger High School Red Devils. You don't skip practice. You don't break curfew when there was one. You don't use profanity. You don't smoke or drink or at least you don't get caught. You hustle or you run laps. You always give it your best all of the time. You play fair or you do not play at all. You do not fight on the field of play. Sportsmanship was as important as winning, and winning was very important! At the end of the day, the players were more afraid of disappointing their coaches than the fear of punishment or losing a game.

For the basketball team, several signs placed in their dressing room echoed some of the Sexton/Mock philosophy. One read, "When your opponent stops your dribble, you're dead. It takes a teammate to revive you." Still another, which reminded the players of the importance of teamwork, "Who passed the ball when you scored?" Or another stated, "Play the game. The officials will referee." And finally, a reminder of the cost of a mistake: "Free throw: the penalty you pay for fouling your opponent."[4]

In 1953, Kinston was slated to play their first game of the northeastern conference tournament against Washington, a city northeast of Kinston often referred to as Little Washington to distinguish it from the big one in DC. Kinston, seeded first in the tournament, was scheduled to play its first game against the Washington Pam-Pac in the second round. In that first game, the Red Devils murdered Washington beating them 69 to 38. One of Kinston's guards, Bert Seville, had an exceptional night hitting six set shot for a total of twelve points. Yank Stallings, sports editor for the *Free Press* at that time, acknowledged the guard's hot hand:

"Coach Sexton was especially delighted over the fine performance by guard Bert Saville.[5] "If Saville has realized he can play basketball with the best guards around here," said Sexton. "He will be a great value to the club. All he needed was confidence and the four first quarter baskets on long set shots he whipped in the hoop should give him that confidence."[6]

"The Grainger High Red Devils were never greater than they were against Washington Friday night. If the boys had been playing with watermelons, they could still have hit the nets with regularity . . . Kinston unleashed an unmerciful attack and racked up 20 points in a fast and exciting first quarter with Bert Saville amazing the crowd with four beautiful long set shots. All of them found the mark and by the time the Red Devils had a 12–3 lead and the rout was started."[7]

At the Red Devil Reunion in March 2010, I met Bert Seville and his wife Bettie. Bert and Bettie (then Bettie Sue Jones) were high school sweethearts. Bettie, who was younger than Bert, was a junior varsity cheerleader at the time. Before the tournament started, Bettie recalled, Coach Sexton called all the cheerleaders together to give them a little talk. As she related the story, Bettie who still had a "who are you to tell us" look on her face. Coach Sexton informed the cheerleaders that if any of them were dating the ballplayers, they were not to break up with them during tournament play because he didn't want their game to be affected. Bert, standing beside Bettie and laughing, said, "Well, the truth of the matter is that I broke up with Bettie before the tournament and ended up having my best game ever."

That night, Bert's father was in the stands sitting beside a man he didn't know but obviously a Washington fan. Bert's dad later told him that after making three straight set shots, the man became very agitated and said, "If that guy hits one more shot, I'm leaving." Well, Bert did just that, and the man got up and stormed out. It probably was a good thing he did since the game continued to go south for Washington.

After defeating the Pam-Pac, Yank Stallings quoted Coach Sexton, "They were loose, relaxed, full of fight and determination and it makes quite a difference in any ball game when those factors are combined." Stallings added, "This sums up Coach Amos Sexton's theory of winning any ball game."[8]

Almost everybody knows about the famous bus trip to Elizabeth City when Dad ousted three players from the bus for playing poker for money. They had been warned. Dad drew a line in the sand, and they crossed it. He had to follow through.

Years later, after alluding to the bus incident, Lloyd Whitfield, a later sports editor for the *Free Press* noted another disciplinary tactic used by the coach. Under the title, Co-Captain Dropped, Whitfield wrote, "On another occasion a co-captain skipped drills before a state tournament. He was not allowed to make the trip and his loss from the squad might have cost Kinston the state title." Respecting the rules and those in authority was always enforced.

During practice, both coaches knew how to motivate the players, sometimes by negative reinforcement. Lloyd also pointed out, "Fans who gather at Mock Gymnasium daily to watch Sexton drill the Red Devils are in for laughs. Perhaps the most amusing thing to create an audible chuckle occurs when Sexton senses a lack of hustle. Quickly, he says, 'You want to get on that black line, don't you?' It's amazing the way the spirit picks up. The black line is the back-court line under the backboard. When drills fail to increase in tempo, Sexton places the players on that line, and they run wind sprints for some fifteen or twenty minutes."[9]

Before Amos Sexton came to Kinston, Frank Mock was the only football coach with no assistant. Fred Williams said the way he handled practice was to get one group, for instance the linemen, and give them certain drills to work on, and then he would go to another group and assign them certain exercises or drills. "There was no goofing around," Fred said. "We did what he told us to do until he came back to our group." Years later, when he himself was a coach, Fred said he thought back on the days Coach Mock had worked with the team, and he realized how amazing it was that one man could work a team by himself the way Frank Mock did.

RED DEVIL TALES

Gene Handy played football at Grainger High from 1953 to 1955. His family moved to Kinston from Virginia in the summer of 1953. Gene played offensive and defensive guard, so he came under the direct guidance of Coach Sexton, who coached the offensive and defensive lines. He said that Coach Sexton was a real believer in using the forearm to attack the opposing lineman. The forearm was used to control the opposing lineman by striking him in the chest. This maneuver gave the player the ability to move his opponent to the right or left or back. The coach had a name for this, the "forearm shiver."

In these early days, most players did not have face masks on their helmets, so if a player went high with the forearm shiver, he might hit the other player in the mouth. After the game, some of the linemen checked their elbows to see how many teeth marks they had. Two linemen, Bob Moore and Bob Church, made a joke out of it so that even students (boys and girls)who didn't even play football were threatening each other with the forearm shiver and showing imaginary teeth marks.

Gene said that when he first came to Kinston, he felt like an outsider, and it seemed hard to make friends. Coach Sexton, he remembered, picked up on his dilemma and took him aside one day to let him know that he understood what he was going through. Coach Sexton said that he was not from Kinston, and neither was Coach Mock. "Baseball players get traded all the time," he told Gene. "Give it time, and you'll get the hang of it." "A lot of what Coach Mock and Coach Sexton taught," Gene reflected, "I have applied to my personal and business life."[10]

Wilbur Mozingo graduated in 1956 and was on the 1955 class-AA state championship football team. His fondest memories are of coming back from out of town games late at night and the whole bus having to listen to Coach Sexton's favorite country music station, WWVA, in Wheeling, West Virginia. It was not the choice of most of the "bebop" group, and it sure wasn't the sound of Bill Haley and His Comets, but Wilbur now says, "Thanks to him, I love country music to this day."

81

One of the Red Devils' biggest rivals was the New Bern Bears. New Bern, North Carolina's second oldest city (1710) is about thirty-two miles east of Kinston. There are two stories that relate to this old Red Devil rivalry with New Bern. Both tales involve Coach Mock and football. The first story concerns one of the Red Devils doing a rather devilish act—repainting the black New Bern Bear.

One Friday night, before a basketball game between the Kinston Red Devils and the New Bern Bears, someone got rather creative, showed up early before the game, and painted a bright-yellow stripe right down the back of the black bear mascot, which stood proudly in front of the basketball gym in New Bern. The unfortunate incident was reported to Coach Mock, who called several boys early Saturday morning to go with him to New Bern and correct the unsportsmanlike gesture. He first called Charlie Lewis early Saturday morning and woke him up. Charlie was not under suspicion for the dastardly deed, but he was president of the K Club. Therefore, he was the proper student authority to see that justice was exacted or restitution was made. Unfortunately, Charlie had a Saturday-morning job, and he said, "We were so poor at my house that if I was going to have any money for the next week, I had to work on Saturdays." Coach Mock certainly understood Charlie's situation, but he was able to contact John Law and Gene Anderson. John and Gene accompanied Coach Mock to New Bern and bravely repainted the black bear. I say *bravely* because while they were painting the bear, they were being laughed at and jeered by New Bern students. But they finished the job and headed back home. Rectifying the problem and taking responsibility were some of the hallmark character traits of Frank Mock.

The other story involved one of the Red Devil football players, Paul Popov. Paul was newcomer of sorts to Kinston. In fact, he was a newcomer to America. Originally from a small village in Pskov province in northwest Russia (near the St. Petersburg area), Paul was not knowledgeable about American sports, but he loved the idea of playing football. He had seen American films of football while in Germany. He even envisioned himself running for a touchdown. I'm sure he must have seen the inspirational 1940 film, *Knute Rockne: All*

RED DEVIL TALES

American, starring Pat O'Brien and featuring a young actor, Ronald Reagan, who played "the Gipper."

Paul's family had emigrated from Russia to Erfurt, Germany, in 1944, during the German retreat from Russia because his dad feared Stalin more than Hitler. Paul still remembers the bombing of cities near the end of the war, and his family came very close to losing their lives in a bombing raid. After the war, with the help of the Christian World Service (CWS) and Joe Casey, a local farmer in the Kinston area who sponsored them, Paul's family immigrated to the United States in 1950.

Paul was about fifteen and worked on Joe Casey's farm plowing fields and clearing ditches. Joe Casey's wife arranged for Paul to attend Contentnea High School, a small rural school outside of Kinston. When farming slowed down during the fall and winter months, the family moved to Kinston with the help of a local Catholic priest. Paul's father found work at the Frosty Morn Meat Company, and Paul worked at the Kinston Loan and Jewry Store. Then Paul began going to school at Grainger High. He wanted to play football, but he didn't know the proper procedure for joining the team.

One day, Paul was standing in the lunch line at the school cafeteria when Amos Sexton came up and gave him a good look over. Paul was a stout, muscular boy, and Coach Sexton, who was the line coach, felt of his arms and told him, "You look like you should be playing football."

In his broken English and Russian accent, he told the coach he wanted to go out for football, but no one had invited him. Coach Sexton said, "Well, son, I am inviting you to come out." So that afternoon, Paul was fitted with headgear (no faceguards) and pads and started playing, even though the junior varsity season was just about over.

The next season, Paul was well-initiated into American football as practices began during the hot days of August and the unrelenting drudgery of "two a day" workouts. Paul played guard, and Coach Sexton showed him how to block and tackle. Coach Mock, he remembers, was the quiet and steady field general but "your dad," he noted, "was a very animated firecracker."

RONALD SEXTON

In 1952, the Red Devils were playing the New Bern Bears in football. Paul was sidelined for much of the game due to burns he received from the lime that lined the field. Apparently, the lime caused an allergic reaction. At some point during the game, Kinston kicked off to the New Bern Bears, and the runner took the ball, dodged several Red Devils, broke out into the open, and started running down the side lines for a touchdown. The fans were standing up, cheering. The New Bern sideline was alive with excitement. The New Bern receiver was running down the Red Devil side of the field. The Red Devils were shocked. The coaches were thinking, *What the . . .?* Paul Papov was on the sidelines watching in shock as the opposing runner was headed for the goal line. This couldn't be happening! Well, Paul figured, he was going to help his teammates, so he jumped out from the sidelines, grabbed the player's ankle, and tackled the guy. Can you imagine the shock and even dismay of the New Bern players and New Bern fans, not to mention the bewilderment of Coach Mock, assistant Coach Sexton, and all the Kinston players some of whom were probably laughing their heads off. Somebody forgot to inform Paul that you can't do that. And what about the poor runner who knew he was about to score a big touchdown and impress all the cheerleaders? Well, the referee blew his whistle, and everybody waited for the call surely expecting a touchdown to be awarded to the New Bern Bears.

However, the referee simply added fifteen yards at the point of the infraction. One can only imagine the disappointment and even fury of the New Bern fans. The game was on the Red Devils' home field, and the visiting crowd was not happy. Coach Mock, having a sense of fair play, told his players that on the next play, they were to do nothing and let the runner make a touchdown. It was a noble gesture, and the New Bern fans never forgot it.

The other story about Paul Popov is most certainly an urban legend. I called Paul, and he insisted that the story was not true. Nevertheless, the story is worth repeating. As the story goes, when Paul first came out for football, he stood by and watched the other players on the field block and tackle. As he observed, the whole affair looked like a good old-fashioned street brawl and slug fest. So when

RED DEVIL TALES

it was time for Paul to get out there and show his stuff as a guard, he started just slugging the opposing lineman when the ball was snapped. The coaches rushed in and pulled Paul off the unfortunate player and said to him, "Whoa, whoa, hoss. You can't do that."

Paul, looking rather surprised, said in his broken English, "Why not? That's what it looked like to me."

"No, Paul, there are certain ways to block and tackle. We're gonna have to show you how," Coach Sexton responded.

Paul Popov learned the game of football and developed into a great athlete. During his junior and senior year, Paul made all conference, and in his senior, he also was honorable mention for all state. After graduating from Grainger High, Paul went to East Carolina on a football scholarship where he majored in French and Spanish. After college, he joined the Marine Corp and was stationed in Quantico, Virginia. He graduated from OSC as a second lieutenant but eventually ended up as head of the foreign language department at Georgia Tech until his retirement in 2001.

"Thanks to your father," Paul told me, "in 1955, I was able to become a US citizen." After five years in America, a person was eligible to become a citizen. Paul said Coach Sexton, along with Paul's boss at Kinston Loan and Jewelry Store, vouched for Paul and served as witnesses so he could become a US citizen in a naturalization ceremony in New Bern.

As a coach, Frank Mock could be very creative. The name of the game was winning, and he was always looking for an edge. In 1957, Elizabeth City was a powerhouse in football. The Red Devils had their work cut out for them when they made the one-hundred-thirty-mile to play the Yellow Jackets. Tom Mosely was an assistant coach, and some say he had a good feel for the game. Tom would go and scout a team, come back, and, without any notes, give incredible details about the team's strengths and weaknesses. For the game against the Yellow Jackets, Tom had designed a trick play that he hoped would give Kinston the edge against the more powerful Elizabeth City. They called the play the Davy Crockett. It was designed to cause the opposing team to think the Red Devils had made a mistake and were confused about what play to run. Kinston took the kickoff and managed to get the ball up to the thirty-five-yard line. Now the play unfolded as the team huddled sort of aimlessly a few yards to the side of the ball.

They looked like a bunch of junior high kids not even knowing how to huddle up. What happened next looked like a play you would see in a cartoon. With the team still standing around in some sort of huddle, the center broke out and headed for the ball.

Now this was all legal. He then snapped the ball to one of the half-backs in the huddle, and off they all went down the field. The play worked for the Red Devils who took the ball all the way down to the five-yard line. On the next play, the ball was snapped to John Laws. He took the ball but got nowhere. He was dragged down from behind. The Red Devils went on to score but had stirred up a hornets' nest and got stung by the Yellow Jackets, who beat the Red Devils. Maybe the play should have been called Laurel and Hardy.

John Laws, who also helped repaint the New Bern bear, graduated from Kinston High School and went on to the University of North Carolina and played on the Freshman basketball team during Dean Smith's first year as coach. He credits Amos Sexton for teaching him the fundamental skills that helped him make the team. John went on to work for Exxon and is now retired and living in Texas. John underscored the fact that Coach Mock and Coach Sexton were great teachers and motivators of young men. He added, "They taught me how to be gracious in victory and how to learn from defeat."

Pedro Brinkley played football and baseball under Coach Mock. Pedro was a free spirit who often did things the unconventional way. It seems that everyone has a Pedro story. Along with Emmitt Morton, Pedro was the typical Dennis the Menace, full of mischief, always pulling pranks or teasing someone. Since he was a good athlete, his shenanigans were tolerated, but you just never quite knew what he might do.

On my visit to Morehead City to see Gary Holt, Charlie Lewis, and Pat Wright, Pat told me his Pedro story. Charlie said, "After Pedro graduated, I inherited the center-field position, and I remember Coach Mock telling all those 'Pedro stories.'" He said Coach Mock had to be careful what he said to Pedro because he never knew what

RED DEVIL TALES

Pedro might do. If Coach Mock said, "Guys, we need to get somebody on base, Pedro was the kind of player who would go up to bat and stick his head across the plate and get hit so he could get on base. One time, he took an extra ball with him to centerfield, and when he caught a fly ball with one hand, he threw the other ball instead. One time, when Kinston was playing at Edenton, he went for a fly ball and ran through the fence and knocked it down to catch the fly ball. Then during a football game against Goldsboro, Pat remembered, the Red Devils were "just getting the tar beat out them." Goldsboro at that time had a team that was big, rough, and looked like players in college. "They could put a real hurt on you." Pat added, "On this particular night, they were playing in the pouring rain, and it looked like a mud-wrestling contest."

Pedro was the running back and just getting clobbered. The rain, the mud, and the relentless beating finally got the best of him. Near the end of the game, Pedro, who was bleeding from the nose and around his eyes, hobbled back to the huddle and announced, "Boys, we're getting the crap beat out of us, so, everybody, pick one because we're at least going to win this fight." Pat said, "The next play ended with the biggest slug fest you have ever seen."

Gary Hocutt played football and graduated in 1956. Another football player, Bobby Orr, had broken up with his girlfriend, so Gary started dating her. One night, Gary was over at Mary Jenney's house, and they were on the couch in the den reading poetry to each other (wink, wink). Gary looked up, and out the window, he saw Bobby perched in a tree, looking in. So he got up and ran out the door trying to catch Bobby. He never caught up with him that night, so the next day at football practice, Gary finally caught him and had him pinned down and was hitting him. Coach Sexton had heard about the "peeping Tom" incident and pulled the boys apart, telling them, "All right, boys, I want you to take your helmets off and go over there and settle this right now." So Gary and Bobby got over to the side, and everybody gathered around them, and they went at it. Gary was bleeding; Bobby was bleeding, but they continued to slug it out. When it was all over, it was over. From then on, Gary said, they were good friends. Pat interjected a comment, "Coach Sexton used to keep a pair of boxing gloves around just for such an occasion. Bobby Stanley and I must have gone after it twenty or twenty-five times," Gary said, "Well, that day, there were no boxing gloves."

Around 1954, a group of boys started an organization to help promote friendship and the Red Devil spirit. They called themselves the BBBs (Brother of the Beer Bottle). I am sure the new club was inspired during a time when they were "in the moment." The founders were Bob Church, Tom Tucker, John Southerland, Reid Parrot, Billy Curle, and Eion Faelten, and they still have an annual meeting at Atlantic Beach. Bob Church said that when his father was killed in an air crash, these boys sent flowers with the name from The Brotherhood for the Betterment of Boys. Bob's grandmother told him that she was very proud of his being associated with such a fine organization.[11]

Sylvia Jones Wheless (class of '55) remembers Coach Sexton's strict rule concerning walking on the gym floor. "We were at no time to walk across that floor in street shoes. If we did and got caught, we were to get on our knees and clean it up. Fifty years later, I still cannot get used to people walking on a basketball court with street shoes."[12]

There was the occasion when Dad taught us some "gentleman's etiquette." Morgan Peoples, who taught history at Louisiana Tech University and was a member of our church, Grace Methodist, came over to our home one day for a visit. At the time, my older brother was in high school. I was in junior high school, and my younger brother was in elementary school. We were all sitting in the den, watching television. Dr. Peoples was greeted at the door heartily by Dad, and as they both made their way into the den, we gave him a brief nod hello and then went back to watching television. We were nice but just not aware of the proper protocol for greeting adults. After all, this was an adult and one of Dad's friends. Dad and Dr. Peoples visited for a while and then he got up to leave. He said good-bye to all of us, and we casually said bye, I think, probably never taking our eyes off the television. Dad didn't say anything until Dr. Peoples left. As soon as he was gone, Dad returned to the den, turned off the television, and said, "Boys, the next time an adult enters this

RED DEVIL TALES

house, I want you all to stand up, firmly shake his hand, and, with a big smile on your face, welcome him. And when he gets up to leave, you stand up again until he leaves. Dad was not ugly, but it was a stern statement that carried an inherent warning. Until this day, I always stand up to greet someone, especially an adult, and firmly shake their hand with a warm smile. Dad only had to tell us once.

In 1964, I was in the sixth grade. I was just on the edge of those wonderful teenage years when life really starts to change for young boys. That year, the Beatles conquered America with "I Want to Hold Your Hand," and their mop head haircuts. Like every other kid on the block, I thought I wanted to learn to play the guitar. So I asked for a guitar for Christmas. Now Dad liked music, and his dream was to have a son play at the Grand Old Opry, but I was thinking of going in another direction. So he told me, "Son, if you want to learn to play a guitar, you need to first start with a ukulele. Then if you can play that, I'll get you a guitar." Are you kidding me? A ukulele is not exactly a chick magnet. But that was Dad; you start at the bottom and earn your way up.

I'm not sure how long I had a ukulele, but the next Christmas, I got a guitar. It was a cheap, low-end, six-string folk guitar from Sears and Roebucks I think. I am almost certain it cost less than thirty dollars. My real goal was to play an electric guitar like all the famous bands of the day. When I asked for that, Dad again advised me of the ground rules. He said, "Son, when you can play on that guitar any song I name, I will get you any kind of guitar you want." Well, I now had the goal before me. It was close to another Christmas, several years after conquering the ukulele and learning to play a few songs on that cheap Sears and Roebuck guitar that I told Dad that I believed I was ready for the examination to get me to the next level.

Pat McCarty, one of Dad's good friends and an Acme Boot salesman, came over for dinner one night. I do not remember where Mother or my brothers were at the time. I just remember it was Dad and me and Pat McCarty in the house that night. Dad, of course, was a big country music fan, and I grew up listening to singers like Hank Williams, Eddie Arnold, and Ernest Tubbs. Well, if you know country music, you know you can play just about any song, at least

89

the old classic tunes, if you master about three major chords. I knew Dad loved country music, and I figured he would ask me to play several Hank Williams songs. So I learned "Your Cheatin' Heart" and "Cold, Cold, Heart." I also learned, probably like every child does, that you wait until the most opportune moment to ask for something from your parents. You certainly don't venture to ask them or tell them any bad news when they are in a foul mood. Well, on this night, Dad and Mr. McCarty were laughing and enjoying the evening, so I figured this was a good time. When I announced that I was ready to be tested, Dad thought that it might be good entertainment for the evening and agreed to give me the test. Mr. McCarty liked the idea and looked forward to the audition after learning about the ground rules. Dad said, "All right, go get your guitar, and let's see what you can do."

Sure enough, the first request Dad made was, you guessed it, "Your Cheatin' Heart." After I finished, Mr. McCarty laughed with glee and Dad had that, "Okay, that's fine, but that's just one song" look. "The next song I want you to play is . . ." You got it, "Cold, Cold Heart." I played that one, and I could see that Mr. McCarty was now pulling for me.

He said to Dad, "Amos, looks like the boy knows what he is doing." I think Dad figured that there had to be three songs to win. That rule had not been explained to me, but at least it would not be four or five songs. My repertoire was limited. Dad thought for a moment and came up with a song I'm sure he thought I would never be able to play. I got lucky on the first two, so I knew this one was coming out of left field. Besides, I only knew those two songs. With nervous anticipation, I waited for the next musical challenge.

Then he said, as if he had pulled a fast one, one of those secret plays just for the right occasion, "All right, son, play 'She'll be Coming Around the Mountain.'" Oh my! I thought I had just won the lottery. Jumping Jehosophat! I think I could play that song with any chord. I had not learned that song, but I knew it couldn't be that hard. I was going to have to fake it. So I pulled a move right out of Dad's playbook, "When you don't know what you are doing, at least make 'em think you know what you're doing." But will he buy it?

I confidently said, "Okay, here goes." I had the ball, and I was going in for the last-second layup. I put my fingers around the neck of the guitar and made a *C* Chord and started singing like I knew what I was doing. "She'll be coming around the mountain when comes . . ."

Fortunately, I had hit another chord that sounded like the right one. Pat McCarty jumped up and yelled, "He did it! He did it! Amos, get that boy a real guitar." Well, I'm not sure if Dad was exactly booming with pride, or he just realized he had been had. Yes, I had learned from the master. He looked sort of like he had just lost a state championship, but being a man of his word, he bought me the guitar I wanted. Who knows? Maybe it would pay off. I'm sure he thought I was on my way to the Grand Old Opry.

In 1965, older brother Edison was a sophomore in high school. He played varsity football. One Friday night, we all went to see him play an out-of-town game in Shreveport, which is about seventy miles west of Ruston. In the car that night were Dad and Mother, my younger brother Don, my grandmother Gertrude, and me. You remember Granny Gertrude from chapter 5, right? Well, by this time in his career, Dad had become prosperous enough to buy a Cadillac, a gold Coup de Ville. If you remember, Cadillacs in those days were big, and driving one was like driving a tank. Dad's Cadillac was a classy champagne color. We arrived at the game just a little late, and there were no parking places. Dad pulled up to the front of the stadium and asked the policemen on parking duty, "Hey, do you have a place for the mayor?"

The policeman, obviously seeing the big Cadillac and assuming it must surely be the mayor of Ruston, replied, "Yes, sir, right here up front."

Dad pulls into the VIP parking, grinning like a possum. Mother, horrified that Dad has pulled a fast one, said, "Amos, why do you lie like that? You ought to be ashamed of yourself."

Dad, laughing, said, "Honey, I didn't tell him I was the mayor. I just asked him if he had a place for the mayor."

When the game was over and we were ready to leave, Dad, for some reason, gets the bright idea that I should be the one to drive home. Well, I am in eighth grade, no driver's license, and can just barely see over the steering wheel. I remember Mother sounding off in astonishment, "Amos, you know that he doesn't have a license."

"Well," Dad responded, "this will be a good practice for him." I was stunned, to say the least, and emotionally caught somewhere between excited and scared to death. It was nighttime, and there was a lot of traffic leaving the game. Dad gets in the passenger seat. Mom, Grandmother Gertrude, and younger brother Don are in the backseat. I got in the driver's seat and buckled up.

The first question I asked Dad was, "Okay, which way do I go?" Now this was an opportunity for a hands-on lesson in driving. Dad, a former coach and teacher, now proceeded to tell me how to get home. He assumed his teaching posture, looked at me, and said, "Son, you see the moon up there?"

"Yes, sir," I responded.

He continued, "Well, the moon is in the east. Ruston is in the east, so just follow the moon." I was too scared to question the wisdom of this well-thought-out insight, so I proceeded to drive in the direction of the moon. I did my best to just "follow the moon." Coming to a red light about a mile or so down the road, I asked Dad which way I should turn. Again, he simply said, "Son, I told you that the moon is in the east. Ruston is east, so just follow the moon." By this time, I figured that this advice would be the only directions I would get. Eventually, I found my way to the interstate, basically following the flow of traffic, but the moon was always in front of me. This would become an inside family joke whenever we gave directions to anyone. We would always say, "Just follow the moon."

Coach Frank Mock and Coach Amos Sexton in 1955. This was the final practice before the football team played and won the first state football championship for Grainger High School. Courtesy *The Free Press*.

7

FRANK MOCK

Long before Amos Sexton arrived on the scene, Grainger High School had an established football and baseball coach who was well on his way to legendary status. Coach Frank Mock was nine years older than Amos Sexton and essentially became his mentor and confidant setting an example in both word and deed to this young and inexperienced coach. Coach Mock probably provided in large part Amos Sexton's basic ideas and principles of coaching. Frank Mock set the standards and provided direction for the athletic program at Grainger High School. He was highly principled, patient, and compassionate, and he loved his players, but he was also fiercely competitive and dedicated to winning. These attributes were instilled into his players.

Throughout his career, Frank Mock wore several hats. From 1934 to 1957, he was a coach and teacher. In 1957, he became the principal of Grainger High School, a position he held until the school merged with Adkin High School in 1970 to become the new Kinston High School. From 1970 to his retirement in 1978, he served as assistant superintendent of schools.

Frank Mock arrived in Kinston in 1934 fresh out of Davidson College and became one of the most respected high school coaches in the state of North Carolina. Coaching both football and base-

RED DEVIL TALES

ball, he developed a reputation of winning and sportsmanship, and he helped shaped the lives of several generations of youths who still credit him for giving them a solid foundation for any future success they have had in life.

From 1934 to 1957, Frank Mock established his mark as a legend coaching baseball and football. In baseball, he compiled 317 wins and two state championships. In the twenty-three years prior to Coach Mock's arrival in Kinston, the Red Devils' football teams had a losing record of 44 wins to 104 losses. In the next nineteen years under the direction of Frank Mock, the Red Devils had nineteen consecutive winning seasons with a total of 134 wins and the state championship in 1955. In 1948, the Red Devils had a perfect 10–0 record—the only undefeated team in Grainger High School history. His legendary status went beyond his success as a coach. He was respected around the state of North Carolina for his work as an educator and community leader. He served as president of the Board of Control of the North Carolina High School Athletic Association. He served on the boards of the North Carolina Officials Association and the North Carolina Coaches Association.

As a community leader, he was an active member and president of the Kinston Rotary Club, chairman of the Salvation Army board, and he served as a member of the North Carolina Committee of the Southern Association of Colleges and Schools. He was a member of Phi Delta Kappa and, on the side, became a sports announcer for a local radio station (WELS). One month after his retirement from the Kinston City School system with forty-four years of dedicated service, he passed away in July 1978. In 1991, he was posthumously inducted into the North Carolina High School Athletic Association's Hall of Fame.

Frank Mock was born on December 11, 1912, in a small community outside of Lexington, North Carolina in Davidson County. Frank was the second of four children. He had an older sister and two younger brothers, and all children went to college. His father was a country doctor, and to help make ends meet and help send the children to college during the depression years, his mother rented out rooms, mostly to school teachers. Coach Mock first attended

95

Rutherford Junior College for two years and then finished at Davidson College. His sister finished school at Duke University; his younger brother Harry graduated from Appalachia State University; and the other brother graduated from the University of North Carolina and became a doctor. Frank's dad had graduated from Davidson and wanted Frank to be a doctor. In fact, even after he was married, Frank's dad had him go over to the Baptist Hospital and take an examination to get into medical school. Frank was just not interested in being a doctor. He wanted to teach and coach.

Frank Mock would have made a good doctor. When any of his boys got hurt, he always knew what to do for them. For a long time, a local Kinston physician, Dr. Wooten, who lived close to the Mocks, attended every home football game and was always available to look after any player who was hurt. According to Mrs. Mock, Frank never wanted to be a college coach either.

Mrs. Mock, formerly Mable Blalock, graduated from Grainger High School in June of 1934, and Frank came to the school as a teacher and coach the following September. It was three years later that Mabel met Frank through another teacher at the high school. They dated for six months and were married.

Mrs. Mock said Frank never came home and talked "shop." Whatever problems or issues he encountered at school or on the field stayed there. If Mrs. Mock heard about something, it came from someone else. Frank then might or might not tell her about it. When he was home, Frank was involved with his family. He became very active in his church, Queen Street Methodist, where he taught a couple's class for thirty years.

As a coach, he always said he would rather win or lose a game than end in a tie. He may have been laid back and quiet in personality, but he was a fierce competitor. Even though he demanded good sportsmanship from his players, his goal was to win. The last thing he said to his players before they went out on the field was, "All right, boys, let's go get wet all over!"

As a Sunday school teacher for thirty years, his lessons emphasized strong Christian values and being a follower of Christ. Among some of his notes were found a quote from the German writer

RED DEVIL TALES

Goethe's list of the nine requisites for contented living. This list of values seems to sum up rather accurately the character and demeanor of man who touched so many lives:

1. Health enough to make work a pleasure.
2. Wealth enough to support your needs.
3. Strength enough to battle with difficulties and overcome them.
4. Grace enough to confess your sins and forsake them.
5. Patience enough to toil until some good is accomplished
6. Charity enough to see some good in your neighbor.
7. Love enough to move you to be useful to others.
8. Faith enough to make the real things of God.
9. Hope enough to remove all anxious fears concerning the future.

The quote looked like it was written hastily on a napkin, indicating he was taking notes from a speaker he was listening to. Both Frank Mock and Amos Sexton regularly attended the weekly Rotary Club luncheon, which usually had a speaker give a few thoughts.

Another saying which both Frank Mock and Amos Sexton probably heard a Rotary Club luncheon and embraced its truthfulness was called The Measure of a Man. Dad kept a copy of it in his wallet. The words are generally attributed to Robert Lewis Stevenson and some have given credit to Ralph Waldo Emerson.[1] Whoever wrote these pithy words, it seems to have endured for several generations, and many have found them deeply moving and meaningful:

"That man is a success when he has lived well, laughed often, and loved much, who has gained the respect of intelligent men, and the love of children, who has filled his niche and accomplished his task, who leaves the world better than he found it whether by an improved problem, a perfect poem or a revived soul, who looks for the best in others and gave the best he had."

These became the shared values of Frank Mock and Amos Sexton and values which they set as their goals and tried to live out, as well as, pass down to their Red Devil athletes and students.

"A Red Devil is a most unique person," Amos Stroud would later note. "No matter who she or he might be. There is something special about Red Devil comradeship. No matter whether the person was for the '30s or even the '70s, (1970 being the last year the athletic teams were called Red Devils), they all relate very well. In the 1930s and '40s and most of the '50s Frank Mock was either the teacher-coach or the principal. 1970 was the last year he was the principal. In fact, before that year was completed, he had moved into the central office, relinquishing the duties of principal to his assistant, Bill Peeden.[2]

Bill Peedin, gave a fitting tribute to Frank Mock who had given so much to the youth and to the city of Kinston and whose influence shaped the lives of the boys he coached, the students he taught, and the school he administered. "He was a man of great religious faith and believed this faith to be vital to mankind." Bill Peedin wrote,

"He was a man who believed in the basic integrity of young people and provided leadership for many during the years that shaped them to maturity; He was a man who believed in people and whose spirituality took the shape of serving them; He was sensitive to beauty—the beauty of a rose, of the great out-of-doors, the beauty of truth, the beauty of the little things; He was sensitive to the needs, the suffering, the failures, the joys, the successes of other; He was a confident man and had the gift of inspiring those with whom he worked; He was a man of courage—the courage to live by his convictions; He was a man whose happiness was rooted in the love of a close family and in the loyalty of his colleagues and a host of friends. This man shared the enthusiasm and satisfactions of 44 commencements in the Kinston City Schools. This coach, teacher, principal, associate superintendent served his entire professional career in the city schools. For the past 22 years, he was a platform participant or platform guest at commencement. This is Frank L. Mock, Jr., as I knew him—a gentle man who will always live in the lives of others."

RED DEVIL TALES

A local sportswriter who had followed Frank Mock's career through the years wrote,

"For 42 years of his career this scribe has been closely identified with his work and his great motivating spirit for young men on the athletic field. The first time we followed his team was in September, 1937, when he took a small group of boys who knew little about football to Dunn and held a much stronger team to a 7–7 tie."

"In the years that followed, with exception of a few months he worked at Seymour Johnson Field in Goldsboro during World War II, he compiled one of the most enviable won-loss records in the history of high school athletics. His teams had a win percentage of .721 for his entire career. He did it in good years and bad years—when talent was fair, when it was poor or when it was average. He never complained about the talent. He saw potential in every youth who donned a uniform. He encouraged each to do his best."[3]

Frank Mock had a philosophy in athletics that was integrated with everything that was a part of Grainger High School. He once said, "We try to stress the importance of teamwork in everything here. We try to integrate the athletic program with the school program. We don't try to overemphasize athletics. We think we have a fine music department, an excellent band, and the best in cheerleaders. We like for our athletes to take part in everything. Some are in the glee club. Some are in the band. In athletics, we try to stress some sacrifice. A boy must give all he has, get wet all over, to be successful in anything."

Red McDaniel in his book, *Scars & Stripes,* credits and pays tribute to Frank Mock for teaching him the mental toughness, endurance, and discipline to face adversity. For six years, Red had to endure constant physical and emotional torture as a POW in North Vietnam. Deprived of food, water, sleep for days and weeks on end, solitary confinement, legs put in irons, beaten with a rifle butt or whipped with a thick rubber fan belt, and only receiving minimal medical attention for the wounds that were inflicted just to keep him alive. Red languished,

"How do I play this "game"—locked in the ropes, bleeding, burning up with fever, my life oozing out of broken flesh, my mind so far gone I couldn't concentrate on their questions, could hardly hear them? Yet all my discipline of the past told me I had to try."[4]

"His name was Frank L. Mock. He was my high-school coach. I swung on strike three with the bags loaded and he yelled, "Great damn day!" That was the only time I ever heard him drop a bad word, but I never held it against him. Now, in this hour of darkness, his kindly, rough-hewn face floated before me like a balloon."

"How many times had we practiced under him? How many times had he put me through my paces? How many times had he drilled me in the fact that playing the game is "all in the winning"? And, as if I might miss the point, he added, "To win isn't everything—actually, it the only thing.""

"Every game, every challenge of life was built around that statement for me. The military picked it up and socked it home. You flew to win against the opposing elements of empty space; you flew to win in combat. The American way was to win. 'I never saw an American who lost and laughed,' General George S. Patton said once. I wouldn't lose. I couldn't lose. I had been drilled to win."

". . . I had to hang on to winning. I had to compete, or I was dead in this place. Frank Mock's drive to make me want to win had to count now in the biggest battle of my life. And yet I knew, too, as Grantland Rice put it, 'He marks—not that you won or lost—but how you played the game. Frank Mock had inspired me to win but also to put character into the game, to put all I had into it regardless of the outcome. In my senior year I was to receive a trophy conceived by a concerned citizen for 'the man who gave the most to the game.' I treasured that reward, but I owe it to Frank Mock for teaching me that big lesson in playing the game."[5]

Coach Mock being carried off the field by his players after the Red Devils won the state AA championship in 1955. Courtesy of *The Free Press* of Kinston.

Coach Frank Mock, 1954 *Kay-Aitch-Ess*

Early-morning football practice, 1953. Left to right: Pedro Brinkley, George Whitfield, Joe Mayo, Tony Gerrans, and Coach Frank Mock.

Coach Mock with James Bradshaw
and Cecil Gooding

Amos Sexton and Frank Mock

8

SUPERINTENDENT JEAN BOOTH

During the years that Amos Sexton coached, Jean Booth was the superintendent of schools and had been the one individual responsible for hiring him in the fall of 1948 as the head basketball coach and as an assistant football coach. He became a good friend and confidant of Dad through the years. The first time I met Mr. Booth was in 1981 at the Red Devil appreciation banquet given for Dad by some his former players. I was impressed by Mr. Booth's eloquence and diction.

The way he related how he came to employ Amos Sexton as the basketball coach was especially entertaining. When he was introduced, he gracefully approached the podium, and with a voice like Franklin D. Roosevelt, he began, "Mr. Toastmaster, ladies and gentlemen, we gather here this evening under the canopy of a starlight sky to honor an outstanding individual." Then he went on to tell the story of his hiring of Amos Sexton. "The employment of Amos Sexton," he continued, "is an enduring and bright spot in my professional career."

Mr. Booth called the personnel director of East Carolina Teachers College in Greenville and asked him to send four young men down for an interview. After interviewing these boys, he said that there was no question Amos Sexton was the man for the job.

RED DEVIL TALES

Even knowing that he had not a sliver of experience in basketball, Mr. Booth said he had "charisma, personality and a 'get up and go' attitude." He knew he had the right man for the job.

"Every first week in April, a school administrator has a rather interesting time when he recommends a list of employees to the School Board for the next year," Mr Booth continued. One year in particular after he had made his recommendations, Mr. Booth said that one member of the School Board asked him a question. He said, "Mr. Sexton is on the air every morning on a radio sports program. How about Mr. Sexton's English?" Coach Sexton was not noted for his diction and proper use of the English language. "I said to this School Board member and to the rest of the august members of the Board of Education," Mr. Booth responded, "I did not employ Mr. Sexton as an English major but as an inspiring leader of young men in a program that needs rebuilding. Now do you think that he is rebuilding it?" The board unanimously agreed. And Mr. Booth said, "And that was the last I heard of that! But I said parenthetically, it is just such people as Amos Sexton who popularize new words and new expressions, and it is my opinion that the next edition of *Merriam Webster's New International English Dictionary* will include such words as, *flub* and *flub-a-dub dub*. Amos taught me a lot about the English language."

Dad said that after one particular sports banquet where he was doing some of the speaking, Principal Jack Horne called aside my mother and told her, "Lee, you need to talk to Amos about getting him some help with his English. If he is going to represent Grainger High School, we need to get some training with his diction." To my knowledge, I don't think that happened. If it did, it didn't take. Dad said he had fun on his radio program because in that context, he could just "let it rip," and no one could talk back to him. Apparently, he had acquired an audience that enjoyed his colorful Alabama brogue.

Jean P. Booth had a long and noteworthy career in education, and most of his career as an educator was spent in Kinston. He first came to Kinston in 1928 as the principal of Grainger High School. In 1945, he became the superintendent of education, a position he held until his retirement in 1967. Born in 1902 in Warrenton, North

107

Carolina, he graduated from Davidson College in 1923 with an AB degree, and in 1939, he received his MA degree from New York University. He actually had been a faculty assistant in Greek language at Davidson and taught Latin at Grainger High School. His hobbies were photography, swimming, and beekeeping, and in his spare time, he loved to hunt and fish.

Most of us would not consider it a hobby, but he also enjoyed studying the Greek language and history, as well as the Japanese language and culture. He was truly a unique and amazing individual. He was well educated, cultured, yet he was very warm and gregarious.

Mr. Booth and his wife did not have any children, which afforded them the opportunity to do other things. Once a year, they loved to go hunting for elk or moose in Colorado or other scenic places. They bought the finest hunting equipment available and loved the adventure of going out into nature and "harvesting" worthy game. They enjoyed collecting antiques, and apparently, Mr. Booth did well investing his money because upon his death, he left a generous amount of money to various educational institutions and charities.

Principal Jack Horne's son John remembers him and his dad hunting quail with Mr. Booth. John, who was just a small boy at that time, said he remembers Mr. Booth smoking a pipe and his hair always combed back looking dignified and stately. "He always had dried apricots in his house," John recalled.[1]

In December of 1981, Dad had invited the Booths to come to Louisiana for a good old-fashioned Louisiana duck hunt. Dad made arrangements to entertain the Booths with hunting and fishing trips and introduced them to the Louisiana's original Cajun culture. It was on this trip that I had that opportunity to visit with Mr. Booth over the phone. The Booths came to Louisiana and apparently had a wonderful time as a letter he wrote to Mom and Dad seems to indicate. The following excerpt from this letter tells a little of his adventure and shows that he was not only eloquent in his speech but also in his writing. The letter is written in his own handwriting and looks as if it is done by a professional calligrapher.

RED DEVIL TALES

The letter is seven handwritten pages of oration describing Dad's "illustrious career as a coach at Grainger High School, his accomplishments as a businessman, and his thoughts on his fishing adventure in the rolling hills of north Louisiana, and his exotic duck hunt in the south Louisiana swamps and bayous." Of course, Mr. Booth couldn't pass up the opportunity to review a historical background of the Cajun people. The following is a sample of this letter he skillfully crafted to Dad:

"Amos Sexton and his charming wife, Lee, invited the scribe and his wife, Peggy, for a visit and waterfowl hunt in Louisiana from December 29, 1981, to January 7, 1982."

"He was formerly employed as a teacher and basketball coach in the Kinston, North Carolina City Schools, his teams winning three State Championships during his ten year tenure. His contributions to the many young people were legendary, admired and loved by all age levels as teacher, counselor and friend. On his radio programs and in everyday life his language was intriguingly refreshing flowing in rhythmic strophes—dramatic gyrations symbolic of his scriptural namesake, the Old Testament prophet (Amos), though not quite so orthodox."

"Amos left the teaching profession and in the past quarter of a century has achieved phenomenal success as a business man with headquarters in Ruston, Louisiana, in the areas of furniture distribution and real estate. His friends, who are legion, are proud of his achievements and affluence."

"We were welcomed by Amos and Lee at the Monroe Airport, thirty miles distance from Ruston. Superb hospitality was the hallmark of our visit from the time of our meeting at the exit ramp. We were welcomed at the entrance to a beautiful and elegantly appointed home on Lilinda Drive by a bevy of dogs led by 'Frenchie' and 'Howdy,' and lesser canines who reflected the warm hospitable spirit of their owners."

"The day after arrival, we were cordially received by the Rotary Club where the North Carolina visitor had been scheduled to give the program. After Amos had several times, in reference to me, used the terms "elderly senior citizen" or "age 79," his former superintendent remonstrated, saying that he was neither a senior citizen nor elderly, but was 79 chronologically only."

"In preparation for the hunt, the matter of hunting permits came to the fore. 'No problem,' said our host. We were ushered into the august presence of Sheriff Wayne Houck of Lincoln Parish. He said it would be a privilege to issue to Peg and me a Louisiana hunting-fishing permit, good for life at no cost. As a sequel to his generosity, the permits were lost in the bayous on the first outing. The sheriff obligingly issued duplicates. The original copies were located in our gear later. Therefore, we are doubly protected now legally."

"We embarked from Ruston in the Sexton's beautiful Landau Regency mobile home for the five hour trip to Cameron Parish, south of Lake Charles. Upon arrival at 7:30 p.m., we connected with electric current in the backyard of the Cajun Acadian family of the Savories."

"It was in the yard of Sheriff James R. 'Sono' Savoie of Cameron Parish that we parked the mobile home, well-stocked with groceries and other essentials. The 19 year old son, Bobby, a sophomore in McNeese State University, had been designated as our guide. He met us at Creole with a warm welcome and piloted us to the Savorie place."

"As we prepared to cook supper, at the end of the 250 mile trip, Bobby came to the door and said the family was inviting us to eat with them and that the seafood gumbo was ready. There the traditional Cajun cuisine was delightfully perpetuated by Hazel (Mrs. Savoie) and her 94 year old mother whom we called 'Grandma' falling in love with her at first sight."

"Bob was a guide par excellence, great marksman and one hundred percent gentleman all the way and could handle mud boats with real finesse. I told his parents that if I had a son, I would like for him to be a duplicate of Bob, adding parenthetically that "he must be an exponent of his raising." He always said, 'yes sir,' and even busied himself to brush mosquitoes from you, always seeking your comfort in the blind. On the final safari into the bayous, he connected a flat-bed to a tractor and dragged us to the blind as an expert ferryman. When Peg or I mired into the mud and ooze, he was always ready with a helping hand—probably in deference to chronological ages. New Year's Day was a memorable occasion. The Savoies, with children and grandchildren invited us for dinner: smoked beef, two smoked turkeys, smoked ham, scalloped oysters, shrimp gumbo, many vegetables and side dishes. When time came for the evening meal they insisted that we come for what was left—a plenty."

"Sheriff Savoie is the owner of a very commodious home and 1100 acre cattle ranch. He presides over his holdings with great aplomb[2] and dignity. His wife, Hazel, is a most charming and considerate hostess."

"The writer stacked bags, gun cases and other gear in the dry shower stall. The water came on during the night soaking woolens and guns. Hazel, learning of the predicament said, 'No problem, I'll place the hole works in my dryer.' Soon everything was dry and neatly packed into the bags by this great lady."

"We were saying goodbyes and taking pictures of these choice people, when Grandma hugged us with her benediction. 'May God bless you always. It has been wonderful to know you. We love people.' Four year old Jami's injunction was, 'take care.'"

"After the trip across the state, back to Ruston, the hospitality of the Sexton home resumed in increased crescendo. Amos called a Mississippi connection about flights of waterfowl on the flyway and was told that it did not look well there. When asked about permits, he simply said, 'The same arrangement.' I replied to Amos, 'I have never been so 'sherrified-up' in my life.'"

"After two more hunts at the Sexton home in Claiborne Park, we spent a day on Black Lake in the Ruston Area fishing for largemouth bass, catching enough in the 2–3 pound class for two fish suppers cooked as only Amos could cook them. Much was learned from his cooking expertise. In fact, between duck and fish suppers, the writer added 5 pounds of avoirdupois[3] to his body weight."

"As the ducks brought home from Louisiana are enjoyed, we will strive to emulate the gumbo served by Lee Sexton and the Cajuns along with the Boudin which Amos iced for us with the waterfowl collected on a memorable hunt."

"A most enjoyable day was spent touring Louisiana Tech, Grambling State University and the holdings of Amos in and around Ruston and re-visiting the Rotary Club. As long as life lasts, the zenith of warm hospitality will be a treasured memory of the Sextons in the gently rolling hills of the Ruston area, the Cajun Savoies of the bayous of the south, the Rotarians and so many new friends met in the Bayou State."

"We join Grandma and Hazel as they said, 'We love people.' May all of our friends in Louisiana who were so kind to us continue to be a part of our lives during the years ahead."[4]

Charlie Lewis credits Jean Booth for making a significant contribution to his athletic career. Charlie's father was a barber and cut Mr. Booth's hair (what little he had). When Charlie was five, his dad asked Mr. Booth one day when he came into his shop whether or not Charlie should start school as five-year-old. His birthday fell in November, so he could have started school as a five-year-old. In those days, there was no automatic cut-off date like there is today. Mr. Booth said he could do that, but he advised Mr. Lewis to hold him back until he was six. He said that Charlie's maturity level would be better if he waited one more year.

The advice was taken, and Charlie said that if had graduated a year earlier, his life would be totally different. Charlie said his parents could not afford to send him across the street, let alone send him to East Carolina University. If he had been in the 1956 graduating class instead of the 1957 class, he would have been competing for a scholarship against players like Alley Hart, Bobby Stanley, and Eion Faelten. That extra year, Charlie believes, made the difference, and Jean Booth was responsible for that.

In 1949, Jean Booth was given a leave of absence by local and state educational authorities to serve from February through May as a visiting expert, attached to the staff of General Douglas MacArthur in Japan. He taught educational administration in four imperial Japanese universities and worked as an Army commissioner on the general's staff. Mr. Booth was very active member and supporter of the Rotary Club, and while in Japan, he assisted a district governor,

RED DEVIL TALES

Tomotake Teshima, in reactivating several Rotary Clubs that were disbanded during World War II.[5]

The Rotary Club of Kinston was featured in an article in the February 22 issue of *Look* magazine. Entitled, "Rotary: Big wheel of the service clubs," the article highlighted the Kinston chapter of Rotarians and the exceptional community involvement and service that the organization provided over the years for the local area. Every Thursday at 12:45 p.m., the rotary club met for a luncheon and business meeting at the Hotel Kinston downtown on Queen Street. Superintendent Jean Booth, Principal Jack Horne, and Coaches Frank Mock and Amos Sexton, as well as, many other businessmen in the community were always a part of the weekly ritual of comradery, fun, and good deeds. The *Look* staff writer, Jack Star, noted that the Kinston organization "composed a cross section of the business and professional community of their city of 25,000 in the rich tobacco country 78 miles east of Raleigh."[6] The gathering of over a hundred consisted of the president of the Chamber of Commerce, the commander of the Veterans of Foreign Wars, the superintendent of schools (Jean Booth), the president of the Ministerial Association, and, "a man who owns half the town . . .one of Kinston's leading doctors."[7]

Jean Booth's contribution to the success of Grainger High School was his ability in administration, choosing and working with the right personnel, and implementing his vision for a solid and well-rounded high school program.

Superintendent Jean Booth

9

PRINCIPAL JACK HORNE

It was the first day of school at Grainger High School in 1947, and all the students, grades seven through twelve, were gathered in assembly to listen to the opening remarks of the new principal, Jack Horne. Students were still coming in and mingling around as they slowly made their way to their seats. The roar of chatter echoed over the auditorium when Dr. Horne stepped up to the podium and said, "All right, students, I want everyone to find your seats and give me your attention. If you cannot find a seat, we will find one for you." Gradually, the noise subsided, and everyone began to fix their gaze toward the front.

One student, however, was not paying attention. Emmett Morton continued talking. Dr. Horne looked at Emmett and said, "Hey you, you down there, be quiet. He once again issued a call to order, and once again, Emmett ignored the principal's warning. Then Dr. Horne abruptly left the podium and briskly walked down to where Emmett was seated and still talking. The look on Emmett's face when he suddenly realized that the principal was standing in front of him was priceless. But before Emmett could retreat back down into his seat, Jack Horne had him by the ear and was pulling him up the aisle. As the whole assembly watched in horror, you could have heard a pin drop. Dr. Horne, dragging Emmett up the aisle

115

still holding him by his ear, passed Emmett's mother, a teacher at the school, and said to her, "Mary Douglas, you come with me." Dr. Horne, Emmett, and his mother exited the auditorium.

Frazier Bruton who related this story and was a witness to this first day of the new principal said he did not know what happened to Emmett, but one thing was established: Principal John H. Horne was not a person to cross. He ran a tight ship, and he meant business. In fact, in his younger days, Jack Horne had been a much feared boxer. There was a standing rumor that developed around school that Dr. Horne would take some rebellious and disrespectful kid who needed some discipline into the boxing ring and teach him an unforgettable lesson.

Eion Faelten was one of Grainger High School's prominent athletes. He stood six feet four and played center on the Red Devil basketball team and defensive end on the football team. In 1997, at a Red Devil Reunion, Eion said when he saw Dr. Horne, he never realized just how small a man he was. He said, "In high school, we were scared to death of him. It is amazing how a man of his size could command so much fear and respect."

Dr. John H. "Jack" Horne was the principal of Grainger High School from 1947 to 1957. He was born March 31, 1914, in Rocky Mount, North Carolina. By the age of five, he was an orphan. His mother, Genevieve Hanna Horne, died in 1918, and his father, George R. Horne, died in 1919. They were victims of the flu pandemic of 1918. Many people do not realize that this global pandemic killed more people than World War I. It is estimated that somewhere between 20 and 40 million people died worldwide as a result of this deadly strain of the Spanish flu.[1] Jack Horne also lost a sister and infant brother to this deadly virus. He and his surviving brother George were raised by his father's sister, Mrs. J. A. "Carrie" Hutchins of Spencer, North Carolina.

After graduating from Spencer High School, he attended the University of Chicago and the University of North Carolina at Chapel Hill from which he earned a bachelor's degree in zoology and later master's and doctor's degrees in education. After graduating from the University of North Carolina, he came to Kinston in the fall of 1936 where he coached boys and girls tennis and boxing. While there, he taught chemistry, physics, and biology. He was a faculty sponsor of the Boys hi-Y, a member of First Baptist Church and the junior chamber of commerce.

In June of 1942, he was drafted into the Army where he was assigned to the 315th Combat Engineer outfit, which was attached to the 90th infantry, and he participated in the Normand invasion at Utah Beach and the Battle of the Bulge and other campaigns. He took part in the in invasion of Normandy D-Day plus one and was awarded the Purple Heart, Bronze Star, Silver Star, and the Bronze Arrowhead for D-Day plus one. He was discharged in the fall of 1945 and settled in Polkton, North Carolina, and became principal of Polkton High School for one year. He married former Marguerite Mae Cochran of Lacona, Iowa, in January 1946. In September 1947, Jack Horne returned to Kinston and became the principal of Grainger High School.

In 1957, he left Kinston and accepted a professorship at East Carolina Teacher College where he taught in the School of Education for two years. In January 1958, he was made registrar and director of admissions. He was later promoted dean of admissions.

Dr. Horne served as a trustee at Campbell University where he also taught in the school of education for two years. In January 1960, he was then made registrar and director of admissions. He also a taught men's Sunday school class at Immanuel Baptist Church.

His hobbies were hunting (deer, squirrel, quail, dove), fishing, golf, carving, genealogy, and he loved working in the yard with flows in the College Day Program and work with the Southern Association of Colleges and Schools in evaluating public school programs and facilities in North Carolina. He served on a committee that studied the curriculum of the newly established community college system.

In the eighth grade, Poo Rochelle learned in an unusual way when the Rotary Club met. One day, just before lunch, Poo and Charles Randolph decided that they were going to light and throw some firecrackers out of Miss Betty Nethercutt classroom window. Miss Nethercutt's English classroom was on the ground floor. Well, they lit the firecrackers and threw them, but instead of going out the window, they hit the glass and bounced back into the room. Horrified and scared to death, Miss Nethercutt immediately dispatched the boys to see Principal Horne. They probably would rather have faced God. So the two rascals left the room and headed to the principal's office, which was in the middle of the second floor. The first person the boys came to in the office was Mrs. Smathers, the principal's secretary. Ironically, Mrs. Smathers was related to Poo's mother in some distant way, but that wasn't going to help matters. They walked in and stood in front of Mrs. Smathers, who looks up and smugly says, "Is there something you want?"

This was the last place they want to be, and Poo nervously answers, "We would like to see Mr. Horne." Mrs. Smathers then informed the boys that Mr. Horne has gone to the rotary club meeting and would not be back until 2:15 p.m. So the boys said to Mrs. Smathers, "Okay, maybe we'll just see him when he gets back." Yeah, right. Of course, they never went back to see Dr. Horne, nor did they go back to class, but from that day on, Poo said, "I never forgot that the rotary club in Kinston always met on Thursday at one o'clock." To his students Dr. Horne was affectionately known as "Mr. Uga Uga."

Jack Horne

10

RED DEVIL TALES

The Red Devil basketball team was limited to twelve players. If you were the bottom tier of twelve players, you were either an inexperienced underclass rookie or upper classmen who backed-up the exceptionally talented starters. Frazier Bruton was one of those players who just barely made the team, but he was proud to be the eleventh player on the 1950–51 Red Devil squad. His older brother Doug was a starter and arguably one of the best athletes to ever come out of Grainger High School.

Coach Sexton always tried to play the bench when he could because he had a sense of compassion for every player. However, he had a tendency to lose track of time in a basketball game. On December 18, 1950, the Red Devils played Camp Lejeune in Raleigh. Camp Lejeune was an AAA team, and Kinston at that time was AA. Camp Lejeune had an all-American player by the name of Floyd Propst; and Everett Case, North Carolina state basketball coach, wanted to see Floyd Propst, as well as Bobby Hodges and Doug Bruton, play. So he called Amos and asked him if he could have the game moved to Raleigh's North Carolina State's coliseum. The Red Devils played Camp Lejeune in Raleigh but lost 49–41. Floyd Propst had a great game and scored thirty-two points. The game was close for a while, but near the end of the game, Frazier said Coach Sexton looked at

120

RED DEVIL TALES

him and yelled, "Bruton, take your coat off and get in the game." Frazier looked at the clock, and there were only three seconds left. So Frazier acted like he didn't hear him; and the twelfth player, Kenneth Anderson, got up and went in instead.

Immediately after the game, in the locker room, as he was getting dress to go back, Coach Sexton came over to him, put his arm around him, and said, "Frazier, time just got away from me. I'm sorry. You'll play more next time."

"Sure enough," Frazier laughs. "The next game, I played two minutes."

Kinston was a small community where everyone seemed just a stone's throw away. Frazier and Doug Bruton lived across the street from Coach Sexton, when he lived in a house on Grainger Avenue. Another basketball player, Amos Stroud, also lived next to the Brutons, as well as Bobby "Bowlegs" Grady. Bobby was an outstanding Red Devil football player.

The Brutons lived in a two-story house, and their father worked as a postman. Some considered the job of a postman as a one who was fairly well-off in a small town where many barely scratched out a living. Plus, the Brutons had a cow in their backyard. Frazier was born with some health issues, and he said he needed calcium among other things. So his father had a cow in the backyard that Doug and Frazier had to milk every day.

Another schoolmate who lived several houses from the Brutons was Emmett Morton. According to Frazier, Emmett was the Dennis the Menace of the neighborhood. He was always up to something and full of mischief. Actually, Emmett was a good baseball player who played shortstop on both the 1949 and the 1950 state championship teams. Frazier said every time he rode his bike past Emmett's house, Emmett always came out and playfully hit him upside the head or pulled his hair. If a tobacco truck came down the street, Emmett ran down and pulled off a bail. Then he would go sell it. Emmett's mother, Mary Douglas Morton, was an English teacher at the school; and she also taught Bible.

"You know," Frasier commented, "Emmett's like a typical preacher's kid, sort of wild and mischievous."

Frazier remembered the time Emmett threw a snowball at a passing car when he was loafing around at Shady's Soda Shop one afternoon. This time Emmett was a senior in high school, so he had a good throwing arm. Shady's was the local hangout famous for their chili and hamburgers, hot dogs, and sodas.

One day, when there was snow on the ground, Emmett was at Shady's making snowballs and stashing them behind some bushes. Frazier walked up to him and asked, "Emmett, what are you doing?" He knew he must be up to something.

Emmett replied, "Frazier, that's my business. You go on."

Frazier went on into Shady's to get a hot dog.

Also sitting on the outside on a wooden beach was another student, Carl Bynum, who was reading a newspaper. Well, about that time, a car came down the street past Shady's and Emmett hurled a snowball at the unsuspecting motorist and hit the passenger right square in the head. Frazier saw the whole thing and heard the driver of the car yell, "Oh hell." Then the driver wheeled his car around, got out of the car, and approached Carl who was still reading the paper and totally unaware of what was going on. The man knocked the paper away from Carl and barked, "We saw you do that. Now you act like you haven't done nothing!"

Carl's nickname was Bad Man, and even though he didn't play sports, he was sort of a rugged frontiersman type who spent most of his time in the woods hunting. He was the kind of person that if you got into a bar fight, you would want Carl on your side. So this man was probably about to go head-to-head with a grizzly bear. This boy wasn't afraid of the devil. In the meantime, Emmett had run down to the end of the block and was bent over laughing. To save the day, Shady, the owner of the soda shop, who had seen everything that had happened, ran out of the shop with his little white hat on, waving a foot long butcher knife at the man, yelling in his thick Lebanese accent, "If you, ah, gonna hit, ah, someone, you, ah, hit, ah, the, ah, right damn one!" He let the man know that Carl was not the culprit. Actually, he probably saved the man's life.

In 1949, Frazier traveled with the team to New Bern. At that time New Bern had an all-state player name Sonny Russell who gave

RED DEVIL TALES

Kinston fits on the court. Even the great Bobby Hodges could be intimidated by Russell who had a forty-four-inch jump and could often times block Hodges's shots.

"Sonny Russell," Frazier noted, "could jump at the foul line and dunk the ball—something that you didn't see much in that day."

Hodges was so tall he didn't have to jump much so he didn't. The first meeting between the teams had been won by Kinston 42–33, but New Bern was playing without their star player Sonny Russell. The second meeting between the teams was on January 25, 1949. Dad had just come on board as the new head coach in November. On the bus to the game, Frazier said Bobby Hodges came and sat beside him and Doug.

Bobby told Doug, "Me and you tonight, Doug, me and you." Then Bobby got up and left.

Frazier, sort of bewildered by the comment, turned to Doug and asked, "What did he mean by that?"

Doug told him their strategy against Sonny Russell. "He's gonna pass me the ball more tonight. I'll be the high scorer. You just watch."

"Sure enough," Frazier laughed. "Bobby passed off to Doug more than he ever did against New Bern because of Sonny Russell."

The paper recorded the results as well under the subheadline, "BRUTON SHOWED WAY."

Lloyd Whitfield wrote, "It was the amazing accuracy of Doug Bruton which helped the Devils by-pass the New Bern zone defense. Bruton would break into the foul circle and take a pass and toss the ball into the basket with the greatest of ease. His accurate shooting during the third period enabled the Devils to overcome the Bears lead and win the game. Bruton hit three out of three foul shots and seven field goals to score 17 points for high man of the evening." Whitfield went on to say, "The defensive play of Bobby Hodges was great as he held the great Sonny Russell to 10 points."[1] The Red Devils won the game 34–29. Looks like the strategy worked. As an interesting side note, Lloyd Whitfield was not only one of the sportswriters at the time for the *Free Press*, he was one of the players on the team.

Jerry Kanter graduated in the class of 1944. He played under Frank Mock, and he remembered Amos Sexton not only from his

123

days in Kinston but when he worked in New Orleans in the sixties. Jerry worked the French Quarters for F. Strauss Liquor for seven years. It was there that he ran into Amos Sexton several times when the former coach was selling kitchen cabinets in the area. Jerry remembered one night when he was living in New Orleans. One of his clients in the French Quarters called him late at night and said, "There was a man down here trying to compete with Evel Knievel and says he knows you and he's got a motor cycle in here." The call was coming from Papa Joe's in the 600 Block of Bourbon Street.

Dad traveled over a five-state area selling cabinets. In order to cover such a large area, he got a private pilot's license and bought a single-engine airplane. He found a little motor scooter that would fit into the back of the airplane, and off he would go to some airport, take out his little scooter, ride around the area, and call on his clients. In those days, Dad wore a suit so it looked rather funny to see a man well-dressed and riding on little box-looking scooter down the road. Dad didn't care how it looked. He was having fun with it and saving big bucks. Dad like to tell the story when one of his clients, who was in Arkansas about one hundred and fifty miles away, called him and asked if he could come up and see him. Dad told him that he would be up there that afternoon. Well, in about an hour and a half, the man sees Dad driving up in that little scooter. In great amazement, he said, "Amos, how in the hell did you get up here that fast in that little scooter?" I think Dad's response was, "Bob, this little scooter goes a lot faster than you think it does."

Well, apparently in this French Quarter restaurant and bar, Dad just pulled the little scooter inside for security reasons. This probably brought on the consternation of the management at which time Dad probably dropped Jerry Kanter's name, using it as his "free pass" card. Jerry, upon hearing a description of the man, realizes that it has got to be Amos Sexton. "Okay, I think I know who it is," he said. "I'll be down there in a minute." Jerry said in the seven years that he was in New Orleans, he met some real characters and Amos Sexton could blend in with the best of them. Several weeks later, Jerry said one of his clients said to him, "Jerry, let me know a week in advance when

RED DEVIL TALES

this dude's coming back so I can close this place up. He was in my place with a damn motor scooter."

Jerry also remembered that Frank Mock and Amos Sexton used to umpire games on the side. Jerry played minor league baseball in Houma, Louisiana, for one year. In 1951 he warmed up pitchers in the Coastal Plains League and for the Kinston Eagles minor league team. He played in a few games, but he will never forget the night in Grainger Stadium when Frank Mock and Amos Sexton were umpiring one of the games. Frank was behind the plate, and Amos was at first base. Kinston was beating the daylights out of the opposing team, and in the final inning and the last out, a ball was hit to Jerry, who was at second base. Jerry threw the ball to first base, and the guy was out by a mile. Amos called him out. But the man crossed first base and continued till he got to Amos and just slugged him in the face. Jerry said Amos regained his composure and worked his way back on top of the guy and nearly beat him to death. People in the stands started converging on the scene. Jerry said that one man in the stands came out and pulled out his knife and said, "He'll never do that again."

They finally pulled Amos off the man, but in the process, they broke his belt, split his pants, and had to have a police escort to get him off the field.

At the 1981 reunion, Jerry related these stories and ended his remarks by saying, "Amos, you are not a good motorcycle rider because you don't know where to go, you don't keep it in the right places, and I question your umpiring. But I can say this: Kinston's loss is Cajun country's gain."

Jerry now is almost ninety years old and is still active as a swimmer. He has competed in swimming events at the regional and state level. He also swam several events in the first Senior Olympics in 1987.

George Whitefield and I were eating breakfast one morning at Ken's Grill on Highway 70, between Goldsboro and Kinston, when Joe Whaley walked in. Joe Whaley still looked good for someone who was the starting guard on the 1950 state basketball championship team and a star running back for the football team. We were

125

sitting in a booth consuming, according to George, the finest cooked eggs, grits, and toast in North Carolina. As Joe slowly made his way to a table across the room, George, somewhat startled and surprised like a kid on Christmas morning, looked up and yelled, "Hey, Joe, come over here."

Joe was a little taken back. It was early in the morning, you know, and not everyone was operating on all six cylinders. Joe made eye contact and casually moved toward our booth and managed to say, "Good morning, George."

Now came the big question. It was like we are on one of those game shows, and George was about to ask the contestant Joe Whaley the sixty-four thousand dollar question. George, who was now standing as he was greeting Joe, put his left hand on his shoulder and, with his right hand pointing at me, said, "All right, Joe, now look at this guy. Who do you think he is?" Who does he look like?"

I'm not sure whether Joe was just not fully up yet or whether he felt like some quiz-show contestant unceremoniously dragged from the audience against his will, but he didn't exactly look as if he was playing along. I was a little embarrassed, and Joe looked a little embarrassed. But he looked at me, then at George, then back to me. He finally managed to say, "Well, he looks like a Sexton." Fortunately, Joe hit the mark.

George, like Bob Barker on *The Price is Right*, congratulated Joe and said, "That's right. You got it. Isn't he the spittin' image of Coach Sexton?"

George said he remembered as a small boy when he was about twelve years of age going to the old Grainger Stadium and watching the Red Devil football team practice. He said he remembered seeing Coach Mock with a whistle around his neck and dressed in old baggy trousers, the kind with elastic around the bottom. Coach Mock blew the whistle, and little Joe Whaley from his fullback position blasted off right guard for seven or eight yards. George said he marveled how someone so small could be so powerful.

Joe Whaley graduated from Grainger High School in 1950 and then went on to served in the Air Force from 1951 to 1977. Then he went and graduated from East Carolina University and began another career teaching school from which he retired in 1993. Since then he plays a lot of golf and is an avid participate with the Red Devils and Friends Golf group.

The Red Devils and Friends golf group was started by Amos Stroud, another member of the 1950 state championship basketball team. He and Tommy Cole were also captains of the 1951 team.

Amos grew up in Kinston and attended grade school (1–6) at Harvey Elementary School, the seventh grade at Southwood, and, finally, Grainger High School (grades 8–12). Amos Stroud was sophomore when Coach Sexton came to Kinston in 1948. At that time he was playing on the junior varsity team. He said Coach Sexton even had the JV team running the fast break offense.

They ran it so much, Amos remembered, he could probably run it in his sleep. He can still recall the details of how it was set up. He said, "In this fast break, it was based on the premise that the defensive set up of the team was two defenders at the top of the key with three men, usually the center and two forwards back near the base line. In most situations, one of these three players would get the defensive rebound. When this occurred, the two guards out front would break toward the respective side lines while the two back forwards would start down a separate side line toward their offensive end of the court. The rebounder would pass the ball to one of the out men on a sideline, which in turn would pass the ball to the other out man breaking across the center line toward the passer. This would ideally result in two players breaking down the side lines with the player receiving the out pass in the middle. Theoretically, this would set up a desirable three on two going to their offensive basket. The player who got the rebound would follow the play down the center of the court. If the man in the middle could, he would try to pass off to one of the players breaking down the side lines, or take the shot himself, with the third option being passing back to the trailer following him."

Preparation for varsity basketball didn't just start with the junior varsity. It started with kids playing at Emma Webb Park as soon as they could pick up a basketball. Coach Sexton taught physical education and civics, but even his PE classes were centered on training young boys to play basketball. Grainger started with the seventh grade. Coach Sexton would choose about twenty-five of the best potential players in PE, have them practice the fundamentals of basketball, and have the rest of boys play volleyball or something else. The recreational department was in good hands with the former Grainger High School basketball coach Bill Faye. Bill Faye started the youth playing basketball at Emma Webb Park and introduced them to the fundamental. Charles Lee took them on the next level at the junior varsity. By the time these kids got to the varsity with Amos Sexton, they not only knew the fundamentals of basketball, they also knew how to run the fast break offense. It was a system that worked well and paid big dividends. There was cooperation and coordination at every level.

When Stroud was a junior, the basketball team won their first state championship. It was a most unusual season, he remembered. The team was undefeated in the northeastern conference, but because of a clerical technicality involving a required form not being properly filed, the team had to forfeit the first thirteen games. Nevertheless, the State Athletic Association director Mr. Hap Perry promised this team would get to play for the state championship, even if it meant they would play in the AA instead of the A playoffs.

During his senior year (1951), Amos pointed out that all their home games were played at the Stallings Air Base field house because the school was building a new gym, which would eventually become Frank L. Mock Gymnasium. The team ran laps on the runway—that is, of course, when the airplanes weren't taking off. The Red Men were definitely in great shape as most of these laps were run at or near dark and usually in cold weather.

The first two years he was at Grainger, Amos Sexton coached the JV team as well as the varsity basketball team as Coach Fay had done before him. In 1951, Amos's senior year, Charlie Lee was hired as a seventh grade teacher and JV basketball coach. He also coached the Red Devils' first tennis team. Charlie Lee would later become the head basketball coach and tennis coach at Goldsboro High School.

"Your father was very good to me," Amos said. "I did my practice teaching at Grainger High School with him and the math teacher Mrs. Gladys Sutton. One summer, I went to summer school at East

RED DEVIL TALES

Carolina. Your father was in graduate school at that time, and he let me ride back and forth at no charge, which was very helpful. He was a very kind man."

According to Amos Stroud, Amos Sexton was good at two things: human relations and salesmanship. But one of the scariest days of his life was when he accompanied Coach Sexton on one of his pots and pans selling adventures. The incident occurred that would test both his human relationship ability and his salesmanship.

Coach Sexton's method of selling pots and pans was to set up a home demonstration at someone's house and invite a few ladies to come and watch him cook with these new pots and pans. In the process they all enjoyed the healthy and tasty food one could make using these new stainless steel pots and pans. Coach Sexton usually brought along a black lady to help cook and clean up. On one particular occasion, Coach Sexton told Amos as they were coming back from Greenville that he needed to stop by a house in Ayden to see a lady who had been sold on the pots and pans. All he needed to do now was to convince her husband of the marvelous benefits of these new kitchen products. The coach told Amos that he wanted him to see him sell the man on the new pots and pans. Sort of witness the "great salesman" in action.

It was an impromptu and unannounced visit, but Coach thought this was just going to be an easy deal to close. They found the house and went up and knocked on the door. The little lady opened the door, but she looked as if she had seen a ghost. Somewhat startled and embarrassed, she said, "Oh! Well, I got to go get my husband." The lady went to the back of the house, and the husband came to the door and politely invited Amos and Coach inside. They sat down in the living room, and Coach Sexton commenced telling the man how good the food was going to be using these new pots and pans. The husband was most impressed and thought it all sounded good. It looked as if it was a done deal, and Coach Sexton was beaming with pride over his sales demonstration. However, the man said he needed to speak to his wife for a moment so he got up and left the room. A few moments later the wife came in and announced, "We can't have any of these pots and pans. We just can't buy them right now."

129

Stunned and bewildered, Coach Sexton looked at her and said, "Why can't you? I thought you wanted them?"

The man had told his wife that she could buy the pots and pans, but she would have to pay for them out of her dress and clothing allotment. Well, that little lady wasn't about to pay for them out of her allotment. Amos Stroud said that Coach got about as bewildered and frustrated as he had ever seen him and that included during the ball games when he was on the wrong end of a bad referee call. Coach looked at this little petite lady and, trying to recovery from a good deal gone bad, made one more appeal but to no avail. You would have thought he just lost an important ball game. Well, you can't win them all, so Coach and Amos Stroud sadly retreated to try again another day.

Amos Stroud and Doug Bruton got into some trouble in study hall one year that should have landed them in the principal's office and maybe even got them expelled from school. The study hall was on the third floor, and the library was on the second floor. In between the two floors was a spiral staircase. Amos was put into to study hall with Doug Bruton to help him with his math. Doug was getting a scholarship to Chapel Hill (UNC), and he was taking geometry and algebra II to fulfill the requirements to go to college. Amos had already taken the course, and he wanted to be a teacher anyway, so he was helping Doug with his homework. The study hall teacher was Mr. Luther Howard Whitehurst, a small, frail, but intelligent young man who taught English. In fact, at that time, according to Amos, Mom and Dad lived in the same building with Mr. Whitehurst on Park Avenue. This was before they moved to a house on Grainger Avenue.

With about three or four minutes left in study hall, Doug and Amos asked Mr. Whitehurst if they could go down to the library. Well, what Amos and Doug would do was to go down the spiral staircase, bypass the library and head for the cafeteria so they could be first in line. After a while, Mr. Whitehurst caught on to the scam and told the boys that they could no longer leave early to go to the library anymore. Doug told Amos that he would just write Mr. Whitehurst a letter. Amos still remembers the words: "Dear Killer, we will be

RED DEVIL TALES

going to the library as usual, and you ain't got nothing to do with it, and we are going to go anyway." Then both Doug and Amos signed the letter. Mr. Whitehurst was called Killer because he was so small and frail looking, sort of a Barney Fife appearance. Mr. Whitehurst got the letter, but instead of giving it to the principal Jack Horne, which would have pretty much ended their lives, he gave the letter to Coach Amos Sexton. Amos said Sexton handled it, and he handled it well. He told the boys that they were going to run every time he said run. And run they did. Frazier remembered Doug coming home and complaining about how hard Coach Sexton was running them.

Amos Stroud would go on to have a great career as an educator. Nevertheless, he said that probably the saddest day in Grainger High School sports history was during his first year as a high school principal. Amos was at Union High School in Sampson County. His superintendent asked him to talk some patrons, faculty members, and students to observe some vocational programs. He selected Grainger and North Lenoir High Schools. This way the observers could see what was at an urban setting and a rural setting. However, he recounted, it was on a Thursday morning he would never forget.

He said, "When we arrived at Grainger High we were met by Principal Frank L. Mock. He told me he had all of my observers covered, and asked that I go to his office with him. This seemed as a logical way to observe. When he got to his office, he got each of us a Coca-Cola from the machine he kept there. We went in his inner office and sat down together, he behind his desk and me in front of the desk. He said to me slowly and sadly, 'Moose, there will never be any more Red Devils!' He went on to explain that the Kinston School Board had met on Tuesday evening and decided that the name of the school would become Kinston High School instead of Grainger High School, that the school colors were being changed from red and white to green and white, and that the mascot, Red Devils, would now be Vikings. This man who had devoted all his professional years after graduating from Davidson College was saddened beyond description. This was my first year as a high school principal. Frank Mock did not finish that year. He was replaced in a few weeks by his assistant principal Bill Peedin. Mr. Mock moved

131

into the central office as an assistant superintendent. I could never think of that as a promotion. Part of Frank L. Mock's life, especially his professional education career, seemed to have left him that day."

Times began to change, and all those wonderful men and women who had made the Grainger High School Red Devils a very special group were gradually exiting the stage. It was a part of the inevitable evolution of our society that no culture is constant and unchanging. The social revolution of the 1960s had irreparably altered the times and generation of the 1940s and 1950s. Amos Stroud, like everyone of his generation, would experience and be a part of the some of the unsavory changes in our society during the 1960s and 1970s. A case in point, Amos related one incident that was very troubling to him as a principal and an indication that the times had indeed changed.

"A few years later when I was principal of White Oak High School in Onslow County, we played football against Kinston High School in Grainger Stadium. Unruly Kinston fans surrounded our fans, most specially our cheerleaders, with jeers and slurry language. I approached Assistant Superintend Mock with a request for some assistance. He was helpless in this situation. In desperation I got a Kinston policeman and made him accompany me to the area our cheerleaders were with instructions that he was to help me restore a reasonable amount of order. He did a fair job only. That was the night I nearly called off a game and took my people home. We never played Kinston again while I was at White Oak."

Amos said he always liked and respected Dad, and he added that mother was a fine lady as well. In fact, he had class with two of mother's brothers and one of her sisters when he was at East Carolina. He also became close to my mother's brother Sherrol since both of them were principals in Sampson County. He and Sherrill were principals at a very difficult period, he said, and they both consoled and supported each other during a time when school systems were going through a great transition.

I thought it would be a good idea to play golf with the Red Devils and friends during my visit, so I gathered clubs from two different bags (one had been my mother's) and threw them in the back of the car. Well, I figured I couldn't do that bad since most of players were in there seventies. I was wrong. I forgot these guys are old Red Devils and that means two things: they are very competitive and they are out to win.

On this day they were playing at the Emerald Golf Course in New Bern. When I arrived, I could tell by the golf attire that these guys were committed players. A little embarrassed, I slowly pulled out my golf bag, which any casual observer could tell had not been used in a long time. Fortunately, I wouldn't have to carry this dinosaur of a bag. We got carts, and I was assigned to ride with Amos, who was very patient and understanding. I didn't even take a practice swing, and in our group, I was the first one up. I finally hit the ball on the fourth swing, and I knew then it was going to be a long day. I am not saying how many balls I left in the woods or in the course ponds, but at the end of the day Amos reassured me that he would lend me some of his practice balls, not if, but when, I ran out.

Amos was the perfect gentleman and wrote me a nice note later in which he said, "Like all good players, you won money on your first time with the Red Devils. You impress me as a Christian with an excellent sense of humor. You seem to have all of your priorities in the right place. I wish for you all of the good things life has to offer. Any time you are in the area, it will be a thrill to be in your company. Thanks for becoming a part of my life."

But as a final note Amos would add, "You are the only golfer I ever saw get his golf club tangled up with the brake pedal on the cart. And the only teammate to hit me with his club. I will be more careful next time. And I split my shirt while playing with you! (Nevertheless) I had a great time. Thank you for the memories."

11

FRED WILLIAMS

Fred Williams is the oldest of four brothers who played football and baseball for Frank Mock and basketball for Amos Sexton. Sherrill and Jerry played baseball for Frank Mock. Darwin played tennis for Charles Lee. Ironically, Fred is the only surviving brother. At the 1981 Red Devil reunion, Dad jokingly said that he started his coaching career with Fred Williams and he planned to retire when he had coached the last Williams brother. He didn't miss it by much. The youngest Williams brother, Darwin, graduated in 1955; and within two years, Dad did retire from coaching. All the Williams brothers were good athletes, but it was the oldest brother, Fred, and the youngest brother, Darwin, who seem to push the athletic talent to the next level. Fred indicated that both the other Williams brothers, Sherrill and Jerry, were good athletes, but they came along at the wrong time.

It was the era of people like Bobby Hodges, Doug Bruton, Bryant Aldridge, and Joe Whaley. Fred played with Bobby and Doug, but he was a senior when they were juniors. Sherrill was in the same class as Bobby Hodges and Doug Bruton. Jerry graduated in 1952. Sherrill was the tallest of the Williams boys and played on the 1950 State Championship basketball team. He wasn't in the starting lineup, but he played a lot nevertheless. However, it was Fred who excelled in

134

all three sports: football, basketball, and baseball. He was the first Grainger High School athlete to make All-State, which he did as an outfielder in baseball and played on the 1949 State Championship baseball team, the school's first such team. In football, Fred was a part of that 1948 football team, the only undefeated football team in Grainger High School history.

According to Fred, everyone knew Amos Sexton's football credentials but they were somewhat surprised that he was going to be the head basketball coach. Asked if he knew Coach Sexton was not a basketball coach, Fred said that they had no trouble picking that up. First, he dribbled the ball with two hands. Then the coach said, "Ya'll show me what you did last year." After the team showed him what they did the previous year, he said, "Well, we'll do that again this year."

"Coach Sexton didn't just come out and admit that he did not know anything," Fred recalled. "But he gave the players a lot of latitude to play on their own at first." Coach Sexton was smart enough to figure out that the boys knew what they were doing. After all, these boys had played for the state championship the year before, not to mention the fact that they had been playing basketball for years.

Once Amos Sexton he began to learn the sport, he began to coach. The previous year, the Red Devils had missed being state champions by only two points. Fred remembered that they probably should have won the game, but in the last few seconds, Fred had stolen the ball and Bobby Hodges was out front. Fred threw the ball to Hodges, who took it down for a layup. Hodges made the shot, but one of them was called for a traveling violation—a call Fred still questions. Fred said he didn't travel, and Bobby said he didn't travel. It was just one of those unfortunate calls. At any rate, this team was very capable of playing basketball. They all had grown up playing at Emma Webb Park, so they were street smart players, and they had been well coached and prepared by Bill Faye the previous two seasons. What Amos Sexton brought to the table was a sense of direction, providing motivation and leadership, keeping them in shape, and giving them more confidence. In short order, he would give them what they needed to take it to the next level of play.

"Amos would talk to anybody and everybody about basketball," Fred remembered. "It didn't make any difference who it was."

Fred thought that Frank Mock had even coached basketball several years himself. It was earlier in the forties when the school only had one person to coach all three sports. Mrs. Mock told me that she didn't think that Frank ever coached basketball. Rone Lowe, in his article "1955 WAS BIG YEAR IN SPORTS FOR KINSTON, HOME OF THE CHAMPS" stated, "He (Frank Mock) also coached basketball three years during the war, but was out of the coaching field (1945–46) while serving as principal of the school."[1]

Fred knew of a story that was told about Frank Mock and his basketball coaching days. This urban legend goes like this: One year Coach Mock had a group of football boys on the second team of the basketball squad. Fred said he has no idea who they were playing, but the other team was so rough, just beating up on the starting team, that Coach Mock called a time-out and sent in his football players to give them a taste of their own medicine. So the football players entered the game and proceeded to play like football players and rough up the other team.

When Fred and I began to look at the Red Devil picture album, we came to the 1949 baseball team. Fred began to name the players. He pointed to two in particular: Joe Whaley and Bill Dixon. He laughed and said, "These two guys were in the chorus." He remembered the time that they had to go sing, and it caused them to miss a game. They had to go sing in the chorus, or they would get a failing grade. Joe Whaley played second base, and Bill Dixon played centerfield. The athletic teams met together during third period homeroom. One day, before a baseball game, Coach Mock said to the team in his low-key, soft, but dignified voice, "I understand that two of our players are going to be out for today's game because they have to sing in the chorus. Okay, this is what we are going to do." He had written on the board the lineup, and he had Fred playing second base in place of Joe Whaley.

Fred said he spoke up and asked, "Coach, am I going to play second base?"

Coach Mock replied, "Well, you said you could do it."

RED DEVIL TALES

Fred said, "I can do it." Fred would have played anywhere as long as he got to play. He had been playing catcher, but his senior year was mostly played in centerfield.

Then the next time the team played, Bill Dixon was gone and Coach Mock put Fred in the outfield. Again, Fred questioned Coach Mock. The coach replied, "Well, you said you could do it." Fred had played right field on his American Legion team so he knew he could do it. Fred said his senior year was his best year. He hit over 350. At one point in the season, Coach Mock put him as the number 4 hitter (the cleanup spot) in one game and he never touched the ball. He went to the coach after the game and said, "Coach, I don't want to hit fourth."

"Well, Fred," Mock replied, "where do you want to hit?"

Fred said, "Can I hit third?"

The coach let him hit third, and he had a great year, making All-State, the first Grainger High School player to do so. Fred said he thought it was because he was a senior and they had won the state championship. According to Fred, Jimmy Byrd, who pitched the final game, Doug Bruton and Joe Whaley were all great players and could have just as easily been chosen All-State. But Fred did have a great year and he downplayed his talent and his contribution to the state championship team.

The only cuss word Fred ever heard Coach Mock say was *damn*, and even then, he remembered only one time. Only once in a blue moon did Coach Mock ever say a cuss word, and every one that heard it was always amused because it was so rare and he said it so precisely, like a well-placed adjective. Fred recalls the one time when a fellow teammate, Robert Abbott, dropped a pass, and Coach Mock in amazement said, "Great damn day, Abbott." That's about as frustrated as you would ever see Coach Mock get.

But Coach Mock did have a rule that all his players understood: "If you get in a fight on the field, don't bother to come back to the bench, just go on to the locker room." In other words, Coach Mock would never tolerate his players fighting on the field. He believed in playing and winning by the rules. Fred said one time he was on the ground and another player from the opposing team was hitting him. The referee threw both Fred and the other player out of the game. Fred said he went over to the bench after being thrown out and Coach Mock looked with great surprise as if to say, "You know the rule." But he said to Fred, "What are you doing fighting?"

Fred said, "Coach, I wasn't fighting. I was just trying to get up. I was on the bottom, and they were beatin' on me."

Coach Mock believed him and said, "Okay, you can stay out here." Coach Mock knew Fred didn't fight on the field.

The next story Fred told was about one of his classmates Thomas Piver. "Thomas Piver," Fred said, "loved to sing. He would go to church every Sunday night and sing."

Tommy was on the football team, although he didn't play much. Tommy loved to sing, but he also loved to hunt, especially deer. One year, on opening day of deer season, Tommy decided he was going to skip football practice and go deer hunting. He sent word to Coach Mock that he was sick. Tommy went hunting and killed a nice deer, and guess whose picture gets in the paper with his trophy buck. That's right, Thomas Piver. The article goes on to describe how Thomas went hunting and shot the deer. Now that the news was out, Tommy was scared to go to practice but he went anyway. Fred said that they all were rather tense during practice just waiting for Coach Mock to say something to Tommy. However, Coach Mock never said a word. Practice went on as if Tommy had always been there. Just as practice was coming to an end, someone threw Thomas a pass and he dropped it. Now Coach Mock yelled out, "Come on, deer slayer, catch the ball." Fred said everybody just rolled laughing. That's the only thing Coach Mock ever said to Tommy about it.

It was certainly not uncommon for young boys in the forties and fifties to pick up smoking, especially since they lived in tobacco country. The coaches were strict about players not smoking, and if someone was caught he could face the feared gauntlet or something worse. Fred said almost everyone on that team except him smoked to some extent. Coach Mock knew Piver was a smoker; and one day, when he missed a pass, the coach yelled out, "What's the matter Piver, smoke get in your eyes?" That was Coach's way of addressing the problem on occasion.

RED DEVIL TALES

Unfortunately, Thomas Piver's life came to a tragic end when he was killed in a car accident in December of 1948. Tommy was a junior at the time, and the (1948) school annual would be dedicated in his memory by his friends.

Fred asked me if I had heard the "Frank Mock and his forty thieves" story. That was the first time I had heard it called that, but I remembered a story Dad use to tell, and I remembered Bobby Hodges's version of it. Fred would add a few more details. Fred said Dad loved to tell the story.

It happened on the way back from a football game, he believes from Norlina, and the bus had stopped in Warrington. Several of the players took some items from the place where they had stopped. Fred said one player had taken an electric razor and was talking about how he was going to lather up when he got home and use it.

"That's how stupid we were," Fred said. "We didn't know you didn't have to have lather with an electric razor."

Fred said the next part of the story he didn't remember, but Dad used to tell it this way: A policeman stopped right behind the bus and one of the officers got on the bus and demanded that Coach Mock, who was driving, back the bus up. Coach Mock said, "But..." But he was immediately interrupted by one of officers, who said, "Don't give me any buts. I said back the bus up." So Coach Mock backed the bus up and ran right into the patrol car. When he hit the car, the officer shouted out, "What did you do?" Coach Mock responded, "Well, I was trying to tell you that the patrol car was right behind me." Now, Fred says, they took everyone to jail and then made everyone go back on the bus and get everything that was taken. Apparently, Fred was not one of the culprits.

The road trip story reminded Fred of the time when his youngest brother Darwin was kicked off the bus for playing poker and gambling. Of the four brothers, Fred said Darwin was a little more "rowdy" than the others. Their father had left the family when Fred was about twelve. The family had moved to Kinston during the depression, and his father had worked various jobs, but the last job Fred remembered was driving a logging truck. His mother took a job as a seamstress in the alteration department at Harvey's Department

Store. She walked to work every day from where they lived on Mclewean Street. Fred said his mother came to him one day and told him that his dad was not coming back. She told him, "Now, Fred, you have to remember one thing: whatever you do, your brothers are going to do, and you can either set a good example for them or a bad example for them. Don't you forget that." Fred said he did the best he could. His father never came back, and he never sent them any money. They were poor, Fred remembers, "but, we didn't know we were poor." Everybody else was poor too. His friends Jimmy Byrd and Bobby Hodges were not much better off. Fred did see his father one more time. His dad came to see him play in a football game at Roanoke Rapids during his senior year, and Fred spoke briefly to him after the game. That was it.

In order to make ends meet, all the Williams boys worked. Fred delivered newspapers. He got up every morning at 4:30 and threw over two hundred papers in east Kinston. For breakfast, he traded a newspaper for a cinnamon bun and a glass of milk. He would then go to school, and after school he had about three hours of ball practice. When Sherrill was old enough, he did the same thing and so did Jerry. "Darwin," Fred said, "was a little different." He delivered newspapers some, but not much. According to Fred, Darwin, being the youngest, liked to play more. Sherrill had a temper but got along with everyone all right; and Jerry, like Fred, was more "laid-back." Nevertheless, the boys worked and played hard and managed to make it.

Fred eventually got a job on Saturdays working at G. R. Kinney Shoe Store. When he went to work his first day, he didn't have a dress shirt or neck tie to wear so the lady at the store gave him some money to get some proper clothing. After working there a while, they needed some more help so Fred recruited Jimmy Byrd. Fred and Jimmy grew up together as next door neighbors. Fred said Jimmy was essentially like a brother to him. Fred and Jimmy worked at the shoe store for a while, and when the store needed more help, Fred solicited his brother Sherrill. When Fred finished high school, he began working full-time at the shoe store until he was drafted into the Army. Sherrill, and eventually Jerry, would work and manage

RED DEVIL TALES

the shoe store. Fred went to Korea, but when he came back, he said he was better off than when he left. He had no place to spend his money, so he sent it home. When he returned from Korea, he worked a few months at the DuPont plant then went on to East Carolina College. Sherrill went into the Army about two years after Fred got out of service. Jerry and Darwin were never drafted, although Jerry did serve in the National Guard.

With this as background, Fred told me, "I don't know if you know this or not, but Darwin got into some trouble with your daddy." I told him I knew a little about it but not much. Fred said Darwin was kicked off the bus along with Robert Whaley and Lane Ward for gambling, something they knew they were not supposed to be doing. Fred said his mother was very upset about it. She was upset, he said, "not because he was put off the bus, but because he had no way to get back home." Fred said he has never heard how they ever got home. But the matter was not just forgotten. Apparently Sherrill was upset and went up to the school to address the issue with Coach Mock. Darwin was the youngest in the family, and the older three brothers were very protective of him. And I think we all agree that throwing the boys off the bus was understandable. However, leaving them to fend for themselves was a little risky. Hitchhiking was common in those days, and everybody did it. Nevertheless, by today's standards that would be considered irresponsible. When Fred found out what Sherrill had done, he went to Coach Mock himself. Fred said that Coach Sexton did the right thing, but he thought the boys should have been provided a way back home. Fred said he remembered what Coach Mock said to him. "If you don't watch out," Coach Mock warned, "Darwin is going to cause more trouble than all three of you other boys." Fred said he realized that. Darwin turned out to be not only one of the best guards that the Red Devils ever had, but he went on to play for Atlantic Christian College.

Darwin was also a good pool player, and Kinston had a pool hall where people could play. When Fred was working at the shoe store, he would go across the street to the pool hall to get one of their good sandwiches. He said Darwin always had someone looking out for him just in case Fred came in. Fred said when he was walking in the front door Darwin would be leaving through the back door and when he left Darwin would come back in. Fred said Darwin made somewhat of a living playing pool. Playing for money, whether it was cards, pool, golf, or even games, was a part of the culture of the area and of that era.

Bill Faye, who was the recreational director at Emma Webb Park, had established a basketball league that included all ages. Fred said Darwin started playing as soon as he was old enough. But he said, "You can't imagine how (small) he was. I mean he was so small it was pitiful." Darwin started playing basketball, as soon as he could dribble the ball. He played four or five years at the recreation department, and when he was old enough, he went out for the junior varsity team at the high school. Charles Lee was the coach, and he wouldn't let Darwin play because he was so small. Eventually, Sherrill took his mother up to the school to talk to Coach Lee. This was something his mother never had done before. Fred said his mother never saw him play a football game or baseball game, and she only saw him play basketball one time. "She just didn't have a way to get to the games," Fred remembered. "Once she became friends with George's surrogate mother Ada, she went to every game because Ada made sure she had a way to get there or she would come by and pick her up." Darwin had complained about not playing and threatened to quit the JV team and go back to the recreation department at Emma Webb Park to play. He didn't care where he played; he just wanted to play basketball. Charles Lee told Mrs. Williams that he realized that Darwin was a good player, but he was just too scared to play him because he was afraid that he might get hurt. That's how small he was. Fred said his mother told Coach Lee, "If he gets hurt, then he just gets hurt. But if he doesn't play, he's going back to the recreation department. But I would love to see him play here." Charles Lee relented and began to let Darwin play.

When Darwin was a freshman at Atlantic Christian College and Fred was at East Carolina, he went to see Darwin play. Darwin played the whole game except for the last four minutes on the junior varsity team, and then he was taken out for the rest of the game. Fred didn't know what had happened. He wondered whether or not

RED DEVIL TALES

Darwin had been hurt or if something else had happened? When the junior varsity team finished their game, the varsity came onto the court and Darwin came out with the varsity. When the varsity game started, Darwin didn't start but Fred said he was just surprised that Darwin was even sitting on the bench with the varsity. After about four minutes into the game, Darwin went in and played the rest of the game. Fred said that Darwin loved to play basketball. He was an excellent ball handler. He and his brothers used to talk about it all time. "If Darwin had been allowed to 'palm' the ball like they do today, he could have held the ball the whole game." Fred believed this. Darwin would do anything to play the game, and he couldn't stand to lose. He was a fierce competitor.

Fred showed me a newspaper article that he had saved about Darwin when he had a heart transplant at the age of fifty-two. Darwin's first heart attack came in 1974 when he was only thirty-six. He had come to the Chesapeake, Virginia, area to teach and coach at Truitt Junior High School. He then became a junior varsity coach at Oscar Smith High School. From there he coached the varsity basketball team for two years. Darwin's health issues began with basketball. Darwin was playing in a men's basketball league in Suffolk, Virginia. Darwin was not in the best shape, but he was a driven player and kept playing hard. After a while he would have to sit on the bench to rest, and when the other team began to take the lead, Darwin would go back in. At the end of the game, he had his first heart attack in the locker room. He almost died from this first episode, but he did recover in about five months. However, his heart was irreparably damaged. He went back to work at Forest Glen High School, where he became the head football coach, head of the physical education department, and the school's athletic director.

Darwin had his second heart attack in June of 1977 while playing a pick-up basketball game with some kids. Again, he was lucky to pull through. After his recovery, Darwin had to retire on disability but he still managed to become a volunteer coach. He just wouldn't stop pursuing his passion. Darwin struggled along for a few more years with health problems, and finally, he had to have a heart transplant. On July 2, 1989, Darwin underwent heart surgery at the Medical

College of Virginia, which was successful. However, the doctors told him that he would need to take a certain kind of medicine that would probably kill his immune system. Darwin agreed to take the risk; at least, it would buy him some time. Unfortunately, Darwin eventually contracted cancer due to a weakened immune system. He fought the cancer as long as he could but finally lost the battle and died in 1994, five years after his heart transplant.

The last time I contacted Fred he was on his way to see Darwin's grandson, Matthew Hamlet, play baseball for Boston College against Duke University. Matthew, now a senior, plays second base.

"I regret," Fred noted, "that Darwin did not get to see what a fabulous baseball player his grandson has become."

Matthew was five when Darwin died, but Darwin enjoyed coaching him up to the age of five, and Matthew could hit a baseball at the age of three. Darwin's granddaughter, Meredith Hamlet, is a cheerleader for North Carolina State University and has competed in many cheerleading competitions.

Jerry Williams also has grandchildren that are outstanding athletes. His grandson, Ethan Ogburn, got a baseball scholarship at North Carolina State and is an excellent pitcher. His granddaughter, Alex Williams, is a gymnast at North Carolina State on a gymnastic scholarship. Today, Fred is enjoys watching the Williams's grandchildren in their athletic endeavors. He noted, "The talent continues."[2]

"As I look back on those days," Fred said, "they were great days for the boys who played athletics at Grainger High School. I (have) never considered any of the four of us (Williams brothers) as stars. We were what I call role players. We worked hard and played hard and did whatever we could to help the teams. I thank God for the great coaches we played for. They were outstanding role models and father figures for many of us. As I remember the talented players we were associated with, the memories live forever."[3] The Williams brothers left a great legacy as Red Devils.

From left to right: Fred, Jerry, Sherrill, and Darwin (Family photo)

Fred Williams

12

BOBBY HODGES

In any conversation of the best and the greatest to ever play at Grainger High, the name of Bobby Hodges always comes to the forefront. There were many great athletes at Grainger High School through the years, but Bobby Hodges always heads the top of any list.

On our trip to Wilmington, we met with Bobby Hodges, who was working out at the local Y. M. C. A. I thought, *How amazing! Bobby Hodges, now in his late seventies, is still in shape and still working out.* We went to a designated room to wait a few minutes for Bobby to come in, and as I sat there waiting, I didn't remember ever meeting Bobby Hodges before. Even at the 1981 reunion for Dad, I was more or less an observer and never really interacted with the players. But now things have changed. Twenty-nine years later, I was on a quest and wanted to find out what Dad was like in those years. So I made a major effort to talk to Hodges.

Bobby Hodges played at Grainger High School from 1946 to 1950. He was truly one of the best. Like everyone else in that day, he had a nickname or what we call today a handle. His name was Firpo, actually a name his father was called. I remembered what Tommy Cole had said earlier about Dad calling Bobby Hippo on the first day of practice when he came to Kinston. When someone tried to correct

147

him, Dad made it clear that he was sticking with Hippo. I wondered if he continued to call Bobby Hippo.

Most of the names of Red Devil athletes who had played for Dad were new to me as I made my way through the list of boys I wanted to meet on this journey of mine, but not the name of Bobby Hodges. I had heard his name very early in life. Bobby was inducted into the first class of the Kinston-Lenior County Hall of Fame in 2004. Bryan Hanks noted that he was one of Kinston and Lenoir County's first great two-sport athlete.[1] In 1948 and 1949 he was All-State in football and in 1949 and in 1950 he was All-State in basketball. In 1950, after the Red Devils won the state championship in basketball, Bobby said that "one of my favorite memories is of winning that State Championship in Cameron Indoor Stadium, then riding in the parade down Queen Street when we got back…That really brought the community of Kinston together."[2] He was one of only a few athletes selected to play in both the East-West All-Star basketball game and football's Shrine Bowl. He was recruited by the University of North Carolina, Alabama, and Georgia, but chose East Carolina instead.

Bobby went to East Carolina Teachers Colleg (now East Carolina University) on an athletic scholarship and played both football and basketball, a four-year starter in both sports. In football he played both tackle and end. In 1953 and 1954, he was All-Conference and All-State, as well as the team cocaptain. In 1954 he made All-American. He still holds the East Carolina record for most touchdowns (10) in a season. At the end of his football college career, he was drafted by the Philadelphia Eagles.[3]

When the football season ended each year, Bobby immediately joined the basketball team playing center. In basketball, he was All-Conference from 1952 to 1954. He was the Most Valuable Player in the North State Tournament in 1950–51 and "set the scoring record for the tournament in 1954 with 90 points in three games."[4] In 1953 and 1954, he was All-State and the conference MVP, and he was drafted by the Philadelphia Warriors of the NBA in 1954. When he graduated from East Carolina, he held the school record for career

148

RED DEVIL TALES

points (2,047) and season scoring average of just over 27 points per game in 1953 and 1954.[5]

At East Carolina Bobby earned a degree in health and physical education and was named to *who's Who among students in American colleges.* Although he was drafted for pro football and basketball, he was unable to pursue this career because of an ROTC commitment. Bobby was married to the former Drue Bain of Erwin, an ECU cheerleader who died of cancer in 1993. The couple have three children and five grandchildren.

When his college career ended, Bobby wasn't finished with basketball just yet. He became an officer in the Air Force where he played basketball at Nagoya, Japan, from 1956 to 1958.

In the Air Force Worldwide Championship in 1957–58, Bobby was voted MVP. He also played at Andrews Air Force Base from 1958 to 1961 and in the Pan American Games in 1959–60. His career after the Air Force was still in sports. He coached football and was athletics director at Frederick Military Academy (1961–62). He coached basketball at Frederick College (1962–68), basketball and football at Hillsdale College (1968–71), and basketball at Lenoir-Rhyne College (1971–78). In 1968 he was named Small College Coach of the Year, the Conference Coach of the Year in 1971–72, and the NAIA District 26 Coach of the Year in 1971–72. When he left coaching in 1978, Bobby became the headmaster of the K–12 private school, Cape Fear Christian Academy. From 1988 to 1990 he served as deputy commissioner of the North Carolina Division of Motor Vehicles. From 1991 to 1993 he served as commissioner. Before being inducted into the Kinston-Lenoir County Sports Hall of Fame in 2004, he had been inducted into the East Carolina University Athletic Hall of Fame in 1974. In 1993, he was honored by the North Carolina High School Athletic Association as one of the top fifty athletes in the last fifty years.[6] That's quite a list of athletic accomplishments.

When Bobby walked into the room, it was like coming face-to-face with the Empire State Building. His gigantic six-feet-five-inch structure towered above my five-feet-five-inch (on a good day) small frame. With a big grin on his face, he reached out to shake my hand

149

RONALD SEXTON

with arms that could probably reach across a river and said, "My God, you look so much like your daddy." I had heard those words many times before in my life, and they always brought a smile of pride to my face. But for some strange reason, hearing it from Old Red Devils was different. He seemed to stare into my eyes, wanting to look back into time and remember someone very dear to him. I remembered what Charlie Lewis said the first time he saw Bobby Hodges when he was in about the fifth grade. Charlie's father and Bobby's father were barbers and worked in the same shop. Charlie said he went into his dad's shop one day and Bobby was there. "When I saw him I thought he was the biggest human being I had ever seen," Charlie said.

George and I began with the same routine as with others— looking through the Red Devil album, a notebook of pictures George and I had put together. With George at the helm, we flipped through the pages of pictures of Red Devil history. At the front of the album were the early teams. George showed Bobby some pictures he had forgotten. Shaking his head in amazement and wonder, he found it hard to believe so many years had passed since he had first put on a Red Devil uniform. George began to laugh almost uncontrollably as he thought back on the first meeting Dad had with the basketball team. They met in the old gymnasium, which had the distinctive winding staircases. Every player on the team had just come off a successful football season where they were undefeated, the only team in Grainger High history ever to accomplish that feat.

Bobby, laughing as he remembered the first meeting, said, "We all thought that Coach Mock had hired him as an assistant football coach since he had played at East Carolina as a guard. Well, Coach Sexton called everybody in, and to tell you the truth, he didn't know anything about basketball." Bobby was laughing still. "I tell you, he did not know one thing. I recalled Tommy Cole saying to me about that first basketball meeting. We knew your dad didn't know anything about basketball by the way he was holding the ball when he came out, and he dribbled it with two hands."

Dad was only twenty-seven years old, so he wasn't that much older than the boys on the team. Furthermore, the boys assembled that day were arguably the best high school team in the state. I think the general feeling among the players was that they were hoping that this new guy, Amos Sexton, just wouldn't screw things up.

Kinston had, in those days, the best combination of adults who worked together and who loved to work with kids. George remembered that Bill Faye, who had just taken the job as recreation director, had come up to him one day at Emma Webb Park and offered him a little job. George said that he "hardly knew who Bill Faye was, and it was not long after his father had died, but Coach Faye knew that I was sort of down in the dumps and needed some help."

Every Friday morning at ten o'clock, Bill Faye would appear at Emma Webb Park. George said, "He would stick his hand in my right pocket and put a twenty dollar bill in there—every single week that summer. He was a good man. And this was his money. A kid just doesn't forget that. Because of Bill Faye and the recreation department, we had a great program for the kids in Kinston that was second to none. We had people like Tracy Hart and Capt. Pat Crawford, who also assisted in making the recreation department work so well. Then, on top of that, we had coaches like Frank Mock, Amos Sexton, Charlie Lee, and Tom Mosely, all working together. You couldn't have drawn this up and made it a better situation. We had the right people at the right time with the right stuff."

Then Bobby added, "Yes, those were great days."

Bobby said that his initial meeting with Coach Sexton has been with him all his life and he can't think about it without going into hysterics. "The first thing Coach says to us is, 'Boys...'" Bobby was laughing now so hard he could hardly continue, but he tried. "He said in that Alabama brogue, 'Boys, ya'll take dis shar basketball down that thar court and put it in that thar basket, and I want ya'll to show me what ya'll did last year.'" Now we're all laughing uncontrollably. Bobby said from then on Coach Sexton was known to us as Dis Shar. "Of course, we didn't call him that to his face." The team even had a play they called dis here, that thar, and the other. I can just hear it now as they huddle on the sidelines during a game, "All right boys, let's run dis here, that thar, and the other."

Now Kinston is not exactly Madison Avenue. It was more or less a small rural farming community. So when they say, as Alley Hart did, that Dad was "country come to town," you can imagine just how backward Dad sounded. It was his accent and expressions, of course, that gave people that impression; but he was far from being someone who just "fell off the turnip truck." Dad was definitely street-smart and could be very creative, but like Bobby Hodges said, "The man knew how to win, and he turned out to be one of the best basketball coaches in the State of North Carolina. He read books, we went to clinics, and he talked to other coaches. He learned the game. He didn't know much about the game at first. But he knew a lot about us. He knew what buttons to push and what buttons not to push. And when he finally learned the game, he became a much-feared basketball coach to go up against."[7]

Bobby remembered the football team's road trip to Hopewell, Virginia, in late September of 1949. Hopewell beat the Red Devil football team 39–0, but the Virginia team had players that could have been playing in college. George remembered the game. Somehow he was invited to a Kinston Rotary meeting sometime later and heard Felix Harvey, a local business man, complain to Coach Mock about the game, saying, "Frank, what do you think about Hopewell, Virginia, playing all of those boys so much older than our guys. I would protest if I were you to the Virginia High School Athletic Association." George said he would never forget Coach Mock's comment. Coach Mock responded, "Felix, that's their problem, not mine." George said, "That was the way he felt about it. That was just the kind of man Frank Mock was. He was not the kind of man to whine and complain. He took his licks and went on." Kinston lost big that week to Hopewell, but took it out on an undefeated LaGrange team the next week, beating them 43–0.

Bobby remembered that on the way back from the Hopewell game, the team stopped in Warrington to take a break. It seemed to slip some of the players' minds to pay for certain items like salt and pepper shakers and other useful items. A few miles down the road, the bus was pulled over by a policeman. Coach Mock got out of the bus and, after learning what had happened, made the boys who took souvenirs ante up. Stories like this tend to grow into urban legends, but I remember a very similar story told by Dad, and he said the boys

RED DEVIL TALES

told him that they were just getting Christmas gifts for the coaches. It sounds like some of the boys were a cross between Dennis the Menace and The Little Rascals.

Bobby remembered how frustrated everyone was over having to forfeit nearly all their conference basketball wins in 1950 due to a clerical technicality over the transfer of Graham Philips. It was common knowledge that the clerical oversight had been reported by an administration official from the Red Devils' closest rival, Washington. This official complained to the commissioners of the North Carolina High School Basketball Association that Graham Philips was an illegal transfer. Thus, over a clerical technicality, Kinston's seasonal wins were dismissed. Kinston was allowed to play in the Northeaster Conference tournament, but they were dropped from number one to number eight (last place) in the ranking. Bobby said, "We were so damn mad with the Washington team, who was moved to first place, we went to the tournament and kicked their ass."

Bobby Hodges also recalled the time he went out for high school baseball as a ninth grader. He said that in the seventh and eighth grade he was the "big man on campus" and as a freshman he played on the varsity football and basketball team so when baseball season came around Jimmy Byrd and a few others encouraged him to go out for baseball. So on the first day of practice Coach Mock said to him, "Well, Bobby, what position can you play?"

Bobby answered, "Coach, I think I can play any of them. Just play me wherever you want to put me."

So, because of his size, Coach Mock put him at first base.

Then after dropping several balls at this position, Bobby, realizing that maybe playing first base was not his forte, told Coach Mock, "Coach, I can catch too." So Bobby said he got behind the plate and he wasn't very good there as well. Then Bobby asked, "Coach, you want me to try pitching?"

Coach Mock answered, "No, no, go on to outfield."

Bobby went to outfield, and Coach Mock hit him a few fly balls, most of which he missed. One fly ball even hit him in the head. Mercifully for Bobby, practice came to an end and the boys headed to the dressing room.

In the dressing room, Coach Mock called Bobby over and in his dignified and distinct tone said, "Bobby, I think it would be advantageous for you and our school and our baseball program for you to spend your afternoons in the library."

After about his third year at East Carolina, Bobby said he came back to Kinston to do some research on Kinston's well-respected recreation program as a school project and he made a point to stop by to visit with Coach Mock. Bobby said he told Coach Mock, "Coach, I want to tell you right up front. If you had not cut me from the baseball team in the ninth grade, the two of us would be sitting in Yankee Stadium today." Coach Mock, laughing, said, "Boy, get on out of here!"

Bobby Hodges after the 1950 Red Devil
basketball state championship.

13

DOUG BRUTON

In March of 2010 I made my way back to North Carolina to attend the three-day Red Devil All-Class reunion. On Friday night the group met in Kinston in old high school auditorium and Saturday night they all gathered again in Morehead City. This was my fifth trip to North Carolina in three years visiting and interviewing Red Devils.

After the event was over I decided to make a trip to Washington, D. C. area to visit two Red Devils who have achieved icon status in the school's history. Doug Bruton and Eugene "Red" McDaniel were two players on Dad's first championship team in 1950. Doug lives in Bowie, Maryland, a suburb of the Washington, D. C. area, and Red lives a stone's throw from Mount Vernon, George Washington's home. Red was at the reunion and told me to call him when I got up to Washington and he would see if he could work me into his schedule. I called Doug, and he said to come on up Tuesday and Wednesday the week after the reunion. Fortunately, I was able to visit several days with Doug and his wife Ginny, and several more days with Red and his wife Dorothy. It was one of the best trips and experiences I have ever had. They were both gracious and fun hosts, sharing old stories and serving up good eats—a delightful combination. On top of that, I was able to visit just about every Civil War Battle

155

field between North Carolina and Washington, D. C. and spent one day touring the Capitol itself. It's was a trip I wish I could do all over again.

I finally found my way to Bowie, Maryland, and was graciously greeted by Doug as I drove up into the driveway. It was the first time I had met him in person. We had talked on the phone and through correspondence. I had seen pictures of him in high school, and he looked like the perfect athlete. He was tall, well-built, and looked like a Rock Hudson or young Cary Grant. Now in his late seventies, he still looked like an athlete: in shape and in good health. As I made my way into their beautiful multilevel home, I could tell Ginny was a great decorator and loved antiques. What I would learn later was that the Brutons had started a small antiques business.

Doug and I sat down in the living room while Ginny got supper ready. At the time, I had not put anything in writing and I was not even sure how I was going to write the story. Was this going to be a history of the Red Devils of Grainger High? A task I would soon find out was above my pay grade. Was I going to tell the story of my dad during his coaching years and the athletes he coached? Still, I was not sure. I just wanted to hear stories about those days and what they knew about Dad. What was he like as a coach? Doug showed me his basement where he kept many of his trophies and newspaper clipping from his days as an athlete. The room I stayed in was tastefully decorated with pictures of Doug during his high school and college athletic careers.

Before supper, Ginny called out from the kitchen and asked Doug and I if we would like a Manhattan. I do not drink and never have although I have always been curious about tasting certain adult beverages. I could never understand why people liked it so much. For me it was like taking the cold medicine liquid Nyqil. Well, I wasn't about to insult my guest so I acted like I drank Manhattans all the time. Besides, it was carefully and graciously prepared so I indulged. Surely I wouldn't turn into an alcoholic over one Manhattan. I drank it slowly and investigated the taste as if it was part of my research. Not too bad. I eventually finished it and then came another invitation, "Hey, how about another one?" Before I could say "No sir-ree

RED DEVIL TALES

Bob tale tootle" I had another one in my hand. I took a deep breath and began to sip again.

I felt at home when we had hot dogs for supper, and that night as we were turning in for the evening, they invited me into their bedroom to watch a college basketball game. It was college basketball's most glorious happening: March Madness and the University of North Carolina, Doug's alma mater, was still in the running. They were both in their pj's and told me to pull up a chair beside the bed and watch a game. I felt at home. I was somewhat amused when Doug remarked about a team he couldn't believe had made it to the sweet sixteen. "Who the hell is Butler, anyway?" he wondered. "How did they make it this far!" For a UNC alumni who is used to seeing their team go to the "big dance" on a regular basis, who do these "up and coming" basketball upstarts think they are? Butler, of course, would go on to make the final four although they would lose to Duke. In 2011, Butler would again make it to the final four. This time they lost to Connecticut 53–41. Before we turned in for the night, as the game came to a close, Ginny made Doug and I another milk shake. Manhattans, hot dogs, basketball, and milk shakes—it was a night to remember.

Douglas Bruton was a natural athlete who played and excelled in all three sports: football, basketball, and baseball. I think he could have played anything and achieved greatness. Today, he plays a little golf and I bet he could give Tiger Woods a run for his money. Well, maybe not. Doug is eighty years old now, but in his prime, I might put money on it.

His years as an athlete at Grainger High School were from 1946 to 1950. In football he was All Conference for three years (1947, 1948, 1949), and for three of those years he received the Outstanding Lineman trophy award. In 1949 he was All-State and All-Northeastern Conference. In 1948 and 1949, he was honored with the prestigious George DuBose Defensive Trophy, which is given to the best defensive player in the Northeastern Conference. The winner of this trophy is determined by a vote of the entire membership of the varsity squads of all conference schools.

In basketball Doug was an All-Conference forward from 1948 to 1950. He was a crucial part of the Red Devil State A Championship team in 1950, selected to play in the East-West All-Star game in 1950, and was elected cocaptain of the East team. In baseball Doug was one of the most talented first baseman to ever play at Grainger High School. He was a driving force behind the state championship teams of 1949 and 1950. He became the only high school player ever to hit a ball over the left field fence during a game at the Grainger High School Stadium.

At the end of his high school career, he was offered a five thousand dollar bonus to sign with the New York Giants baseball team. He declined the offer and instead accepted a four-year football scholarship at the University of North Carolina.

At UNC from 1950 to 1953, he started as a linebacker for the UNC Tarheels. But plagued by injuries, he was forced give up football his senior year. However, he played baseball for the Tarheels in the 1954 season. As a pitcher that year his record was 5–4. One of his wins was against the very talented Quantico Marines and another win over Clemson where he also hit a grand slam to win the game 10–8.

In 1957 Doug was the line coach of the Atsugi Navy-Marine Flyers football team in Japan and they competed for the Far East Championship. He pitched for the Atsugi Navy-Marine Flyers baseball team and was selected to play on the Far East All-Star team. In 1958 and 1959 he pitched on the FBI baseball team that won the Washington, D. C. City Industrial League Championship both years. In 2012 Doug was inducted into the Kinston-Lenoir County Sports Hall of Fame.

Doug in 1950 voted "Most Athletic"

14

EUGENE "RED" MCDANIEL

After visiting several days with Doug and Ginny Bruton, I left Bowie, Maryland, and headed south to see Red and Dorothy McDaniel in Alexandria, Virginia. Red and Dorothy live in a multilevel old brick-and-shingle colonial home located on the part of George Washington's original plantation known as Washington's pig farm.

Red McDaniel was born and raised on a small tobacco farm just outside of Kinston. As long as he can remember he was called Red because of his reddish-blond hair. He is the oldest of eight children who subsisted daily as they struggled to make ends meet. The family prayed at meals, but Red remembered that his parents didn't go to church often because they didn't have the "proper" clothes.[1] However, his father, although just a tenant farmer, loved athletics and propositioned Red that he could either plow the fields or play sports. Well, he didn't have to make the offer twice. Red loved athletics as well and poured himself into all three major sports: football, basketball, and baseball. His passion, however, was baseball; and it was this sport that afforded him a scholarship to Campbell Junior College in Buies Creek, North Carolina, some eighty miles from Kinston. Years later Red discovered that Coach Frank Mock had arranged for him to get the scholarship and anonymously paid some of his college expenses.

RED DEVIL TALES

The O. L Shackleford Award created in 1951 was inspired by the commitment to excellence and integrity in character displayed by Red McDaniel as an athlete at Grainger High School. The award was given yearly to the most outstanding athlete who embodied the highest qualities of sportsmanship, ability, and character. The prestigious award began with Tommy Cole in 1951 and was awarded each year to one athlete until Grainger High School came to an end in 1970.

O. L. Shackleford was a local business man in the community who funded and sponsored the award to the athlete who most embodied the values of excellence and commitment. The recipient's name—engraved on a large, elegant, sterling silver bowl—was kept at the school as a tribute to the great athletes it honored. The athletes were given a small replica of the trophy to keep for themselves. Years later, as a POW in North Vietnam, Red McDaniel lived out these values and proved to be the worthy image of the O. L. Shackleford Award.

Red's dream was to be a baseball coach, and while playing baseball at Campbell College, he earned extra money playing semi-pro baseball during the summertime in the Tobacco Belt League. "The farmers from rural eastern North Carolina would gather on Saturday nights to watch the games. When a player hit a home run or drove in the winning run, or did anything else spectacular, they passed their straw hats and baseball caps to collect a reward for the player."[2]

While at Campbell Junior College, Red met Dorothy Howard, a Baptist minister's daughter. Her father also taught Bible at the school. When Red graduated from Campbell Junior College, he went on to Elon College on a baseball scholarship. Dorothy went on to the University of North Carolina at Greensboro and majored in English.

"After graduation, with the draft staring him in the face, Red decided to enter Navy flight training rather than be a foot soldier."[3] Red joined the Navy and finished the first stage of flight training at Naval Air Station Pensacola (Florida).

In June of 1956, Red and Dorothy were married and she said, "He promised to love, cherish, and protect me. He should have added, 'And I promise you'll never be bored!'"[4]

Advance flight training continued in Corpus Christi for three months and then it was on to Virginia Beach where Red flew the A-1

Skyraider for the next four years with the Attack Squadron 25 at Naval Air Station Oceana. Red's first deployment was a three-month exercise in the North Atlantic. Dorothy was expecting their first child. After his stint with VA-25 at NAS Oceana ended, he was assigned as a flight instructor training new pilots in the A-1 Skyraider. From there he went to Georgia briefly to train at the Carrier Air Approach Control Center then back to Norfolk for a tour aboard USS *Independence*. Red was now trained to fly the Navy's new jet bomber, the A-6A Intruder.[5]

From the time Red received his Navy wings in 1956 to his deployment to Vietnam in 1966, he had already circled the globe several times, and he and Dorothy had their three children: Mike, David, and Leslie. When Red settled in aboard the USS *Enterprise* October 1966, Mike was eight, David was seven, and Leslie only four.

The long and trying ordeal of Red McDaniel's capture and six-year imprisonment as a POW in the infamous Hanoi Hilton is movingly told in the two books: *Scares and Stripes* by Red and *After the Hero's Welcome* by Dorothy. Red chronicles in riveting detail his arduous journey from the time his plane is shot down through his long and torturous imprisonment to his final release and joyful reunion with his family. Dorothy's book picks up her side of the story. It was difficult enough just being a Navy wife enduring the long months of separation when Red was on deployment to the agony that comes from not knowing if he is dead or alive and being tortured constantly as a POW. She also relates the anger and frustration they both felt when upon Red's return they eventually learn that there were still POWs languishing in Asian prisons, never to return.

Red was thirty-five years old, a seasoned veteran of twelve years as a naval aviator when he flew his eighty-first and final mission over Van Dien, Vietnam, to hit a truck repair center just south of Hanoi. This was to be an Alpha Strike, a dangerous mission deep into enemy territory.

As I made my way to their home one afternoon, I said to myself, "One can only imagine what this brave couple had to endure in the service of this country. We could never repay nor adequately compensate them for the sacrifice they made for our freedom. I suppose

RED DEVIL TALES

that only those who have endured such a trial can truly appreciate the price of liberty."

Red and Dorothy greeted me as I drove up. They invited me inside, lavishing me with their good old-fashioned Southern hospitality. We sat for a while in the family room, catching up on family and old times and discussing my project. As we sat talking, I glanced around the room to see the numerous reminders of Dorothy's and Red's family history. Pictures of their children Mike, David, and Leslie now grown and with their own families and children grace the walls in the background. Red sat in a reclining chair while Dorothy and I occupied the sofa.

In front of the sofa by the old brick fireplace in the family room was a long table that was handmade from the wood of the original wooden flight deck of USS *Lexington*, dating from WWII. The crew of *Lexington* had handcrafted the table and presented it to Red when he relinquished his command of the old training carrier. The brass plaque on top of the table commemorates Red's tour as Lexington's captain from 1977–1978. Over the brick fireplace hangs a ship's wheel made from the same old wooden flight deck and it too has Red's name and the dates of his command. On the wall well-known aviation artist William Phillips's famous painting *Intruder Outbound* hangs as a reminder of Red's final mission over North Vietnam, presented to Red on his sixtieth birthday by the American Patriots Association. Prints of the painting cosigned by Red and the artist can be found today in aviation art shops around the world. Red's numerous military medals, including the Navy Cross (the Navy's highest award for bravery), two Silver Stars, the Distinguished Flying Cross, and two Purple Hearts for wounds received during torture sessions while he was a POW and numerous framed photos of the McDaniel children and grandchildren complete the room's collage of memories.

The first time I remember hearing Red McDaniel's name was from Dad. After Red retired from the Navy, he and Dorothy made a trip to Louisiana to visit Mom and Dad. At the time, I was away at seminary. Red had recently written his book. Dad thought it would be a great idea if he could get Red to speak at church and relate his experience to the congregation. Mom and Dad were members of

Temple Baptist Church. The pastor there, Dr. Robert S. Magee, was noted for his fine oratory. I could tell Dad enjoyed telling me the story. He went to Dr. Magee and told him about Red and wondered if the pastor might allow Red say a few words or give his testimony. Dad told me that he knew Dr. Magee was very protective of his pulpit and wouldn't let just anybody take it. Dr. Magee politely told Dad that he would consider it. Dad gave the pastor a copy of Red's book *Scars and Stripes: The True Story of One Man's Courage Facing Death as a POW in Vietnam*. The next day Dr. Magee called Dad and enthusiastically asked Dad if Red could not only give his testimony but take the whole service. He had read the book. He knew this man had a story to tell and that this difficult and painful experience had severely tested his character and faith. Red did speak, and Dad was very proud to be a part of his life. Dr. Magee was a real patriot himself and had been won several awards for his patriotic sermons.

Red was invited back in June of 1989 to speak at a celebration of America event sponsored by Temple Baptist Church. Dad had passed away in March of that year, but Red still came and was the featured speaker. He shared his experience and gave a moving tribute to America. This was the first time I had met Red McDaniel, and I had the privilege to introduce him at the event.

As Red, Dorothy, and I sat in the family room, now some twenty years later, I marveled at this giant of a man who survived six years of torture, severe and brutal beatings, isolation, and malnourishment, physical and emotional pain. Very few of us, if any, have any idea the extent of all he had to endure. At nearly eighty years old, he still looked amazingly fit. His tall and lean six-feet-three-inches athletic frame showed no visible signs of his tumultuous six years (2,110 days) of North Vietnamese imprisonment, but I knew he had suffered numerous physical injuries, not to mention the psychological and emotional scares inflicted upon him as well. Even today, he continues to struggle with health issues incurred as a result of six years of unrelenting torture for six years. Just recently, now nearly forty years later, he had yet another back operation, an injury he incurred when he had to bail out of his crashing aircraft. His parachute had hung in a tall tropical banyan tree some forty feet from

RED DEVIL TALES

the ground. When the parachute suddenly broke free, he had fallen to the ground crushing vertebrae in his lower spine.

There was nothing in Red's demeanor that betrayed his skills and accomplishments. He is rather soft-spoken and humble, not exactly the image I would think of a top gun jet pilot who had skillfully flown a complex machine like an A-6 Intruder. That in itself is quite an accomplishment. But to be able to land that jet aircraft, loaded sometimes with thousand-pound bombs under your wings on a moving runway smaller than a football field, and moving up and down with the waves is even more amazing.

Red McDaniel was on Dad's first basketball team when he arrived at Grainger High School as the new basketball coach in November 1948. He was an outstanding forward who played on the Red Devils' first state championship basketball team in 1950. He played on coach Frank Mock's first state championship baseball team in 1949. He was the catcher and, if you know anything about baseball, you know that this position is arguably the toughest and most demanding place to be on any baseball team.

In 1978 Red, now captain of USS *Lexington*, took the aircraft carrier eighty-nine miles up the Mississippi River to New Orleans to host a Navy Admiral's retirement ceremony. The trip happened to coincide with the Mohammed Ali-Michael Spinks boxing world championship bout. The ship docked at Poydras Pier in front of the New Orleans Hilton, and Red and Dorothy were ensconced in the presidential suite, one floor above Mohammed Ali. Their meals were prepared in the presidential suite's kitchen, and Red invited Dad down to dinner one night. He and Red had decided that they had "come a long way" since Red's high school athletic days.

Actually, this was Dad's second visit aboard USS *Lexington* while Red had command. The first time was when he and my younger brother Don went to sea with Red for several days and left the ship with a catapult shot on their way home. As Don tells the story, he and Dad were home at the time going over some important cabinet business when Red called and invited Dad for visit aboard *Lexington*. A pressing business obligation was going to interfere, so he had to decline the invitation. Well, so he thought. Red McDaniel now insisted, "Amos Sexton, you

165

are going to come down here if I have to send one of my pilots off of the carrier, commandeer your ass, and fly you down here." Laughing, Dad consented and said, "All right, Red, I'll be there." It was a fascinating and memorable trip for Dad and brother Don, to say the least. I remember him telling me about his days on *Lexington* with Red. He could not get over how orderly and "spit and polish" Red commanded his ship. Dad, shaking his head in amazement as he described to me this occasion, said, "You should have seen it when Red walked onto that ship. Every sailor saluted and stood at attention. It was a sight to behold." Dad was most impressed.

In March 1982 Red decided to run for Congress after his retirement, and Dad came up to North Carolina to campaign for him in the Sexton motor home, which became the "Red McDaniel for Congress" campaign bus. People in eastern North Carolina became very familiar with the bus and the loud speaker that let everyone in earshot know that they should vote for Red McDaniel for Congress. Red says today that having Coach Sexton come to North Carolina to campaign for him was a "high honor" and "one of the highlights of my life."

Coach Mock and Red McDaniel

Lieutenant Red McDaniel in his flight suite aboard USS *Intrepid* (Courtesy of Dorothy McDaniel's private collection).

15

TOMMY COLE

Tommy Cole was another one of the great athletes who played in the late forties and early fifties. He was a student at Grainger High School from 1947 to 1951. Tommy was a gifted athlete who excelled in every sport. In 1950 he was an All-Conference end, awarded as the most valuable lineman and selected to play in the Optimist Bowl. In basketball, he was on the 1950 state championship basketball team but it was in baseball that his talents really came to the forefront. He played third base with the finesse and grit of a Brooks Robinson, both at base and at bat. He was a part of the Red Devils' first state championship baseball team of 1949. In 1951 he was an all-conference player and was selected to play in North Carolina's All-Star Game.

His peers recognized his talent and, as a senior, he was voted Most Athletic and recognized by the community by being the first recipient of the O. L. Shackleford Award. George said Tommy was just a natural athlete. For example, on a Saturday night he played in the 1950 state championship basketball game in Durham, North Carolina, and on the following Tuesday he played in the first game of the baseball season against Wilson "without missing a lick." He hit three line drives off the left field fence at Grainger Stadium. "They took off like rockets," George remembered. He had an unbelievable

RED DEVIL TALES

throwing arm from third base, and he was a power hitter who could drive the ball over the fence. George said you just have to be a natural athlete to go from one sport to another sport without any transition period or practice and perform well.

After graduating from Wake Forest in 1955, Tommy pursued a lifelong career in banking and finance. He eventually became regional manager for Cape Fear Mortgage Services but is now retired. He is still active in civic, fraternal, and church activities in Goldsboro and Wayne County, North Carolina.

It had been a few years since George had heard from Tommy, but he suggested that I give him a call and see if I could make contact. Tommy was a quiet and rather private individual, so I wasn't sure I would be able to see him. I called what I thought was his residence and left a message on the answering machine, not really expecting anyone to return my call. I told him who I was and what I was trying to do and left him my cell number. To my surprise, he called me back that afternoon and we arranged a meeting for the next day. In the meantime, George filled me in on just who Tommy Cole was as a Red Devil.

Listening to George talk about some of these athletes is like listening to an old soldier describe a great general and warrior. There is a sense of awe and reverence in his voice. To hear him speak of a particular game is like hearing the story of a great battle won at great cost that has lasting significance. By the time George had prepped me on each player, I always felt like I was visiting one of the immortals of Greek mythology.

Tommy Cole went on from high school to play baseball at Wake Forest. It was there in 1955, he became captain of the baseball team that won the College World Series, which still remains the only Atlantic Coast Conference team to ever win it all in baseball. He was voted All Conference in 1955 and led the conference in home runs.

I made it to Tommy's place early the next morning, and he greeted me with big smile as if he was looking into the face of Amos Sexton. We went in, and as we sat down, he began to tell me about Frank Mock and Amos Sexton. For him these men were father figures who demanded the best from their players, but in an encourag-

169

ing way. Each of the coaches was different, but together they made a perfect winning combination. Frank Mock had been at Kinston since 1934, nine years older than Amos, soft-spoken and laid-back, whereas Tommy indicated that Dad was this young, enthusiastic, and driven field general who could get the most and the best out of his players. It was like having Dwight Eisenhower and George Patton on the same battlefield. Tommy remembered Amos Sexton as a Jim Valvano, the famous NC State coach who was known for his enthusiasm and his ability to motivate players. He said Jim Valvano's memorable speech in which he said, "Don't give up; don't ever give up," didn't start with him. Tommy said, "Amos Sexton started that."

Tommy Cole was on that first team that Dad coached when he first arrived in Kinston. Did he know that Dad was not an experienced basketball coach? Tommy said, "No, but we soon found out the first day when he met with both the junior varsity and the varsity. I knew that he didn't know the rim from the basket by the way he dribbled the ball. He dribbled the ball with two hands. He made no bones about the fact that he did not know basketball, but he made it clear that he was the coach."

He had been studying the roster and trying to learn everyone's name. Obviously, Bobby Hodges stood out at six feet five inches and was well-known. His nickname was Firpo because his father was called that after the famous Argentine boxer Luis Angel Firpo. Dad said, "I am going have to take some time learning you guys, but I know there is Hippo…"

Bobby interrupted and said, "No, Coach, that is Firpo."

To that the coach responded, "Well, I'm going to call you Hippo."

Tommy said, "We knew then who was boss."

Tommy remembered Dad's dedication to learning basketball by reading every book or article available on the subject, especially anything by or about the St. Louis Billikens, after whom the Red Devils patterned their fast break offense after. "Your Dad came knowing nothing about basketball, but even before I left in 1951," Tommy said, "he knew everything about basketball. He was a self-taught basketball coach."

RED DEVIL TALES

In an attempt to find a notable coach to compare the two, I suggested that Coach Mock was like a Bud Wilkinson, the famous football coach at Oklahoma, and maybe Dad was like the then Kentucky basketball coach, Rudolf Rupp.

Tommy said, "Well, maybe a little bit but your Dad was never vulgar like Rudolf Rupp. He never said a profane word in front of us. And the only time I heard Frank Mock say anything was after I threw a wild pitch from third base. When I came into the dugout, he said, 'Great damn day, Tom!'"

Tommy remembered a side of Dad that revealed just how close he was to Frank Mock and how tenderhearted he was. It was during the football season of 1950 and they were going to play Roanoke Rapids. Because it was so far away, the team had to leave early in the afternoon. At the time Mrs. Mock was expecting a baby, and Tommy said Dad announced to the players just before the bus was to leave that Coach Mock would not be coming on this trip. He was at the hospital with his wife who was in labor about to deliver their baby. At half-time, Coach Sexton announced to the team that Coach and Mrs. Mock had lost the baby. Tommy said that as he gave them the news he had tears in his eyes. It really affected him. Mrs. Mock later told me that it was October 6, 1950, and the baby was a boy.

One year, when some of the boys were playing Legion ball, Tommy said he, Bryant Aldridge, and Graham Philips hitchhiked from Kinston to the beach on Highway 70. They were going to spend a day at the beach, but they had to get back because they had a game that night. He said they made it back all right, but all three of them got sunburned. In those days, the uniforms were wool and that was not a good combination with sunburn. Somehow Coach Mock got wind of the boys' little side trip to the beach and about their sunburns, so during pregame warm up when Coach Mock was hitting balls to the infield, Tommy said he was fumbling and missing most that were hit to him. Coach Mock, about to hit another one, yells out to Tommy, "All right, beachcomber, let's see if you can get this one."

I received a letter written by one of Tommy's sisters, Betty Cole Keaton, who now lives in High Point, North Carolina. She said that growing up in Kinston was the best place for their family. Her father had accidentally drowned at the age of thirty-seven, and her mother bravely raised three daughters and a son. She said since Tommy was left without a father figure, Frank Mock and Amos Sexton were the perfect role models for him to look up to. "I never heard of a Grainger High athlete express anything but admiration and respect for Amos Sexton and Frank Mock," she recalled.

She was a year older than Tommy and remembered when the Sextons first moved to town in 1948. They lived in an upstairs apartment of her friend Varion Herndon's family home. "What a coup it was," she said, "to be able to see Coach Sexton and Lee somewhere more personal than at school." As a cheerleader, Betty said the pep rallies and the out of town games were very memorable. The year 1950 was the year the Red Devils won the state championship in basketball, and it was the year the team had to forfeit all their conference games to Little Washington. She especially remembered that the cheerleaders made up a rather spiteful cheer: "Wheaties, the breakfast of champions. They got the conference, but we got the State!"

In 1961 Betty and her husband, Martin Keaton, and their three sons moved to High Point, North Carolina. They lived next door to Charlie and Crystal Rich. Charlie was the general manager of Marsh Kitchens. She remembered one morning when Chrystal told her that she was having the wife of one of Charlie's salesman over for lunch since the men were at work. She told her that this salesman was "quite a go-getter. He flies his own airplane to a city, gets out his little motor scooter, and rides to call on his customers."

Betty said she almost fainted when she told her that his name was Amos Sexton. "Needless to say," Betty noted, "I finagled my way to lunch with her also."[2]

Tommy Cole voted "Most Athletic" in the 1951 *Kay-Aitch-Ess*.

Tommy as right fielder on Wake Forest's
national collegiate championship team
in 1955 (courtesy *The Free Press*).

16

BRYANT ALDRIDGE

Bryant Aldridge was inducted into the Kinston-Lenoir County Hall of Fame in 2007, along with Coach Amos Sexton, Eugene "Red" McDaniel, and George Whitfield, among others. George Whitfield said of Bryant, "There is no question that Bryant Aldridge was one of the greatest all-around athletes to play at Grainger High School." Bryant was a starting player on every varsity team from the time he was in the ninth grade, and he was the captain of every single team that he ever played on. And he is the only Red Devil ever to receive twelve athletic letters, which he earned during his high school career from 1948 to 1952. He was the only athlete to be cocaptain of the football, basketball, and baseball teams. During the 1951 football season, Bryant made all-State, all-Southern, and all-American honors. He was a cocaptain in the 1951 Shrine Bowl game, and he played in the 1951 East-West All-Star game. In baseball he was a part of the teams who won the state championship in 1949 and again in 1950. In Legion baseball, he was a part of the 1950 team with a .575 batting average. He was president of all his four classes in high school and all his four classes at Duke University.

George said as a fullback Bryant was a "holy terror." One night, as a sophomore, George was to run a reverse. In the huddle, Bryant

175

told George, "You just stay behind me. I'll take you into the end zone." Bryant weighed about 205 pounds and was like a rock, George remembered. "When he hit someone, he really put a hurt on them. It was like following a Mack Truck through the line. With those broad shoulders," he added. "Bryant laid people out left and right."

When George was a sophomore in 1952, he shared a cubical locker with Bryant during football season at Grainger Stadium. The special little cubical room belonged to the manager of the Kinston Eagle's minor league baseball team. It was given to Bryant during football season since he was a senior and captain of the team. Bryant asked George if he would like to share the locker with him. George remembered that after every game that they played there would be coaches from all over the country coming into that room to see Bryant. Coaches from Tennessee, Notre Dame, Duke, and many others would show up to see Bryant play. Of course, he finally chose Duke.

Bryan Hanks, managing editor of the *Free Press*, noted that "Of the thousands of athletes who've played on the courts and fields of Grainger and Kinston High School, there hasn't been one more decorated during his prep career than Bryant T. Aldridge." And he adds, "There probably hasn't been one as humble as the soft-spoken Aldridge, either."

"After high school," Byran Hanks continued, "Bryant was awarded a football scholarship to Duke University. He spent the 1952-1956 years at Duke and continued to excel as an athlete and scholar." Bryant was also a three-year varsity letterman, All-State 1955, All-ACC 1955, and led the Duke Blue Devils to a 35–7 victory win over Nebraska in the 1955 Orange Bowl game. Bryant again won honors at Duke as a student and an athlete. He was a member of the Red Friars (Honorary Society) and included in the listing of Who's Who in American College and Universities in 1955. During College Bryant was also a member of ODK and Kappa Alpha Fraternity.

"From 1960 to 1963, Bryant was the assistant administrator at Watts Hospital in Durham, North Carolina, and then moved to Greenville, South Carolina, and served as director of internal operations at Greenville General Hospital from 1963–66. From 1966 to 1998 he was president of Nash General Hospital in Rocky Mount, North Carolina. Bryant T. Aldridge literally helped to build Nash Health Care Systems. Aldridge is known throughout the state for his visionary leadership in health care. He conceptualized the all-private room hospital, and the country's first freestanding outpatient hospital, Nash Day Hospital.

"In 1999, a new 23-bed rehabilitation center, located adjacent to Nash General Hospital, was named the Bryant T. Aldridge Rehabilitation Center honoring the president of Nash Care Systems as a testimony to his years of leadership. A long time fan and supporter of Duke University, Bryant has served in many leadership capacities, guest lecturer, Iron Dukes, and the Gridiron Society. In 2002 the offensive backs coach's office located in the Yoh Football Center was named the Bryant T. Aldridge Family Coach's Office. Bryant was named Tar Heel of the Week in 1996, is a 1997 Paul Harris Fellow, and 1999 Rocky Mount Distinguished Citizen."[1]

George concluded, "His life was impeccable. He always did the right thing. In high school he was the recipient of the coveted O. L. Shackleford Award and received many honors as an athlete and student scholar, not only at Grainger High School, but at Duke University."

Left: After a football game Coach Sexton playfully teasing Bryant (40) in front of his locker as George Whitfield (20) looks on. Right: In his senior year Bryant is not only captain of the football, basketball, and baseball teams but is also selected as "Most Versatile," "Most Popular," and "Most Athletic."

17

GEORGE WHITFIELD

My earliest memory of George Whitfield is from the time I was two or three years old. I remember watching Superman on TV in the fifties, and George would come home from school and tell me that he was Superman, the man I saw on television. And, of course, I believed him. For years I thought George Whitfield was the real Superman. Well, George may not be faster than a speeding bullet or more powerful than a locomotive or able to leap tall buildings with a single bound, but he is, in many ways, a "superman."

George Whitfield is the most generous, thoughtful, and appreciative person I have ever met, and he has accomplished more feats during his career as a coach than Superman could have ever pulled off. He has lived an amazing life. George has spent his entire adult life living his dream: coaching. For forty-seven years, through six decades, he has guided hundreds of young people through the trials and triumphs of athletic competition. As a coach he has won nine state championships and fifteen conference titles. His latest state championship was in 2015 when, at the age of seventy-eight, he came out of retirement to lead Arendell Parrott Academy in Kinston to their first baseball state championship. He has been named Conference Coach of the Year thirteen times and has been inducted into eight different Halls of Fame. He coached all three major sports (football, basketball, baseball), but his life's passion has been baseball, and it is in this arena that he has a 77 percent winning record (954–286).

George has now retired (somewhat) from coaching, but you wouldn't know it by his involvement in promoting the sport of baseball with his yearly clinic, which he has been conducting every January since 1974. During his long coaching career, ninety players have received college scholarships and three of those have reached the major leagues.

Another amazing accomplishment that is usually left out of any George Whitfield bio is that he has the names and address of every player he has ever coached. The list contains over six hundred names.

The story of how George Whitfield came to live with us has almost become mythological. It is a story of rescue and redemption, and it gives some insight into why George conducts his life in such a noble manner. He will never forget Amos Sexton and Frank Mock. These two men he credits for saving him from a life headed for destruction, and they are largely responsible for pointing him in the right direction. In every award or achievement that he has ever won, George has always given credit to these two men. George never tells this story without nearly breaking down. The defining moments of his life include these two coaches.

George was born in New York City on August 21, 1936. The announcement of his christening at St. Patrick's Cathedral is in the *New York Times* on October 21, 1936. His father was a dentist who had practices both in New York City and in Miami, Florida. When George was eighteen months old, his mother died of a heart attack. She was only thirty-four years old. Her mother's dear friend Ada Haynes was with her when she died. Because George's father traveled between New York City and Miami, he was not home very often so he asked Ada if she would be willing to stay with George and his older sister Katherine and help raise them. George's father is actually from Lagrange, North Carolina, which is not far from Kinston. He brought George's mother back to Kinston to be buried. And it was in Kinston that George, his sister, and Ada Haynes settled, as George's father traveled between New York City and Miami.

RED DEVIL TALES

Ada became the only mother George would ever really know, and she raised and took care of George and his sister from the time of his mother's death until his father died in 1948 when George was twelve. George would take care of Ada until her death at the age of eighty-seven. Ada loved and adored George and followed him wherever he went during his career as a coach. Even at the age of seventy-five she was dragging his baseball fields with a wire mesh behind her 1948 Oldsmobile, preparing the turf for the next game. When George accepted his first coaching job in Goldsboro, he took Ada with him. George was single at the time, and they bought a house on 704 Pittman Street for $12,500 with monthly payments of $152. Then George met Mary Lou Ward on a blind date, and they married in July of 1961. When George left Goldsboro to go to Richmond County at the end of 1967, Ada came with the family.

In 1978 George would lose two of the most important people in his life—Ada, the only mother he ever knew died on March 10, and Frank Mock died on July 11. Mrs. Mock told me that George calls her every year on July 11.

Growing up in Kinston, George has always loved sports and it was his dream to go to Grainger High School and to play ball like the boys he admired watching as a youngster. In the late forties, athletics was big in Kinston. There was a semi-pro baseball team, the Kinston Eagles, who played at Grainger Stadium. The city parks and recreation department had one of the best athletic programs for youth in the country. In those days kids started playing baseball, basketball, and football year-round at Emma Webb Park. In 1948 the Midget basketball team in Kinston won the state championship, and many of the boys on that Little League team would finish their athletic careers playing for Amos Sexton. The year 1948 was also the year that the Grainger High School Red Devils, under the coaching of Frank Mock, went undefeated in football. It was also the year that Amos Sexton came to Kinston to be the head basketball coach at Grainger High School. Sports were the talk of the town, and Kinston had a big fan base, so twelve-year-old George was growing up in a great place.

181

George's father was away most of the time, so George always looked forward to the times when he would meet his dad at the Wilson train station, knowing that he would be home for a while. His dad took the Orange Blossom Special from Miami to Wilson, and the New York Special from Wilson to New York. His dad loved horse racing, and he also used to gamble, especially on horse racing. He got to know all the jockeys and people would call and ask him who they should bet on in the Belmont Stakes or the Kentucky Derby. On the mantel in his house, George has a marble statue of the great racehorse Man of War. That statue belonged to his dad. It had been given to his dad as a gift by the famous racehorse jockey Eddie Arcaro. At his dad's funeral, there were beds of roses similar to the ones placed on winning horses that were sent by racehorse jockeys.

As far back as George can remember, his dad never drove a car. Even when he was home and would go to the Elks Club to play cards, he would walk from his house to downtown. When his dad was home, George cherished the brief moments he got to spend with him. He would go to his dad's room first thing in the mornings, and they would tussle playfully. It was on one of those mornings that George said his dad sat him at the end of the bed and said to him, "Son, I want you to promise me something. I want you to promise me that you will never smoke a cigarette, never chew tobacco, and that you will never touch alcohol, beer, or wine. I want you to try to do that, and if you able to do that, then when you are twenty-one years old and you can honestly and truthfully say that you have done it, I will leave you ten one hundred dollar bills at the Branch Bank." George said that, without a doubt, this was the greatest thing his dad did for him. It was not, of course, promising him the ten one hundred dollar bills. It was getting him to make a commitment to abstain from the vices that could ruin his life.

George's dad would get to see him play only one athletic contest in his life. It was a day he would always remember. When George was about eleven years old, he was playing right field in a Little League game and he saw his father walking up the ramp at Grainger Stadium. George said that he was so excited to see his dad that he wet

RED DEVIL TALES

his pants. It was the only time his dad saw him play. His dad died a few months later.

On September 23, 1948, George's dad was in the hospital suffering from his second heart attack. He asked the nurse where his son and daughter were. The nurse replied, "Mr. Whitfield, your daughter is practicing her piano lessons and your son is out playing ball." He responded, "Fine." The nurse said he never said another word. His dad died about 11:00 p.m., but George was not told until about 8:00 a.m. the next morning.

George's world just seemed to collapse at that point. He was crushed and became distraught. He could not understand why God would take his mother away from him when he was only a baby and then take away his father as well. To add to the trauma, George and his sister were placed under the control of two aunts, who were virtually unknown to him and who had no interest in raising a young adolescent boy. A mutual hate developed between George and his two aunts. He said, one day when he was about thirteen, one of his aunts slapped him. In those days, women wore blouses with big collars and a bow. George reached up and grabbed her by the collar and said, "If you ever put your hands on me again, I'll kill you." And he meant it. He was a bitter and angry adolescent. "There is no question in my mind," George remembered, "had I not been taken under the care of Amos Sexton, I would have done something that would have put me in a lot of trouble." He did whatever he could to make his aunts' lives miserable, like unscrewing the lugs off their tires so they would fall off when the car pulled out of the driveway. Unable to handle such a rebellious young teenager, his aunts were determined to send George off to prep school so they would not have to deal with him.

In 1948 George was in the seventh grade for part of the year at Grainger High School. His picture is in the 1949 annual. At some point, his aunts sent him to Woodberry Forest prep school in Madison County, Virginia. George said it was a good school and they had a good athletic program but that was beside the point. He was forced to go and prohibited from going to the school where he wanted to go: Grainger High School. Furthermore, he was being isolated from seeing the one person who really cared about him, Ada

183

Haynes. He felt that His aunts did whatever they could to get him away from the one person he could call mother. Removing Ada from his life was like losing another family member.

George, distraught and frustrated, eventually ran away from Woodberry Forest and returned to Kinston, but his return didn't last long. As soon as arrangements could be made, he was sent to another prep school. This time it was Virginia Episcopal school in Lynchburg, Virginia. Again, George would not cooperate. He said he remembered well his plan of escape from the Virginia Episcopal School in Lynchburg. It was in mid-April in 1951, around eleven o'clock at night when the hall monitors made one final check on the students. George had placed some pillows under his covers to fool the monitors. He quietly left his room and walked down the hallway. He climbed down the fire escape and then down some ivy to freedom. He managed to get the highway and started trying to bum a ride home. After a while, a Thurston Truck driver stopped and asked him where he was going. George told him he was going to Kinston. "Well, son," the trucker said, "you are in luck. I am going to New Bern. Climb in and I'll take you to Kinston." George climbed in and tried to sleep while the truck driver drove all night to Kinston.

At 7:30 in the morning, the truck finally arrived in Kinston and the driver let George out at the steps of Grainger High School. George, bedraggled and tired, sat on the steps and waited for someone to open the school. Mrs. Smathers, the principal's secretary, finally came to open up the school. George went in, and Mrs. Smathers introduced herself. She asked him if there was anything she could do to help him. George told her that his aunts had sent him off to school and that he had been trying to get back to Kinston so he could attend Grainger High School. Mrs. Smathers told George that he would have to see Coach Mock and Coach Sexton, who should be in any minute to check their mail before school. So he sat down and waited to see the two coaches.

George had never met either man, but he knew of them as the revered coaches of the Kinston Red Devils. He had heard of them only through the newspaper and sometimes he observed them as he sat on the outside of the fence at Grainger Stadium to watch ball

RED DEVIL TALES

practice. For some reason he was sure they would help him. In a few minutes, both Coach Mock and Coach Sexton walked in the office to get their mail and saw George sitting in the chair all disheveled and dirty. They walked over to him, and Dad asked him, "Son, what in the world are you doing here? Where have you been?" George told them that he had been sleeping all night in the cab of a truck. They wanted to know why. After George told them his story, he said Dad looked at him and said, "Son, we're gonna put a stop to this." Then Amos told Coach Mock, "Frank, I am going to take him home with me today." George was enrolled in Grainger High School and immediately that night he was brought home to our house. I wasn't born yet, and my brother Edison was only about a year old.

George remembered that my mom knew nothing about what was going on until Dad brought him home for supper. He did something a little unusual when they arrived at the house and knocked on the door. He stuck his head in and said, "Lee, what are we having for supper?"

My mother, somewhat surprised, yelled back, "Amos, you know what we are having for supper. It might be pot luck. Why do you ask? You never ask. Are we having company?"

Dad said, "Yes, we are."

And my mother responded, "Well, who is it?"

Then Dad made the big announcement. Dad said, "It is a boy I am bringing home to raise."

George said there was a long silence.

Finally, Mother stuck her head out of the kitchen and said, "Amos Sexton, have you lost your mind?"

And that is how George Whitfield was introduced to mother. It was a part of Dad's nature, I suppose, and reflected some of the values of that generation that he didn't ask Mother for her approval or even give her a heads-up. Nevertheless, George said my mother was a little cold to him at first, but it did not take long before she warmed up to him, and he began to feel like part of the family.

George's father had a close friend in Goldsboro, Dr. Eddie Bizzel. He was an eye, ear, and throat doctor; and he had been like a brother to George's dad. His father's will stated that if there were to be any changes in the guardianship of George and his sister, it would have to be approved by Dr. Bizzel. That same week George said Dad met with Dr. Bizzel. Dr. Bizzel and a lawyer named Alley Whittaker were responsible for getting the court to approve the transfer of guardianship of George to Amos Sexton. Dr. Bizzel said that he was sure that, if George's father knew about the situation, he would want George to live with the Sextons. Dr. Bizzel told the courts that it was much better for George to stay with the Sextons than for him to stay with two half sisters who really didn't want him. And it was just causing a lot of problems.

To this day George does not know, and he thought he would never know what made my dad take him into his home and raise him. He said he had asked Dad that question several times, and Dad would always change the subject. I think I know why. My dad had a heart for the underdog and for those who struggled in life. He had experienced some of that himself as he grew up in a poor Alabama family. He knew what it was like to have nothing. I think it was such a natural reaction that Dad did not even think about it. Someone was in trouble and he was going to help. Maybe George as a thirteen-year-old boy without a father and a mother tended to tug at his heart. I think the reason Dad did not want to talk about it was because he knew he would get emotional. Maybe it was the way George looked that morning, like a little beaten puppy. Maybe it was the way George looked and explained his plight, a scared little rabbit with no home. Whatever the reason, Dad reacted as a father would to a lost and wayward son. He responded with his heart, and I doubt that he could have articulated his feelings anyway. Maybe he just didn't have the words.[1]

Years later, George was back in Kinston, drinking a milk shake and eating a hot dog at Carolina Dairies. Carolina Dairies had the best milk shakes and hot dogs in the country, according to George. The last thing on his mind had been to go to see his aunts, but for some odd reason, the thought entered his mind. The pull to stop by and see them came to the forefront of his thinking. He had carried the hate for these two aunts for thirty years. As far as he knew, these were the only two people on the face of the earth that he hated and he hated them with a passion. Everything they had ever done to him was mean-spirited and unkind. There was just no forgiving them. Just out of nowhere, the thought of seeing his aunts hit him. "It was almost as if God was saying to me," George recalled. "'If you ever want to get this off your mind and out of your conscience, now is the time." He finished his hot dog and his milk shake, walked out, got in his car, and drove to where his aunts lived, a mere two blocks away.

Having no plan of what he would do or what he would say, George parked in the driveway, got out of his car, walked up to the door, and rang the door bell. George could see through the screen door. His aunt was sitting in the living room. Her hair was as white as snow. And she had a walker. George had not seen her since the day she had driven over to the Sexton's home and delivered his last belonging. She slowly made her way to the door using her walker, not really recognizing the visitor behind the screen door. When she opened the door she looked as if she had seen a ghost. There in front of her stood a man she had known as a little boy. She invited him in, and they made some small talk, not speaking of anything in the past. After a while George told her that it was time for him to go. They both got up, and she walked him to the door. When they got to the door, she held the door open with her walker and said to George, "I just want you to know that everybody who knows you in Kinston is proud of what you have accomplished, and so am I." George said, "Those were the last words she said to me. Several weeks later she died."

George said he realized that when you dislike somebody, it doesn't hurt anybody but you. Hate and bitterness are poison to your soul, and the poison eats away at your heart and it will paralyze your life. "Chances are," George admitted, "the other person doesn't even know it. I doubt seriously that she or her sister knew how much I disliked them. The only person it hurt was me."

In July 1978 Coach Mock died. On the morning of Frank Mock's funeral, George told Coach Mock's daughter Peggy that he hoped that her father somehow knew how much he loved and respected him. I think George regretted not being able to express to Coach Mock how much he appreciated all that he had done for him through the years. When George went to Goldsboro to coach, he often visited Frank Mock, who had guided and encouraged him through the initial stages of his career. George was going to make sure he got the opportunity to publically say thank you to Mom and Dad before time slipped away, so the 1981 appreciation banquet was his opportunity to do just that. At the end of the banquet that night, George turned to Mom and Dad and said, "I am only thankful tonight that I could be here to tell Amos and Lee Sexton how much I love and respect them and how much I appreciate all the years they have given me." That night George gave Dad several things as a way to remember his nine years of coaching the Red Devils of Grainger High School. The most unique memento, I thought, was a full-sized basketball goal with the names of every basketball player Dad had coached during his nine-year tenure. That night was a great tribute to Dad, which he never forgot. After both of my parents had died, I found in their collection of special mementoes a letter they had saved and certainly must have cherished. It was a letter written by George the day after we left Kinston for the last time to move to Louisiana. In the letter he tried to express his appreciation for what they had done for him and what they meant to him. George felt that my dad had rescued him from a troubled and aimless existence. George's life is a story of redemption, and he credits people like Amos Sexton and Frank Mock for giving him a second chance at life. And he never forgets it. All of life, he has been saying thank you.

In the letter, written on yellow notebook school paper and dated July 15, 1958, George wrote to my parents:

"Before you all pulled away last night there were many things in my heart which I wanted to express to you in words, but as the days drew closer for you to leave, I guess it grew harder for me to brace up and say them. As long as I live I could never do enough for you and the boys to repay you for the wonderful years we spent together. Since coming to you we have lived in three different houses and each has its set of wonderful memories. I am sure though that the house on 1903 West Road will always be our favorite. We have shared happiness and sorrow since we have been together, but life has so much of these things in it and how wonderful it is when we can

RED DEVIL TALES

share it with those we love. Your having to move to Louisiana was a real blow to me, but I know that you wouldn't have gone if there had been any other way you could have given your family the type of life you wanted them to have and stayed here."

In the last part of the letter, George talked about us three boys and how much we three meant to him.

"Having to give up the three boys will be one of the toughest things I've ever had to do. One of the things I wanted most in life was a brother, but Donnie, Ronnie, and Edison have been as close to me as any real brother could have been. The boys and I have had many good times together. I guess because of his being the oldest and his real love for athletics, I have spent more time with Edison. Each of them, though, has a deep and everlasting spot in my heart. I hope the day will never come that I can't do things for them. As they leave for Louisiana my one hope and prayer for their lives is this: that each of them will live close to God at all times, never failing to acknowledge that He is the source of everything that can be good and wholesome for them. And that no matter what task they undertake they will give to it everything that they possess. Unless you can do that it will never be of any lasting satisfaction. That they will never let athletics be the ruling force in their lives, but will integrate it with many activities so they will be well-rounded men. When they play (they will) play with all their heart and when they work (they will) do the same. (I) Guess I would be the happiest person in the world to see them be good athletes, mainly because I know what great lessons it will teach them. Nowhere else can they learn fair play, sportsmanship, and sacrifice for others as they can by participating in athletics. If they could do these things I am sure they will grow up to be fine young gentlemen like their father."

I think I understand now why George Whitfield is such a committed Red Devil. All our lives George has lavished us three boys with gifts and acts of kindness and generosity. Every Christmas he would send us gifts which would include toys, athletic equipment, or clothes. Dad finally called George aside and told him not to do so much for us. Dad said George was outdoing Santa Clause. George still sends us gifts at Christmas. Even after we had our own families, he sent our kids gifts. He has attended not only our weddings, but he has attended our children's weddings. It doesn't matter how far he has to travel. He'll be there. One year, when I was very young, George gave us all a $25 dollar savings bond. I had no idea what it was, and you can imagine how disappointed a seven-year-old would be with such a gift. But after I had graduated from high school and my mother gave it to me to cash in, I understood its significance. With interest added on, the savings bond was worth more than $100.

George's generosity is legendary. If you go out to eat with him, there is a 99 percent change that he will pick up the tab for everybody. There is no telling how many people he has covered, supported, or helped in his lifetime. If there were a Hall of Fame for the most generous people, he would be at the top of the list. From time to time I have tried to be creative and bypass his attempt to cover the meal, but I am rarely successful.

George has a lot of Red Devil stories to tell. One of the stories he likes to tell about Dad is the time when the basketball team was coming back from a game and they made a "Pepsi stop" to get something to eat. At this particular little side joint, the boys all ordered hamburgers. The man, obviously delighted that he was about to sell a shipload of hamburgers to a hungry bunch of athletes, puts on the grill about seventy-five burgers. In the meantime, Dad decided to have a little fun and pulled out his little dog whistle. It was a small flat piece about the size of a quarter that you put in your mouth and make a sound like a squealing pig or dog. You usually find this sort of thing at county fairs. Dad put the whistle in his mouth and began to make a noise that sounded like the yelping of a sick puppy.

The cook, hearing the loud cry, came out and said, "Okay, guys, there are no dogs allowed in this restaurant."

Dad, putting on his face of bewilderment, looks at the man and said, "We don't have a dog in here."

The man returned to the grill and in a few minutes Dad started playing the whistle again.

This time, the man was a little more agitated and repeated his warning, "Now, fellows, I told you that there are no dogs allowed in

RED DEVIL TALES

the restaurant." As he was saying this he was looking around, almost sure there was a dog under one of the tables.

The players were in on the scam and all looked puzzled, trying to hold back from bursting out laughing. Again Dad reassured the man that there was no dog in the restaurant. The man returned to the grill cooking his seventy-five hamburgers. Apparently, Dad couldn't resist doing it just one more time. I am sure this time he really bore down on the whistle and made the dog sound like he was being skinned alive.

Finally, the man came out, and this time, he was outraged. "All right, boys, that's it. If you got a dog in here you got to leave."

Dad, not amused that the man couldn't take a joke, said to the team, "All right, boys, let's go."

The boys all got up, and they left the man with seventy-five hamburgers on the grill.

When George finished high school, he and some of his friends thought it would be a good idea for them to go college at the Citadel, a military college in Charleston, South Carolina. George and Bert Saville were planning to play on the basketball team. The other boys were Gene Pate, Bob Curtis, Bob Brafford, and George Henry. George said he had no idea what he was getting into. The first night on the campus, he had to shine twenty-nine pair of shoes. The next morning the first sergeant, an upper classman, came up and, with his shoe, stepped on all those carefully-polished shoes George had worked on all night and took off all the shine. Then he sarcastically barked out to George, "Well, you didn't do a very good job, did ya, knob?" George said this little squat stood about five feet five inches tall, and he really wanted to punch him out. After a few days of being humiliated and abused, George called Dad back in Kinston and told him that he didn't like the place and he wanted to come home.

The first thing Dad said to him was, "Well, son, do you remember what we taught you at our house?"

George said, "Yes, sir, I do."

Dad said, "Okay, repeat it."

George answered, "You don't ever start something that you are not going to finish."

"That's right," Dad told him. "If at the end of this year you decide that you don't want to go back, I will come down and pick you up and bring all of your stuff home and we'll make arrangements to go to another school. But until then, you may as well settle in and get to work."

At the end of the first semester, George made four Fs and one D on his report card. Dad called him up and said to him, "George, I am really proud of you. Why did you study so hard in that course you made a D in?"

In the military school, they made you retake the courses you had failed, but with a different professor. George struggled through the year, but he stayed. The second semester George made four Cs and one D. He had survived the year, and with no hard feelings toward the little squatty sergeant, George chalked the experience up as "a lesson learned the hard way." The next year he went to Lees-McRae Junior College in Banner Elk, North Carolina. Dad knew the basketball coach there and told him that he was sending him two good players, George Whitfield and Cecil Gooding. They were roommates. Later, George would finish his college career at East Carolina.

George remembered one particular game where Dad had instructed the players not to shoot the ball for several minutes until they knew the kind of defense the other team was running. Kinston was playing Jacksonville. George said the last thing Dad said before the team went out on the court was that he knew Jacksonville was going to be playing some kind of zone defense. He told the boys that when they got the ball, he didn't want anyone to shoot until the team knew how they were going to shift in that zone. They were to pass the ball around in order to see how Jacksonville was playing the zone. The Red Devils got the opening tip. Buddy Potter tipped the ball to Cecil Gooding, who in turn threw the ball to George. George was wide open at the top of the key. He took the shot and missed. George said Dad must have jumped three feet high off the bench and called time-out. He motioned for George to come out of the game, and as George made his way off the court, he said Dad grabbed him by the seat of the pants and practically threw him on the bench. He stuck

RED DEVIL TALES

his finger in George's face and barked, "You will do what I tell you, or you won't play. I told you not to shoot." George sat on the bench the whole first half. He said Dad didn't say a word to him until the start of the second half, when he looked over at George and said, "Now do you think you can do what I tell you to do."

"Yes, sir."

"All right, get back in there."

All the above stories are interesting and amusing but really do not do justice to the amazing life and career of George Whitfield. One only has to Google his name on the Internet or peruse through years of newspapers articles throughout his long and illustrious career to realize he is a well-established legend in the State of North Carolina and around the country.

In the last seven years I have spent a great deal of time in North Carolina and with George Whitfield. Other than his family and many friends, I have learned that George has several passions that drive and define him. First, his passion for baseball is second to none. He knows and understands the game, and his record proves it. As a Red Devil, he is competitive and wants to win but his love for the game runs deep and wide. For the last few years I have joined him in Omaha, Nebraska, to watch the College World Series. It does not matter who is playing, George watches every inning of every game. In fact, he insist on getting to the game early to watch the teams warm up and take batting practice. I have often joke with him that his funeral should be held on a baseball diamond and his home, with all of his memorabilia, should be turned into a baseball museum.

Second, as mentioned earlier, and throughout, George loves being a Red Devil. His experience as a Red Devil during his high school years in Kinston and his relationship with Frank Mock and Amos Sexton forever made him humble, appreciative, and the consummate Red Devil. This is his family and he continually draws strength from being around Red Devil friends.

Third, George loves country music. This affection probably goes back to having to listen to country music on the Red Devil bus when Dad was driving. For George, Nashville and the Grand Ole Opry is his Mecca, which he periodically makes pilgrimages to.

Fortunately, my brother Don lives in Nashville and is able to get him tickets. He called one day to inform me that someone had died, and it took me a few moments to realize that it was not a family member, but a country music star. But for him it was as if one of his own family members died.

Fourth, George has a great appreciation and respect for the military. He respects their love of country, commitment to excellence, and the willingness to sacrifice their life in service to others. These are values he played out in coaching baseball, and the values became his compass in life. Every year in his annual baseball clinic, George honors someone from the military. This he has done for over forty years. Going to tour the battlefields of Normandy is on his bucket list.

Finally, George loves a good steak. Now everyone probably loves a good steak, but for George a good steak meal is a part of his regular routine. I believe we have eaten at every top steak house in North Carolina. In Omaha, George not only experiences his passion for baseball but he enjoys the famous steak houses located throughout the city. Of course, I have also learned a few things he is not fond of: Chinese or Mexican food and cucumbers. He is strictly a steak and potato man.

Basically, George just has a passion and love for life. It is a part of his DNA. He is always optimistic and positive. He is driven, and everything he does, he does it 100 percent. Every day is like Christmas morning. Every day is a celebration of something. It's like every day is someone's birthday. Every boy he has every coached is like his own son. He never forgets, and he always remembers.

Amos Stroud, who played on the 1950 state championship basketball team, was instrumental in starting the Red Devil and Friends golf group. For years Red Devil alumni would meet once a month at some North Carolina golf course and play. Amos was also responsible for putting together a Red Devil booklet for the 1999 Red Devil Class Reunion. Red Devil alumni from 1937–1970 were encouraged to write an update on their life after graduation. Amos wrote about George. This is what he said:

"All of these write-ups are in alphabetical order except for this one. George Whitfield may be the prime reason Red Devils still exist;

RED DEVIL TALES

the Grainger High School brand that is. George has been instrumental in getting the Red Devils together most, if not all, the times they meet as a group. Without a doubt he owns more Red Devil information, materials and paraphernalia than any other. He is also the most recognized Red Devil in existence today. If anyone has something to report about a Red Devil, you can be assured George will be at least one of the first to be informed. You can count on George to keep up with every Red Devil possible. If there is such a thing, George Whitfield has the reddest Red Devil blood of all.

"George says he has been involved in athletics all his life and he still enjoys it as much as he did as a high schooler. He did not say it, but I bet you can wager that he was involved in athletics as a small child. In his own words, he describes his love of sport and organized athletics best: 'I will forever be indebted to my wonderful coaches, Frank L. Mock, Jr. and Amos R. Sexton, for all they did for me during my formative years. They are the reason I chose coaching as a life's work. Bill Fay gave me my first job at Emma Webb Park, and the first competitive game of sports I ever played was under Captain Pat Crawford. They were wonderful men. All of us were so lucky to have their types for major influences in our lives.' I suspect the number is legion that could attest to the same or a very similar statement."

Coach Sexton giving instructions to the 1954 starting five. Front row right to left: Robert Whaley, George Whitfield, Darwin Williams, and Coach Sexton. Back row right to left: Cecil Goodwin and Buddy Potter.

Coach Sexton giving a "chalk talk" to George Whitfield and Douglas Gregg in 1953. Courtesy *The Free Press*.

The 1954 Kinston Red Devils, the Eastern AA champions, whoop it up in the dressing room at the state tournament.
Front row, left to right, Manager Jim Heard; Darwin Williams; Edison Sexton, son of the coach; George Whitfield; and Bert Saville.
Second row, Assistant Coach Charles Lee, John Carter, Wayne Anderson, and Coach Amos Sexton.
Back row, Marshall Happer, Billy Tripp, Robert Whaley, Billy Evans, Cecil Gooding, Buddy Potter, and Poo Rochelle.
Staff photo by Roy Matherly. Courtesy of the Greensboro *Daily* News.

Coach Sexton (center) instructing
Buddy Potter (left), and George
Whitfield (right). Courtesy of the *Free Press*

George Whitfield as an assistant baseball coach at University of East Carolina University under Coach Keith LeClair.

18

MARSHALL HAPPER

I heard about the all-class Red Devil reunion in March of 2010 from my correspondence with Marshall Happer. Marshall had been on my short-list of people to meet and interview, but he lived in Florida, so I was unable to meet him personally. The first time I had taken notice of Marshall was in a picture of the 1956 basketball team taken right after they won the state championship. The whole team, including Dad, is gathered in the back of the old Kinston Red Devil team bus and right up front, holding the trophy, with a smile bigger than Texas, is Marshall Happer.

Marshall was not only the starting guard in both the 1955 and 1956 state championship basketball teams. He also played in the 1956 East-West All-Star basketball game in Greensboro. The coach that year for the East All-Stars was Amos Sexton. However, as talented as he was as a basketball player, Marshall's most notable accomplishments would be in tennis.

In 1955 and 1956, he won the NCHSAA (North Carolina High School Athletic Association) junior championship and the North Carolina junior championship. He then went on to play tennis for four years at the University of North Carolina where he was a vital member of four consecutive Atlantic Coast Conference championship teams (1957-1960).

In 1956 when Marshall was a senior the tennis team played Wilmington Hanover High School at Emma Web Park. Marshall played Wilmington's first man, Jerry Taylor, and the first set was very competitive and close, but Marshall pulled it out winning 7–5. This seemed to arouse Marshall, and he played the second set like a man possessed wining 6–0 without the loss of a single point. This is sort of like bowling a 300 game, you simply cannot improve on the performance. It's a perfect game. Marshall calls it his golden set. Eion Faelten, who also on the tennis team with Marshall, said that in 60 years of watching tennis he had never seen anyone at any level repeat such a feat.

In the spring of 1960, Marshall was a senior at the University of North Carolina and arguably one the best tennis players in the state. His old high school Red Devil teammate, Eion Faelten, was a junior in North Carolina State. The two schools met in Raleigh that year, and Eion was up against Marshall. Eion recalled that he was having his best day against Marshall, "playing out of his mind," winning the first set. Eion said, "I found myself thinking that I am about to beat Marshall Happer. This can't possibly be happening and sure enough that was a self-fulfilling prophesy! Marshall hit a good serve and came to the net, but I got a fairly good racket on the ball, and he volleyed my return, but not a winner. I was able to line up a shot that I thought was going to be a winning passing shot. To my dismay, my shot clipped the top of the net and fell back to make the score deuce. It was like a balloon had been pricked by a pin and all the air rushed out (of me). He eventually tied the game 5–5. He then went on to win the set and proceeded to roll over me in the third set 6–0. It was then I realized once and for all that as a tennis player, I just was not in his class."

After graduating from the University of North Carolina, Marshall practiced law in Raleigh but he continued to play tennis. And in 1966 and 1967, he won the North Carolina Men's Doubles Championship. After practicing law for seventeen years in Raleigh, Marshall went on to serve as the first and only administrator/commissioner for the Men's Tennis Council, the governing body for men's professional tennis worldwide and later as the executive director and

RED DEVIL TALES

chief operating officer for the US Tennis Association. In 1981 he was inducted into the North Carolina Tennis Hall of Fame, and in 1995 he was inducted into the Southern Tennis Hall of Fame. In 2010 he was inducted into the Kinston-Lenoir County Hall of Fame, and in 2012 into the North Carolina Sports Hall of Fame.

I was looking forward to meeting Marshall in person at the 2010 Red Devil reunion. After wandering around with no luck, I finally asked someone who said, "Oh, yeah, Marshall is here. You can't miss him. He is wearing a pair of solid red pants." I finally got to meet Marshall and recognized that familiar smile and, yes, bright Red Devil red pants with a red-and-white knit shirt. He said, "You know I don't understand. This is a Red Devil reunion, and I don't see anyone wearing red. It just doesn't make sense." Well, the only thing missing from Marshall's attire was a red hat. However, I did see one fellow, Jay Tripp, sporting a red pompadour hat that stood out. Marshall was the reunion chairman and president of the Grainger High School Red Devils Foundation and obviously had done a great job in putting this event together. Of course, he had a lot of help from other loyal Red Devils. Marshall also started a website for all former Red Devils of Grainger High School where alumni can stay in touch with each other, post blogs and pictures, and relive the long and lustrous history of Grainger High School. (www.ghsreddevils.org)

Like Poo Rochelle, Marshall Happer grew up in Kinston in the 1940s and 1950s living across the street from Emma Webb Park. "He was a 'playground rat.'" For many kids in Kinston, Emma Webb Park was the training ground and farm league that forged the future athletes of Grainger High School. Marshall said, "We all went to that park every day, and we played everything available, including midget football, midget baseball, which were Kinston's predecessors to the Little League." But the recreational department at Emma Webb Park had other activities as well: basketball, tennis, swimming, pool, ping-pong, and even bridge playing. The recreational director Bill Faye and Tracy Hart, his associate, were well before their time in promoting youth sports, according to Marshall. He said that they regularly competed against other cities in eastern North Carolina in football and baseball. In 1950 the midget football team traveled to Shamokin, Pennsylvania to compete in the 1950 Second Annual Piggy Bank Bowl, but play was cancelled because of snow. In 1951, the midget football team lost to Canton in the finals of the North Carolina State Midget Football Tournament in Burlington. The Kinston recreation department sponsored a pre-high school Jaycee basketball league played at a local church gym, as well as a summer men's tennis team that played home matches at Emma Webb Park and away matches throughout eastern North Carolina.

As a basketball player, Marshall was as skillful and agile on the basketball court as he was on the tennis court. And if a player had a good idea on how to execute a play or defend an opponent, Amos Sexton was open to change or adjustment. A case in point, according to Poo Rochelle, was when he took Marshall Happer's suggestion on two new defensive setups the young player had designed himself to use against big centers. Marshall was five foot eight as a sophomore but within a year had soared to a height of six feet two inches and had become a talented and intelligent guard on the court. Poo said he still remembers the time in practice as they are working on their defense that Marshall asked Coach Sexton as he pointed to a spot on the court, "Coach, would you consider having someone here and let me play in front of this guy?" They were practicing to play against one of their most formidable foes, Greenville. Poo said Greenville had two good players who beat six of theirs, but the Red Devils always managed to beat them for the state championship bid. The Red Devils always figured a way to beat them when it counted. When Kinston got to the state playoffs that year in Enka, they played Mount Airy who had two six-foot-five forwards and three guards who were good shooters. Marshall called that same defense to Coach Sexton's attention. Mount Airy had one good outside shooter who missed the first several shots he took. They then decided to back away from him and leave him open until he scored. That allowed Kinston to have three players under the board against their two. The defensive adjustment worked, and Kinston won the game. One of the benefits of growing up and playing street basketball at Emma Web Park is that Kinston

RED DEVIL TALES

players learned how to think on the court and improvise to various situations and conditions.

Eion Faelten said that in basketball Marshall "was the consummate team player and if one of the big men got open in the paint, he could expect a pass from Marshall. In our day the scorekeepers did not pay much attention to assists as they do today, and the typical boxscores included FGs, FTs, total points, fouls and sometimes RBs but never assists. If they had, Marshall would have had many double doubles (points and assists) and a few triple doubles (points, rebounds, and assists). He most certainly would have been the team leader in assists."[1]

Also in 1956 Coach Charles Lee who had been the junior varsity basketball coach and the tennis coach left Grainger High School to go to Goldsboro as the new head basketball coach. In his place Amos Sexton was appointed as the new tennis coach. Like his beginning basketball career as a coach, he knew nothing about tennis either. He made no pretense of trying to coach the players. He told the boys to just do what they had always done, go out there, "kick butt," and win matches. He was more of a chaperon than a coach. Eion Faelten said that if he had had the time to study and learn tennis as he did basketball, he most likely would have become a tennis coach genius also. Marshall told me that on one occasion as he was about to serve and the ball was up in the air, Coach Sexton yelled out, "Knock the hell out of it, Marshall." Marshall cracked up and had to stop and regain his composure before resuming play.

As Marshall reflected on his time as a Red Devil, he made a few observations:

"In the 1950s, we first played basketball on recreation department teams at a church gym. Remember Bill Fay, who was the director of recreation, had been the Red Devil High School basketball coach, so we had some coaching early on. We played outside on the dirt basketball court at Emma Webb Park. In addition to the small size dirt court, the wooden backboards were not offset so it was hard not to hit them when shooting a layup. Coach Charles Lee, the Red Devil JV (Red Imps) coach worked at Emma Webb in the summers.

205

He was very good at coaching the fundamentals, and he was always sizing us up for his JV team.

"The first encounter at GHS was on the JV Team for the ninth and tenth grades. If there were ten players on our ninth grade JV Team, I am sure I was the last one selected as then I was only about five foot two and maybe eighty pounds. Because I was so short and so small, I started and always stayed as a guard even though I was six foot two by my senior year (still only about 130 pounds). Usually one or two of us would move up to varsity to sit on the bench at the end of the tenth grade season for the state championship tournaments. The Red Imps won most of the games under Coach Lee who enhanced everyone's skills. Coach Lee was also Coach Sexton's assistant for the Red Devil varsity.

"The importance of the Mock Gym cannot be overstated. It was the only full-size basketball court in our conference. All the other schools in our conference had very small gyms, and in New Bern, we played in a National Guard armory with a very low ceiling and sorry lighting. Our greatest rival was always Greenville, and they had the smallest gym. We called it the Match Box. The goals were attached to an overhang from the balcony, so the Greenville students liked to wave their hands near the top of the backboard and scream when we shot foul shots. Even though we won two state championships, we always considered Greenville to be the second best team in the state. All our games were tough. I believe that except for us, Greenville could have won two state championships. But there was us.

"The large size of the Mock Gym court gave us an important advantage. Coach Sexton took advantage of that. He got us into shape to play a full game at full speed on our large court. A typical practice after some offense and defense drills would end with the 'whistle drill' where we would start running full speed from one end of the court towards the other end until he blew the whistle, and we had to reverse on a dime and run immediately in the other direction until the whistle blew, and blew, and until we got tired and had accumulated a few stone bruises. After that we had to shoot around one hundred foul shots and then finish with something like twenty laps around the court. I was pretty sure that I became immune to running

RED DEVIL TALES

laps, and it just did not matter how many I had to run. I got into such good shape at GHS that it took me years to lose it.

"To take advantage of our conditioning, we began running at the first tip-off and never stopped until the last buzzer at the end of the game. If an opponent was going to guard any one of us, he had to have his running shoes on because we were going to keep on moving every minute. No standing around for anyone.

"Our most effective offense was our fast break, and it was our responsibility as guards to make it happen. Since our tallest center was never more than six feet three inches, we were relatively small under the boards, but they learned to work together to block out and get defensive rebounds. The instant, and I mean the instant, that one of them got a defensive rebound it was my job (or one of the other guards, Darwin Williams in 1955 or Alley Hart in 1956) to be crossing between the foul line and the top of the circle to receive the immediate (did I say immediate) outlet pass from the defensive rebounder. At the same instant that the rebound was secured and was being passed to a guard in the middle, the other two rebounders (two forwards or one forward and the center) had to immediately take off to fill the two lanes on each side of the court. As soon as the first guard got the ball, the second guard had to be in the center of the court to receive the second pass and then dribble the ball up the center of the court. If we had a three on one or a three on two when the guard got to the foul line at the offensive end of the court, there was an easy pass to one of the big guys in the outside lanes for a layup, or if there were two defensive players backing up to block the side lane, then the shot was open for the guard inside the foul line. If there were three defensive players back, we would probably hold up the fast break and set up our regular offense, which was also run, run, run.

"Now we did this on every defensive rebound and usually by the end of the third quarter or the beginning of the fourth quarter, the other team was exhausted and just could not get back. Often we could run up a lead at this time if not before. The secret was constant pressure as we were in such good shape we could run seemingly forever. Now this was much more of an advantage on our large home

207

court, but it also worked on the smaller courts as running constantly is running constantly.

"Our 'slow break' would occur after our opponent scored and while they were congratulating themselves on a wonderful score, our big guys filled the outside lanes and we moved quickly to get the ball down the court so if they got there first we had a quick return score. This added more to the constant pressure.

"Our regular offense was basically pick-and-roll against man-to-man defenses and fast passing of the ball for zone defenses as we moved closer to the basket. Everyone was moving all the time. We tried to get the ball to our big guys in the middle, and they were all good scorers inside. We learned early that it was not necessary to shoot every time you got the ball, and if you continued moving and passing, you would get the ball back for an even better shot. We did not care who scored. We just wanted whoever got the best shot to take it, and if someone else was in a position for a better shot, it should be passed to them. If a shot was missed, we fought like hell for the offensive rebound with us as guards protecting back on defense. We learned that playing as a team was more lethal and more effective than playing as individuals. We always had five guys on the court who could score and that balance was very important.

"Our defense as Coach Sexton used to say was a man-to-man zone. What he meant was make sure that your man is covered no matter what and let's keep our sort of big guys guarding players under the basket so they can get to important defensive rebounds to start our fast break. We were free to pick up our offensive opponents as soon as we wished and often as guards we just started on them at the inbounds after we scored.

"We studied our opponents, and we learned that most high school teams only had one, two, or, at most, three of their five players who would score from outside, so we began to invite sorry shooters to shoot a lot while we backed into the middle to keep the ball away from their big guys who could score inside. We found that inviting a bad shooter to take a free outside shot made a bad shooter even worse. A bad shot from a poor shooter from outside always made a good rebound for us to start our fast break.

RED DEVIL TALES

"I discovered that after we scored, one opposing guard would take the ball out and pass it in to the other guard. A few times each game that act got so monotonous for them that they quit paying attention, and so I liked to linger back, and I could, a few times each game, either turn quickly and intercept the inbound pass or steal the ball from the guard who received the negligent inbound pass. Either Darwin Williams in 1955 or Alley Hart in 1956 would be aware and paying close attention, so if I got the ball, I could give them an easy pass for a quick layup. This worked a lot.

"We were a AA level school, and Coach Sexton always scheduled us with AAA teams before our conference games began with Wilmington, Goldsboro, Rocky Mount, Raleigh, and Wilson, who were all AAA. We also played some college freshman teams like Atlantic Christian. We lost some of those games to AAA teams, but it made us tougher for our AA league. My personal attitude was that we were never going to lose, and until the final buzzer in a game we would lose, I was still trying everything I could think of to win.

"When Coach Sexton was selected to coach the 1956 East-West Game, for the first time he got three really tall centers, and I mean tall. Coach Mock was coaching the East-West football team, and he had Rochelle as his quarterback so Poo could not play on the basketball team. Coach Sexton asked me to play to run the ole Kinston fast break with Ike Riddick, Greenville's best player. Coach Sexton felt certain that since he finally had the tallest big men he ever had, we would kill the West team. Well, the West team destroyed us on the boards by getting most of the rebounds, and we lost badly. You can't run a fast break unless you get a rebound. By the way, August 1956 was my last chance to play in the USTA National 18 and under tennis tournament in Kalamazoo, but it conflicted with the East-West Game. If we had known we were not going to get any rebounds, I am sure that Coach Sexton would have insisted that I go to Kalamazoo.

"In the 1950s Kinston was about the finest high school town anywhere. It seemed that everyone in town attended every football, basketball, and baseball game, every chorus presentation, every school play, and everything else. The first close television station was in Norfolk so TV was not really available, and attending high school stuff was the thing to do. That is also why the Kinston recreation department and the public parks were so important.

"Every time we won a state championship in anything, we were met at the city limits for a parade throughout Kinston. I still remember that after my 1955 state tennis championships I returned with Coach Lee in his Studebaker convertible. There was a sign at the Kinston City Limits "Kinston Home of Champions." When the new mayor of Kinston attended my induction into the North Carolina Sports Hall of Fame in 2012, I mentioned that and he promised me that he was going to get the sign replaced. I do not know if he did or not."[2]

In 2014, Marshall was inducted in the North Carolina Sports Hall of Fame. The write-up on Marshall is worth noting:

"They say character is more easily kept than recovered, and that notion captures the essence of Marshall Happer. Across his lifetime, through decades of achievement, whenever he has found himself confronted by tall challenges, Happer displayed unshakable integrity. Few men of his statue have been more revered.

"Happer grew up in Kinston, twice winning high school state championships in both basketball and tennis. During 1957-60, he played tennis for the ACC champion North Carolina Tar Heels. He joined the Manning Fulton Raleigh law firm in 1964, but kept playing tennis, winning the North Carolina State Championship with two different partners in 1966 and 1967. But Happer's passion for tennis took him beyond the court. He was president and founder of the Raleigh Racquet Club in 1968, and later president of the North Carolina Southern Tennis Association. From 1972-79, he staged professional tournaments in Raleigh as part of the Southern Prize Money Circuit he administered; in 1979, he organized the USTA's national secondary prize circuits. His stock is rising.

"The Association of Tennis Professionals (the men's players association) was founded in 1972. Happer believed the ATP was not meeting the needs of up-and-coming new players, so he negotiated for and won approval for the awarding of ATP ranking points at satellite tournaments in 1978, creating a crucial pathway for players to compete on the major international Grand Prix circuit. Happer's pursuit of that goal was unwavering. His most far-reaching work commenced in 1981 when he was named as independent administer (commissioner) for the Men's Tennis Council, the international governing body for men's pro tennis. Happer was responsible for the administration of the worldwide Grand Prix of Tennis, including the code of conduct. He employed the first pro tennis officials and developed the first drug testing program.

"As New York Times columnist Dave Anderson wrote in 1983, 'The most important person in tennis is a rangy forty-five-year-old North Carolina attorney with a soft Southern accent and a soft button-down shirt. M. Marshall Happer 3rd is the administrator of the Men's Tennis Council, the closest thing to a commissioner that this fragmented and footloose sport has had...Marshall Happer is slowly restoring law and order.'

"Happer remained exemplary in that post until MTC dissolved in 1989; the ATP Tour was formed and the Grand Slams became independent. But the rules of tennis, code of conduct, and structure of officiating today all came out largely through his leadership

"From 1990 to 1995, Happer returned to the USTA as executive director, the governing body of American tennis. He was in charge not only of the staff, but also hundreds of tournaments and events, plus the US Open, the US Davis Cup, Fed Cup, and Olympic teams. Happer retired as COO of the USTA in 1995, but remained as USTA outside counsel until the end of 2009, involved with nearly all TV, sponsorship and business contracts for the US Open.[3]

In Grainger High School's 1956 yearbook, the *Kay-Aitch-Ess*, featured this picture along with a list of Marshall's 1955 tennis accomplishments. It reads: "Marshall Happer is one versatile Grainger High athlete who, besides being a regular on the basketball team, has established quite a reputation in tennis circles throughout North Carolina. During 1955, Marshall's long list of trophies included:

1. The state high school tournament singles championship
2. Northeastern Conference high school singles championship
3. State Jaycee tournament (Earning a trip to the National tourney at San Antonio, Texas, and advancing to the second round)

4. State closed singles championship
5. Sandhills Invitation junior singles championship (Teamed with Billy Hollowell of Kinston to win doubles crown)
6. State Open junior singles championship

The 1956 North Carolina Class AA basketball state champions smile gleefully before leaving the bus after arrival in Kinston from Asheville Sunday night. The Red Devils copped the state crown for the second straight year by running over Sanford 74-62. Members of the squad shown from left to right are: Front row: Eion Faelten, Poo Rochelle and Marshall Happer. Second row left to right: Tim McLaren, Charles Lewis, Billy Evans, Bobby Stanley and team manager, Herbert Hilsinger. Third row left to right: Steve Creech, Coach Amos Sexton, scorer Verner Abbott, Alley Hart, David Adkins and Roger Hobgood. Courtesy of *The Free Press*

19

VERNON "POO" ROCHELLE

After having lunch with Charlie Lewis, Gary Hocutt, and Pat Wright, I met with Poo Rochelle in the afternoon at his home in Morehead City. For most of his life, he was a resident of Kinston, born Vernon H. Rochelle on March 7, 1938. His childhood friends in kindergarten gave Vernon the nickname Poo, which has stayed with him his entire life. Poo attended Kinston city schools from grades one through twelve, graduating in 1956. In 1953 he became an Eagle Scout, an achievement reached by very few. Poo left Grainger High School after graduation and attended Duke University. He played one year of basketball as a freshman at Duke and received a degree in Business Administration in 1960. After serving two years in the Navy, Poo went to the University of North Carolina, where he received his law degree in 1965. He was a law clerk for Justice Carlisle W. Higgins, North Carolina Supreme Court, for two years before he established his law practice in Kinston in 1966. In 1970 Poo was appointed Kinston City Attorney, a position he held until his retirement in June of 2005.

On August 14, 2010 Vernon H. "Poo" Rochelle was inducted into the Kinston-Lenoir County Sports Hall of Fame, a well-deserved recognition of his achievements as a Red Devil athlete and of his professional career as a lawyer and civic leader. He was very

RED DEVIL TALES

honored and humbled by the experience, noting to Bryan Hanks, "I am obviously very pleased to be inducted, but I also feel like, 'Why me?' The teams I played on were really good all the way through the years. It is sort of like, how do you pick one guy and not all the other guys? But I am real pleased and honored that someone would think I am worthy of such an honor."[1]

At the ceremony Poo also had something to add about the team he played with and the community of Kinston. He said, "We (the Red Devils) were successful, in part, because we worked. We pushed ourselves in most cases beyond our capabilities as individuals. Individually we were good players, but collectively we were a great team. But beyond that, people drove out of town to see us play ball. That kind of support is something you don't think about, but it is there and you know that it there...Athletics is the window to schools. If you have lousy athletics, people don't care much about your school, (but) if you have good athletics, good coaches, and administrators, they are very supportive."[2]

In high school Poo Rochelle excelled as an athlete in both football and basketball. He played varsity football even as a freshman, and in 1955, he was the quarterback and cocaptain of the NCHSAA State Championship football team. Both in the eleventh and twelfth grades, Poo was All-Northeastern Conference, and as a senior, he was selected on *The News and Observer* All-Eastern Team. In 1956 his senior year, he was the quarterback of the East team in the NCHSAA East-West All-Star Football Game.

In basketball, Poo was the starting forward of the Red Devils basketball team in 1954, the State Runner-Up Team in the state championship, and he was a vital part of the state championship teams of 1955 and 1956. He was selected as All-Northeastern Conference in both his junior and senior years, and he was selected to *The Greensboro Daily News* All-State Team in 1956.

He now realizes that he learned a lot about life during his high school days under Coach Mock and Coach Sexton but did not realize it until he was much older. It would come to him when he had to make some decision that affected other people and many times he would ask himself, "What would Coach Mock do or what would

Coach Sexton do?" The principles and discipline Poo learned from the coaches of Grainger High School have served him well as a lawyer and throughout his public service career.

When he was in the tenth grade, Billy Tripp had moved to Kinston from Virginia and, he noted, "His sister was my girlfriend. Both of us were quarterbacks. I was a passing quarterback, and he was a running quarterback. We were playing Goldsboro at Grainger Stadium. We would shuttle plays back and forth. On one particular play, Billy was to run a fullback counter play. The next down I was going to run the same play, but instead of giving the ball to the full-back, I was going to pass the ball. Well, the quarterback took the ball, went down the right side of the line, and faked a hand-off to the right halfback who was diving straight ahead. He then turned around and handed the ball to the fullback. Well, Billy fumbled the ball. I was standing beside Coach Mock and, not realizing that I was standing that close, said, 'I'll be damned.' Coach Mock turned to me and said very calmly but sternly, 'Son, if there is to be any cussing on this team, I'll do it.' I felt like crawling under a rock."

The most famous road trip story, which has evolved into an urban legion, is when three players were kicked off the bus for gambling, left to fend for themselves in the middle of nowhere, and had to hitchhike back home to meet Coach Mock or Jack Horne in the snow, depending on the version of the story. I have heard so many variations of this story, I began to think it might have happened three or four times.

According to Poo, it was his junior year and the basketball team was on the way to play Elizabeth City, which was about 135 miles from Kinston. He thinks it was Elizabeth City because he remembered they left early. On this trip he said Coach Sexton did not go his usual route. He went to Greenville, then down to Washington, then down toward Bath and then he turned sort of northeast and went to Edenton.

"Well," Poo recalled, "he had told Darwin Williams, Robert Whaley, and—I forget the other person, maybe Buddy Potter—that they were not allowed to play poker for money." The players in question were all seniors, and furthermore, they were starters. Since Poo was a junior, this had to be 1955. As the bus rolled on down toward Elizabeth City, these guys had put a stool in the aisle near the back of the bus and began playing poker for money. They had traveled as far as Greenville, and as they approached the campus of East Carolina College, the bus came to a stop at a red light. Robert noted years before at the 1981 Red Devil reunion that this was on a "Pepsi stop."

At this point, Coach Sexton, who always kept an eye on the players in his rearview mirror, saw that there was some real hanky-panky going on in the back of the bus. Poo said Coach got out of the bus and walked around to the back and opened the door where he caught the boys in the middle of their crime.

Robert Whaley would later say, "Coach Sexton caught us playing cards, and some money just happened to fall out of my pocket. And what is worse, I had a full house."

Poo said that Dad made the culprits get off the bus and they were to get home the best way they could. When they got back to Kinston, the first person they were to see was Jack Horne.

Another version has the boys getting off the bus in the middle of nowhere about one hundred miles from home and it was snowing. This version also says they were to meet Coach Mock on the steps of Grainger High School. And they were told that if they couldn't find a ride home they would to stay right there and they would be picked up when the team came back through town later that evening.

Poo noted that Elizabeth City at that time was not a very good a team. Elizabeth City was so bad that the second time they played them that year, this time in Kinston, the opposing coach, Bob Brooks, got up in the second quarter and came over and sat with Dad on the bench where they just "shot the bull" for the rest of the game. The coach had told his players on the bench that they could go into the game whenever they wanted to, but he was going over to visit with Coach Sexton. Poo said they beat Elizabeth City the second time 99–23.

Robert Whaley lives in Florida today and works in real estate. I did get a chance to talk to him, and he verified some of the parts of the story and, like all of us, had forgotten some of the details. After all, it was over fifty years ago. Robert did believe that it was on the trip to Elizabeth City, which he said took just about all day. He believes they were about sixty miles from Kinston, which would put them way past East Carolina and closer to Edenton. They were playing poker, which they had been warned not to do, but he figured it was a good way to pass the time on a long trip. They came to one of those "Pepsi stops," and he and Darwin were so involved in the game they didn't realize they had stopped and Sexton was on top of him before they knew it. He told the boys, "All right, that's it, you're not playing tonight and you're going back to Kinston." And when they got back, they were instructed to call the principal. Robert said having to call the principal was "the killer" because at the time Frank Mock was the acting principal. And Robert pointed out, he was also the baseball coach, and Robert played baseball. How did they get back to Kinston, and who did they see when they got back? Robert said they bummed a ride back home, which in those days was fairly normal and not considered that risky. He said they thought nothing of hitching a ride back home. Kids with no cars in those days used to hitch a ride to the beach all the time. When they got back to Kinston, they called Frank Mock.

He said, "Mock chewed on us. He didn't hesitate. You certainly wouldn't do anything like that today. Today, he would have said, 'Fellows, I am very sorry this happened. The coach went overboard. He shouldn't have done that. I'll just have a little talk with him.' No, sir. Wasn't like that. There was no boo-woo, cry me a river. That's the way Coach Sexton was. He did it straight, and you knew you weren't supposed to be doing it."

"Wasn't it rather radical to get kicked off the bus sixty miles from home?" I asked.

"Well," Robert said, "it was sort of a 'spur of the moment.' A couple of things: Sexton had 'theories' of the way he did things. He would get it from a book or get it from another coach. And at the time, I am sure he was sending a message to the other younger players. You just didn't question it because the very next day he was looking after you."

When the boys got home, they called Coach Mock.

Robert continued, "Coach Mock chewed on us about being seniors and setting a bad example and said, 'You guys better get your heads on straight. And, Robert, you really better get straight because you are about to come to me in baseball, and I'll remember this.' He didn't mince words. That's just the way it was."[3]

Robert said he never told his parents about it. If he had, his dad would have beaten him with a belt. Oh my, now Robert was about eighteen and six foot three and he knew his father would beat him? The discipline in those days was hard but swift. But when it was over, it was over, and the next day it was forgotten. Robert said that he never played cards on the bus again.

I related the story to Mother's brother Theron. Theron, who was in high school himself at the time and often visited Mom and Dad said that Dad worried that night about those boys until he knew that they had gotten back home safely. In the end, Theron remembered, Dad felt he had probably overreacted, but he had drawn a line in the sand, and the boys had crossed it. He had to make good on his threat.

On the way back from Elizabeth City that same night, as Poo remembers, Dad pulled in front of a black nightclub, or some sort of a drinking joint. It was about 11:30, and something was wrong with the bus. This bus was about on its last leg. Coach pulled into this place and stopped. Maybe he was just going to find a telephone and call for help. He went to door of the nightclub and knocked. Poo said a guy opened the door and looked out and said, "Amos, what are you doing here?"

Coach replied, "Well, I got some trouble with my bus, and I got my ball team out here, and we need to get on back home."

Several of the black men came out, and within about ten minutes, they had the bus fixed and the team was back on the road.

In another occasion, Poo remembered, "We went through a little place called Bear Grass. It was just a little cut-through between Greenville and Washington, and it only had a small gas station. Well, as we were going through this little crossroad, Coach Sexton blows the horn, opens the window, and yells, 'Hey, Jerry, how ya doing?' The guys in the bus are saying, 'Wait a minute, you don't really know this guy, do you? thinking that Coach was just pulling their leg. So Coach Sexton stopped the bus and said, 'All right, come on, I'll show you.' He backed the bus up, and this guy came out, and Coach opened the door for him and this guy said, "Amos, what are you doing in the part of the neighborhood?" Now, the boys are dumbfounded, thinking, *This guy knows everybody.* It turned out that during the summer months, Coach Sexton peddled pots and pans through the countryside and he just got to know a lot of people all over eastern North Carolina and everybody liked him. He would always make friends and 'shoot the bull' with them." Poo, shaking his head and laughing, said to me, "Your dad was a piece of work."

Another story related by Poo involves Robert Whaley's secretly exiting from the bus one night. The team was coming back from Rocky Mount, and the bus came to an intersection. Robert had persuaded several boys to go up and stand behind Coach Sexton and sort of lean over him so he couldn't see Robert opening the back door and jumping out and getting in the car with his girlfriend, which was behind the bus.

Poo said, "After Robert had successfully pulled off this caper, it wasn't ten minutes before Coach Sexton called out for Robert. Robert's nickname was Sunset Carson. Coach calls out, 'Tell Sunset to come up here. I want to chew his ass out about something he did tonight.' The boys yelled back at Coach and told him that Robert was fast asleep. They talked the coach out of it. If Coach Sexton ever knew what had happened, he never said anything about it. He probably never knew it because getting off the bus like that was something you just didn't do. We just did stuff like that all of the time."

One night Poo stole a basketball. He said he was so mad when they got beaten by Greenville one time and somehow the game ball ended up in their dressing room after the game, so he just took it home with him. He said he thought he just might shoot the ball with his rifle or something, but Coach Sexton came to him the next afternoon and said, "I want you to give me the ball, and I'll just send it back."

When Poo was either in the ninth or tenth grade, he recalled, he played on the varsity football team. One night, after they really got their tails beat, they stole all the towels. On the way back home, the bus was just outside of Edenton when they were pulled over by a deputy sheriff. Coach Mock and Coach Sexton made every player unload his duffle bag and lay everything out on the highway. Then every player took the towels one by one and handed them to the sheriff. This is the way the coaches handled things like this. They made a public spectacle out of this episode in order to make a point. If you did something wrong, you made it right.

Another time, Poo said, he skipped practice and went to a movie. He said he was sitting there watching the movie when all of a sudden he looked over and Coach Sexton was sitting nearby. "I don't know how he found out. He probably saw that I was missing and somebody told him that I and a friend had decided to go to a movie." Poo said the next day he was put in a tackling line where you would run down a line of boys and each one would just slam you to the ground. Poo said that he weighed only 140 pounds at the time. That was the only time he had to go through that, but that was enough—lesson learned. "They taught us," Poo remembered, "that there were always consequences to our actions."

There was always something that seemed to happen on the way to Elizabeth City, which was the longest trip to make. The team usually left Kinston around 1:30. Ceiling Ray Gooding's family was an actual tenant farmer on the edge of town. Cecil was six foot three and weighed about 220 pounds and didn't have an ounce of fat on his body. His family did not have a lot of money, so on these long road trips his mother would make him collard sandwiches. Well, Cecil was in the back of the bus and about halfway to Elizabeth City the odor of those collard sandwiches began to kick in, and everyone had to open their windows and moved more to the front of the bus. Cecil ended up sitting by himself at the back of the bus. At some point Coach Sexton got wind of the problem, and all of a sudden he shouted out, "Good gosh a-mighty, Cecil!"

Poo said, "We all thought this was a good time to submit our complaint, so we told Coach that he was going have to do something about Cecil and the collard sandwiches or we were going to start riding in our own cars.

"When we got to Elizabeth City, we stopped at a little hotel to have a pregame meal. Well, those collards had just about done Cecil in, so he was spending much of the pregame meal in the bathroom. At the end of the meal, we were ready to go and we couldn't find Cecil. We thought he might have gone back to the bus, but when we couldn't find him, someone suggested that we check the bathroom because if he had not gone he needed to go. When we got to the bathroom, we found Cecil stuck above the door transom unable to move. He had one leg inside the bathroom and the other leg hanging outside the bathroom. He got into this predicament because the bathroom door was locked and required ten cents to get in. Since Cecil had no money, he had to find a way to get in. He managed to get in the bathroom crawling through the small window above the door, but he got stuck trying to get out. We thought we would have to take the door down to get him loose, but we finally managed to get him free."

Poo said Dad was very superstitious, especially around tournament time. He always wore a red vest and red socks, and if they won the first game he wouldn't even change his underwear. He remembered some of the players got on him about it in Asheville. In Poo's senior year, they played in the state tournament at Enka, a manufacturing place with a very nice gym. The team was staying at a nice hotel downtown, and as they sat around waiting to go to the gym, they asked him, "Coach, why don't you change those red socks?" And he said, "Boys, I'm not changing these (socks) unless ya'll loose, and if you lose, you have a long walk home.'"

The people of Kinston were always big supporters of the Kinston Red Devils. It was a matter of city pride that the Red Devils do well, besides everyone's sons and daughters went to Grainger High School. Poo recalled that during his senior year they played Roxboro in the state football tournament.

"We were supposed to play at Roxboro, which is just north of Durham. If we won that one, we were to play in Clinton, and then if we won that one, we were to play the eastern champions. We were supposed to play three games in the tournament. The businessmen of Kinston raised eight or nine thousand dollars and paid Roxboro

RED DEVIL TALES

to come to Kinston. When we beat them they raised enough money to pay Clinton to come to Kinston. Finally, the state championship game was played in Kinston. We played thirteen games that year, and nine of them were home games.

"The community support was phenomenal. When the team bus was on its last leg, the Rotary Club raised money to buy the school a new bus. There were people in Kinston who went to every ball game, and it didn't matter if they had a son or daughter in the program. There were nine thousand people from Kinston at every playoff game that year and that included the black citizens of Kinston who came. Adkin High School, which was the school for the black students had a team in 1952 that was not only undefeated, but no one had even scored against them. Adkin High School would play at Grainger Stadium on Thursday nights, and Grainger High School would play on Friday night. Both blacks and whites would attend each game. Bill Brice was the Adkin High School football coach, and he was a legend in his own right. His teams were top-notch. In fact, the night before Kinston played for the state championship in 1955, Adkin played Chapel Hill for their conference championship. The ballpark was full, and many of the Grainger High School fans were there. The Adkin team lost their game, but the next night, when the Red Devils played for the state championship, many of the Adkin people were there to watch them play."

When Poo was twenty-one and studying at Duke University, his father came to Durham to visit him. Poo said they went out to eat and somewhere in the conversation his father asked him, "Well, how does it feel to be twenty-one?"

Poo said, "Great! Now I won't have to kiss anybody's ass anymore."

His father smiled and informed him, "I hate to tell you this, son, but now that you're grown, you're going have to kiss everybody's ass."

The high school hangout in Poo's era was Johnny's Drive-In. Johnny's was owned and operated by Johnny Kassouf, who was known for his gambling and betting on Red Devil games. Everybody liked him, and he was considered a good guy. He had married one of the Pharo girls when he was a Marine at Camp LeJeune, and they were both of Greek or Lebanese decent.

This is how it got started. Some of the Red Devils would be at Johnny's, and Johnny would come up to them and ask, "Who are ya'll playing tonight?"

Then one of the players would say, "We are playing Roanoke Rapids."

"Okay," Johnny would say in his a Mediterranean accent. "I'll give you a hamburger and a drink for every point you score over fifteen."

Poo said "We would go out to Johnny's and ask him, 'Johnny, who do you have tomorrow night?' He would say, 'I bettin' on you clowns, you know that.' Then we would say, 'Johnny, they got the worse gym of anybody in the league. The floor is slick, the lights are so high in the ceiling that you can't see anything. It's an armory. I need a ticket for a hamburger for every point I score over twenty.' So Johnny started giving us a ticket for a hamburger for every point over twenty. I remember we went to Roanoke Rapids one night, and I had twenty points in the first half. I had thirty at the end of the game. I came in the next day and told Johnny, 'That's ten hamburgers and ten Pepsi-Colas.' He was the only person who bet on Kinston when we played Elizabeth City in football one year and we beat 'em 21–19. He was the only person in Kinston that bet on the Red Devils to win. I bet he made a pile of money on that game. He wasn't dealing with us, and he never asked us to throw a game, but he was giving us an incentive to play hard. It only cost him a few pennies for hamburgers, and there is no telling what he made in betting on the games."

Poo remembered only one run in with Coach Sexton. When he was a sophomore, he was also a member of the school chorus, as well as playing basketball. Occasionally, there would be conflicts between the two activities, and most of the time, things could be worked out. In December 1954 Jim Hall, the choral director, got the opportunity to have the group sing in Norfolk, Virginia, on television just before Christmas. Television was still a relatively new phenomenon, and there were not many television stations at the time. The Norfolk station could only be received occasionally in eastern North Carolina.

RED DEVIL TALES

Nevertheless, the choral group traveled to Norfolk, spent the night, and the next day sang on television.

Well, the trip caused Poo to miss a basketball practice. He said when he returned Coach Sexton jumped all over him and told him that he had to make a choice of being a singer or a ballplayer. Poo said he remembers telling him, "I don't think this is a choice that has to be made, but if I had to choose one over the other I guess I would choose singing because I would be able to do it longer." Well, the result was that Poo sat on the bench the next game. This was early in the season before conference play and they were playing Raleigh. Poo was not a starter yet, but he was beginning to play a lot. In this game Wayne Anderson, a Kinston forward, was having trouble guarding a Raleigh player named Fred D. Barrett, a left-hander who also played first base in baseball. He actually ended up going to Clemson to play baseball. Poo said, "He was eatin' Wayne's lunch so bad that Coach Sexton had no choice but to put me in the game." Poo went in and absolutely stopped the Raleigh player cold on defense and even scored fourteen points on offense.

The music versus basketball issue was forgotten. Then Poo added, somewhat dumbfounded, "And Amos loved music. My God, we had to listen to country music on every single bus trip. There was a station out of Cincinnati, WCKY, that had a strong signal, especially at about 11:30 at night when we were coming home from a game. We had to listen to Hanks Williams, Ernest Tubbs, Lefty Frizzell, Eddie Arnold, and all that crowd. We used to get on to him about his country music."

Oh, I hear you on that, Poo. Growing up, it was country music or no music. There is a picture in the 1954 *Kay-Aitch-Ess* annual of this chorus group singing on TV in Norfolk. All the girls are up front dressed in a white blouses, looking like angels, and in the back are two rows of boys in their Sunday finest, coats and ties. And there in the back is Poo Rochelle singing away, a definite Kodak moment. Poo was right, he shouldn't have to make a choice. It is not like he missed a championship game. Besides, how many times do you get the opportunity to sing on TV?

In those days kids may have been mischievous and at times pulled cranks, but they didn't get into the kind of trouble that kids do today. Parents kept a tighter rein on their children, and there just wasn't enough time to get into too much trouble, especially if you played ball. And in those days, you played every sport if you could. Football practice started in the middle of August when it was a hundred degrees, twice a day.

The first game was right after or before Labor Day. At the end of every football practice, Poo said they ran what was called the gauntlet. "We started at the goal line running five yards," he said. "Then five yards back, ten yards, ten yards back, fifteen yards, fifteen back. This went on until we ran ninety-five yards, then ninety-five yards back. And finally, we ran one hundred yards and one hundred yards back. And this is at the end of practice when you are already dead tired. But you pushed yourself, and you got faster and in better shape. We worked hard. This is all we knew to do. Then when football season was over, basketball season began."

"One year," Poo continued, "football season ended on Friday, and they had a basketball game scheduled for the next Tuesday. They had one day, Monday, to practice for the game. During basketball practice we ran, ran, and ran some more. At the end of practice, you had to make ten foul shots and then run twenty-five laps around the gym every day. As soon as basketball season was over, most played baseball too. There were players who left high school and went straight into the service and felt that boot camp was a breeze compared to what they went through in sports training in Kinston."

In Poo's house there were only two acceptable grades, A or B. That reminds me of something my dad told me when I made a C. I was rather satisfied with the grade when Dad told me, "Son, just remember when you make a C you are just as close to the bottom as you are to the top." Our parents set high standards.

One year, Poo said, he decided not to prepare for an English assignment, which consisted of reciting a poem in class. He did not prepare, and the teacher knew it. The English teacher, who was a friend of his mother, gave Poo a D. As a result, he said he had to rake the yard every day for the next six weeks, which was the length of a grading period. His parents gave him fifteen minutes to get to school and fifteen minutes to get home after school. When he got home, he had to work. He lived right across the street from Emma Webb Park, and for six weeks he had to watch his friends play while he raked the yard. The teacher had taught him a lesson, and his mother enforced it. "I was never in trouble at school," he said, "and neither was either of my brothers."

At one point in our conversation, Poo looked at me and said, "Did anyone ever tell you about your dad getting into the 1957 Final Four college basketball game in Kansas City?"

I said, "No, I haven't heard that one yet."

It was the year North Carolina played Kansas in the Final Four basketball game.

"Someone told him, 'You're not going to be able to get into that game.' He goes out there with no ticket. I mean nothing!" Poo recalled. "Well, a group of us were watching the game on television over at Anne Parrott's house when, lo and behold, he appears on television sitting behind one of the team benches. We couldn't believe it. Someone said, 'Well, that SOB got into that game!'"

Yep, I am not surprised. That reminds me of the story told earlier when Dad finagled his way to get a VIP parking space at a football game. He was a very determined person and seemed to find a way either by hook or by crook to get what he wanted. We learned more than just right and wrong from Dad. A few years after Dad had passed away, my mother took all of us and our families to Disney World. My older brother was doing something that did not exactly follow the instructions at Disney World and his wife said to us, "Edison thinks rules are made just so he can break them." My brother, laughing, responded, "I can't help it. I just learned it from the master."

There is an addendum to the Kansas City story. I have an AP wire photograph taken of the game showing a particular controversial moment. The caption under the photo reads: "TENSE MOMENT. Kansas athletic officials argue it out with game officials after a tense hassle broke out on the floor of the Municipal Auditorium at the N. C. A. A. Championship finals here tonight. The tense moment occurred after Kansas's Wilt Chamberlain and North Carolina's Pete Brennan collided, fell to the floor, and then exchanged words. Shown above is the game official Hagan Anderson arguing with one K. U. official while in back of him is Coach Dick Harp of Kansas talking with a student as a K. U. player looks on."

To the far left in the picture is Dad observing with his head almost in the middle of the conversation between the referee and the University of Kentucky official. You would think he was one of the coaches involved.

As gifted an athlete as Poo turned out to be, he said learning basketball was the hardest thing he ever did. Playing basketball did not come naturally to him. He had to learn how to play it. He was coordinated, but he did not have the "natural flow" it takes to play the game at first. He had to learn it and practice a lot. Football was very natural to him. It was like, he said, he was born with a football in his hand, but basketball was a different story.

The first time he discovered his football prowess was in the eighth grade when he went out for the junior varsity football team. He weighed 126 pounds. He saw someone throwing the ball, so he figured since he had big, soft hands he could be an end and catch the ball. After about twenty minutes of catching balls, he said Dad called him over and said, "Let me look at your hands." Poo held his hand up, and Dad told him, "You're not an end, you're a quarterback. Here's the ball. Go start throwing it." That's how he ended up playing quarterback. From then on Poo found his niche as a quarterback, and in that position, he did very well.

His learning basketball started with Coach Charles Lee who was Poo's history teacher in the eighth grade, but he also coached the junior varsity team. Poo didn't go out for basketball, but after class one day around Christmastime, Coach Lee persuaded him to come to the gym and play on the basketball team. Poo said learning basketball was the hardest thing he ever had to do. Basketball was just not "natural" for him like football was, but Coach Lee encouraged him to try it. There were fifteen players on the team, and Poo was in the last three of the fifteen. He said these last three players called themselves the Fighting 69th, after the famous fighting group of World War II.

RED DEVIL TALES

These boys got to play when the score was about thirty points either way. The group consisted of Poo, Billy Evans, and Wendell Malpass. They had a running battle over points for the year. He can't remember who finally won the contest, but he believes that eight points for the year was the highest score in that threesome.

However, the next summer, as Poo was going into ninth grade, Charles Lee ran the recreational department at Emma Webb Park. Poo lived right across the street from Emma Webb Park. The park had a dirt tennis court, but Coach Lee took the tennis net down and put up two basketball goals at either end. Coach Lee found four other boys who were going into the ninth grade the following year, and we all showed up every morning at nine o'clock that summer in shorts, sneakers, and T-shirts and practiced basketball every day, all day long. Together, this group of five boys—Poo Rochelle, Marshall Happer, Billy Evens, Robert Whaley, and Darwin Williams—practiced basketball as a team under the coaching of Charles Lee. By the end of that summer, basketball was becoming familiar to Poo. One of the benefits of playing street-type basketball is that the player learns to improvise and become a more thinking player. You do whatever it takes to win.

Charles Lee was the junior varsity coach, but he, of course, assisted with the varsity basketball team as well. Charlie Lee was the son of a Methodist minister, so he was somewhat sensitive to any profanity that might slip out of a player's mouth. When Poo was a junior and playing varsity basketball, Coach Lee virtually went into orbit over Poo saying an "expletive deleted" during practice one day when the team was working a rebounding drill.

The fast break, to be successful, worked by getting the rebound, so the team relentlessly practiced on a grueling rebounding drill. In basketball, the most dangerous area is under the board when players are competing for a rebound. On this particular drill, Coach Sexton was at half-court, observing and directing players. Coach Lee was under the basket watching and advising players as they came off the board. Buddy Potter, who was six foot three and weighed 220 pounds, was an aggressive rebounder; and he and Robert Whaley had the sharpest elbows of anybody. Buddy Potter or Robert Whaley would come off a rebound and, according to Poo, "absolutely take your head off with precision" with their sharp elbows.

Well, on this particular occasion, Buddy Potter came off the board and hit Poo squarely in the nose. Poo said he thought his face was gone, and with tears coming from his eyes, he grabbed his face in pain. Charlie Lee was, at the same time, screaming and screaming from under the basket, "Get the rebound, get the rebound, get the ball out, get the ball out."

Poo, with his face in his hand and still grimacing in agony, cried out, "Well, just wait a damn minute."

The cry, not necessarily meant to be heard, was picked up by Coach Lee, who starting running down court like Barney Fife chasing a jay walker, shouting to Dad, "You heard what he said, you heard what he said. Now you punish him, punish him for that!"

Dad, somewhat dumbfounded, looked at Poo and demanded, "Well, what did you say?"

Poo sheepishly responded, "Well, I said, 'Just wait a damn minute.'"

Dad, still focused on getting the drill right, retorted, "Well, that has nothing to do with it. Why didn't you get the rebound?" Then Dad looked at Coach Lee and very calmly said, "Charlie, go back under the basket. I think Buddy has already punished him enough."

Poo paid a nice tribute to Coach Charles Lee at the 1981 reunion when he said, "Charles Lee made a lot of us into better basketball players before Coach Sexton got us." Eion Faelten added that Coach Lee could play one on one with any of the players on equal terms. He certainly was responsible for getting Poo Rochelle to play basketball, which definitely paid off for the Red Devils in two state championship seasons.

Charles Lee came to Kinston in 1950 after a successful year at Central High School in Elizabeth City. He was born in Seven Springs, the son of a Methodist minister. He graduated from Randolph-Macon Academy in 1944 and then entered the service for two years. He graduated from East Carolina in 1949 in physical education. Along with coaching the junior varsity, assisting with the varsity team, teaching PE to seventh and eighth graders, he was also the

RED DEVIL TALES

head tennis coach. By 1955, Charles Lee was only twenty-eight and his junior varsity basketball teams had won 85 percent of their games (102–18). "The Lee-coached cagers had thirty-six straight home victories to their credit over a four-year period."[4]

Dad acknowledged how much help Charlie Lee was with his coaching. He jokingly used to say that Coach Lee's problem was that he never had a basketball game officiated right. He was always going head to head with referees' calls. Dad said, "You know, those officials are human just like we are and some of them are rather sensitive like me." So he was concerned that Coach Lee would upset the officials during the junior varsity game, and then they would take it out on Dad during the varsity game.

Dad remembered one game they were playing at home to a "packed house" and one of the referees, Red Benton, had what Dad called rabbit ears and could easily hear the coaches' catcalls coming from the bench. Charlie kept "hollering" at Red Benton, the referee, coming down the line and then suddenly jumped up and stomped his feet. Dad quickly grabbed him by the coattail and slung him back against the wall, being afraid that they were about to get called for a technical foul. "His wife," Dad said, "had to rub his back the rest of the night."

On Thursday, March 8, 1956, the Red Devils traveled to Enka to start the state playoffs in basketball. They were playing Myers Park of Charlotte. It was the only afternoon game the Red Devils played in that tournament. Midway through the first quarter, the Red Devils were down 16 to 4. Coach Sexton called a time-out and the five starters—Poo Rochelle, Alley Hart, Marshall Happer, Bobby Stanley and Eion Faelten—huddled around Coach Sexton. He told them, "Fellows, these other five guys have sat on the bench all year while you played. They have practiced and made you what you are, and right now you are playing like a bunch of bums. You have till the end of this quarter to take these people apart, or you are going to sit down and these other guys are going to play the rest of the game as a reward for the work they have done."

Poo said they went back in and caught up with the other team and went on to win the game 86 to 79. The interesting comment in

231

the paper read, "The taller Myers Park five had things pretty much its own way in the first quarter as it took a three point lead at the outset and held on until the waning minutes of the period when the defending champs moved out front, 17-16, as the quarter ended on a shot by Bobby Stanley."[5]

The *Free Press* headlines from that game read, "ROCHELLE AND HART LED KINSTON IN STATE AA TOURNEY AT ENKA."[6] Poo had the highest score that afternoon with twenty-six and Alley Hart had sixteen. The threat worked.

"When we all reflect on who we are today and what we do," Poo summarized, "we remember the lessons we learned from those days of athletic competition. Winning, adversity, endurance, teamwork, dedication, discipline, persistence, and selflessness are values that, at the time, when you are sixteen, seventeen, or eighteen years old, are meaningless, but when you are thirty-five, forty, and forty-five years old, you understand these lessons and are better prepared for the competition of life. Today, I play a lawsuit like I played a ballgame. I play to win."

By the time the 1956 team took the court, Dad had been coaching for nearly eight years and he had certainly become more confident as a basketball coach. His reputation for winning ball games was well-established. Nevertheless, Poo noted that he still was learning the game and was always open to new ideas, even from the players. He had made light years of progress since his first day on the job when he essentially threw the balls out on the court and told the players to continue to play as they had the year before. After eight years of reading books, going to clinics, and learning from other coaches, not to mention what one learns by experience alone, Amos Sexton still considered himself a student of the game and was always trying to make himself and his players better.

"Perhaps the best part of Coach Sexton," Poo continued, "was that he knew what 'buttons to push' to get his players to do their best on the field and on the court. It is true that when he first came to Kinston that he did not know the shape of a basketball. But the one thing that I recall in all of the years that I played is the fact that he never stopped learning the game, and he never stopped learning about us."

At the 2010 Kinston-Lenoir County Hall of Fame ceremony Poo Rochelle concluded by saying, "I felt like, and I think that most of my teammates felt like that when we went away to play ball we represented you, the community of Kinston, and those who came before you. We tried to conduct ourselves in a way that was good… and acceptable…I was surprised when I went to college, then to law school, and eventually around the state how much respect this community was held in by others I did not know…We were known for what we were: a town of champions."[7]

1955 Strategy Huddle, Coach Amos Sexton, with pencil, plans some Kinston strategy with three of his players the night before the championship game with Clinton at the State Class AA tourney at Sanford. Left to right, Darwin Williams, Coach Sexton, Poo Rochelle, and Robert Whaley (photo by Lawrence Wofford. Courtesy of *The Free Press*.

1955 Cocaptains Poo Rochelle and Bill Hill receive State AA trophy as Coach Mock watches proudly.

To the far left Dad managed to get in the middle of a controversial moment at the 1957 Final Four championship game between North Carolina and Kansas.

The 1955 Class AA North Carolina High School State Champions Kinston Red Devils. Members of the team (left to right) are, front row: Pat Wright, Lee Becton, Marshall Happer, Assist Manager Dempsey Hodges. Second row: Assistant Coach Charles Lee, Coach Amos Sexton, handyman Louis McAvery, Assist Manager Walter Poole. Third row: Poo Rochelle, John Carter, Buddy Potter, Billy Evans, Eion Faelten, Robert Whaley. Fourth row: Darwin Williams, Tim McLaren, Jimmy Hodges. (Photo by Lawrence Wofford) Used by permission the *Free Press*.

20

ALLEY HART

As with all my interviews, George helped me make the connection and set up the meetings. Our usual plan was to arrange a meeting with several former players who were living in the same area. It was sort of kill-two-birds-with-one-stone strategy. George knew there were several people we could see in Wilmington, a beautiful and historic city on the East Coast. I remember Wilmington well because as a young boy visiting my North Carolina kinfolk in the summertime, we usually came down to Wrightsville Beach at Wrightsville, which is right outside of Wilmington. On this mission we had made arrangements to see Alley Hart and another Red Devil great, Bobby Hodges, both living in Wilmington.

We made an appointment to meet Alley in the morning, then see Bobby Hodges at noon, and finally, meet another Red Devil alumnus, Talmage Jones, that afternoon. So this was going to be a full day. On this trip, both George and his son Geff would be going with me. We left early Thursday morning, June 25, and met Alley at Whitey's Restaurant in Wilmington. For George, this place brought back a ton of memories. During the days when he was coaching Legion ball, his teams played in a tournament at Wilmington every July. The team stayed in the hotel beside the restaurant, both of which were owned by eighty-year-old Whitey Prevatte. The restaurant has been a

236

RED DEVIL TALES

popular eatery since 1954. George said, "We would always come in this restaurant, and Whitey would always have a place set up in the back for our pregame meal. We ate breakfast and lunch in here every day, and he would always cut us a deal."

As we walked into Whitey's, we were ushered to the back where we met Alley Hart wearing an orange knit shirt and looking very preppie. With the exception of his graying hair, he looked as if he could still be in college. I bet he still has a great jump shot. Along with the usual restaurant sounds of background chatter and the clatter of plates and silverware, music from the 1950s played in the background. It was probably just incidental but rather ironic as we sat down at the table and ordered breakfast against the background sounds of Buddy Holly, Frankie Avalon, and the Platters.

Of all the players that I interviewed, Alley was the only one who showed up with handwritten notes. In fact, he had jotted down five pages of his thoughts about his days as a Kinston Red Devil. He was prepared, and he knew what he wanted to say. He had put a lot of thought into it.

Alley began by stating that he had played basketball in the ACC (Atlantic Coast Conference) in college because of Kinston and Amos Sexton. He learned, he noted, the fundamentals of basketball beginning with Bill Faye, Kinston's recreational director; Tom Mosely and Charles Lee, the junior varsity coaches; and, finally, Amos Sexton.

Alley Hart was an incredible basketball player. He was quick, a gifted ball handler, and he had a jump shot second to none. On defense, if you blinked, he would take the ball away from you; and because of his speed, he helped make the fast break work for the Red Devils. By most assessments, Alley really blossomed in his final year, especially during the state tournament. Even though the Red Devils failed to win it all in 1957, Alley was selected All-Tournament in both the Northeastern Conference and All-Tournament in the state finals. He would go on to Wake Forest on a scholarship in the first recruiting class of the legendary Bones McKinney.

As a freshman at Wake Forest under Coach Charlie Bryant, Alley averaged twenty points a game. Under Bones McKinney, he averaged almost fourteen points a game and he holds two Wake

237

Forest University NCAA Tournament records: most free throws in a game without missing and most assists in a game. From 1959 to 1961 he was a part of the team that won the regular season title, and the Dixie Classic Championship.

In 1961, when Alley was playing, Wake Forest won its first ACC Tournament Championship and went as far as the Elite Eight in the NCAA Tournament. Against eighth-ranked St. John's in Madison Square Garden in the NCAA Tournament that year, Alley scored twenty-eight points, and had twelve rebounds with nine assists. If he had had one more assist he would have held the record for the first triple double in the ACC. For his accomplishments, Kinston had Alley Hart Day on April 14, 1961, and on August 14, 2010, Alley was inducted into the Kinston-Lenoir County Hall of Fame.

From 1962 to 1963, Alley went into the Army and played on Fort Jackson's first undefeated team where he averaged twenty-one points a game. After serving his stint in the Army in 1964, he entered the insurance business, a profession he is still in today. His accomplishment in the insurance profession reflects the competitive and winning spirit of his athletic career. He is president of A. L. Hart and Company, and in 1974 he received the CLU Designation and has become a life member of the Million-Dollar Roundtable.

But Alley was not quite through with basketball. In 1998, thirty-seven years after college, he started playing in the 3-on-3 Senior Olympic Basketball Games with the 56's out of Raleigh. This team won the North Carolina State gold medal five times. They won the National Gold Metal of the fifty-five-and-over class in 1998, and if that wasn't enough, they won the National Gold Metal of the sixty-and-over class in 2003. Alley says he is retired now from competitive basketball, but he still has a mean jump shot. But like all Red Devils he likes to win and he is fiercely competitive. From 1997 to 1999 he was leader and Coxwain of the Three-Time Champion "Young Executives" of the internationally famous Whale Boat race in Banks Channel at Wrightsville Beach, North Carolina.

Alley did not play football in high school, but he wanted to play the sport his senior year. Having concentrated on basketball and seeing some of his friends playing football, he thought he would "give it

RED DEVIL TALES

a shot." It made sense. Alley had played midget football as a halfback and led the league in scoring. On the first day of football practice, his senior year, Coach Sexton was handing out equipment. Alley got in line, and when his time came, the coach looked up at him and, being somewhat startled, said, "Alley Hart, what are you doing here?"

Alley said that he told him, "Coach, I think I can pass a football."

Coach Sexton looked at his hands and then turned around and picked up a basketball. He put the basketball in Alley's hand and told him, "Alley, you get your fanny upstairs and start passing that basketball toward the goal." And that was the end of that. Alley was not that big, and if he had gone out for football and gotten injured, his basketball career might never have happened.

"There are just so many good stories that come out of this era." Alley reflected. He turned to George and said, "You know, I was going to get with you some time and tell you we need to write a book together."

I interjected, "Yeah, the best people to write a book on this era are the people who lived it. George tells a good story. If you had someone to follow him around with a recorder and just let him reminisce, you would have a pretty good book."

Now laughing, Alley commented, "Oh yeah, we tell a good story. We just exaggerate a little bit."

I thought of that saying I have heard people say in Louisiana, "Well, let's not let the truth ruin a good story."

At any rate, Alley continued, "If I wrote a book I would call it *The Other Guard.* In high school the other guard was Marshall Happer. Then in college it was Billy Packer, who went on to become a famous sports broadcaster for CBS. I was always the other guard. But somebody ought to write a book. We could do it if we really got serious about it."

I interrupted again. "Well, you guys need to hurry up and get with it. The sand is running out of the hourglass."

Alley, now in deep thought and ignoring my passing comment, said, "But along with athletics you have to have the Peyton Place. You know we couldn't write some of these stories until my wife Nancy dies."

We were all laughing now.

Alley, looking at George, continued, "And after Mrs. Mock dies, since she has you on such a high pedestal."

Now we were really laughing. Alley said that's what Bones McKinney use to say after I asked him one day, "Coach, when are you going to write your book?"

He said, "I'm waiting for Edna to die. When she dies, I'm going to write a good book."

But Alley said, "Then he came out with his book, and I said to him, 'Coach, I thought you were going to wait until Edna died before you write your book?'"

He told Alley, "But it doesn't look like she is ever going to die."

We all laughed, and George added, "By the way, I ran into one of your old little league baseball friends, Jay Tripp, the other day at the barber shop. He told me to say hello to you."

Alley, with a big smile on his face, responded, "Oh yeah, that boy cost me a no-hitter in a game one day."

Alley recalled the story. He said, "This was in Little League, and in fact, Amos was my coach."

This was news to me because I never realized that Dad did anything other than coach basketball and assist in football.

In 1951 Alley was in the sixth grade, and he said it was the first year they had a Little League program. He was on a team sponsored by the Rotary Club, and they were at that time undefeated. Two other men helped Dad coach, Alley recalled: Jim Hartis, the fellow who had given us our dog Rebel, and Horace Newman. Alley led the league in hitting, pitching, and home runs. Interestingly enough, he was the only player on the team, except for Talmage Jones, who never played high school baseball.

"But," Alley remembered, "Jay Tripp was the last boy coming up to bat and I had a no-hitter."

Jay got up and started playing like he was going to bunt. Alley said he knew he wasn't going to bunt, so he pitched to him anyway. Well, he bunted the ball. Alley went forward from the mound to get the ball, and, realizing that he might not be able to throw him out, threw a wild pitch to the first baseman, hoping to get an error and

RED DEVIL TALES

save his no-hitter game. Even as a sixth-grader, he understood the game. However, the scorekeeper that day was his dad, and after the game his dad told him, "Son, I'm sorry, but I had to give him a hit."

I would later remember that when I had visited with Jim Hartis a few days earlier he had told me about coaching Little League baseball. He also had commented that he believed that Alley Hart was the most talented baseball player he had ever coached.

Well, after this brief side note, we continued. The next thing we did was peruse through the Red Devil picture album that I had put together. I had assembled dozens of photographs of Red Devil players and teams, primarily covering the years Dad coached (1948–1957). There were also school pictures of the band, cheerleaders, and old hangouts like Shady's or Johnny's Drive-In. Anything, image or picture, I could collect I put in the album. Most of the pictures had been taken from the school annuals, but many had been sent to me by ex-players or from George's vast collection of Red Devil memorabilia saved over the years. It was always enjoyable to watch as every Red Devil pondered over each photograph. Emotions of joy and nostalgia were only tampered by the sadness of realizing that some of their friends had since passed away. Inevitably, most would try to see if they could still name every player in some old team photo. Oftentimes they would see a picture of a fellow player that they had not remembered for a while or they would see a face and remember some humorous anecdote. Sometimes they simply commented on a common experience shared but never forgotten. It was a joy to see them relive the glory days of the past as they turned each page of the Red Devil album.

Alley pulled out his notes and glanced down his list. There were several points he wanted to make sure he covered. He began by saying that at Grainger High School they were taught the fundamentals of basketball. They were taught how to shoot, how to dribble, and how to pass the ball. And they were taught teamwork. "But most of all," Alley added, "we were taught the fast break." They didn't spend a lot of time on defense. They just ran and ran and drilled and drilled and practiced the fast break.

Alley said in his senior year, Everett Case, the famous basketball coach at N. C. State who brought "big time" basketball to North Carolina, came to Kinston to watch the team practice. Afterward, Everett Case told Dad that the Red Devils had the best fast break offense he had ever seen in his life, including high school, college, and professional. Everett Case, nicknamed the Grey Fox, coached at N. C. State from 1946 to 1964 and compiled a record of 377–143.

Alley said they were good because just about all they did in practice was master the fast break and run drills in order to get in shape. In fact, he noted, Dad started prepping players on the fundamentals and even the fast break before they got to the varsity. Dad had coordinated with Bill Faye, who was the city recreational director, and Charles Lee, who was the junior varsity coach, so that by the time players reached the varsity level, they were already schooled in the fundamentals of playing basketball and running the fast break offense.

Dad believed in conditioning and teamwork, two elements that made the fast break work. A team had to be in shape in order to constantly run up and down the court the whole game. Timing was also important in the fast break because every pass had to be a smooth transition to the next player. As one player passed the ball, you had to hit the guy at the right moment. There was a rhythm and timing that must take place between the players. Like a finely-tuned orchestra, teamwork was a critical ingredient. By the fourth quarter, many teams were flat worn out trying to keep up with Kinston's fast break offense. George remembered one coach on an opposing team who, after being pounded the whole game by Kinston's fast break, stood up near the end of the fourth quarter, waved a white towel, signaling that he had had enough and he was giving up.

According to Alley, Dad had gone out to Dallas or somewhere during his first year of coaching and paid someone a hundred dollars for them to teach him the fast break. This could be an urban legend, but I am sure that Dad did learn a great deal about the fast break from Everett Case.

George added, "I can remember sometimes getting up in the night to go to the bathroom and Coach Sexton would be at the kitchen table studying the fast break from a book by Eddie Hickey. He also read other books on basketball and went to any available basketball clinic or visited with other coaches, but he learned the game."

Alley also recalled Dad wearing bright red socks, which he pulled up to his knees, and a red vest, both of which he superstitiously wore for good luck. Also, he added, Coach Sexton always wanted to get the basket close to the bench during the fourth quarter. He wanted the goal close to him so he could communicate with the players better in the fourth quarter. In order to accomplish this, the varsity players would rush out on to the court as soon as the junior varsity had finished. They would start shooting under the basket away from their bench so as to give them the other goal closest to the bench during the second half.

The next point Alley noted concerning Dad was his enthusiasm, a quality recognized from the start by Superintendent Booth when he first interviewed Dad for the job. Coach Sexton was always outgoing, gregarious, and never met a stranger. His Southern hospitality style was to call everyone Hoss (probably to cover not remembering their name) and slap them on the back while shaking their hands enthusiastically with a big smile on his face. He would have made Dale Carnegie proud. His enthusiasm, Alley noted, was contagious; and he had a good relationship with other coaches, teachers, cheerleaders, parents, students, and even fans.

Alley said Coach Sexton was a real go-getter and just a bundle of energy. He had a radio program from 5:00 a.m. in the morning till 7:30 a.m. And he went out and sold his own advertising. He sold anything that wasn't nailed down: encyclopedias, pots and pans, even shrubbery. He did anything to bring money in for the family. And he did most of building his new home and built a boat in addition to that.

Finally, Alley said, his father, the Rotary Club, and Dad helped raised the money for a new Red Devil bus.

Alley remembered when Dad left coaching and went to work for Marsh Furniture Company. "In the beginning he went up there (High Point, North Carolina) and they didn't hire him," Alley said. As Alley remembers it, Dad asked them if they were selling anything in Louisiana. "They told him they didn't have anything in Louisiana so your dad told them, 'All right, you let me come up here for two weeks, let me learn the business and then I am going to Louisiana. It won't cost you a dime, except for what I sell.' Two years later, they called him back up to High Point and said, 'Amos, would you like to come to the home office and be vice president in charge of sales?'" Alley said that Dad told them, "I can't afford the pay cut." He was doing so well on his own they couldn't offer him more than he was making selling in Louisiana. Of course, Dad had five states covered.

Alley's point was that Dad was a real go-getter. But along with that, these were times when young athletes really looked up to their coaches. In those days, Alley recalled, the players respected the coaches and the coaches showed respect for the players. In fact, both Coach Mock and Amos Sexton considered every student important, not just athletes. Also, every athlete was allowed and encouraged to play all three sports: football, basketball, and baseball. And the coaches of each sport supported each other.

"Coach Mock," George added, "was just as proud of Coach Sexton when he won a championship as if he had won the championship himself."

There was never any animosity or competition between Coach Mock and Coach Sexton. They were not only partners as coaches, they were good friends. Egos were not involved. And there was never a competition for a player's loyalty to one sport. This cooperation and mutual respect even extended to other school activities. For the most part there was a great working relationship between the athletic department and other school activities such as the band or the school chorus. In fact, some of the athletes were also in the school chorus, and if there was a conflict in scheduling between the school chorus and an athletic event, they would get together and work something out. Teamwork was not just an athletic concept, it was a philosophy that permeated throughout the entire school system. From the superintendent to the principal to the teachers and down to the administrative staff and students, there was a cooperative spirit that was understood and accepted.

RED DEVIL TALES

Alley looked down at his notes and said, "Well, the next thing I have down here is George Whitefield. How many coaches would have taken a strange and troubled kid into their home and raised him? It says something about the character of a man who opens up his home and his heart to rescue a wayward soul. The only one other person in town who wanted George as much as your father was my mother." Alley's mother and George's surrogate mother, Ada, were very good friends. He said his mother loved George and understood his predicament. In fact, Alley lamented that his mother had told Dad on one occasion that she would trade Alley for George. She was joking, of course, but she loved George. In fact, Alley noted facetiously that he thinks his mother loved George Whitfield so much that she named his younger brother George after him.

Alley mentioned that Kinston was a great place to grow up. Even though it was a small town there were plenty of things to do to keep a young boy occupied. On the occasion of his induction into the Kinston-Lenoir County Sports Hall of Fame in August 2010, Alley was asked by Bryan Hanks, the managing editor of the *Free Press* in Kinston, what he's most proud of in his life, he said "I'm proud that I'm from Kinston, the home of champions."[1]

Kinston had a great recreational program with several places to hang out, and during the summer months, many of kids played sports at Emma Webb Park. During the era of the 1950s, Kinston was a typical small-town community where kids could grow up and feel safe, and most people lived hardworking simple lifestyles. As we look back on it today, we realize, of course, that it was not perfect. In those days, segregation was the accepted norm, and we never realized the hardships and struggles of growing up as a black American. It was just the way it was. George added that both Coach Mock and Coach Sexton, however, were friends with the black high school coaches at Adkins High School and they were always giving them athletic equipment to use.

There are two movies made back in the 1980s that seem to typify Kinston in the 1950s and high school basketball. The first movie, *Porky's*, was made in 1982; and although somewhat crass and sophomoric, it still shows some of the typical shenanigans and pranks of high school students in a small town. Alley said *Porky's* could very well have been Kinston in the fifties. In fact, he buys the movie to give to his friends. The other movie which George believes so typifies high school basketball in the fifties is *Hoosiers*. George said some of the drills they used in the movies were the same drills they used to run. Though the setting is in Indiana, the small-town farming community could very well have been Kinston. And going to the big city to play a higher class team was not unlike Kinston playing teams like Raleigh or Wilmington.

There is a television series that I would add to the list the help us understand Kinston in the fifties: *The Andy Griffith Show*. Kinston, like the fictional town of Mayberry, had a certain small-town spirit and down-home family values that were not unlike many small rural southern communities, where people helped their neighbors, loved their country, worshiped on Sundays, respected authority, and honored their soldiers and their elders. Mount Airy, North Carolina, is where Andy Griffith actually grew up; and it is supposed to be the small town which Mayberry was more or less modeled after.

For every character you remember from Mayberry, you could probably find an exact replica in Kinston. Even today in Kinston you can walk into a barber shop and feel like you are in Floyd's Barber Shop of Mayberry. In Kinston, it's the Model Art Barber Shop that has been cutting hair for over fifty years. Pearlie P. H. Pigford has been cutting hair in Kinston since October of 1953. He probably cut Dad's hair. On my first excursion to North Carolina in August of 2008, George insisted that I experience Pig's full beauty treatment. George has been going to Pig for a haircut since he was in high school. No matter where his career has taken him throughout the byways of North Carolina, he always comes back to Kinston for his haircut, shampoo, and Pig's famous face massage. "I can guarantee you one thing," bragged George. "If you are feeling down and in the dumps, you let Pig give you 'the treatment,' and when he is through, you'll feel like fighting the great Rocky Marciano."

Well, who could turn that down? We loaded up the next day and headed for Kinston. The Model Barber Shop is actually located in the Kinston's Vernon Park Mall, so you don't exactly get the feel-

RED DEVIL TALES

ing at first that you are walking into Floyd's of Mayberry. But after you meet Pig, as he is known to his patrons, you feel like you have stepped back into the fifties. There's nothing vogue about his six feet-by-six feet cubical. There are sports magazines like *Field and Stream* and *Sports Illustrated* piled high in the corner. The smell of Old Spice permeates the air, and I would swear there is a spittoon in the corner. Here, you feel like a man again. It's not like these modern sissified, perfumed, unisex beauty salons where the lady that styles your hair looks and talks like Liza Minnelli. No, sir, here you get the full manly treatment. The conversation is about the latest baseball scores or the stock market. Of course, there is the usual talk of "looks like our country to going to hell in a hand basket" saga. The only thing missing is the smell of cigar smoke and hearing the voice of Vin Scully or Dizzy Dean calling the play-by-play of the Brooklyn Dodgers and the New York Yankees on a black-and-white TV set. Hallelujah! Happy days are here again!

One of greatest feelings he ever had in his life, Alley recalled, was during his junior year when Kinston played in Enka for the state championship. Kinston had won the state championship the year before. During the next year, when the team was certain they were going to win a game, the cheerleaders would start singing, "Go, state champs, go." In the final game of the 1956 season, and with only a few seconds left on the clock, Kinston had enough lead to know they had the game won. The cheerleaders started singing again, "Go, state champs, go." Alley said he got chill bumps and hot flashes as they sang, and he knew they were winning another state championship. That feeling, he remembered, was better than anything he experienced, even in college at Wake Forest when they won the ACC championship.

I recalled reading in the *Free Press* an article by sports writer Lloyd Whitfield in which he referred to the chant, "Go, state champs, go." This was when Red Devils had beaten the Washington Pam Pack cagers 72-60 in 1957 to win the Northeastern Conference basketball tournament and the right to go on to the state championship finals. After the game, "fans swarmed the floor."

hitfield wrote, "To congratulate Coach Amos Sexton and the Red Devils, a group of enthusiastic Kinston rooters ripped the nets from the rims, and Keith Sparrow, a Grainger High Student, was elevated on the shoulders of other fans. He placed a red-and-black sign over the rim that read, 'Sanford, here comes Kinston.' Streets in Greenville resounded with Kinston chants until after midnight. All of the cheers were the same, 'Go, state champs, go.' A bit early for that yell."[2]

Well, maybe, at any rate, the Red Devils were undefeated in conference play and Coach Sexton wanted to schedule a game before the playoffs that would test the team's mettle and hone their skills. The year before at this time, he had scheduled a similar game against Atlantic Christian College (March 5, 1956). Atlantic Christian had three ex-Red Devils playing: Douglas Gregg, Darwin Williams, and Robert Whaley. In that game, the Red Devils went head-to-head with this college freshmen team and lost by only two points, 69–67. For whatever reason, this then undefeated 1957 team, loss to the East Carolina Freshman 91–63, the worst lost of the coach's nine-year career and the most points scored against a Red Devils basketball team in fifteen years. The one bright note was Bobby Stanley. Days before the game, Bobby Stanley had been questionable to play since he was "under the weather." By game time he was well enough to play, and play he did. He ended up being the busiest Red Devil on the court with twenty-five points. His performance caught the eye of East Carolina's coach Earl Smith, who was very impressed with his performance. By the way, Alley had nine points.[3]

When he was a junior and a senior playing basketball, Alley would not allow his father to come to practices because he didn't want anyone to think he was playing because of the friendship between his dad and Coach Sexton. His dad was a tobacconist (a tobacco dealer who would calculate the worth of the crop of farmers) and he and Dad became good friends through the years.

Alley believes that the final team (1956–57) Dad coached was the best team in the state and arguably the best team Dad ever coached, even though they failed to win the state championship. The team was undefeated, at least by high school teams, until they

RED DEVIL TALES

went to the state tournament in Sanford, where they lost to Clyde A. Erwin, a rural school in Buncombe County.

As we discussed that game, George lamented and said, "Oh my, Clyde A. Erwin got hot on that night and couldn't miss a goal even if they had kicked the ball." Clyde A. Erwin had a six-foot-six-inch center named Horace Medford who George said got hot and seemed to hit everything he threw up. George continued his lament by adding that this school had never won a state championship before nor since. Clyde A. Erwin had been a fifteen-point underdog, and for the Red Devils to lose to this team was a tremendous blow. This team probably had the potential go down as one of the best teams ever. But they needed to win that state championship.

The Red Devils took out their frustration and disappointment during the consolation games against East Mecklenburg High School with a decisive win of 104 to 78—a new tournament record, which still stands. Charlie Lewis had the most points scored with thirty-two and Alley Hart had twenty-two.[4]

All five starters could shoot the ball and all five were gunners. Every player had at least one 25-point game. With that much talent and every ballplayer wanting to score, it was difficult to keep everyone from competing with one another. Dad, realizing the situation, had called Alley aside at the beginning of the season and told him he had to help keep the peace. That team still holds the North Carolina record for the number of free throws made in a game. In the game against Washington, North Carolina, this team went to the free throw line 47 times and made 45. The only two missed were by Bobby Stanley, who hit 8 out of 10. Alley said the next day in practice, Coach Sexton made Bobby work on his free throw shooting. In this game also, Charlie Lewis hit 16 out of 16 free throws, which stands as a record to this day. Ironically, Coach Sexton had said in the paper that day that he was worried about the team's free throw shooting. That night before the game he told us to really concentrate on our free throw shooting.

I can still remember Dad telling me that this team was so good that they would purposely allow the other team to score and keep the game close so substitutes wouldn't be allowed to go in the game.

249

Alley added that all eleven players on that team went on to graduate from college. All five starters on that team graduated from college and got extra degrees. "Every player got an additional degree except one," Alley said. "But he married well, and he is richer than all of us put together."

Since 1949 the North Carolina High School Athletic Association has sponsored the East-West All-Star Basketball Game, which over the years has become very prestigious and the envy of every high school player to be selected to play. In 1957 Alley Hart was selected from the Kinston team, but the NCHSAA wanted one other player from Kinston. They were going to choose either Bobby Stanley or Eion Faelten. They wanted the coach to choose. Dad told the committee that they needed both of them. In the end neither one was chosen, to the great disappointment of the players.

It was years later, Alley said, that Dad told him the reason neither one was selected. It was some eight years later (around 1965) that Alley went down to LSU in Baton Rouge for an insurance meeting, and he called Dad. Alley said Dad flew down in his single-engine airplane from Ruston and picked him up. In their reminiscing of old times, Dad told him of the incident and said that he had told the committee that they should take both players or take neither. The committee would only take one more so they ended taking neither. That is the reason neither Eion Faelten nor Bobby Stanley was chosen. Dad was trying to protect both players.

Alley said at the 1981 reunion that it was ironic that "Here we are, a bunch of ex-basketball players honoring an ex-football player. He couldn't shoot. He couldn't dribble, and he couldn't pass. All he knew how to do is win ballgames, and in the nine years that Amos Sexton was in Kinston, he has probably ended up being the greatest high school basketball coach in the history of North Carolina."

Co-captains Alley Hart and Jerry Steele accepting Wake Forrest University's first ACC Championship trophy in 1961.

The celebration continues as Alley Hart is hoisted onto his teammate's shoulder

Alley at Whitey's Restaurant sharing his
thoughts on the Red Devil legacy.

21

EION FAELTEN

Eion MacGregor Faelten was born in Danbury, Connecticut, and lived near White Plains, New York, until the death of his father in 1945, when Eion was only six years old. His mother was born in Edinburgh, Scotland. And after his father's passing, she and Eion went back to Scotland to visit his grandparents. The visit ended up lasting about eighteen months, long enough for Eion to go through a year of school. In those days most school children in Britain wore uniforms that consisted of shorts; school ties; long, argyle-style socks; and a little beanie cap.

Eion's father had been a professor of architecture at Yale University from 1922 to 1934. He had hobnobbed with famous architects such as Frank Lloyd Wright and achieved many architectural awards for the school. From 1936 until his death, he was a professor of architecture at the University of Pennsylvania. Jack Rowland, one of Professor Faelten's students, came to Kinston and opened up an architecture partnership with James MacGregor Simpson. James MacGregor Simpson was Eion's uncle and his mother's brother. His mother and her brother had immigrated to America in the 1920s, and she met Eion's father when she was working at an architecture office in New York City. It was Eion's father who had encouraged his uncle Jim to go into architecture. While in Kinston, he designed many

RED DEVIL TALES

buildings in the area, including the Fairfield Recreation Building. When Eion and his mother came back to America, they came down to Kinston to visit Uncle Jim. They liked Kinston and ended up staying.

Eion moved to Kinston in November of 1947 and started third grade. All he had to wear to the old Harvey Elementary School was his Scottish school uniform. You can imagine the reaction of the local children. I am sure the teachers and students at Harvey thought the circus had come to town. In the first few days Eion was teased, and three or four fights took place. As the story goes, when Eion finally had had enough, he beat the crap out of one of his tormentors and that was the end of that. His mother finally got him into some acceptable attire. Eion always jokes that he introduced Bermuda shorts to North Carolina. Apparently, however, the beanie cap didn't take.

Eion said the first time he met Coach Mock was when he was in the seventh grade. It was more or less an encounter rather than an official introduction. Eion loved football and went to every Grainger High School football game as a youngster. His mother always gave him twenty-five cents to get into the game. However, in those days twenty-five cents could buy a couple of candy bars and a soft drink. Eion, not about to waste the money on an admissions fee, always jumped the fence into the game and used the money to buy snacks. There was a place on the south side of Grainger Stadium that had only a seven-foot wall next to the restroom. It was here that two or three of the spikes had been either hammered down or removed, leaving a gap of several feet. Even as a twelve-year-old, Eion was tall enough to get both hands on the wall and haul himself up and over the fence. On one occasion, after taking a quick look to make sure no one was watching, he pulled himself up, swung over the wall, and jumped down the seven-foot wall. Unfortunately, as he leaped over the wall and landed, Coach Mock was standing there.

Eion said that Coach Mock promptly grabbed him gently and escorted him to the entrance, saying some words of wisdom that he can't remember.

"If I had been one second later," Eion remembered, "I would have probably landed right on him."

RONALD SEXTON

Well, the "words of wisdom" didn't take because Eion went right back and leaped the fence. He was never caught again and never paid a dime to get into Grainger Stadium.

Eion became one of the best-rounded athletes at Grainger High School. He matured quickly and, in the eighth grade, reached a height of six feet one inches. In 1952, Charles Lee, the junior varsity coach, put him on the JV team; and he was off and running. By the time he was a sophomore in 1954, he had reached the height of six feet four inches and Dad wanted to put him on the varsity. Eion resisted, believing that he would simply be practice fodder and sit on the beach most of the time. He pleaded with Coach Lee to intercede for him, knowing he would play more on the junior varsity. Coach Sexton, he said, relented; and he played on a junior varsity team that went undefeated (20–0). However, with two games left in the regular season, Coach Sexton had his way and elevated Eion to the varsity in time for the conference and state tournaments, although he admits he didn't play much and did not "letter." He became the starting center on the 1956 state championship basketball team and the 1957 team, Dad's last year. He was also a formidable defensive end on the Red Devil football team, and he played tennis alongside state champion tennis player Marshall Happer.

Eion graduated from Grainger High School in 1957. He earned ten varsity letters—four in football, two in basketball, and four in tennis. In his day, tennis was considered a minor sport. Marshall Happer would change that, at least in Kinston and in the state of North Carolina. Eion enrolled in North Carolina State University and earned a BS and MS degree in physics and nuclear engineering. He played tennis for NC State through his junior year.

In 1963 Eion went to California to work for North American Aviation, which later became Rockwell International. In 1967 he moved to T. R. W. Electronics and Defense Systems, where he remained for twenty-seven years. During his professional career, he worked on such projects as the Apollo moon mission, MX Peacekeeper program, Minuteman ICBM systems, Ronald Reagan's SDI program, and numerous satellite programs (military defense and commercial). He also participated as an experimenter in under-

RED DEVIL TALES

ground nuclear tests performed at the government's Nevada test site. When anyone asked him what he did for a living, Eion would facetiously respond, "Well, I could tell you, but then I would have to kill you." Upon his retirement, he became a semiprofessional chess player, as well as continuing to play tennis, until injuries forced him to lay that sport aside. Today, Eion loves to play chess and study Civil War history and quantum physics.

One of the Red Devils' biggest rivalries in basketball was the Phantoms of Greenville. Located in the same city as East Carolina College and directed by a fearless coach named Bo Farley, the Phantoms were always a challenge to beat, especially from 1955 to 1957. *The Free Press* noted that the Phantoms had their own version of the fast break, although Eion Faelten didn't remember it that way. Their version of the fast break, as he recalled, was Ike Riddick, Greenville's talented guard, just dribbling rapidly down the court.[1] Nevertheless, in 1956, they would give the Red Devils a run for their money. Greenville also had a talented center named Hal Edwards, who often dominated the boards and could make the difference in any contest. During the regular season, Kinston played this conference team twice and could meet them again in the conference tournament. In 1956 they did just that.

The first encounter was on the Red Devils' home court, Mock Gymnasium. Unlike most, if not all conference gyms, Mock Gymnasium was built to accommodate a sizable crowd of 2,500 and the court itself was regulation size. Built in 1951 at a cost of $211,000, it opened its doors in January of 1952.

Unfortunately, in 1956, the Red Devils lost the first game with Greenville 69–62 in Mock Gymnasium. It was déjà vu for the home team, who had lost to Greenville the year before. That had been their first conference loss since the new gym opened in 1952.[2] Greenville was a real thorn in the flesh.

The next meeting between the two rivals was in Greenville. The Greenville school had a substandard gym nicknamed the crackerbox, which the Kinston cagers considered to be the worst in the conference. The undersized building had a court that was not regulation size, and it was definitely not suited for the Red Devils' "run-and-

257

gun show." It was difficult to run the fast break in what the Red Devils called a midget court. They joked that it only took about three dribbles to get from one end to the other. Eion Faelten, who is six foot four, amusingly noted that if he was at the foul line, he could probably stretch out and touch the half-court line. On one side of the court were three or four rows of bleachers while the other side was standing room only. If a player lost control while running, he could have easily crashed into the wall. Most of the spectators were in a balcony that circled the gym, which was still standing room only. Unfortunately for the fans of Kinston, there was a quota for how many of them could enter the gym to watch the game. The rest had to stand outside the building, usually in the cold.

After the second meeting between the two teams that took place in Greenville's substandard facilities, the Kinston paper commented that "it was shameful to see the some two hundred fans outside the Greenville gymnasium during the game. The 'crackerbox' was jammed to its capacity and at 7 p.m. the doors were closed."[3] The game was one of the top prep games in the state, and Kinston fans were a little irate that the venue was not more accommodating. The East Carolina gym was available; but Greenville, having home court advantage, probably figured the best way to clip Kinston's fast break was to play on a court that worked against that offense. In preparation for the game, Dad held practice at Wheat Swamp and Contentnea schools, where the courts were similar. It paid off.[4]

Therefore, in spite of having to play on a second-rate court against a well coached and talented team, the Red Devils managed to edge out their opponents in the second contest 69–66. It was "nip and tuck" all night with the lead changing six times. By the end of the first half, the teams had battled to a tie (34–34). In the third quarter, the Red Devils managed to pull ahead, and by the quarter's end, held a 55–46 lead. Then, Hal Edwards, the Greenville center, began to find his range again; and with four minutes left in the game had brought the Phantoms to a 59–59 tie. Two reserves, Charlie Lewis and Billy Evans, were brought in to shore up the Red Devils' rebound strength. With 2 minutes and 35 seconds left in the game, Eion Faelten, Kinston's steady center, scored two free throws giving

RED DEVIL TALES

the Red Devils a 63–61 margin. The Red Devils nervously held a one-point lead (67–66) with 1 minute and 30 seconds to go when Poo Rochelle took a Greenville rebound and sent the ball game into a freeze. Eion was fouled with only 5 seconds remaining and from the free throw line hit both free throws for the final score, 69–66. It was the Phantoms' first defeat in three years on their home court. The Red Devils now shared the lead in the conference with Greenville, and the Kinston paper summed it up, "KINSTON FIGHTS UPHILL BATTLE; EION FAELTEN SINKS 'CLINCHER.'"[5] Poo Rochelle had the hot hand for the Red Devils with the top score of 24 points. Marshall Happer added 10 more.

At the end of the regular season of play, all seven teams in the conference participated in the conference tournament. The Northeastern Conference teams included Kinston, Greenville, Jacksonville, Elizabeth City, Roanoke Rapids, Washington, and New Bern. The teams' records determined their seeding at the tournament championship with the top team drawing a bye in the first round, which was given to Greenville.

In 1956 Kinston and Greenville were tied for first place at the end of the regular season. There was a conference ruling that the league winner and the tournament winner would meet in a one-game playoff for the right to enter the state tourney. Therefore, with Kinston and Greenville tied at the end of the regular season, the winner of the tournament would go to the state AA playoffs. If another team other than Kinston or Greenville had won the conference tournament, the situation would have been a little more complicated. If that had happened, Greenville and Kinston would have played and the winner of that game would play the tournament winner. Fortunately, that did not happen.[6]

Therefore, before the Red Devils could defend their title as last year's state champions, they had to win the conference tournament. Fortunately for Kinston, the tournament was being held at Memorial Gymnasium at East Carolina, a place that could accommodate all of the Kinston fans and the regulation court that could facilitate the fast break. Sure enough on February 25, the Red Devils and the Phantoms met for the tournament championship. Memorial

259

Gymnasium was filled to its capacity of 2,500. The Red Devils were scrappy and aggressive. "Moving the ball swiftly, they ripped the cords consistently…and took an early lead that was never relinquished."[7]

In the first 3 minutes of the game, the Red Devils jumped out to an early lead, 10–3. In the second quarter, Kinston began to pull away "as they hit from all angles" and it looked as if a rout was in the making with a half-time score of 33–25. In the second half, however, Greenville went on a streak and pulled the game to within four points, 47–43. Kinston seem to lose its shooting accuracy in the final minutes of the game as the Phantoms pulled within 2 points, but the Red Devils matched their opposition basket for basket as both clubs tallied 19 points in the final period; the Red Devils won the Northeastern Conference Tournament Championship, 76–72.[8]

Poo Rochelle and Bobby Stanley were named to the All-Tournament team selected by the coaches. In three games they scored 50 and 42 points, respectively. Greenville added two of its players, Hal Edwards and Ike Riddick.

Eion Faelten had the top score in the championship game with 21, knocking down 8 shots and making 5 out 6 from the foul line. In addition to this, he held Hal Edwards, the All-Tournament center, to one rebound in the first half. Eion said one disadvantage of being listed as a center was that he almost always played second fiddle to Hal Edwards, who was a great player. At any rate, now as Northeastern Conference champions, the Red Devils, were off to Enka to play for the State AA championship.

Enka is a small town west of Asheville in the western part of the state and nestled in the scenic Appalachian Mountains. The three-day tournament was held in early March, and there was still snow on the ground in Asheville. The snow combined with a bitter cold wind would keep some fans away. The Red Devils arrived in Ashville on Wednesday evening before Thursday's game against Myers Park. After checking into the Ashville-Biltmore Hotel, the team had a 45-minute practice session at a local high school gym. Early Thursday morning they worked briefly on backboard drills.[9]

In the state playoff of 1956, eight teams qualified to enter the tournament. Along with the Red Devils there were Mt. Airy, Roxboro,

RED DEVIL TALES

Myers Park, Clinton, Granite Falls, Sanford, and Hendersonville. Kinston's first game was against Myers Park of Charlotte.

The game began at 4:00 p.m. before a scant crowd of about two hundred. The trip from Kinston to Enka was about three hundred miles, and the weather was still in winter mode. In most tournament contests, it is the final games that draw the crowds. Nevertheless, there were several dozen Kinston fans on hand, including former Red Devil players George Whitfield and his roommate Cecil Gooding, who were now students at Lees-McRae College in Banner Elk, North Carolina.

The taller Myers Park team controlled the first quarter and held a slim lead until Bobby Stanley put one in the bucket, giving the Red Devils a one-point lead (17–16). Alley Hart made the final shot of the second quarter to give the Red Devils a slim 37–34 advantage. The Red Devils looked very sluggish and listless. This was the game where Dad felt that the starters were flat and not playing up to their potential and called the starting five to the bench to give them a stern lecture. Near the end of the first quarter, Coach Sexton called a time out. The starting five came in, and Coach Sexton looked at the boys with disgust and told them, "Boys, I don't know what you think you are doing out there, but you are not playing basketball. And let me tell you something. You see these boys over here on the bench. They work every day in practice just as hard as you do, but they don't get any of the credit. Now I'm telling you that if you do not start playing basketball, I am going to sit your butts on the bench and put these boys in the game because I know they want to play. I don't care if we lose by 25 points. I want players who hustle and want to win! You make the call. Now get back out there and show me that you can play basketball."

Well, it must have worked. In the second half, the Red Devils went on a roll, scoring 30 points in the third quarter while holding Myers Park to 18 points. By the end of the third quarter, the score was 67–52. However, in the fourth quarter and with only four minutes left, Myers Park put on a full-court press. But at game's end the Red Devils held their ground and won 86–79. All five starters were in double figures. Poo Rochelle held the high-score honor with 26.

Alley Hart pumped in 18 while Eion Faelten, Bobby Stanley, and Marshall Happer all had 14 each.

The next game was against Mt. Airy who were expected to be the team to beat since they were both big in size and experienced in tournament play. The big guns for Mt. Airy were a six-foot-six center named Jack Smith and a six-foot-four forward and center named Ken Norman. The serious half-time talk in the Myers Park game must have carried over to the next one against Mt. Airy because the Red Devils hammered the slightly favored Granite Bears.

Eion Faelten would have one of his best games against Mt. Airy. He ended the game with 25 points and managed to restrain Ken Norman in scoring and rebounding. He held Norman to 1 rebound in the first half and most of Norman's 23 points for the night came when Eion was on the bench. George Whitfield was in the audience that night and, being a meticulous record keeper, counted 21 rebounds from Eion. The paper also noticed the performance, "Eion Faelten, the tallest man in the winner's starting lineup, was the man that cracked the Mt. Airy defense in the first half and poured in 18 points in the initial two periods to provide the defending champs with an early lead."[10]

Four of the starting five scored in double figures that night with Poo Rochelle again having the big gun, shoving in 27 points, 18 of which came in the second half. Along with Eion's 25, Marshall Happer had 16 and Alley Hart had 15. At the end of the first half, the Red Devils' fast break had strapped the Granite Bears 57–38. Early in the fourth quarter, the starters were pulled and the bench cleared to give the first five a rest for the championship game the following night. The Red Devils had a comfortable lead, 90–68. As the starters came off the court to allow the reserves to finish the game, Eion sat by Coach Sexton. At one point Kinston had moved ahead by 27 points, but with the starters on the bench the reserves managed to add only two points. As the fourth quarter dragged on, Mount Airy began to close the gap and eventually came within ten points. With the reserves in the game, Ken Norman managed to get hot and scored 11 points in 3 minutes. Eion said Dad got very nervous and almost put the first team back in the game, but the final buzzer

RED DEVIL TALES

sounded to end the game with Kinston beating Mount Airy 92–82. If the starters had played a full game, there is little doubt that they would have broken 100. The 10-point difference at the end of the game didn't reflect the rout it really was.

The championship game was against the Sanford Yellow Jackets, coached by Bob Cook, a former N. C. State basketball standout. As the game got underway, the Red Devils struggled in the early minutes of the game, committing more fouls than usual and missing their first seven free throws, giving Sanford an 18–14 lead at the end of the first quarter. The score went back and forth in the second quarter, and at halftime, it was all even at 37–37. In the first minutes of the second half, the Red Devils quickly moved ahead 41–37 before the Yellow Jackets could score. But Jack Crutchfield, the Sanford forward, pumped in two baskets to tie the game. The lead switched hands several times after that until Kinston pulled ahead 54–48 by the end of the third quarter. The Red Devils, constantly running up and down the court with the fast break, finally began to have an effect on the Yellow Jackets. In the final quarter, the Red Devils would score 20 points to Sanford's 14. Russell Fasick, Sanford's six-foot-five center, was held to 14 points by Eion and the tight zone defense. In the last four minutes of the game with the score of 58–53, the Red Devils seemed to find their second wind. Rochelle and Faelten hit on successive baskets to increase the spread, and Kinston had its third state championship in basketball. The final score was 74–62.[11]

Poo Rochelle and Marshall Happer were named to the All-Tournament Team in the NCHSAA Class AA Championship Basketball Tournament. "Poo Rochelle was the only unanimous choice for the honor squad as he sparked the Grainger High School Red Devil team to its second successive State title. He tallied 77 points in three games for an average of 25.6 points per game. Happer shoved in 43 points from his guard position and performed well as the quarterback for Kinston's fast break offense."[12] Eion Faelten did his fair share, as well, contributing 49 points in the tournament.

Over one thousand fans were gathered, waiting to greet the returning champions back to Kinston. A host of students, school and town officials were on hand to congratulate the state champions, who were escorted into town and down Queen Street by the highway patrol and followed by hundreds of well wishers.[13]

If the 1956 semi-final game against Mt. Airy was one of Eion Faelten's best games, he laments that the next year's State semifinal tournament game against Clyde A., Erwin was one of his worst. It was Dad's last loss and maybe the hardest to swallow. He just hated to lose, especially this one. Poo Rochelle and Marshall Happer had graduated in 1956, and the starting five of the 1957 team were Eion Faelten at center, Bobby Stanley and Charlie Lewis as the forwards, and David Adkins and Alley Hart as guards. It was in many ways a dream team.

The Red Devils had just beaten one of the best teams in the tournament by one point. After that game, most picked the Red Devils to win it all. Alley Hart and Charlie Lewis got the headlines in the game against Hildebran, but Eion made his own contribution as the paper noted, "Eion Faelten dropped four straight free throws in the last four minutes to keep Kinston in the running. The Red Devil center was held to one field goal in the contest but he more than made up for it with 14 of 16 from the free throw line."[14]

The four seniors were talented enough to catch the eye of college scouts so each wanted the opportunity to demonstrate his abilities. Coach Everett Case of N. C. State was on hand at the state tournament and very interested in Eion, who the paper said, "showed the Wolfpack mentor plenty with his rebound work and accuracy from the free throw line."[15] Al Porter of Wake Forest was looking at Alley Hart, who had pumped in 20 points against Hildebran and 22 points against Clyde A. Erwin. Even junior Charlie Lewis was coveted by college scouts. Howard Porter of East Carolina was attending the tournament and talked about how much he would give to get Charlie Lewis.[16] David Adkins and Bobby Stanley were also being observed. David, along with Alley, had "impressed the crowds as the top two guards in the three-day classic."

Clyde A. Erwin was a rural school in the foothills of the Smoky Mountains in Buncombe County, near Hickory, North Carolina. They were not supposed to beat the Red Devils, who were favored by 15 points. N.C. State coach Everett Case watched the Red Devils

RED DEVIL TALES

beat Hildebran and predicted the Kinston team would win it all, but the Warriors of Clyde E. Erwin had a stellar night with their six-foot-six forward/center, Horace Medford, posting the highest score of 38 points. Their other forward, Jack Blazer, had 24 points for the night. Together the two players accounted for almost 75 percent of Erwin's score. It was definitely an off-night for the Red Devils defensively, and the Clyde A. Erwin team had their best game of the season. "Fans who packed the gymnasium Friday night to watch Kinston's highly publicized fast break saw the Red Devils operate Coach Sexton's offensive attack almost to perfection for the first half," the paper noted. "In the meantime, the Kinston team was apparently forgetting the game included (defense) and allowed underrated Erwin to score at will."[17] At one point during the game, Kinston held a 26–18 margin but the two Erwin forwards seemed to hit everything they threw up at the goal.

After the game, Coach Sexton's comment to the press was, "I never thought I would get beat by two men (Horace Medford and Jack Blazer). I tried every defense I know in an effort to stop the big boy from Erwin. He is a fine ball player." Then, with some frustration he added, "My boys did not think. The offense was up to par, but the defense was as poor as I have seen it all season."[18]

The normal defense the Red Devils ran was a Coach Sexton concoction, which Eion called a man-to-man zone, a sort of a hybrid between a pure zone and a man-to-man defense. The defense appeared to be a 2–3 zone, but each player guarded whoever was in his area man-to-man. If the opposing player left your area, you did not follow him. You guarded your area. This defense tried to utilize the best parts of a zone and man-to-man defense. Most teams seemed to get confused by it.

"Medford," Eion noted, "played like a center even though he was listed as a forward."

In addition to the team's poor defensive performance, their free throw shooting was also unusually off. "Failure to hit from the free throw line here cost the Red Devils the semifinals," the paper lamented.[19] The Red Devils went to the line 22 times and made only 12. That difference alone would have been enough to win the game.

265

RONALD SEXTON

Bobby Stanley was the Red Devils' high scorer against Clyde A. Erwin with 24.

With Eion, the problem started when he had four fouls called on him in the first quarter. However, operating with four fouls, Eion still dominated the boards with 17 rebounds against 11 for Medford.[20] After getting four fouls in the first quarter, Eion wondered why Coach Sexton left him in the game. Twenty-four years later at the 1981 reunion, Eion visited with Dad and asked him why he had left him in the game that night. Dad told him that he thought about pulling him but he looked down the bench at Roger Hobgood, Eion's six-foot-eight substitute and saw that he was as white as a sheet and shaking like a leaf. Dad thought it best just to leave Eion in the game. Eion managed to play the rest of the game without fouling out.

During the regular season, when the Red Devils were playing Washington, Eion was fouled at one point during the game and went to the free throw line to shoot. At the free throw line, the referee called out, "One and one." Eion somewhat startled looked at the referee and said, "But I was shooting," meaning he should be getting two shots regardless. The referee simply held up his hand and again said, "One and one." Eion, shaking his head, simply turned to shoot the foul shot, mumbling to himself, "But I was shooting." For that the referee threw him out of the game. As Dad and Eion visited in 1981, Dad also told Eion that the same referee that had thrown him out of the game against Washington was also one of the referees the night that the Red Devils were playing Clyde A. Erwin. Eion never made the connection. I suppose that, in the heat of a game, all referees look alike. Dad told Eion that he knew the Red Devils were in trouble when he recognized the same referee who had worked the Washington game.

The Red Devils, obviously devastated and disappointed that they had lost to Clyde A. Erwin, took out their frustrations in the consolation game by absolutely mauling East Mecklenburg High School of Charlotte 104–78. The Red Devils started off slow, as if still stunned by their loss to Clyde A. Erwin. At the end of the first quarter they were behind 19–18, and with one minute into the sec-

266

RED DEVIL TALES

ond quarter they were down ten points. Apparently coming to their senses, the Red Devils pulled it together and began to play like a championship team. By the end of the first half, they held a 46 to 39 lead. The Red Devils came out in the second half with fire in their eyes, scoring 26 points in the quarter and 32 points in the fourth. It was Amos Sexton's victory number 202, but in the dressing room after the game, the boys realized they had missed their opportunity. The paper noted, "The Red Devils shed a few tears in the dressing room after the game. They realized that the 104–78 victory over East Mecklenburg was anti-climatic to what they came to Sanford to accomplish."[21] It was Amos Sexton's last game as a coach.

Eion remembered the 1957 basketball team as a talented group of boys who had the potential to win it all, but it was also a very disappointing year since they failed to win a third straight title for Kinston and Coach Sexton. The team was not only incredibly talented, but they were highly competitive. The trouble was that at times they tended to compete against each other. Eion recalled the time during practice, two days before they were to play Washington for the second time near the end of the regular season, when things came to a head. Tempers flared during an intense scrimmage, and Coach Sexton immediately ended practice and called the starters into his office.

Near the end of the season there was some friction developing among the players as the play-offs loomed and competition became more intense. Bickering and irritation was becoming more noticeable, especially among the four seniors. They were doing a lot of trash talking, which for boys who grew up together competing on the playground and at Emma Webb Park was not unusual.

The tension was caused, in part, by having five starters who could shoot well and everyone wanted his time to shine. Basketball practices were both strenuous and intense-filled drills, scrimmages, and wind sprints. The boys came out of the dressing room with a few warm-up shots, layups, and free throws. But this was only a prelude of things to come. Then came the scrimmage. These scrimmages could be as intense and as competitive as a real game. They played to win even in a scrimmage. Tempers could flare. After a grueling scrim-

267

mage with tongues hanging out, the boys then had to run ten laps around the gym. When this was over, and they thought they could do no more, the dreaded wind sprints began. With Coach Sexton holding a stopwatch and blowing his whistle, the boys sprinted at full speed from one end of the court to the other. They stopped at the other end just long enough to turn around and get set to go back to the other end. The coach then blew his whistle again to signal another wind sprint back to the other end. This went on until the coach decided that the boys had enough. The actual games seemed like a break between practices.

It was during one of these scrimmages, toward the end of practice, that Eion went a little too far. Eion went up for a shot, and Roger Hobgood fouled him. In the process Roger almost broke Eion's thumb. Eion went ballistic, yelling and screaming at poor Roger who said he didn't mean to do it. Eion believes he may have even taken a swing at Roger. Coach Sexton immediately called off practice and called for the starting five to come to his office. They all paraded into the small room, and the coach closed the door. In no uncertain terms he told the team (Eion said, "Especially me") that if they couldn't settle down and start playing as a team he would bench them and play the reserves. Coach Sexton said he would no longer tolerate bad behavior, and if there was any repetition, the guilty party would be dismissed from the team. And he wasn't bluffing. Eion said it got his attention, and he felt like crawling in a hole.[22]

In the next game against Washington, Eion sported an improvised splint on his hand but the team played well and went on to win the final three games of the season. They ended the regular season with a winning streak of thirty games. From there the Red Devils won the Northeastern Conference Championship and then on to the state play-offs where disaster lurked in the semifinal game.

1956 Red Devils departing to Enka for the state championship.
Photo by George Denmark, Jr. Courtesy The Free Press

1956 Red Devils departing to Enka for the State
championship. Photo by George Denmark, Jr.
Courtesy the *Free Press*.
*Eion Faelten goes in for a lay up as
Marshall Happer looks on.*

*Bobby Stanley and Eion Faelten surround
Mount Airy player fighting for the rebound.*

22

CHARLIE LEWIS

In 1950 Charlie Lewis was eleven years old. That was also the year Little League baseball came to Kinston. Charlie remembered that kids from all over town descended on Emma Webb Park to try out for the teams. During the tryouts, players were put through a series of drills, like fielding, batting, and base running. Prospective coaches stood by, observed, made notes, and prepared for the draft, which was the selection process for choosing teams. The Little League would consist of four teams, each sponsored by a Kinston civic club: the Kiwanis, Lions, Rotary, and Civitan. Charlie was selected to play on the Rotary Club team. To his surprise, his coach was Amos Sexton. Charlie certainly knew of Amos Sexton, the head basketball coach of the Grainger High School Red Devils. The year 1950 was the year of the first state championship for the Red Devils in basketball under Coach Sexton's guidance. In 1951 he was coaching a Little League baseball team on the side. The boys were all eager just to play baseball, whoever the coach was, but having Amos Sexton, the Red Devil basketball coach, was special. Charlie can't remember exactly how many games they played that summer. It could have been eighteen or maybe twenty. What he does remember is that they were undefeated.[1]

"Now," Charlie recalled, "fast forward five years to the Grainger High School baseball team who lost the state championship to

Charlotte North Mecklenburg by only one run. That team had five starting players from that old Rotary team. Alley Hart was our best Rotary pitcher, but he had given up baseball in high school in order to concentrate on basketball. It seems to me that someone back in 1950 who watched a bunch of eleven-and twelve-year-old kids try out for a couple of days had an uncanny eye for talent."

That someone was Amos Sexton. Charlie said it was Coach Sexton who placed him in center field on the Little League team when he was only eleven, and he would play that position throughout his high school career.

In 1958 Paul Jones had replaced Amos Sexton as the head basketball coach, and it was Charlie's senior year. In a game against Elizabeth City Charlie scored 50 points, a record that has never been broken. When Charlie scored his 50th point, Paul Jones took him out of the game. There was still six minutes left on the clock. If Charlie had stayed in the game and if the game had been played by today's rules with longer quarters and the three-point shot, you can imagine what his total score would have been. Charlie was 23 for 32 from the floor for a shooting average of almost 72 percent. The Red Devils mauled the Yellow Jackets 104–49, with Charlie Lewis scoring more points than the entire Elizabeth City team.

When Charlie was a freshman, he was already a starter on the varsity baseball team. He played center field, of course; and in the very first game of the season, a ground ball was hit to him. He misplayed it, and it went right between his legs. Charlie remembered, "It should have been a routine play for me, field the ball and get it back into the infield. I must have thought I was a shortstop." He turned around to chase the ball down as it rapidly made its way to the center field fence. He finally caught up with the ball, picked it up, and turned around only to see the runner crossing the plate. "There I was, a fifteen-year-old freshman playing in my first varsity game, misplaying a routine ground ball, which ended up being a home run. My self-inflicted embarrassment had just begun. Coach Mock came out of the dugout, called time-out, and slowly walked out to center field. With my head down, I watched as he walked toward me. I thought he would never get there, and I wasn't sure I wanted him to."

273

When Coach Mock finally got to center field, he looked at Charlie and very calmly said, "Charles, haven't I taught you in practice how to field a ground ball?"

"Yes, sir."

"Well," he continued, "you're going to play center field for the rest of this year and for three more years after that. Now, don't let any more get through."

"This," Charlie remembered, "was vintage Frank Mock—calm, but to the point."

Charlie said that in the next four years playing center field, he never missed another ball.

In 1956 Charlie was a sophomore and a reserve guard on the Red Devil basketball team. He still got a lot of playing time and was considered vital to the squad as the *Free Press* noted after the last game of the season with the Greenville Phantoms: "Two reserve players, Billy Evans and Charlie Lewis, proved to be the difference for the Kinston team as they entered the ball game early in the first half and brought the Devil team back into contention."[2]

Kinston beat Greenville 69–66 on a final "clinching" pair of free throws by Eion Faelten.

Now with the regular season over, Coach Sexton scheduled one more game with the Wake Forest Freshmen in order to get the team ready for the state tournament. Earlier in the season, the Red Devils had lost in overtime to another college freshmen team, Atlantic Christian. These college freshmen teams were playing at a level that would challenge the Red Devils and help fine-tune their skills as they headed into the state play-offs.

For some reason on the day of the game with Wake Forest, Charlie decided he could take a day off so he skipped school. Charlie, Len Smith, and Bill Dawson got into Bill's old Ford Model A and went to New Bern for a day of fun and frolic. Charlie said, "To show you how dumb I was, I didn't figure on Coach Sexton seeing that I was on the absentee list at school, and then that he was going to call my house to find out what was wrong and see if I was going to play that night." Well, Coach Sexton did call his mother, and she told him he was supposed to be in school.

274

RED DEVIL TALES

Kinston lost that night in overtime, and looking over the newspaper account, sure enough, Charlie was not on the list. He watched the game from the stands. The headlines read, "DEAC FROSH DEFEAT RED DEVILS."[3] The paper noted that the Red Devils "could not match the superior rebound ability of the visitors." Rebounding was one of Charlie's strong areas.

Charlie knew he was going to catch hell come Monday. So on Monday, at practice, Charlie got dressed and hustled out on the court to start drills, hoping Coach Sexton would just get busy and forget about it. That didn't happen. Charlie said the coach blew the whistle and told the boys to start doing layups. He turned to Charlie and said, "Lewis, come over here." Charlie said he was petrified, and the coach was madder than a hornet, and he didn't know if he was going to go get hit or what. But he said he deserved every bit of whatever he had coming. "Coach Sexton was a great coach, and we respected him, but he was not necessarily warm and fuzzy, and I was about to get a good dose of what I deserved from Amos Sexton. To this day I have never had a lesson in life explained to me in such clear terms and with such enthusiasm as befell me on that day. He ripped me wide open, and I knew that I deserved it all. I had let my teammates and my coach down, not to mention my parents."

I asked Charlie if he could remember what Dad told him. "Well," he said, "as best I remember, he rattled off statements like 'What were you thinking? You let the team down! You know better than to do this sort of thing! Do you know what responsibility is?' And then I remember at one point he asked, 'And how many cigarettes did you smoke?'" Charlie said he was so confused and scared that he said the wrong thing, "I don't know, Coach. I wasn't counting. But I also remembered how that session ended. It was something like 'Now, that's the end of it. I hope you have learned something from this. Don't let it happen again. Now get out there and apologize to your teammates.' When it was all over, he repeated, 'Now that's the end of it. I will never mention it again.' And he didn't. As I left his office that day, I asked myself, 'How dumb can you be at seventeen?'"

Charlie said one day in civics class, which Coach Sexton was teaching, there was a boy in the class that would never speak up. He was sort of "mousy" and very shy. "Of course, your dad didn't have a 'mousey' bone in his body," Charlie noted. Coach called the boy up to the front of the room, took him to the window, and said, "You see that guy walking over there? Yell at him!" The boy finally did, and Charlie said Coach Sexton then told him, "See there, you can do it. Now go sit back down."

Charlie Lewis was just a freshman at the time of the famous bus incident, but he was on the bus. His version of events is a little different, actually, a lot different. They all agree that they were going to Elizabeth City. And everybody agrees that it was Darwin Williams and Robert Whaley who were kicked off the bus. There is disagreement about the third player. Of course, we now know it was Lane Ward. An additional fact that Charlie brought out was that both Robert and Darwin were sophomores and starters on the JV team and, furthermore, both players became All-State players. It is not very often that you have two players from the same team make All-State and also get kicked off the team bus. These guys weren't some third-string riffraff. Also, Charlie says they were all prohibited from playing cards period, not just playing cards and gambling. Coach Sexton knew that if there were cards involved there would be gambling. According to Charlie, they had come as far as Edenton when the boys got nailed. That's about a hundred miles from Kinston. It was about four or five o'clock in the afternoon. When the guys got their bags and exited the bus, Charlie said they asked Coach Sexton, "Coach, how are we going to get back?" Charlie said Coach Sexton told them, "I don't care. You can thumb a ride or catch a ride, or if you can't find a ride, we'll be coming back through around ten o'clock tonight and you can stand right here on this corner and we'll pick you up."

at the end of the game, we came back through and they were standing right there on that corner. Can you imagine what impression that made on a fifteen-year-old freshman like me?" Charlie reflected. "My God, if he would kick those guys off the bus, he would have probably sent me to Mars."

Okay, I give up. I am giving up history. I thought I could sort this out, but it just keeps getting more complicated. I did watch an

RED DEVIL TALES

episode on the Science Channel about parallel universes, black holes, and dark matter. Maybe that's got something to do with it. I just don't know. But this has got to be the most convoluted story I have ever tried to put together. And these guys were all eyewitnesses!

Lloyd Whitfield, who was a Red Devil that played on the 1949 basketball team and became a sports writer for the *Free Press*, recounted his own version of the bus incident in a 1957 article. The article appeared before the state play-offs in 1957 but before the Red Devils' loss to the East Carolina JV team. You would think that Lloyd would be more of an insider who should know what really happened. And this was only about four years after the incident, not fifty years later when memories do tend to fail and stories get embellished. This was Lloyd's newspaper spin on the event: "One year, two basketball players (nope, it was three) were getting out of hand (yeah, right, a hand of cards) on a bus trip to Elizabeth City. Coach Sexton stopped the bus, gave them bus fare (more like "fare-well, boys") back to Kinston and left them in Greenville (no, it was further than that) waiting for a bus to Kinston and with instructions to see Jack Horne (no again, it was Frank Mock). The two players were starters"[4]

Can you imagine his actually telling the story as it really happened? Or do you think he really knew the truth? Well, that's newspaper spin for you.

Charlie did contribute an addendum to the story. He said that at one of the Red Devil reunions back in the eighties, Dad was asked about the incident, and someone commented on how much trouble a coach would be in if he did that sort of thing today. And then Charlie asked Coach Sexton if he ever had any repercussions from the episode. Dad told Charlie that on Monday morning, when he came to school, Jack Horne, the principal, told him that there was a minister outside who wanted to see him about the Friday-night incident. Dad said that he wasn't looking forward to meeting this minister because he knew he was probably going to get chastised. The minister came in and introduced himself and then asked Amos about the incident and if he had kicked the boys off the bus. The coach told him yes he did. The minister then asked him if he had warned the boys not to do this, and again Dad told him yes he had. He had

277

told them many times. They all knew it. Dad said the minister then shook his hand and said, "Fine, we need more people like you in the world." Then he left.

Charlie said, "You will not find many boys who were not thankful that they grew up in Kinston when they did and had people like Amos Sexton, Frank Mock, Jack Horne, and people like that in our lives, because most of us needed a lot of guidance. I know I did."

The success of Grainger High School was a combination of many things. Like in the perfect recipe, there was a blending of the right ingredients. Grainger High School not only had great coaches, the school also had great teachers who left their mark on students. Charles sent me six typewritten pages of stories and reflections of his years as a Red Devil. Most of them are included somewhere in this work. But one story of a teacher who meant a lot to him is certainly worth telling. It is his "tribute to a special lady." He writes,

"High School athletes naturally look to their coaches for guidance. I was no exception, and my respect and devotion to Coach Mock, Coach Sexton, and Coach Jones was deeply rooted. There is another person in my past to whom I owe a great debt of gratitude. Her name is Gladys Sutton, and she was my geometry teacher at Grainger High. Her daughter Marie was my high school sweetheart, and I suppose Ma Sutton had a vested interest in me since she thought there was a chance I would possibly someday become her son-in-law. She was a kind and gracious lady, and we had a special relationship. She would do little things like "Come by the house tonight after the game. I'll bake a chocolate cake." I was very fond of this lady because of her acceptance and kindness toward me. She also knew what made me tick, and I want to relate the following story as an example:

"Ma Sutton always directed the senior class play. She had done it for years. This year's production was *The Return of Captain Kidd*, and she wanted me to play the role of Captain Kidd. I really didn't want to do it, and I told her so. Not one to accept rejection easily, she said, "Well, think about it. I'll check with you later." Well, I had already thought about it, and I still didn't want to do it. A few days passed, and she approached me again. "I need an answer. Are you going to do it or not?" "No, ma'am, I don't want to do it." She

RED DEVIL TALES

looked me straight in the eye and said, "I know why you don't want to do it. You can stand on the free throw line at the end of a close game and make the free throws necessary to clinch victory, but you don't have the courage to learn your lines and go on the stage and deliver them." She had hit my hot button. She had challenged me. I instantly told her I would be her Captain Kidd and, when the time came, I thoroughly enjoyed doing it. As a matter of fact, I received the Lion's Club Dramatics Trophy for my performance. Here was a lady who had probably never had a psychology class in her life, but who was an expert at the psychology of finding what drives a person to do what they don't want to do.

"Ma Sutton died in 1964 and is buried in the same cemetery as my parents. I often go to Kinston and place flowers on my parents' grave and I always place flowers on her grave as well, and I talk with her and thank her for all she did for me. She was a special lady."

In March of 1957, Dad's last year of coaching, the Red Devils were going for their third straight state championship. The Red Devils ended the regular season with a perfect winning record of 20–0 and a 32-game-winning streak against high school teams that reached back to the previous year. If this team had won the state championship in 1957, by many accounts, it probably would have been considered the best team of Coach Sexton's career, and arguably the best basketball squad in the history of Grainger High School. The talent was spread out evenly and deep. As Alley Hart noted earlier, "We were all good shooters, and everyone was a gunner." During the regular season the team had an 81-point average per game.[5] This was during the days when there were no three-point shots.

"Even the reserves are unbelievable," noted the *Free Press*. "The coach can close his eyes and pick any five of the 12 players on the bench and win. They are good rebounders, good shooters and good defensive men. They play alert basketball and run with the fast break all the time."[6] The Red Devils would enter the tournament with each of the starting five averaging in the double figures and a 47-percent accuracy from the floor for 20 games.[7]

The starting lineup for this 1957 team was guards David Adkins and Alley Hart, forwards Bobby Stanley and Charlie Lewis, and center Eion Faelten. Chubby Cummings, Gene Anderson, Jimmy Dail, John Laws, Fletch Somers, Roger Hobgood, Pat McLaren, James Brake, and Bill Dawson completed the roster. There were four seniors on the starting squad. Charlie Lewis was the junior.

The first game of the state tournament was against Hildebran. The game was close, but Kinston would edge out their opponent by one point. Hildebran was one of the better teams of the tournament, and this was the second year they had been knocked out of competition in the opening round by just one point. They were tall and ran the fast break like the Red Devils, averaging over 50 points per game and had a season record of 22–1. Their only loss was by one point.[8]

"ALLEY HART AND CHARLES LEWIS SPARK LOCALS IN 66–65 THRILLER," the paper delightfully reported. "The hearts of 1,200 fans fluttered like whirly-gigs in the Sanford gymnasium yesterday afternoon as the Grainger High School Red Devils opened defense of the N. C. High School Class AA state championship with a spine-tingling 66–65 victory over a towering Hildebran."[9]

It was a refreshing victory for the Red Devils after being humbled by the East Carolina freshman teams in a "warm-up" for the state tournament. Alley and Charlie were "the men of the hour" as the paper put it. Alley was the top scorer with twenty points and "dropped the winning bucket after he stole the ball with fifteen seconds left in the game."[10] With nine seconds left and Hildebran with the ball, Charlie "sneaked the dribble away from Charles Van Horn" and the Red Devils ran down the clock to win.

"The small gathering of Kinston fans," Lloyd Whitfield wrote, "could have kissed Charles Lewis when he stole the ball with less than 10 seconds and saved the day."[11]

On August 14, 2010, Charlie Lewis was inducted into the Kinston-Lenoir County Hall of Fame. That night, George Whitfield, as the master of ceremonies, introduced Charlie and listed his athletic accomplishments:

"He was a three-sport athlete, winning nine varsity letters. He was All-State in basketball and baseball. He was the first and only All-American basketball player in the history of Grainger High School. He was a cocaptain in football, basketball, and baseball. He

RED DEVIL TALES

played in the East-West All-Star Basketball game. As a senior he won the coveted O. L. Shackleford Award. He was a class officer for two years. He was president of the Varsity Club, and he is the only Red Devil to have ever played for the three Kinston-Lenoir County Hall of Fame coaches: Frank Mock, Amos Sexton, and Paul Jones. He went to East Carolina on a basketball scholarship and as a senior he was cocaptain of the team. As a college basketball player, Charlie was an All-Conference player, being recognized as an outstanding offensive player, leading scorer and received an MVP award. After college, he has had a successful career as teacher, coach, and administrator in North Carolina public schools. He served as the head basketball coach and assistant football coach at Rockingham High School from 1962–1966, and later head basketball coach and assistant football coach at Charles B. Aycock High School from 1966–1971. In 1970 he was selected by his fellow coaches to coach the annual East-West All-Star Game. At the time he was the youngest to ever coach the East team. From 1971 through 1976, he was principal at East Montgomery High School and in 1973 he was selected as Montgomery County's 'Outstanding Young Educator.' From 1976 until his retirement in 1991, he was principal at Clinton High School and two elementary schools with Clinton County Schools."[12]

According to one prominent athlete that I interviewed, there were many great athletes to come through Grainger High School over the years but the two most talented, well-rounded, and greatest he believed where Bryant Aldridge and Charlie Lewis. Both athletes excelled in all three sports. In fact, Bryant Aldridge and Charlie Lewis were the only athletes in the history of Grainger High School who were High School All-Americans.

1957 Starting Five: from left to right: David Adkins, Bobby Stanley, Eion Faelten, Charles Lewis and Alley Hart. Courtesy *The Free Press*.

Starting five retake at a 2009 Red Devil reunion at Morehead Beach, North Carolina. Courtesy of Charles Lewis' private collection.

23

COURTSIDE

If there is one person who is as much a "dyed in the wool Red Devil" as George Whitfield, it is Reid Parrot. Reid has probably been a part of every Red Devil reunion and social event since he graduated from high school in 1956. What I remember about Reid is that he is an eternal optimist, always has a infectious smile, and a good story to tell. George said that Reid is "the type of person that on your death bed you could be lying there, almost unconscious, and he could walk in and smile and tell you some story about Grainger High School, and I swear you would laugh."

Reid loved Amos Sexton, Frank Mock, and Charles Lee, who he remembered as being positive role models; and he says they all had a great influence on his life. These men were not only coaches, but also teachers who influenced more than just athletes. If you add, along with George and Reid, Amos Stroud, who heads up the monthly Red Devils and Friends Golf matches, and Marshall Happer's Red Devil website you have a cluster of old Red Devils who help keep the legacy alive.

Reid Parrot did not play basketball, but he was on the tennis team. Reid was also the scorekeeper at home games and the cofounder of the famous BBB club. He loved sports and wished he could have played every sport, but he said, "I was slow, nearsighted, and had

RED DEVIL TALES

asthma growing up." Yet he was a loyal fan and supporter of all Red Devil teams. And he played an important role from the sidelines.

He said, "I hauled a lot of water, furnished fresh towels at basketball tournaments, and wrote sports every year in high school for the school newspaper."[1] Reid still loves sports and, along with being a loyal Red Devil, he is a fierce East Carolina Pirate fan.

Reid was one of the first persons George encouraged me to visit on my first trip back to North Carolina. George made the arrangement for us to visit Reid and his wife Margaret in Rocky Mount where they now live. Reid and his wife were high school sweethearts. Margaret Allen was a freshman when Reid graduated in 1956.

Reid has been in education all his adult life. He taught in public schools in Wayne County and Lenoir County from 1960 to 1966. He was an instructor and administrator at Lenoir Community College in Kinston for three years. From 1969 to 1971 Reid was in graduate school at North Carolina State University. For eight years he served as a lobbyist for the North Carolina Community College Association. From 1980 until his retirement, he was president of Nash Community College in Rocky Mount.

One of the most enjoyable moments was watching George and Reid go through the picture album that I had put together. They went through every picture, laughing and reminiscing as they turned the pages of the past seeing if they could recall everyone's name.

Reid remembered Dad as a "rugged, plain spoken, ex-Marine who espoused middle class values and a strong Christian faith." He attended the same church in Kinston that we did, Queen Street United Methodist Church. He said he remembers that Mom and Dad sat in the balcony with three small boys, and as young boys we tended to leaned too close to the brass rail. He was always afraid that one of us was going to fall over into the congregation below.

The first time Reid ever met Amos Sexton was when his dad and the new coach went to milk cows on a Sunday afternoon. Reid's father, Jake, ran a hardware store in Kinston for years. Well, this "milk the cow" adventure took place not long after Dad had moved to Kinston. Reid was about ten years old. He said the owners of Carolina Dairies, the Edwards family, had just opened a dairy farm

285

on the Greenville Highway. As a part of a promotion, several men, among them Reid's dad and Amos Sexton, "engaged in milking cows the old-fashioned way," as Reid put it. Being very country themselves and familiar with this sort of thing, both men filled up their pails rather quickly. What impressed Reid so much is that Amos Sexton was still in his Sunday suit and just pushed back his coat sleeve to milk the cow.

Reid may not have had Amos Sexton as a coach, but he did have him as a teacher. In the ninth grade, Reid was in his health and physical education class. One class period in particular stands out. That was when Coach Sexton, in his own Alabama country-boy way, explained how a man had surgery and became a woman named Christine Jorgensen. Reid said he would spare me the details, but the class got the message.

Reid's brother Donald also had Amos Sexton as a teacher. He said Coach Sexton stepped out of his health class one day for a few minutes with explicit instructions to the students to work on a class assignment. It wasn't long before the class felt the freedom of no adult in the room and began to become a little rowdy. In order to cover themselves they had posted a fellow student, Mike "the Pelican" Sparrow (everybody had a nickname), to stand outside the door to be the lookout and warn the class when Coach Sexton started to come back down the hall from the teacher's lounge.

vidently, the sounds of a "class gone wild" permeated into the teacher's lounge. All of the rooms on the first floor had huge windows that allowed one to climb out of one room and into another. So, instead of coming back down the hall, Coach Sexton climbed out the window of the teacher's lounge, crept down the ledge, and climbed into the classroom whereupon civility returned to the classroom. However, Pelican, unaware of the teacher's return, was still at his post, loyal to the end. Donald said the look on poor Pelican's face was priceless when Coach Sexton slipped up behind him and tapped him on the shoulder. Pelican spent the rest of his recess period that week picking up paper on the playground and mopping the gym floor.

RED DEVIL TALES

Reid remembered Dad as a natural salesman and motivator, which was certainly a plus when the Red Devils needed a new bus. It was in 1953 when Coach Sexton had his own radio show and playing country music when he met another radio personality Carl Caudill, and together they led a drive to buy a new Red Devil athletic team bus. Funds were raised by interested Red Devil citizens. The bus was finally delivered on Tuesday, January 12, 1954. The *Free Press* took a picture of the new bus in front of Mock Gymnasium showing H. J. Hearn handing the keys to Dad. In the background are Carl Caudill, Jake West Jr., Coach Mock, Coach Lee, Ray Barbre, and Tom Hewitt. The bus seated thirty-three plus the driver in "blue leatherette seats" and cost a whopping $5,376. Reid noted that there was a great deal of pride by all the Red Devil faithful when "the shiny red-and-white Red Devil bus arrived."

Dad mentioned the bus at the 1981 reunion, and he said he was determined that they were going to take care of it. He sternly warned the players that there would be no "horsing around" or jumping up and down in the back of the bus. The players were going to act like gentleman. Yeah, right. Well, Dad said that the next year he had a large rearview mirror installed so he could keep an eye on the boys in the back.

On one road trip in December of 1954, the team was coming back from playing Rocky Mount. It was a cold night, and it was sleeting. Dad said he heard some commotion in the back and switched on the inside lights just as Robert Whaley was falling into his seat. He stopped the bus along the side of the road and yelled, "Robert, get your bags and come up here." Robert slowly started toward the front of the bus with tears coming out of his eyes because he feared Dad was going to throw him off the bus in the cold sleeting weather. He had been thrown off the previous year, so he was sure this was going happen again. Apparently, he didn't get thrown off.

The first time I met Reid Parrot was in 1981 at the special appreciation banquet held for Dad. The occasion was organized by some of his former players, mainly George Whitfield. Ironically enough, it was held in the old Grainger High School cafeteria. The night before everyone had met had Walnut Creek Country Club for a social gathering. The next morning, Saturday, they all played golf together. My younger brother Don and I toured Kinston and took in some of the local sights. Since Reid was the MC for this event, this is probably the best place to revisit that night when many of Dad's players from his nine years of coaching were together for this reunion. There was a broad representation of friends and colleagues who came. Among the players, there were fellow coaches, teachers, ex-cheerleaders, school administrators, and even an ex-referee and a sports broadcaster. It was a special night for Dad, who had been away from coaching for nearly twenty-five years.

The format for the night was for players from each year, starting with 1949, to come forward to speak. Listening to the audio recording from that night now seems so surreal. And listening to Dad's voice and the voices of so many who have since passed on make the audio recording priceless. You hear the voices of former Principal Jack Horne, former superintendent of education Jean Booth, and players like Darwin Williams, and former coach Charles Lee were all there. The first thing on the program was Reid leading everyone in the old Kinston Fight Song. But first they made Dad put on his old red vest and red socks, which he wore religiously at every ballgame. This was his "rabbit's foot" for good luck. Well, with no accompaniment, they all struggled through the fight song but there were many teary-eyed Red Devils remembering a great era.

> Fight, Kinston High School,
> Cheer down the field,
> Come on, Red Devils
> Out to beat the foe—rah, rah, rah!
> Faithful, ever loyal
> Deepen our fame;
> O Kinston High School
> We love thy name.

Following this, the invocation was given by Rev. Jimmy Miller. His words were aptly chosen and seem to capture some of Dad's core values as a coach. He said, "We come tonight from many places

RED DEVIL TALES

to honor Amos Sexton who we have known as a successful coach, teacher, and friend, who has taught us love of athletic competition, a desire to excel, the importance of teamwork, a willingness to be disciplined, and, above all, has shown us an exemplary life. We rejoice in the way relationships such as this have enriched our lives. Our hearts are sad as we remember those of this fellowship who have died in the intervening years: Frank Mock, Lewis McAvery, Buddy Potter, and Lane Ward. May their memory inspire this occasion. Bless all of those who are gathered here, and this food which is a symbol of the bounty of your goodness to us."

After the meal, the program continued with Reid asking each class, starting with 1949, to stand and introduce themselves. As I listened to the recording, I heard the voices of those who played such an important part in winning games and championships. The names did not mean much to me at the time, but now that I have met and spoken to many of these players and understand the significance of these years, listening to their comments on tape is very meaningful and even nostalgic. I was there that night over thirty years ago, but I never really understood nor appreciated at that time his years as a coach. I believe Dad wanted us to be at this reunion in order for us to see the life he and Mom lived in Kinston. He knew we were too young to remember that part of our family history. I certainly have come to new level of understanding and appreciation for what he accomplished, and I am overwhelmed by the expressions of love and respect that come from men who are now in their seventies and still have such affection and show such gratitude for this man.

I listened to the comments made by his players or his colleagues, some who are no longer with us, and I am thankful someone recorded these speeches that night. That night I was just an observer, never really briefed on the history of those times nor introduced to the players. This was Dad's night, and I was just happy to be there. He was busy renewing old friendships and catching up on old times. I don't think Dad realized that it would take more than a casual encounter for me to come to a place where I would understand his life as a coach, but now I do, and I am glad that I have made this journey.

After all the players and some cheerleaders in the audience had introduced themselves, it was time for a parade of individuals to come forward to the podium and say something to or about Dad. It was both a friendly roast and meaningful tribute to Dad. There was a lot of laughter, as well as words of appreciation for Amos Sexton. The first person up was former superintendent of education Jean Booth, followed by former principal John H. Horne, then the Doug Bruton, Graham Phillips, Red McDaniel, Frasier Bruton, Bryant Aldridge, Ray Barbre, Jerry Kanter, Bobby Stanley, Pedro Brinkley, Bert Saville, Darwin Williams, Lee Abbott Robert Whaley, Poo Rochelle, Alley Hart, Charlie Lewis, Mary Lou, and George Whitfield, then finally Coach Amos Sexton.

It was a night to remember, and I know how much it meant to Dad.

Twenty seven years after this event, I was making my way around North Carolina interviewing many of these players and many others. Reid was the first person I visited with in 2008. From Rocky Mount, George and I traveled to Wilmington to see Alley Hart and Bobby Hodges. We met Alley at Whitey's Restaurant and later met with Bobby at the Y. M. C. A.

After visiting with Alley Hart and Bobby Hodges, George, and I went to meet with Talmage Jones. Talmage is now a lawyer who resides in Wilmington. As a youngster, Talmage played Little League sports, but did not participate in any sports in high school. However, he followed athletics closely and knew a lot about the game. His observations about Dad's teams and various players were well thought out and interesting. Like any good lawyer, he was analytical and prepared.

Talmage graduated from Grainger High School in 1957. He lost his mother at a young age, and as a result, he was raised by his sister Barbara Ann and her husband Jim Hartis. Jim Hartis and his wife were also good friends with Mom and Dad and, of course, loyal Red Devil fans. In April of 2007 at the Hall of Fame Induction ceremony, I remembered as I made my way through the crowd a man coming up to me and introducing himself as Jim Hartis. He told me that he was the man who had given us Rebbie. It took me a moment

RED DEVIL TALES

to realized that he was talking about a dog we called Rebel. Rebel was a golden-colored boxer that we kept as a pet for many years and have many fond memories of as a family pet. I can still remember the first day Dad brought Rebel home. I was absolutely terrified as a three-or-four-year-old (can't exactly remember) and distinctly remember crawling on the top bunk bed and crying as if I had just been attacked by a bear. A boxer does look a little more intimidating than most dogs, but they make great pets. They are very friendly and loyal. Dad liked to tell the story of how Rebel probably saved my life at the beach.

One morning while he and Mother were asleep, Edison and I had made our way out to the beach. Dad was awakened by our laughter, and as he looked outside the window, Rebel was grabbing us by the seat of our pants and pulling us away from the water. For us, it must have been a game. And every time we tried to run into the water, Rebel would run and grab us by our pants and pull us back away from the water. Dad believed that if it had not been for Rebel, I probably would have drowned.

Growing up in the Hartis home put Talmage in a unique position to witness Dad in a more "out of school" setting. He shared some of his recollections as an outside observer. His first memories are of Emma Webb Park and seeing guys playing basketball even in the summertime when it was over ninety degrees. He said he remembers people like Vernon Harris out there in the middle of July playing basketball in a part of the country where no one generally picked up a basketball until after football season. Emma Webb Park had basketball goals even though the court was dirty. People played year round, which helped turn Kinston into "the basketball capital of North Carolina." Talmage said he will never forget the time when Kinston beat Raleigh or when Kinston beat New Hanover, who claimed to be the number one basketball power in North Carolina. "Oh, yeah," George remembered, and with some well-deserved pride, he said, "I threw in the winning shot against Raleigh-Broughton with only one second left on the clock."

Talmage said the first time he saw the Red Devils play basketball was in the late forties when they were playing in the old gymnasium. Talmage said at the time he wasn't that interested in seeing the Red Devils but his brother-in-law encouraged him to come along. He said as he sat in the stand "all of sudden these Supermen started to come out onto the court." Talmage was only about nine years old at the time, and he said these men looked like giants, They came out in their bright-red warm-up jackets which had flaps on the back that sort of looked like capes. Talmage said Dad had a team that every coach in North Carolina would have given their eye teeth to have. This was probably Dad's first year, and the 1948-49 team with Bobby Hodges and Doug Bruton and the like. Talmage went on to say that guys like Hodges and Bruton he thought as a nine-year-old were made out of "different stuff" than ordinary people. "And I guess to some extent, they were," he said. "Bobby Hodges went on to college and made Little All-American in two sports: football and basketball."

Talmage said the next thing he remembers was going with his brother-in-law to see the Red Devils play basketball at Stallings Air Force Base,[2] the year Kinston was building a new gymnasium. He followed this team well, he remembered, since Jim Hartis worked for a man named Charlie Wickham who had a son who was on the team that year. This is the team, Talmage remembers, that broke his heart. "This was the only team of your dad's," he recalled, "that did not win the conference championship." Unfortunately, that's probably how they are remembered. He said he was there the night that it happened in Greenville. Kinston had a one-point lead going into the final seconds of the game against the Washington Pam-Packs, and a guy name Dick Cherry of Washington threw up a "Hail Mary" shot from half-court and banked it in. Talmage said he cried all the way back home. Dick Cherry would go on to play football at East Carolina (1952–1956) and as a quarterback made first team Little All-American.

Talmage remembered that Dad gave a little speech in the school auditorium before he retired from coaching, saying, "Some people think that I am leaving because I believe 'the well is running dry.' Pay no attention to that. I see what's coming, and I can win with what's coming. I have no doubt about it, but I just can't pass up this opportunity that's come my way." In fact, the next year after Dad left,

RED DEVIL TALES

the Red Devils went to the state championship game against Tri-City under Paul Jones, and lost it in the last second.

Talmage turned to me and said, "Well, I guess they have told you how much energy your daddy had. You couldn't wear him out." I laughed and said, "Oh yeah, I remember that too." Then I factiously added, "Today, they probably would have tried to put him on some kind of medication for his hyperactivity, but he wouldn't have taken it." At one time he had a radio show on WLAS that started a 5:30 a.m. and went to about 7:30 a.m. in the morning. Then he had to go to school. He sold encyclopedias at night, sold pots and pans, and, at one time, even sold shrubbery and umpired semi-pro baseball games. He did anything to put food on the table for his family. He sold anything that moved. If he could make a profit, he would sell it. And Talmage added, "The man couldn't sit on his ass—he had to work."

Talmage went on to say that he saw a side to Dad that did surprise him one day. He had never played any sports under Dad, so he said he couldn't speak about how he was on the court or on the field, but he figure being an ex-Marine and being a line coach, he had to be pretty tough. He had just not seen that side of him until one day before school started several guys sitting on a car saw Coach Sexton coming across the parking lot. One of the boys was challenged to call Coach Sexton by his first name. The boy yells out "How ya doing, Amos?" Talmage said he was in the seventh grade and Dad was at the height of his productivity and he was a radio personality. This kid was not an athlete or on any of the teams, but he was probably thinking that this was Amos Sexton of the "Amos Sexton Show" and "the man about town." Talmage said Dad walked over to the car and grabbed this boy by the hair of his head, pulled him off the car, and sternly warned, "Don't you ever call me Amos again. You call me Coach Sexton, or you don't called me nothing." About eight or ten other boys witnessed that incident, and Talmage said, "I can guarantee you that from then on, no one ever addressed him except as Coach Sexton."

I could tell Talmage was student of the game and remembered a lot. He was sort of like an ESPN analysis. He remembered one occasion when Mom and Dad were over visiting Jim and Barbara

293

Anne one Sunday afternoon, the conversation turned to basketball. Talmage said he became like a "fly on the wall" because Dad started talking about his team and assessing some of the players. He believed that out of all of his boys on the team either Charlie Lewis or Bobby Stanley had the most potential to go on to the next level. He thought that maybe Alley Hart had leveled off. He said that Alley had been playing for so long he did not think he would get any better.

"Amos," Talmage said, "underestimated Alley's potential."

Alley Hart was the one who went on and did well at Wake Forest. Talmage said Alley began to evolve to a higher level of play in the later part of the 1957 season. He had perfected his jump shot, getting more lift whereas in his junior year, Talmage noted, he had sort of a push shot like Darwin Williams.

Talmage said Darwin was a lot like Alley Hart in that he was a "gym rat" who probably had been playing midget basketball since he was in the second grade. He was one of those boys with great leadership ability, a tremendous ball handler, and had the guts of a "burglar." When it was all on the line, Darwin could do it. He played a game in Rocky Mount one night against Greenville for the right to see who was going to the state championship. Greenville had one of the best teams in the state at that time. Darwin started coming down the court in the fourth quarter with the game on the line, and he was shooting like ole Bob Cousy[3] and just stripping the net. He and Robert Whaley were on that team. They called Robert, Sunset Carson because he was good-looking like the movie star who was popular at the time. Darwin could flat put on a show with his ball handling. In those days you could freeze the ball and the other team would have to come get you. Nobody could get Kinston when Darwin Williams and Marshall Happer were playing guards with Robert Whaley as a forward.

Both Darwin and Robert ended up playing at Atlantic Christian College. Talmage said he went to see them play one time when they were sophomores and playing the Wolfpack of N. C. State. Talmage was a freshman at NC State at the time. Not to say that either one of them shouldn't have been playing in the ACC. They were borderline.

RED DEVIL TALES

Robert wasn't big enough, and Darwin probably wasn't fast enough, but the thing that disappointed me was that they were out of shape.

"I know your dad would have like to have beaten Tri-City just one time," Talmage lamented. "If he had stayed just one more year, I think he would have done it. With him at the helm, I think we would have beat Tri-City in that final game in 1958."

The game Talmage is referring to is the 1958 basketball team. It was the year after Dad left, and it was Paul Jones' first year. The team struggled through the regular season with a dismal ten wins to nine losses. When it came conference tournament time, no one expected Kinston to get past the first round. Kinston won the tournament and advanced to the state playoff's final game only to lose to Tri-City by four points. Their record of 15–10 does not look that great in the record books, but the team showed a lot of courage in the playoffs and almost pulled it off.

But regarding Tri-City, Talmage continued, "He lost to them bad one time"

George chimed in and added, "Yeah, we lost to them bad when I was playing. They beat us bad. They had three guys over six foot six."

"That's right," Talmage recalled. "They had Roy Searsey and Nick Nichols. I mean that was just too much."

George remembered a road trip to Elizabeth City, which was a long drive from Kinston. Cecil Ray Gooding's family were raising some chickens in their backyard, and the night before, a dog had raided the coop and killed about thirty-eight of them. Well, some of the boys on the team that year heard about the tragic mishap, and on their way to play Elizabeth City decided to write a poem in memory of the chickens. Jerry William got in the back of the bus and came up with this poem: Pedro Jerry Williams, Bobby Faulkner, Mickey Hill, "One bright and sunny day, in the home of Cecil Ray, thirty-eight running mad dogs, pounced upon their prey, thirty-eight innocent hens while roosting in their pens fell victims of a slaughter mad, made the Gooding family sad."

George said, "It made Cecil so mad I thought he was going to beat the crap out of all of us."

I asked Talmage if he remembered any stories about the road trips.

He said there was only one story that he was told about and that was about Lee Abbott. "Lee was very afraid of the dark and ghost and the like," he said. "And your daddy would not drop him off at his house but at Emma Webb Park, which was close to his house."

George laughed and finished the story, "Yeah, that's right, and Coach Sexton would stop the bus and say, 'All right, Lee, get your bag.' And Lee would get off that bus and run as fast as he could to his house. That boy would be in his bed before Coach was in second gear. Your dad knew he was scared, and he always pulled that stunt on him. I think your dad got a kick out of it, seeing Lee frantically run through the dark to avoid the ghost and the goblins."

But Talmage noted that Lee was a great athlete. He ended up playing second base at Wake Forest on the National Championship baseball team along with two other Kinston Red Devils: Buck Fichter, a pitcher, and Tommy Cole, who played third base. This was the only time Wake Forrest or any Atlantic Coast team went to Omaha, Nebraska, and won the College World Series. The year was 1955.

I asked Talmage which team in his opinion was the best one Dad had ever coached. Out of nine years there were three state championship teams and eight out of nine had been Northeast Conference champions. He agreed with Alley Hart in selecting the 1957 team that fell short of winning the state championship. That was the team that was undefeated and no one before tournament time had given them a close game. The team had not really been tested. For that reason Dad arranged for the team to play the jayvees of East Carolina College. The Red Devils got beat with East Carolina, handing the Red Devils their biggest loss in fifteen years. Talmage said your Dad wanted them to get knocked around. They needed it, and he thought the loss got their attention. Talmage said he heard Dad tell Jimmy Hartis that one day.

That was the game where they got beat by Clyde A. Erwin High School. Clyde A. Erwin had a player named Horace Medford, a six-foot-six forward who scored thirty-eight points that night. They got hot and couldn't miss. George added that Kinston was playing a 2–3

RED DEVIL TALES

zone. Eion Faelten said the 2–3 zone was a hybrid man-to-man zone that was Coach Sexton's invention. He went on the say, "Medford posted up on the foul line, and they got the ball to him, and he could have shot the ball from anywhere, and it would have gone in. He made hook shots from the foul line, and it looked like he wasn't even looking at the basket, and it would go in. He made jump shots. He took us down low and would scoop it in and make a layup. After we fouled him a couple of times, we started playing him soft but he would shoot it from anywhere and it would go in. He scored thirty-eight points that night, and nobody had ever done that against Kinston. It was unreal. He went on to play college ball and did well, but that night he beat us."

Talmage noted, "The year before Kinston had played Hildebrand who had a six-foot-four forward named Art Whisnant, and they were lucky to beat that team. That was a close game. Whisnant went on to play forward for the South Carolina Gamecocks and from there played for the Los Angeles Lakers. He was a great player. He was all ACC when he played at South Carolina. They called him Elvis because of the way he combed his hair.[4]

Talmage said he had talked to Eion Faelten several times about that game and asked him, "How in the hell did you all get beat by Clyde A. Erwin?" Well, Eion, who was the center in that game, told him that he had two fouls made within the first two minutes and before the end of the first quarter he had four fouls. So, basically, that took Eion out of the game and they did not have anyone to step up and face Horace Medford. The officiating was questionable, which in any game can certainly make a difference.

Well, that is interesting because I recall reading a comment by Lloyd Whitfield in the *Free Press* who said, "There was a lot of complaining at Sanford during the three-day North Carolina High School AA state tournament, especially on the part of eastern coaches, over the officiating. To begin with, the representative coaches in the tournament were not allowed to choose four officials for the tournament." Whitfield went on to say that "It was apparent that the officiating was not the best available. One fan suggested that referees from the higher bracket such as the Atlantic Coast Conference should be used for state championships."

After the consolation game when the Red Devils slaughtered East Mecklenburg High School 104–78, Dad's comment was, "My only regret is that we were not in the finals. The way our boys played tonight there would not have been much question who the state champion would be. We played below par in the Thursday afternoon match and were helpless on defense Friday night. We had four seniors on the court tonight (Saturday) who are top ball players in my book. They had a lot of guts to come from behind the way they did…All of them gave their maximum Saturday night, and I think it s a wonderful thing the way they played after the letdown Friday."[5]

The paper's final comment on the game was that "The Red Devils shed a few tears in the dressing room after the game. They realized that the 104–78 victory over East Mecklenburg was anticlimatic to what they came to Sanford to accomplish."[6] The talent was there, but it just was not in the cards. They would have been the team to make it three in row for Kinston and probably would have been enshrined as the best team ever in the annals of Red Devil history.

Now it was time to look through the Red Devil album, although most visits began with viewing the book. George is like a Red Devil encyclopedia, and his mind is like a warehouse of Red Devil names and facts. So when George was with me he took the album and walked through the photos. It was always fun to watch.

As Talmage opened the album and turned to the first page, George began, "Now there is Coach Sexton when he played at East Carolina, and look, here he is sitting among all of his championship trophies." Coming to the first team-photo George began pointing to each player from the forty-eight basketball team and rattled off the names, "Okay, this is Doug Bruton, Zollie Collins, Vince Jones, Fred Williams, Bobby Hodges, Charlie Larkin, Buddy Turner, Joe Aldridge, Robert Abbott, Pee-Wee Whitfield, P. A. Cameron (that's the Cameron sisters' brother), Frank Seville, Bill Faye, and Bucky Carter." Pointing to the next photo, he continued, "All right, here is the forty-nine state championship baseball team: Jackie Hudson, Carroll Dubois, Vincent Jones, Zollie Collins, Joe Whaley, Bobby

RED DEVIL TALES

Horton, Bill Dixon, Jimmy Byrd, Red McDaniel, Dick Tyndall, Joe Aldridge, Doug Bruton, Bobby 'Bowlegs' Grady, Fred Evans, Fred Williams, and Bill Cole."

With every picture George could list the names and give a running commentary on the players and team highlights. Then he saw a picture of an early football photo taken during a game. "Look here, that's when they wore those old helmets with no face guards. There is Bobby Hodges, and there's Jimmy Byrd. I don't know who that is. It looks like they are playing Elizabeth City. Then this had to be about the '46 or '47 team. Look how young Hodges looks back then. There's John Langely, Sterling Gates, Paul Bennett. Both these guys became famous doctors." He continued, "There is R. A. Phillips, Vince Jones, Zollie Collins, Cecil Roberts, but I cannot picture who that boy is. Probably Vince Jones could tell us, but I don't know who that guy is.

"All right now, here's one of an All-Tournament team. There is Sonny Russel. You remember him? There are John Langley, Paul Bennett, Sterling Gates, and..." Looking bewildered, he said, "I don't know who that is. He looks like he could be from the Pam-Pack. But there are three Kinston boys right there who were on the All-Tournament team."

He continued to peruse another picture. "There's Bill Faye." Then George, looking surprised, said, "And there is Bo Farley,"

"How about that?" Talmage inserted.

"There is Howard Porter," George continued. "Okay, there is the '49 team: Zollie Collins, Fred Williams, Bobby Hodges, Doug Bruton, Bryant Aldridge, and Joe Whaley. Okay, now this one is at some banquet. There's old Pea-Head Walker. There is Mr. Mock and Horace Ipock, Tommy Cole and Carroll Dubois. They must have won some football award." He looked at another picture. "That is the first team he coached. Here is a picture of Coach Sexton's first East-West All-Star Game. There's Graham Phillips. Remember Floyd Proach from down at Camp LeJeune. He's the one Everett Case liked so much. That is Cecil Heath from Greenville. Okay now, this boy was a Thornton from Raleigh and also a Peebles from Raleigh. Albert Long is from Durham, but I don't know where these other boys are from. There's a picture of the 1950 team after the state champion-ship: Charlie Wickham, Joe Whaley, Doug Bruton, Bobby Hodges, Sherrill Williams, Byrant Aldridge, Red McDaniel, Amos Stroud, Bucky Carter, Charlie Brand, and I think that is Jimmy Tyler."

They come to a picture of the 1953 team, and George sighed with grief as he realized how many players are no longer living. "There is a picture when Darwin played. God knows, look at the boys that are gone: Darwin Williams, John Carter, Bill Tripp...three, four, five. Five of the ten players are gone."

George continued, "All right, here is the 1955 championship team."

Talmage intervened with a comment, "Your dad always liked John Carter. He thought a lot of him. He told my brother-in-law (Jim Hartis) that having John out on the court was like having a coach out there. He stays cool, and he is a good thinker. He knows how to think a good basketball game."

George, still looking down at the album, lamented, "Look at this, Dempsey Hodges gone. Darwin Williams gone." He pointed. "Gone, gone, gone."

It was a typical reaction as I showed each former player the album I put together. You could see both joy and sadness as they reflected on the years of their youth.

Edison (a month before his third birthday) featured in the local newspaper as being a familiar figure around Red Devil practices (Courtesy of the *Free Press*, Feb. 28, 1953).

24

BETWEEN THE CHAMPIONSHIPS

It is unfortunate but just the reality of life that we tend to remember and honor only the champions and those who win the final game. In the nine years that Amos Sexton coached, it is the championship teams that are remembered and honored. The 1950, 1955, and the 1956 championship teams have carved out a special place in our memories, and well they should. But many times, at the end of the day, the only thing that separates immortality from anonymity is a last second "Hail-Mary" bank shot that just happens to go in. Some teams are so evenly matched one could just flip a coin to determine the winner. Or a good team can have a bad night, and a mediocre team can play above their "pay-grade." You just never know. The variables are endless. Even so, any one of the teams that did not win the state championship during Coach Sexton's tenure could have with a little luck.

Between the first state championship team (1950) and second state championship team (1955), there were, nevertheless, four good teams with talented players. All had winning records.

The 1951 team had the personnel and the talent to win a championship similar to what Alley Hart had said concerning the team of 1957. This team included such outstanding athletes such as Bryant Aldridge, Tommy Cole, Graham Philips, and Charlie Wickham. Jerry

RED DEVIL TALES

Trott, Jimmy Tyler, Lee Abbott, Gary Scarboro, Jerry Williams, Amos Stroud, Kenneth Anderson, and Frazier Bruton completed the team roster. This team won the Northeastern Conference Championship, the regional play-offs and advanced to the state finals only to lose to their arch state rivals Hanes of Winston-Salem, 35–31.

The 1952 team had a winning record 19–8, but in Amos Sexton's nine-year run, this was his least successful team, at least on paper. Nevertheless, Talmage Jones thought that the 1952 team was actually better than the 1953 team, who won the conference title. He remembered that the '53 team had a strong opponent in Roanoke Rapids. But, he said, Kinston got lucky and was able to play the conference tournament on their home court. The 1952 team started out on the wrong foot with four straight out-of-town losses: Wilson, Raleigh, Wilmington, and Goldsboro. Their first home game was a win against Goldsboro that started them on a five-game winning streak before losing number 5 at the hands of Roanoke Rapids. The 1952 Red Devils bounced back and seemed to come together as a team taking the next eight victories. However, their momentum was broken in a nail-biting contest against the Washington Pam-pac losing by only one point (65–64). In the final conference game of the season, the Greenville Phantoms got their revenge against an earlier shellacking by the Red Devils (60–38), beating them 66–62. By the end of the regular season, Washington and Greenville had a record of 10–2 and became cochampions of the Northeastern Conference, the first time Kinston had been denied that spot in four years.

The Red Devils would have their own revenge against the Greenville Phantoms in the conference tournament beating the cochamps 54–43 in the semi-finals, but the finals was against the Washington Pam-Pac who unraveled the Red Devils 64–53. However, one of the stars that night was Charlie Wickham. The tournament was played at East Carolina College in Greenville and not the notorious "crackerbox" of the Phantoms. The paper noted Charlie Wickham's outstanding performance: "The Red Devils' Charlie Wickham, playing one of his better ball games of the season, kept the Sexton-coached Kinston quint in the ball game and made

303

it a serious threat at all times. Wickham topped all Kinston scorers with 21 points."[1]

Even though the Red Devils season was over with the conference and tournament titles lost, the Red Devils played one final game against the Class AAA Wildcats of New Hanover. Just as the season had started, the Red Devils ended with a loss being outclassed by the taller and more experienced Wildcat team. "The GHS cagers fought desperately to protect their undefeated home record but Wilmington slapped a black mark on the Red Devils for the first time in 12 ballgames."[2] Nevertheless, Charlie Wickham was the team's high scorer with twenty-three points.

Among Dad's Kinston memorabilia that survived over the years were the school annuals, the *Kay-Aitch-Ess*. In Dad's 1952 *Kay-Aitch-Ess* annual, I saw that some of the students had signed it and it is Charlie Wickham's note that caught my attention.

Above the team photo, he wrote, "Coach, I really have enjoyed playing ball under your fine leadership and I appreciate all the help you've given me both on and off the court. I am really sorry we let you down and didn't get to Durham, but I'll be pulling for you next year."

Here's a young boy who felt like he had let his coach down. Make no mistake, you play to win. Winning was always what you strive for, but if you lose or fail, you show character by picking yourself up and moving forward. You only fail if you quit. The old adage plastered on the locker room wall is still true: "Quitters never win and winners never quit." I know Dad was just as proud of this group of boys, as much as any other team he had coached. Eion Faelten said that Charlie Wickham was also Kinston's best tennis player until Marshall Happer came along.

Winners do not always come in first place. There is a difference between losing and losers. Both Amos Sexton and Frank Mock were big on sportsmanship and fair play. If you beat someone you beat them "fair and square." Those who win by cheating or cutting corners (like some modern-day athletes) are not really winners. I know that sometimes there can be a fine line between "looking for an edge"

RED DEVIL TALES

and downright cheating, but I think we know when we have crossed that line.

Douglas Gregg (nicknamed Crummy) and George Whitfield were cocaptains of the 1953 team when George was a junior and Doug was a senior. George said, "I gonna tell you what, that 'son of a gun' could shoot better than anybody I have ever seen. He shot the ball over the top of his head, and he'd have a fast break on a fast break layup and then he wouldn't take it. He would dribble to the corner and set that ball over his head and shoot it. It would drive your daddy crazy until the nets just moved. I'm telling you that you never saw anyone shoot like that in your life."

Eion Faelten said that Douglas Greg had the strangest shot you ever saw and was deadly accurate from what would be a three-point shot from the corner. "Early on, a few of us tried to copy him," Eion noted. "But it was impossible. His shot was unique, and he was the only one who could pull it off."

The 1953 team had a record of nineteen wins with five losses. They regained the Northeastern Conference crown with 10–2 record and then went on to win the Northeastern Tournament title. Along with cocaptains Douglas Greg and George Whitfield, the team consisted of Bert Seville, Ray Barbre, Allen Heath, Bobby Hover, Wendell Malpass, Cecil Gooding, Buddy Potter, Wayne Anderson, Lane Ward, and John Carter.

As I perused the 1953 edition of the *Free Press*, I came to the February 28 issue and there staring me in the face was a picture of older brother Edison when he was two years old, dribbling the basketball wearing a Red Devil basketball shirt. The picture was titled, "Fancy Dribbler," and under the picture was a caption which says, "Two-year old Amos Edison Sexton Jr., energy-filled son of Coach and Mrs. Amos Sexton, is already making plans to be on his pop's Grainger High School basketball team in future years. He is pictured above with a calm eye on the ball, and steady fingers, directing its vertical path. Edison is a familiar figure around the local gymnasium. He is pulling for his dad's Red Devils to defeat Roanoke Rapids Saturday night."[3]

RONALD SEXTON

This 1953 Red Devil team had just routed Washington 69–38 in the Northeastern Conference Tournament semifinal game with the paper commenting, "The Grainger High Red Devils were never greater than they were against Washington Friday night. If the boys had been playing with watermelons, they could have still hit the nets with regularity and dumped in point after point. The varsity quint of Gregg, Potter, Gooding, Whitfield and Saville opened the ball game and quickly ran up a 6–0 lead before the Pam Pack came through with its first basket of the ball game. Kinston unleashed an unmerciful attack and racked up 20 points in a fast and exciting first quarter with Bert Saville amazing the crowd with four beautiful long set shots. All of them found the mark and by that time the Red Devils had a 12–3 lead and the rout was started."[4]

The conference tournament title game was not so easy. The Red Devils were up against the Roanoke Rapids Yellow Jackets who had beaten them during the regular season. "Douglas Greg came off with 20 points…to pace the Red Devils against Roanoke Rapids. Bert Seville took second high with 14 points. The two Northeastern Conference ball clubs were at each other's baskets the opening seconds of the championship game and when Gregg tied it 2–2 with one of his famous side shots the battle was on. Kinston scored 17 points in the first period. The Jackets scored 14. The Red Devils held a 28–26 lead at halftime and pushed it to 31–26 early in the third quarter before Roanoke Rapids came up with four points to close Kinston's lead to one point 31–30. From the moment until the close of the third quarter both clubs were fighting for the lead."[5]

The fourth quarter began with the teams tied 40–40. George Whitfield opened the fourth quarter with a driving layup shot and Kinston took a 42–40 lead early in the final frame. With only four minutes left the Red Devils took a 56–44 lead. Roanoke fought back with five points, 56–49, but the Red Devils ended the game with 59–52 win. The game was a thriller with the Red Devils making a great fourth quarter drive. Once again the press and the fast break paid off the Red Devils. Joe Talley, secretary of the conference, presented cocaptains Douglas Gregg and George Whitfield with the championship trophy. The seven coaches representing each competing school selected the top five players for the All-Tourney team, and Douglas Greg was selected from the Kinston squad. The next stop was to Winston-Salem for the state basketball tournament.

The Red Devils went into Winston-Salem where they faced a talented Tri-City team. From the very start the Red Devils were cold and struggled to contain the taller Tri-City players. They failed to win any quarter, and three Red Devils fouled out in the fourth period—Potter, Gregg, and Saville. Cecil Gooding managed to put in only six points before he also fouled out. The taller Tri-City team dominated throughout the game.[6]

At the reunion in March of 2010, I met many of these Red Devils. Most are now in their late seventies, and it is fun seeing their pictures in the annuals when they were teenagers and then reading of their adventures on the court or on the field. One of George's good friends and Red Devil teammate is Ray Barbre. I have known Ray through the years because of his friendship with George and I knew he played for Dad. Everyone in those days had a nickname, and Ray was always called Razor Blade by George. I asked Ray to give me his Red Devil story. He said, somewhat apologetically, that he was on the team but he was never a starter. However, he said that he did have one game when he was put in and he got hot. He said that was his only claim to fame. I went back and searched through the *Free Press* and there it was, "RAY BARBRE SHINES." That must have been the moment, and it is worth quoting. The paper stated: "Sexton took his regulars out of the contest at the start of the final period and played his second stringers the remainder of the contest. Little Ray Barbre was as hot as a forest in a runaway fire as he drove in for three field goals and won the admiration of the crowd with his flying style of basketball."[7]

Both Frank Mock and Amos Sexton treated every player with respect, even if they were not starters. As good coaches they recognized that talent was not the full measure of an athlete. Talent without dedication and commitment is useless. We have all seen players who are gifted and talented and never push themselves to their full potential. They hold back and are just lazy. They do just enough to get by. And we have all seen players who are not that talented but who give 110 percent, and we cheer them on and want to see them win. These are the players we champion and who really make us proud. The great thing about the Red Devils is that through the years they not only had talented athletes, but these talented athletes were dedicated and committed to a winning tradition and they reflected the values of their coaches.

The 1954 Red Devils dominated the conference winning both the conference and tournament title. The team's record that year was 21–4. It was George Whitfield's senior year. He and Cecil Gooding were cocaptains and returning starters. Buddy Potter, Wayne Anderson, John Carter, and also returning players. Bill Tripp was a talented player who had transferred to Grainger High School his senior year when the Dupont plant opened in Kinston. He had been a starting guard on the football team. Several new and talented players from the junior varsity moved up and proved to be a valuable asset to the team and would eventually become a nucleus for the 1955 state championship team, namely, Darwin Williams, Robert Whaley, and Poo Rochelle. At tournament time, Coach Sexton added two more players from the junior varsity: Billy Evans, the high-scoring center who stood at six-four, and Marshall Happer, who played guard and was at the time five-six who was the JV team captain and had been a consistent scorer and playmaker. Within a year, Marshall's height would shoot up to six foot two. The junior varsity had a phenomenal record of 19–1 the previous year.

The Red Devils began with a tough schedule meeting six AAA opponents before beginning conference play after Christmas. Two victories over Goldsboro, one each over Raleigh and Rocky Mount, and losses at the hands of Rocky Mount and Wilmington gave the team a 4–2 mark in nonconference play. The Red Devils would start a winning streak of 14 games on December 11, 1953 when they beat Class AAA Goldsboro 47–39. They beat another Class AAA team, Rocky Mount, in overtime 56–54.

When conference play began after the first of the year, the Red Devils won their first eleven games. After ten games Buddy Potter led in individual scoring honors with a 12.8 average per game while Poo Rochelle came in second with an 11.4 average. George Whitfield was close behind with a 10.3 average. By tournament time, Poo Rochelle, then a lanky sophomore forward, was averaging 13.4 points per game. With fourteen straight victories, he Red Devils already had the conference title, but the last conference game of the season was against their archrival, the Greenville Phantoms. The game was played in the notoriously small and badly lit Greenville High School gym known to the Red Devils as the crackerbox. For whatever reason, the Red Devils were off their game and got swamped 68–54, a sweet revenge for Greenville who had been beaten by the Red Devils earlier in the season, 48–43. The Red Devils shook off the lost and prepared for the northeaster conference tournament

In the northeastern conference tournament, Kinston earned a bye on the first round and then beat Jacksonville with comparative ease 61–45. Buddy Potter had the high score of 24 points. But then the Red Devils had to face again the Greenville Phantoms for the conference tournament championship game. If the Red Devils were off their game in the previous contest with Greenville, they were really off on this night. This time the game was held at East Carolina College in Greenville not at the high school. With 2,600 fans cheering their respective teams, the Red Devils played the Phantoms goal-for-goal in opening two minutes then moving ahead 7 points and ending the quarter leading 16–12. However, the Red Devils got cold or confused and managed to score only 5 points in the second quarter. Poo Rochelle had one goal and coupled with it only three foul shots were made. The half-time score was 24–21, certainly not insurmountable, but the Red Devils needed to fine their "mojo."

With their attack blunted by Greenville's foolproof zone, the Devil defense too folded in the third quarter and Greenville romped ahead with 15 more points while permitting the GHS'ers a meager six points, again mustered almost entirely from the foul line. A four-quarter comeback that netted the Grainger squad a dozen points was too late however, and Greenville did not consider it a threat for the Phantoms burned the cords for 19 more in the end box to come out way ahead, 58–39, at the buzzer.[8]

Because the Red Devils had won the conference championship they were still going to the state tournament, but they needed to find their groove before this tournament got underway. The Red Devils played a post-season game against the East Carolina College's junior varsity in order to sharpen their skills for the state tournament. Besides, the state tournament this year was hosted by Kinston in the newly built Mock Gymnasium. Grainger High School Athletic Director Frank Mock served as the tournament manager.

On March 11, 1954, the seventh annual North Carolina State Class AA basketball tournament began for the first time in Kinston's Mock Gymnasium with eight teams competing in the double elimination event for the ultimate crown of state champions. Sanford and Kannapolis were paired first to play while Henderson and North-Mecklenburg were second followed by Kinston and Canton, and finally Whitesville and Tri-City (from Draper, Spray and Leaksville) completed the first round. In the first round Kinston, Kannapolis, Tri-City and Henderson advanced.

The Red Devils beat Canton in a close contest, 67–65. "Canton's unheralded Black Bears almost sent Kinston's Red Devils into lower bracket hibernation in (their) first game as they played them closely from the outset, going under only by virtue of a foul called against them in the final three seconds. Poo Rochelle took full advantage of his 'golden opportunity' to provide the two-point victory margin. In the fastest and most thrilling contest of the day, Canton and Kinston tied it up six times and shared the lead eight times during the action-packed battle."[9] Buddy Potter was the team's high scorer with eighteen while Poo Rochelle was close behind with seventeen. The Red Devils would have to ratchet up a level if they were to overcome their next opponents: the tough Henderson Rebels.

The Friday night game was the day's most hair-tearing thriller with a fourth quarter comeback by Henderson who had an eleven point deficit (54–43) as the final quarter began. The Henderson cagers "came within one point of taking the lead midway in the period but fouls kept them behind, except until the remaining 30 seconds when, with the score at 65–63, Kinston, Rochelle fouled Center Maurice Capps, who converted two to knot it up at 65–up. As the clock ticked away the final six seconds, the Devils hurriedly moved the ball down-court and with one second remaining (Cecil)

RED DEVIL TALES

Gooding took the pass, jumped from one leg and shot—success-fully."[10] The Red Devils won!

Meanwhile, Tri-City beat Kannapolis 57–53, which set the stage for a rematch with the Red Devils. Tri-City had three returning players from the previous year: Roy Searcy, Tri-City's outstanding six-four Center; Carvel Nichols, the team's talented forward, and Tommy Harris, their sharp-shooting guard. Returning for Kinston was Buddy Potter, Cecil Gooding, Bert Saville, and George Whitfield. In the end, Tri-City's five senior, two-inch taller squad overpowered the Red Devils 69–51, to take the state crown for the second consecutive year. The Red Devils managed to hold the Tri-City Black Panthers to a close 27–24 lead at half-time, but the big break for Tri-City came in the third quarter when they garnered 20 points to the Red Devils mere five. Ten of the Panthers points came from 13 attempts at the foul line. The Red Devils came back strong in the fourth quarter with 22 points, but it was not enough to cover the deficit of the third. Overall, Kinston shooting average was 28.2 per cent. Kinston only made 11 of 23 free throws while Tri-City made 27 out of 28 attempts. That alone could have been the difference in the game.[11]

The next year the Red Devils would start their own two-year state title run, but these teams between the championship years were nevertheless good teams and had good runs for the crown but always fell short.

RONALD SEXTON

Kannapolis' "Wonders," undefeated in 22 games, are pictured here discussing last-minute Tourney details with Amos Sexton (third from left), Kinston coach. Also shown (left to right), are Frankie Black: Coach D.N. Hamrick; Sexton; Basil Howard; Gene Thompson; Delmas Petrea; Bill Lippard, assistant coach: Ray Richardson; and Charles Benfield. Courtesy of the *Free Press*.

25

"THE LUCKY FEW"

The boys who played for Amos Sexton and Frank Mock from 1948 to 1957 were all a part of a generation that has been called The Lucky Few.[1] Sandwiched between Tom Brokaw's *Greatest Generation* and their children the Baby Boomers, this generation has largely gone unnoticed and unrecognized. They were, according to one sociologist, "the luckiest generation of American history."[2] This was the generation born from 1929 to 1945.

In his book, *The Lucky Few: Between the Greatest Generation and the Baby Boom,* Elwood Carlson, a sociologist and demographer at Florida State University noted that this generation slipped between the cracks of history, but their contribution to American society runs deep and wide. Raised by the Greatest Generation, they also held to traditional values. This generation was the first American generation smaller than the one before, and yet they were, according to Carlson, productive, successful, and optimistic about the future. They were born in a period when the birth rates were unusually low so they were few in number. Smaller numbers meant "more parental attention to children; smaller class size at school, and greater opportunities for extracurricular prominence, such as making the team, being selected for a leading acting role, becoming editor of the school paper, being elected class officer

313

and so on."[3] Also, being small in number, they had greater opportunities for jobs and promotion. They were the beneficiaries of an exceptionally long post World War II economic boom and the absence of significant competition from immigrants.[4]

However, this generation was not so "lucky," at first it would seem, having been born during the depression era of the 1930s followed by the turmoil of World War II. But these two historical events helped to shape their lives in ways that would prepare them to meet the challenges of the future. Eleven of the twelve astronauts to walk on the surface of the moon, (including Neil Armstrong, the first man on the moon) are members of the Lucky Few. Martin Luther King, General Norman Schwartzkopf, Supreme Court Justices, David H. Souter, Athony M. Kennedy, Antinon Scalia, Cabinet Officer Donald Rumsfeld, and former Vice President Dick Cheney are just a few public figures who are a part of that generation as well. Country music was certainly shaped by this generation with people like Johnny Cash, Waylon Jennings, Merle Haggard, Willie Nelson, Tammy Wynette, Charlie Pride and Kenny Rogers. Sports has its share of Lucky Few members: Bart Starr, Joe Namath, Gayle Sayers, Johnny Unitas, Hank Aaron, Mickey Mantle, Willie Mays, and jockey Willie Shoemaker to name a few. But it was in the world of business and finance where this generation really excelled.

The Lucky Few finished school and started their careers during the largest and longest economic boom in American history. Investment tycoon Warren Buffett, media mogul Ted Turner, fashion designer Calvin Klein, and corporate executive Michael Eisner are just a few examples.[5]

In November of 1951 *Time*'s cover story labeled this group as the Silent Generation. Gertrude Stein wrote: "Youth today is waiting for the hand of fate to fall on its shoulders, meanwhile working fairly hard and saying almost nothing. The most startling fact about the younger generation is its silence. With some rare exceptions, youth is nowhere near the rostrum. By comparison with the Flaming Youth of their fathers and mothers, today's younger generation is a still, small flame. It does not issue manifestos, make speeches or carry posters."[6]

RED DEVIL TALES

Labels sometimes, however, are like noses and opinions—everybody has one. Gertrude Stein notwithstanding, this generation has blossomed into one of the most industrious and productive group ever. They became the force and initiative that pushed forward civil rights, an unparalleled national wealth in the arts and commerce, and unimaginable advances in science and technology.[7]

These boys who played for Amos Sexton and Frank Mock during this period were a part of this Lucky Few generation. Their lives were certainly influenced by an era that included the Depression and World War II, but they were fortunate to be a part of a community that helped nourish their character and shape their lives. Kinston, a town with rich historical roots that reached back before the country, was even founded. Every athlete will tell you that Kinston was a great place to grow up. The people of the community were family oriented, hardworking, and patriotic. And when the city of Kinston formed the recreation department in the 1930s, it provided facilities and programs for the Kinston youth. Kids could play all day at Emma Webb Park and feel safe. It created a healthy environment to grow up in, and their athletic programs helped develop some of the finest athletes in the country. I remember Dad saying that when our family moved to Louisiana, he looked for a town like Kinston to raise a family. He chose Ruston, a city of about the same size and had many of the same characteristics he and mother loved about Kinston. Ruston is also a great place to raise a family. I'm still here.

As I visited with these Red Devils, I found a few common threads that helped me to understand why they are such an outstanding group of men who have lived their lives in such a way that would have made Amos Sexton and Frank Mock very proud.

Everyone I met was gracious, hospitable, appreciative, and a joy to get to know. One of the first common characteristic I found is that all these men remembered their roots. They knew where they had come from and who had helped them along the way. They take pride in their family history and in the country they grew up in. No one I interviewed was cocky or boastful about their accomplishments. Their coaches had grilled in them the importance of teamwork, and

315

they were always aware of the importance of others in their success. They gave credit not only to Amos Sexton, but to Frank Mock, to other assistant coaches, to the city of Kinston, the recreation department, their school teachers, school administrators, and their parents. Many of them themselves went into coaching or became teachers, school administrators, or principals. The rest became lawyers, it seems. Well, maybe not all, but there seemed to be a lot of them, too. Most of them came from little or nothing, and they acknowledge that without the help and guidance of their parents, coaches, and teachers, they would have never have achieved any level of success in life.

Another characteristic that I notice among these men was they all possess a good work ethic. Listening to their stories and watching the way they carry themselves, I could see they believed in hard work. And they still work hard, even in retirement. Work is a way of life. Persistence, determination, struggle, sweat, overcoming adversity, competitiveness, and achievement are ingrained into their nature. They do not want something given to them. They want to earn it. As athletes they were fierce competitors and that seemed to carry over into their careers. They were taught that you have to work hard to win. It is a value that, once acquired, stays with you. This work ethic was evident even in their play, as well. When I played golf with a group of Red Devils, they were having fun but they played to win. They are still competitive after all those years.

Dad told us that when we grew up we could do whatever we wanted to in life but as long as "we lived under his roof" we were going to learn his business and work. The family was like a team, and everybody had to do their "fair share." For instance, most kids looked forward to a week of fun and play during the Thanksgiving break. Nope, not us. My brothers and I had to rake and clean the yard, which took us about a week to finish. And when Dad built an apartment complex, we were responsible for cleaning the vacant apartments. We painted, scrubbed toilets, scraped and cleaned dirty ovens, toilets, carpets, and refrigerators, mowed grass and pulled weeds. Dad's mantra was, "Boys, I want these apartments in tip-top shape." I wonder what he would have done with three daughters.

RED DEVIL TALES

Also, these former Red Devils (now senior citizens) know the meaning of loyalty. They are loyal to their faith, to their friends, to their family, to their community, and to their country. And they are loyal to certain ideas and principles. I often had the opportunity to accompany them to ball games, family dinners, playing golf, or civic meetings. They routinely prayed before every meal, bear hugged friends they hadn't seen in a while, stood at attention with their hands over their hearts as they recited the Pledge of Allegiance, and visited old friends in the hospital or in retirement homes. They faithfully returned to class reunions when they could, and if they couldn't, they would find ways to keep in touch with fellow Red Devils.

Respect for authority characterized this group as well. You could notice it in their conversation when they talked about former teachers, coaches, or even their parents. Call it old-fashioned family values or just good Southern tradition, they still say "Yes, sir and no, ma'am" where it applies, open doors for the ladies, and greet strangers with a smile. On June 1 of 2012, Mrs. Frank Mock turned ninety-five and nearly a hundred former ballplayers returned to honor her birthday. She was overwhelmed by the loyalty and affection these boys showed her.

She said she would have expected them to do this for Frank, but she never imagined they would show such devotion to her. Well, they did. Good manners and civility mark these former Red Devils, school mascot notwithstanding. In the end, they try to live by the maxims and principles they learned in their youth.

For the most part these boys grew up to be strong and responsible men because they grew up in a time and place that helped shape and nurture their character. Parents, teachers, coaches, and community leaders were generally on the same page when it came to discipline and values. There was a clear distinction between right and wrong, and athletics played an important part in shaping character and developing the skills necessary to win in life.

American newspaper columnist George Will aptly noted in his book, *Men at Work,* that "Greek philosophers considered sport a religious and civic—in a word, moral undertaking. Sport, they said, is morally serious because mankind's noblest aim is the loving contemplation of worthy things, such as beauty and courage. By witnessing physical grace, the soul comes to understand and love beauty. Seeing people compete courageously and fairly helps emancipate the individual by educating his passions."[8]

26

AN IRRESISTIBLE OPPORTUNITY

In 1957, nine years after Dad first walked on the basketball court as the head coach of the Kinston Red Devils, the country continued its post-war economic expansion and new position as a world power. The national concern was halting the spread of communism. Russia now had the atomic bomb. Nevertheless, small communities like Kinston benefited from this era of peace and prosperity and continued to maintain their traditional values and simple way of life. More families were able to acquire televisions and buy a car, two inventions that would help shape national life in the future.

In 1957 the average income was $4.454.00 per year. A gallon of gasoline was 24 cents and a US postage stamp was 3 cents. Tuition at Harvard University was now $1,000.00 per year and a new car was $2,157.00 on average. You could buy a movie ticket for $1.00. A new house cost on average $12,225.00 Bacon was 60 cents per pound, and you could buy a fresh-baked loaf of bread for 19 cents.

Dwight Eisenhower was inaugurated for a second term as president in 1957 and suffered a mild stroke later in the year. The life expectancy in 1957 was 69.6 years. Elvis Presley sang "Jailhouse Rock" and Buddy Holly and the Cricket put out "That'll Be the Day." *The Bridge on the River Kwai* won the Academy Award, and Miss South Carolina, Marian McKnight, was selected Miss America.

In sports, the University of North Carolina won the NCAA basketball championship while Auburn and Ohio State were the college football champions. The Milwaukee Braves won the World Series, and the Detroit Lions won the pro-football championship. The Heisman trophy winner in 1957 was John David Crow from Texas A & M.

Dad once told me that the nine years he served as a coach and teacher at Grainger High School (1948–1957) were some of the best years of his life. I remember him saying that when he retired, he wanted to coach again. I know he missed it. Ten years after Dad retired, the landscape of athletics had changed and coaching took on a whole new dimension. Dad would have been out of his element. Late in his career, at Grainger High School, he had been offered a coaching position at Wake Forest University. But the opportunity was not as attractive as another opportunity that offered him a more challenging and lucrative future.

In 1957 Dad was only thirty-six years old and had other mountains to scale. During his years as a coach, he did other things to supplement his income. He sold pots and pans, encyclopedias, shrubbery, as well as umpire baseball games and host an early morning radio program at a local station in Kinston. But while he felt he had to do other jobs to make ends meet, Dad was nurturing another drive in his competitive nature. He was a natural entrepreneur. He not only loved to win ball games, he loved to "turn a dollar" and make a sale. And he wanted to start and grow a business. For him that was a mountain he wanted to scale. It wasn't just having more money. It was the satisfaction that comes from growing your own business and enjoying the benefits of hard work. Like so many people of his generation who struggled through the Depression years and grew up with very little, he wanted security for his family. With a wife and three small boys at home, Dad knew he could not provide the security for them on his teacher's salary alone.

Dad's decision to leave coaching was primarily economic. By all accounts he was quite happy being a coach, but an opportunity came up that he could not turn down. Along with Dad's many side jobs like selling pots and pans, shrubbery, or encyclopedias, he had

RED DEVIL TALES

a morning radio program at W. I. S. P. in Kinston. Apparently, he bought up the time for the radio spot and then went out into the community and solicited sponsors who paid him. He was rather inventive on getting sponsors, and he obviously had a knack for selling, marketing, and promoting. I was told that when Dad was building our first home in Kinston, he traded out or bartered household items such as light fixtures and the like for advertising. If he wanted something, he found a way to get it.

Plumer Daniels, a 1950 Red Devil alumnus, told me the story of how Dad was first introduced to Marsh Furniture Company. Plumer's dad owned a plumbing and appliance business on East Blount Street in Kinston. He said Dad used to sell them advertising spots on his radio program.

After graduation, Plumer went off to college. When he returned home after his first semester, he was informed that he was about to be conscripted into the Army. Instead of being drafted, he and seven other Red Devils in the 1950 graduating class decided to join the Air Force. When he came home on leave in 1952, he went out to the football stadium to watch the team practice. Plumer had become good friends with Dad. When Dad saw him sitting in the stands, he ran up the bleachers to visit with him. Dad told him that he had just built a house on West Road and there was a vacant lot beside him. He suggested that Plumer buy the lot and build a house there. Plumer told him, "Amos, I am still in the Air Force, and I don't have the money to buy that lot." Plumer returned to Kinston in 1954 and took over his father's business. His wife went to work for the Perry family who owned the lot. Eventually, Plumer was able to buy the lot and build a house. He remembered watching us boys outside bouncing a basketball. He said, "As soon as you boys were old enough to handle a ball, you were outside dribbling a basketball."

One day in the spring of 1957, Dad was in the store selling advertising for his radio program and a sales representative from Marsh Furniture Company was also there. Plumer looked at Dad and said, "Amos, Marsh Furniture Company makes a great product, and I think they are going places. You should look into working for this company. You are a natural salesman, and I think this would be a perfect fit for you." Plumer said Dad got the number of the salesman's boss right there and immediately called Marsh Furniture Company from the store. When he reached the man's boss, he asked if he could come up and interview for a job. Overhearing the conversation, Plumer said that the man on the other end of the line was not really interested in talking to him, but Dad persisted and finally convinced him to grant an interview.

Marsh Furniture Company is located in High Point, North Carolina, and manufactures kitchen cabinets. It is a large family business founded in 1906, employing hundreds of people who built kitchen cabinets sold all over the country. They needed a sales representative who would promote and sell their line of cabinets over a certain region of the country. The salesman collected a percentage of anything sold by the company in that region whether he did it directly, had other salesman working under him, or through distributors located in the region. If Dad could get that job, he knew he could do very well. The opportunity and the possibilities were too promising to pass up.

The president of the company was an elderly and crusty old gentleman name Eric Marsh, founder of the company. He had a reputation for running "a tight ship" and controlled the company from the ground up. Like most large companies, getting in to see the president was not easy if you had no connections. You have to get through the "gatekeepers" (usually the president's secretary) in order to see the man in charge. Dad had trouble getting an appointment for some reason, so he figured out a way to bypass proper protocol in order to get in to see Eric Marsh. Persistence and determination were qualities Dad possessed and served him well through the years. If he wanted something, he worked hard at it and eventually found a way to get it. He always said, "There is more than one way to skin a cat." He was determined to get in to see Eric Marsh.

Dad found out that Eric Marsh left for lunch down the back stairway from his office. Dad waited one day at the back entrance until Mr. Marsh came out. After introducing himself, Dad told him he heard about the job opportunity but had a hard time getting in to see him. Dad made him an offer he could not refuse. "Give me a month, and if I haven't produced, then I will walk away and you don't have to pay me anything." Mr. Marsh consented and the rest is history.

Dad told us boys, as we were growing up, that he did not care what profession we went into when we grew up; but he said, "As long as you live under my roof, you will work for me and learn my business." Well, that we did. In the summer of 1969, Edison and I were shipped off to High Point for the summer to learn the business. There we started from the ground up, working in the factory making cabinets on the assembly line from 7:00 a.m. to 3:00 p.m. They gradually worked us through each department down the assembly line until we learned how the cabinets were made from the ground up. I think the only thing we didn't do was go out into the woods and cut down the oak trees they were made from.

Mother certainly played an important role in the success of Amos Sexton. She was the silent partner who stood on the sidelines "holding down the fort" at home, supporting and sometimes just tolerating or enduring Dad's personality and professions, both as a coach and as an businessman. Coaching took Dad away from home often, and when he left coaching and hit the road selling kitchen cabinets, he was gone even more. My mother raised three boys. That is her trophy. Every game he won and lost and every successful business venture he accomplished and some that went south, she was there and deserves credit for standing with him through it all.

Like Dad, mother had a fun loving, vivacious, and an outgoing personality. Together, they made a unique team. Mother was always a great hostess, and she lit up a room when she entered. She wanted to teach school and, in fact, taught the sixth grade for a while when she and Dad first moved to Kinston. However, raising three boys and managing a home put that on the back burner. She would have made a great teacher. Mother did her best to keep three boys and a husband on "the straight and narrow," which could be a tall order at times. She fed and clothed us, made sure we did our homework, broke up fights, and took us to church. Raising three boys was a handful, and she often had to be the disciplinarian when Dad was away. When Dad gave us a spanking, he always hit us right on target—the rear end. But with Mom, we often had to cover our heads with our arms because you never knew where you might get hit as she swung her sword (switch), making sure she hit somewhere. Of course, we were always trying to escape her wrath, so she was forced to swing on the run. Then, there was always the ominous pronouncement, "When your dad gets home, he'll deal with this." One of her favorite sayings when we tried to explain to her who started a fight was: "I don't care who started it, as far as I'm concerned 'the kettle can't call the pot black.'"

She made sure we all went to church and said grace at the dinner table. And she always made our birthdays special. Mother was a good cook and the most cleaning-driven woman I have ever known. She could take someone else's recipe, add or change a few ingredients, and make it her own. But it was her propensity for neatness and cleanliness that marked her sons for life. Our house was always organized and clean. In her own way she was driven like Dad. It was a standing joke in our house that if any of us got up in the middle of the night to go to the bathroom, our bed would be made up by the time we returned.

In our early days as children we wore blue jeans to school with the bottoms turned up in cuffs. Wallowing in the school playground during recess often filled the cuffs with dirt. Every day when I would come home from school and opening the door I would inevitably hear, "Don't come in the house until you have emptied those cuffs." I'm afraid much of that organization and neatness is instilled in her three boys. To this day the first thing I do when I wake up in the morning is make up the bed, sometimes with my wife still in it.

I asked Edison what he remembered about Dad that stands out. Of course, he has a lot of great memories and stories he could tell but two things in particular came to mind. First, he said he remembered noticing that Dad carried a lot of cash in his billfold when they were on business trips. He asked him why he carried so much cash with him. Dad told him that when he was growing up he didn't have two nickels to rub together and if he every got to a place where he had some money he was going to have plenty enough in his pocket. I suppose there always was a fear of running out of money. The other

RED DEVIL TALES

thing he remembered was that Dad told him on one occasion that no amount of money is worth breaking up a family over. Don said Dad was always pulling someone's leg, and he remembered Dad told his sister Hazel that he buried a bunch of money in the backyard. He said that after Dad died she insisted we go in the backyard and start digging. Dad would have gotten a "kick" out of that. I think I'm going to tell my kids the same thing.

In May of 1957 the *Free Press* had a final comment on the nine-year coaching career of Amos Sexton:

"The resignation of Amos Sexton as basketball coach at Grainger High School to accept more (lucrative) employment as a furniture salesman is not only a blow to the local school and its athletic program, but it will be felt as a sectional loss as well. Sexton has coached eight teams which competed for state honors and his ninth was ruled ineligible because of a technicality involving one player. Three teams from Kinston have earned the state title under his leadership.

"The brand of basketball played by teams in the Northeastern Conference has improved steadily. Sexton and others have improved the standards of officiating which have also affected the loop's competition. His goal has long motivated the whole Athletic Department at the local school and we are confident it will continue to do so—whoever may succeed Sexton.

"Sexton has found time to participate in civic and community activities in addition to his coaching duties. He will be sorely missed. It will not be easy to find another coach with his ability nor his high standards of character training for the students who compete under him.

In regretting his decision to leave the coaching field, local friends of Amos Sexton will wish for him and his family continued success in his new line of work. Kinston and Eastern Carolina, to say nothing of the state cage tournament he has dominated for the past several years, will miss him."[1]

Lloyd Whitfield added, "In the loss of Sexton, the teaching profession is losing one of North Carolina's leading basketball coaches. He's recognized as the 'baron of prep basketball in North Carolina.' He realized his duty was not to merely build a winning basketball team, but to mold character, develop a youth and teach him to use his physical capabilities to the fullest advantage.

"The way Sexton figured to accomplish this was to have strict discipline and strenuous physical exercises. As the result he relied on the fast-break offense and would not (hesitate) to suspend a star performer for any deed out of character.

"(I was) a member of the basketball team that Sexton first coached when he came to Kinston in 1948. He's the first to admit that he was scared stiff and knew very little about the sport. He had never played a game in his life and had inherited a team that had been all the way to the state finals the year before.

"In his initial year here, Sexton brought Kinston its first state championship. There were two more to come and his illustrious career ends with a total of 25 cage trophies in the case at Grainger High School that were won during Sexton's tenure.

"His capabilities were so respected that twice he as called on to coach the east squad in the annual all-star classic at Greensboro. A total of 19 Sexton-coached-cagers have gone on to play college basketball.

"Seven years after graduation, (I) returned to Kinston and have worked with Sexton since then. It is remarkable the strides he has made in basketball. He knows the game like an old master and time and time again (I) have seen his strategy win a game in the last few seconds.

"He has been offered jobs with various colleges and he has turned them down because he felt the teaching profession could not afford him with the income needed to give his family the type of life he wanted the family to have . . .

"Coach Frank Mock will miss him. Sexton has assisted Mock all these years with the football duties. Sexton knows Mock's system thoroughly and it has taken nine years to learn it.

"It will just seem strange to attend a basketball game at Mock Gymnasium next Winter and not be able to watch Sexton and his antics on the bench. The old red vest and red socks that Sexton has worn all these years seem a part of Grainger High School basketball tradition now."[2]

This picture was taken by a neighbor only moments before Mom and Dad left Kinston for Louisiana in July 1957.

APPENDIX A

THE RED DEVIL FAST BREAK

The mechanics of the Red Devils' fast break under ideal conditions are illustrated in the diagram below. Of course, things did not always go as drawn up on the blackboard, but the optimum conditions were achieved in a surprisingly high percentage of attempts.

The basic idea was to beat the defender back down the court after one of their missed shots and achieve a three of us against two of them at our end of the court. It would be even better if we were able to get three of our players against only one of theirs, down court, which often happened. If this was achieved, it usually led to a field goal or at least a foul shot. A secondary goal in running the fast break was to physically wear down the opposing team by the relentless execution of this attack. Even if the opposing team managed to get three or four defensive players back down the court in the early part of the game, it was hoped that by the third or fourth quarter they would "run out of gas" reaching the point of sheer exhaustion. An example of this was when the Red Devils played Sanford in the 1956 championship game in Enka. Sanford managed to keep the game close for the first half of the game, but late in the third quarter they simply gave out. They Red Devils pulled away and won by 12 points 74–62.

Following the diagram (Figure A), an opponent, X, has just shot and missed, and C has snagged the rebound. At this point the two guards (G) break out of their position in a curl to the side of the court as shown in Figure A. The rebounder then snaps a pass to one of the guards. Sometimes the rebounder would throw a hook pass (which Coach Sexton liked), but Eion Faelten, (who authored this description) often used a two-handed overhead snap pass, which was quicker. The guard who did not receive the ball ran a curved route to a midpoint at half court and received pass number two from the first guard. It was important for the second guard not to run a straight line path to half court as that would usually get the second guard too far out in front and make the second pass difficult and disrupt the flow. Timing was very important. At this point, ideally, there has been no dribbling. It was also very important to get that first pass from the rebounder out to the guard as quickly as possible.

Meanwhile, the two forwards (F) would take off "hell-bent for leather" down court. The object, of course, was to get out in front of the opponent's big men (X), but not too far out in front of our guards as that would disrupt the flow of the fast break. The guard receiving the pass at half-court would then turn up-court and with two or three dribbles reach a point somewhere around the top of the key with our forwards parallel or slightly ahead. Now assuming the defensive guards (X) managed to get back in defensive position and the opponent's big men had not kept pace (which was often the case), a three on two situation was created. If one "X" committed to stop the ball, one of our forwards had to be open for a bounce pass and easy bucket. If both defensive players (X) committed to stop the forwards converging from the wing, the guard was left free to continue to the basket for a layup or an easy jump shot.

Of course, things did not always work exactly as drawn up on the blackboard, but we learned to improvise and adjust to different circumstances. If one of the forwards got the rebound, the center had to fill his lane, which slowed things up a bit. During the Sanford game, I got too far out in front and received the ball wide open but too far under the basket. I had to make a reverse layup even though I was unguarded. It looked as if I was "hot-dogging." Even when opponents tried to anticipate the play and get back quickly with three or four defensive players, it tended to disrupt their offense and ability to rebound. The opponents were often distracted and "taken out of their game plan."[1]

RED DEVIL TALES

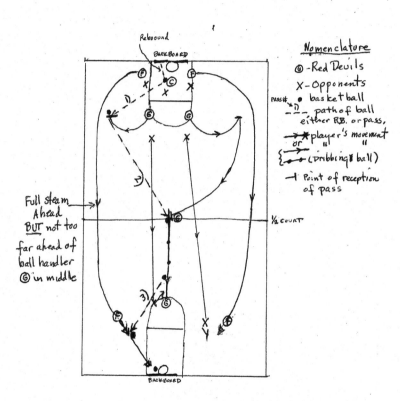

Figure A: Red Devil Fast Break (Ideal Conditions)

APPENDIX B

AMOS SEXTON'S
BASKETBALL RECORD
1949-1957

Year	Record	Accomplishments
1948–49	25–4	Northeastern Conference Champions
		Northeastern Tournament Champions
		District Champions
		NCHSAA State Runner-up (Class A)
1949–50	30–3	Northeastern Conference Champion
		Northeastern Tournament Champions
		NCHSAA State Champions (Class A)
1950–51	19–6	Northeastern Conference Champions
		NCHSAA State Runner-up (Class AA)
1951–52	19–8	Northeastern Tournament Runner-up
1952–53	9–5	Northeastern Conference Champions
		Northeastern Tournament Champions
		District Champions
1953–54	21–4	Northeastern Conference Champions
		Northeastern Tournament Champions
		District Champions

RONALD SEXTON

1954–55	25–2	NCHSAA State Runner-up (Class AA) Northeastern Conference Champions District Champions
1955–56	20–5	NCHSAA State Champions (Class AA) Northeastern Conference Champions Northeastern Tournament Champions District Champions
1956–57	24–2	NCHSAA State Champions (Class AA) Northeastern Conference Champions Northeastern Tournament Champions District Champions NCHSAA 3rd place State (Class AA)

APPENDIX C

1950
NORTH CAROLINA STATE CLASS A BASKETBALL CHAMPIONS
25-4

Bryant Aldridge
Joe Whaley
Eugene "Red" McDaniel
Tommy Cole
Edward "Bud" Bradshaw

Graham Phillips
Bobby Hodges
Douglas Bruton
Sherrill Williams
Amos Stroud

RONALD SEXTON

APPENDIX D

1955
NORTH CAROLINA STATE CLASS AA
BASKETBALL CHAMPIONS
25-2

The 1955 Red Devils: From left to right front row: Darwin Williams, Lee Becton, Marshall Happer, John Carter, Billy Evans and Coach Amos Sexton. Second row: Jimmy Hodges, Robert Whaley, Buddy Potter, Eion Faelten, Tim McLaren, Pat Wright and Poo Rochelle (Courtesy *The Free Press*).

APPENDIX E

1956
NORTH CAROLINA STATE CLASS
AA BASKETBALL CHAMPIONS
20-5

RONALD SEXTON

This is a preseason photo. By the time of state playoffs, Roger Hobgood had replaced Jimmy Hodges The 1956 varsity basketball team forms a "V" around Coach Amos Sexton. From left to right are Billy Evans, Jimmy Hodges, Bobby Stanley, Charles Lewis, Steve Creech, Alley Hart, David Adkins, Marshall Happer, Poo Rochelle, Eion Faelten, and Tim McLaren.

NOTES

Chapter 1

1. *Free Press* (hereafter KFP), March 5, 1957, pg. 2.
2. "Red Devils Need Many More Drills," *Free Press*, November 30, 1948, pg. 2.
3. Seek Publishing, *Remember When: 1948 Memories*, 1055 Ridgecrest Drive, Millersville, Tennessee, 37072-3621, www.seekpublishing.com
4. "First Television Set Purchased by E.E. Rowe of Jacksonville, *KFP*, January 6, 1949, pg.
5. Seek Publishing,
6. Ibid.
7. "Sexton Earns Basketball Baron Title During 9-Year Stay Here," *KFP*, March 5, 1957, pg. 2
8. Ibid.
9. Amos Sexton as quoted by Lloyd Whitfield, KFP, March 5, 1957, 2.
10. Lloyd Whitfield, KFP, March 5, 1957, pg 2.
11. Ibid.
12. Ibid.
13. Ibid.
14. Ibid.

Chapter 2

1. http://www.hoophall.com/hall-of-famers/tag/edgar-s-ed-hickey. How to Improve Your Basketball by Dr. Forrest

C. "Phog" Allen, Harold E. "Bud" Foster and Edward S. "Eddie" Hickey (1950)

2. "Kinston Tops Bears; Will Play Washington," KFP, February 26, 1949, pg. 2.

3. "Kinston Wins Loop's Cage Tourney 46-34," KFP, February 28, 1949. pg. 2.

4. "Red Devils Cop Tourney: Top Chapel Hill in Final Game of Regional Meet," KFP, March 7, 1049, pg.2.

5. "Kinston Cagers Defeat Hanes by One-Point Margin," KFP, March 12, 1949, pg.2.

6. "Hendersonville Downs Grainer in State Tourney," KFP, March 14, 1949, pg.2

7. "Cagers did Well," KFP, March 14, 1949

8. "Boys Cage Loop Will Be Formed," KFP, November 28, 1949.

Chapter 3

1. "Kinston Wins Opener At Snow Hill," KFP, December 8, 1949.

2. "Devils Top Wilson," KFP, December 10, 1949.

3. "Fayetteville is Kinston's Victim Here On Monday," KFP, December 13, 1949.

4. "ECTC Freshman Gain Revenge for Earlier Defeat," KFP, December 17, 1949. pg.2.

5. Bob Lewis, "ECTC Freshmen Gain Revenge for Earlier Defeat," KFP, December 17, 1949, pg. 2.

6. Bob Lewis, "Goldsboro Gets Cage Victory in Contest Tuesday," KFP, December 21, 1949, pg. 2.

7. "On the Sports Front," KFP, December 21, 1949, pg. 2.

8. Ibid.

9. Dick Tyndall, "Kinston Wins by 42-31 in Initial Conference Game," KFP,January 6, 1949, pg.2.

10. Ibid.

11. Dick Tyndall, "Red Devils Given 45-44 Set-Back in Rocky Mount Tilt," KFP, January 7, 1950, pg. 2.

RED DEVIL TALES

12. Dick Tyndall, "Red Devils Given 45-44 Set-Back in Rocky Mount Tilt," KFP, January 7, 1950, pg. 2.
13. "On the Sports Front," KFP, January 11, 1950, pg. 2.
14. Dick Tyndall, "Grainger Plays its Best Home Game Tuesday," KFP, January 11, 1950, pg.2.
15. Dick Tyndall, "Girls Game is Called Off by the Pam-Pack," KFP, January 13, 1950, pg. 2.
16. Dick Tyndall, "Beat Washington Easily in League Contest Friday," KFP, January 14, 1950, pg. 2.
17. "On the Sports Front," KFP, January 17, 1959, pg. 2.
18. "Kinston to Play League Contest on Home Court," KFP, January 19, 1950, pg.2.
19. Bob Lewis, "Kinston Defeats Conference Foe Friday by 55-28," KFP, January 21, 1950, pg. 2.
20. Dick Tyndall, "Visitors are in Position to Dump Devils from Lead," KFP, January 23, 1950, pg. 2.
21. "E. City, Kinston Battle for Lead in Contest Here," KFP, January 24, 1950, pg.2.
22. Bob Lewis, "Accurate Shooting and Quick Passes Allow Kinston to Chalk up Fifth Loop Victory," KFP, January 25, 1950, pg. 2.
23. "Grainer Cagers Play Goldsboro on Friday Night," KFP, January 26, 1950, pg. 2.
24. Dick Tyndall, "Kinston Avenges Earlier Defeat on Friday Night," KFP, January 28, 1950.
25. Dick Tyndall, "Kinston Takes a Big Lead in 1st and Then Coasts, KFP, February 1, 1950. pg.2.
26. Ibid.
27. "Plays New Bern There on Friday in League Game," KFP, February 2, 1950, pg.2.
28. "Takes on Bears in League Game on Friday Night." KFP, February 3, 1950, pg. 2.
29. Ibid.
30. "On the Sports Front," KRP, February 3, 1950, pg. 2.

31. Dick Tyndall, "Bears Hold Three-Point Lead After One Quarter, But Kinston Flashers Back to Take Game," KFP, February 4, 1050, pg. 2.
32. Dick Tyndall, "Red Devils Can Virtually Capture Title With Victory Over Strong Pam-Pack," KFP, February 7, 1950, pg.2.
33. Dick Tyndall, "Kinston to Play Final Home Tilts Here This Week," KFP, February 6, 1950, pg. 2.
34. Dick Tyndall, "Kinston Closes its Home Season with an Easy Win," KFP, February 9, 1950, pg. 2.
35. "On the Sports Front," KFP, February 9, 1950, pg.2.
36. Dick Tyndall, "Kinston is Too Power-Laden for Edenton Cagers," KFP, February 11, 1950, pg. 2.
37. Dick Tyndall, "Team Play Beats Roanoke Rapids as Kinston Wins," KFP, February 16, 1950, pg. 2.

Chapter 4
1. Graham Phillips, interview with author, January 15, 2011.
2. Dick Tyndall, "End Conference Play Unbeaten; Juniors get Win," KFP, February 18, 1950, pg.2.
3. Ibid
4. "On the Sports Front," KFP, February 20, 1950, pg. 2.
5. Ibid.
6. "Group to Meet in Greenville Monday After Local Appeal," KFP, February 20, 1950, pg. 2.
7. "Loop Votes Kinston Into State Playoff: But Conference Meeting Fails to Give Clean Slate Asked," KFP, February 21, 1950, pg. 2.
8. Ibid.
9. "On the Sports Front," KFP, February 21, 1950, pg. 2.
10. "Kinston Devils Play New Bern at 9:30 P.M." KFP, February 23, 1950, pg. 2.
11. Dick Tyndall, "Doug Bruton and Bobby Hodges Pace High-Scoring Kinston Attack as Grainger Registers 72-46 Win Over the Phants," KFP, February 25, 1950, pg. 2.
12. "On the Sports Front," KFP, February 27, 1950. pg. 2.

RED DEVIL TALES

13. Dick Tyndall, "Play Roxboro In Regional Finals; Game at 8 P.M.," KPF, March 4, 1950, pg. 2.
14. Dick Tyndall, "Joe Whaley and Doug Bruton Lead Grainger High to Regional Championship: Play in Durham on Friday," KRP, March 6, 1950, pg. 2.
15. Ibid.
16. Ibid.
17. Dick Tyndall, "Meet Hanes On Saturday After Semi-Finals Win," KFP, March 11, 1950, pg. 2.
18. "On the Sports Front," KFP, March 11, 1952, pg. 2.
28. Dick Tyndall, "Red Devils Beat Hanes Saturday for N.C. Crown," KFP, March 13, 1950, pg. 2.
29. Ibid.
30. Ibid.
31. Ibid.
32. Ibid.
33. "Three Red Devils Gain Places on All-Tourney Five," KFP, March 14, 1950, pg. 2.
34. "On the Sports Front," KFP, March 13, 1950, pg. 2.
35. "Kinston Fans Give Cage Champs Welcome," KFP, March 14, 1950, pg. 2.
36. Graham Philips, 1981 Grainger High School Reunion, tape recording,

Chapter 5
1. Leviticus 11: 9-10
2. Deuteronomy 23:18, KJV

Chapter 6
1. Ron Lowe, "1955 Was Big Year in Sports For Kinston, Home of Champs," The News and Observer, December 25, 1955.
2. Ibid.
3. Lloyd Whitfield, KFP, February 25, 1957, pg. 2.
4. Lloyd Whitfield, "Sidelights," *KFP*, February 2, 1956, pg.2.

5. "A Salute To Frank Lowe Mock"
6. Ibid.
7. Ibid.
8. Yank Stallings, KFP, Feb. 28, 1953, pg.2.
9. Whitfield, KFP, March 5, 1957, pg 2.
10. Mary Ellison Turner, Community News Editor, KFP, May 12, 1998, pg B3.
11. Bob Church e-mail, Sept 11, 2008.
12. Sylvia J. Wheless, personal letter, Sept. 30, 2008.

Chapter 7
1. If you google the phrase "That Man is a Success," you will find a variety of sites that give credit for this saying to various individuals. See http://www.chebucto.ns.ca/Philosophy/SuiGeneris/Emerson/success.htm,
2. Amos Stroud, *Grainger High School Red Devils*, unpublished booklet, 1999.
3. Jake Strother, Weekly Gazette, "A Salute To Frank Lowe Mock" July 20, 1978, pg 3-4
4. Red McDaniel with James L. Johnson, *Scars & Strips: The True Story of One Man's Courage in Facing Death as a Vietnam POW*. Formerly published under the name of *Before Honor* by A.J. Holman Company, a division of J.B. Lippincott Company, Philadelphia and New York, 1975, pg. 113.
5. Ibid. pg. 112-113.

Chapter 8
1. John Horne, phone interview
2. "Aplomb"is a noun a literally means "perpendicularity, equilibrium," or as it is applied here, "self-possession, assurance, poise." See Webster's New World College Dictionary.
3. "heaviness or weight."
4. Letter from Jean Booth, nd, in author's possession
5. KFP, January, 6, 1949.

6. Jack Star, Look, Feb 22, 1955, pg. 91.
7. Ibid.

Chapter 9
1. See http://virus.stanford.edu/uda

Chapter 10
1. Lloyd Whitfield, *KFP*, January 26, 1949, 2.

Chapter 11
1. Rone Lowe, "1955 Was Big Year In Sports For Kinston, Home of Champs," *The News and Observer*, December 25, 1955, 3.
2. Fred William, E-mail to author, April 10, 2011.
3. Fred Williams, E-mail to author, May 24, 2011.

Chapter 12
1. Bryan C. Hanks, "Hodges Was First Great Two-Sport Athlete," *KFP*, April 4, 2004.
2. Ibid.
3. Ibid., 8.
4. Ibid.
5. Ibid.
6. Ibid.
7. I know in his business Dad was a good problem solver, and he definitely knew how to work with people. I watched him dealing with irate clients who were upset over typical business issues and he always managed to solve the problem and satisfy the customer. He had an uncanny ability to look over the business landscape and know what he needed to do. He seemed to know all the "tricks of the trade," so it was not easy to "pull the wool over his eyes."

Chapter 14
1. Eugene B. McDaniel, *Scares & Stripes: The True Story of One Man's Courage in Facing Death as a Vietnam POW*, Formerly

published under the name of *Before Honor*(Philadelphia and New York: A.J. Holman Co., 1975), 28.

2. Dorothy McDaniel, *After the Hero's Welcome: A POW Wife's Story of the Battle Against a New Enemy* (Chicago: Bonus Books, 1991), 12.

3. Ibid., 12.

4. Ibid., 11.

5. Ibid., 19.

Chapter 15

1. Betty Cole Keaton, Personal letter, September 30, 2008.

2. Betty Keaton, personal letter to author, September 12, 2008.

Chapter 16

1. Bryan Hanks, KFP. October, 2007. see also http://www.legacy.com/obituaries/kinston/obituary.aspx-?pid=166350143#sthash.BF1x8SZo.dpuf, and *Free Press,* "Obituaries," August 14, 2013.

Chapter 17

1. I have watched Dad respond to some vagrant who came into the office, and usually around Christmastime. Dad would always help them. He just could not turn them away.

Chapter 18

1. Eion Faelten, E-mail to author, April 24, 2016.

2. Marshall Happer, E-mail to author, June 9, 2016.

3. Steve Flink, http://ncshof.org/2015/01/15/marshall-happer-2014/, April 27, 2016.

Chapter 19

1. Bryan Hanks, *KFP*, August, 11, 2010, 15.

2. Poo Rochelle, Kinston-Lenoir County Hall of Fame Induction Ceremony, August 14, 2010.

RED DEVIL TALES

3. Whaley, tape, 7, 27.2010C
4. *KFP*, March 15, 1955, 2.
5. *KFP*, March 8, 1955, 2.
6. *KFP*, March 8, 1955, 2.
7. Poo Rochelle, Kinston-Lenoir County Hall of Fame Induction Ceremony, August 14, 2010.

Chapter 20
1. Bryan Hanks, KFP August 6, 2010.
2. Whitefield, KFP February 25, 1957, 2.
3. *KFP*, March 11, 1957, and
4. Lloyd Whitfield, "Red Devils Slaughtered 81 (91)-63 as ECC Jayvees Go Undefeated," *KFP*, March 8, 1957, 2.
5. *KFP*, March 18, 1957.

Chapter 21
1. Eion Faelten, E-mail, May 3, 2011.
2. "Locals Drop First Conference Game of Season in Local Clash," *KFP*, January 25, 1956, 2.
3. Lloyd Whitfield, "Sidelights," *KFP*, February 20, 1956, 2.
4. Ibid.
5. "Kinston Fights Uphill Battle Eion Faelten Sinks 'Clincher,'" *KFP*, February 18, 1956, 2.
6. Lloyd Whitfield, "Sidelight," *KFP*, February 21, 1956, 2.
7. "Locals Top Greenville, 76-72, For League Crown Before 2,500," *KFP*, February 27, 1956, 2.
8. Ibid.
9. Lloyd Whitfield, "Sidelights," *KFP*, March 9, 1956, 2.
10. "Locals Seek 2nd Straight Title After Blistering 92-82 Victory," *KFP*, March 10, 1956.
11. "Locals Defend Title with 74–62 Triumph over Jackets Saturday," *KFP*, March 12, 1956, 2.
12. "Rochelle, Happer Are All-Tourney Choices at Enka," *KFP*, March 12, 1956.
13. "State Champs Greeting By Home Town Fans," *KFP*, March 12, 1956, 2.

14. "Alley Hart and Charles Lewis Spark Locals in 66–65 Thriller," *KFP*, March 15, 1957, 2.
15. Lloyd Whitfield, "Tourney Sidelights," *KFP*, March 16, 1957, 2.
16. Ibid.
17. Lloyd Whitfield, "Locals Dropped to Consolation Bracket in State AA Tourney," March 16, 1959, 2.
18. Lloyd Whitfield, "Tourney Sidelights, *KFP*, March 16, 1957, 2.
19. Ibid.
20. Lloyd Whitfield, "Locals Dropped to Consolation Bracket in State AA Tourney," *KFP*, March 16, 1957, 2.
21. "Lewis Stars as Kinston Breaks Scoring Mark; Hart is Honored," *KFP*, March 18, 1956, 2.
22. Eion Faelten, E-mail to author, April 29, 2011.

Chapter 22
1. *KFP*, February 17, 1956, 2.
2. *KFP*, March 1, 1956, 2.
3. Lloyd Whitfield, "Sexton Earns Basketball Baron Title During 9-Year Stay Here," *KFP*, March 5, 1957, 2.
4. *KFP*, February 25, 1957, 2. (Caption under picture of starting five)
5. Lloyd Whitfield, *KFP*, March 5, 1957.
6. Lloyd Whitfield, "Winner in Today's Play Moves into Semi-Finals at Sanford," *KFP*, March 14, 1957, 2.
7. Ibid.
8. Lloyd Whitfield, "Alley Hart and Charles Lewis Spark Locals in 66–65 Thriller," *KFP*, March 15, 1957, 2.
9. Ibid.
10. Ibid.
11. George Whitfield, Kinston-Lenoir County 2010 Sports Hall of Fame Ceremony, August 14, 2010.

Chapter 23
1. Red Devil book, 60.

RED DEVIL TALES

2. In May 1952, Air Training Command renamed Kinston Airfield as Stallings Airbase in memory of Kinston natives Lt. Bruce Stallings, a P-51 Mustang pilot killed in March 1945, and his brother, Lt. Harry Stallings, a B-29 Superfortress navigator, killed in April 1945.

3. Bob Cousy was the legendary point guard for the Boston Celtics known for his "razzle-dazzle" showmanship in his ball handling. Considered one of the greatest passers and playmakers in NBA history. He was called the "Houdini of Hardwood."

4. In 2001 Whisnant was inducted into the South Carolina Athletic Hall of Fame. At six foot four, Whisnant was a three-time All-Atlantic Coast Conference athlete, first team 1962, second team 1960-61...ACC All-Tournament team 1961-62...averaged 19.1 points in 79 games over three varsity seasons...claimed 723 rebounds...his 1,505 career points ranks in top 10 on all-time list... attempted a record 880 career free throws (more than 10 per game), made 567...throughout his career he averaged 17.0 points per game as a sophomore, 19.1 as a junior and 21.0 as a senior...He was from Icard, N.D. http://gamecockson-line.cstv.com/trads/scar-hof.html.

5. Ibid.

6. Ibid.

Chapter 24

1. Yank Stallings, KFP, March 3, 1952, 2.

2. Yank Stallings, "Guard Charlie Wickham Gets 23 Points Against Wildcat Cagers," KFP, March 4, 1952, 2.

3. Yank Stallings, KFP, February 28, 1953, 2.

4. Ibid.

5. Ibid., March 2, 1953, 2.

6. Ibid., March 13, 1953, 2.

7. Yank Stallings, "Ray Barbre Shines,'" KFP, February 28, 1953, 2.

351

8. "Red Devils Fall before Strong Phantoms as 2,600 Fans Watched," *KFP*, March 1, 1954, 2.

9. "Devils Enter Semi-Finals with 67-65 Victory over Canton Five," *KFP*, March 12, 1954, 2.

10. John Foltz, "Score in Final Three Seconds by Gooding Furnishes Victory," *KFP*, March 13, 1954, 2.

11. John Foltz, "Tri-City takes AA Title with 69-51 Win over Devils," *KFP*, March 15, 1954, 2.

Chapter 25

1. Elwood Carlson, *The Lucky Few: Between the Greatest Generation and the Baby Boom*, (Springer Science+Business Media B.V, 2008). Elwood Carlson is a sociologist and demographer with the Center of Demography and Population health at Florida State University.

2. Ibid., 24.

3. Richard A. Easterlin, introduction to *The Lucy Few: Between the Greatest Generation and the Baby Boom*, by Elwood Carlson, xvii.

4. ECarlson, *The Lucky Few.*

5. Ibid., 1-7.

6. Gertrude Stein, *Time*, November 5, 1951.

7. See James R. Brett, http://jamesrbrett.com/TheSilentGeneration/

8. George Will, *Men at Work: The Craft of Baseball* (New York: Macmillan Publishing Company, 1990, reprint ed. HarperPerennial, 1991), 2.
194 "A Sectional Loss," *KFP*, May 1957.
195 Eion Faelten, Personal letter, April 19, 2016.

Chapter 26

1. Lloyd Whitfield, "Sidelines," KFP, March 31, 1957.

Appendix A

1. Eion Faelten

SELECTED BIBLIOGRAPHY

Brokaw, Tom. *The Greatest Generation*. New York: Random House, 1984.

Elder, Glen. *Children of the Great Depression: Social Change in Life Experience*

Halberstam, David. *Summer of '49*. New York: HarperCollins Publishers, 1989.

Johnson, Talmage C. and Charles R. Holloman. *The Story of Kinston and Lenoir County*. Raleigh: Edwards & Broughton Company, 1954.

King, Clyde. *A King's Legacy: The Clyde King Story*. Chicago: Maters Press, 1999.

McDaniel, Dorothy. *After the Hero's Welcome: A POW Wife's Story of the Battle Against a New Enemy*. Chicago: Bonus Books, Inc., 1991.

McDaniel, Eugene "Red." With James Johnson. *Before Honor*. New York: A. J. Holman Company, 1975.

Perry, Dan E. *More Than I Deserve*. Chapel Hill: Chapel Hill Press, 2008.

Powel, William S. *Annals of Progress: The Story of Lenoir County and Kinston, North Carolina*. Raleigh: State Department of Archives and History.

Strauss, William, and Howe, Neil. *Generations: A Future History of America from 1584 to 2069*.

Will, George F. *Men At Work: The Craft of Baseball*. New York: HarperCollins Publishers, 1990.

ABOUT THE AUTHOR

Ronald Sexton was born in Kinston, North Carolina. He moved to Ruston, Louisiana, when he was five years old where he still lives. He has a BA and MA in history from Louisiana Tech University in Ruston. He has a ThM from Dallas Theological Seminary, an advance diploma in local history from Oxford University, and a PhD from New Orleans Baptist Theological Seminary. He is a member of the Phi Alpha Theta History Honors Society. He is an ordained Baptist minister who has served both Baptist and Methodist Churches. He has taught history at Louisiana State University in Shreveport and Delta Community College in Monroe. He and his wife, Lucy, have been married for forty-two years and have three grown children—David, Rachel, and John Mark—and five grandchildren. He loves to fish and bow hunt and continues to study and write local history.

CPSIA information can be obtained
at www.ICGtesting.com
Printed in the USA
FSOW04n1219130117
29431FS